HUNTER'S MOON

BOOK **TWO** IN THE **HUNTER** SAGA

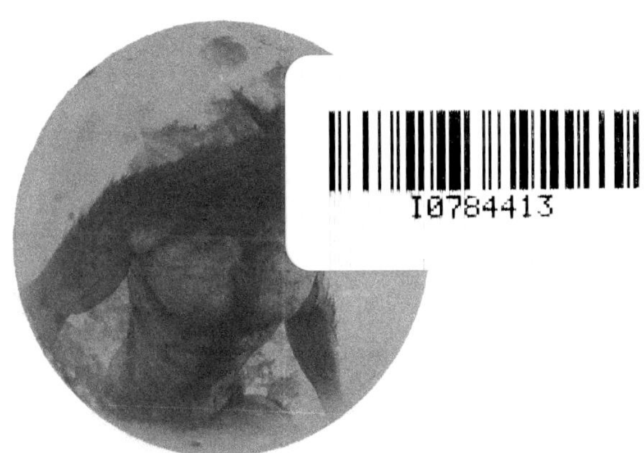

INTERNATIONAL BESTSELLING AUTHOR

JAMES BYRON HUGGINS

WILDBLUE PRESS

WILDBLUEPRESS.COM

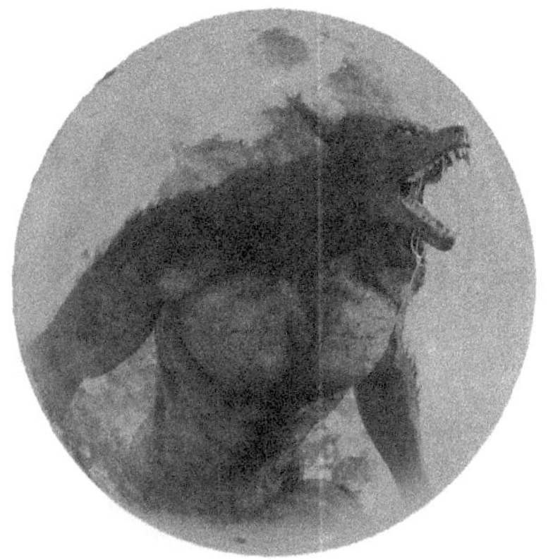

This book is dedicated
To my very special editor
Rowe Carenen

'And when the old poet was so tired,
and could go no further,
the angel quietly picked up his pen,
and finished the page'

PROLOGUE

A white shroud cast by the dying moon laid an icy pallor over the surface of the moor's unmoving night, but the pale imitation of light was only reflected by the impenetrable darkness.

Standing alone, staring through the picture window of his immense trophy room, Major Augustus Milton held a shot of whiskey that he had not tasted although it was his secret for a long life – a whiskey and a cigar before the troubles of the day began. No, the major did not know if it were true. He did, however, know that he had practiced his ritual for most of his 83 years and he was still alive.

Gazing down into the glass, Milton mumbled to the man walking into the chamber, "Be mindful this morning, my friend. False light can be more deceiving than the night."

With his habitually long face Angus Staford opened the flap of his cardigan to reveal the World War II Webley revolver at his waist. "You and me been mindful since the war, governor. And it's five days 'till the Hunter's Moon. It's too early for the dead to be up and about."

"It's not the dead I fear, Angus, but the living."

"I hear ya, governor. Be back in a jiff."

The old man's servant secured the towering door of the immense mansion and walked spritely through the quickening cold to the black Rolls Royce parked on the cobblestone drive. Then he paused to stare up at the transparent tombstones of cloud as he hoarsely rasped, "No, sir, we won't be seeing ghosts this early to the blood moon."

Rounding the rotund hood of the imperious machine, Staford opened the rear door and carefully deposited the briefcase of his friend and employer. He spent a moment to crank the world's most reliable engine and methodically adjusted the heat, cushion and dash. Then he shut the front panel with his habitual reverence before hesitating once more as the moon emerged like a shrouded skull in a graveyard of sky.

His good eye squinted as he focused on the image. "You don't scare me." he muttered. "I'm too old to be scared 'a the likes 'a you …"

A snap caused the old man to turn, searching the dark, but no leaf moved in the dead night wind and, with a dismissive grunt, he turned back. He took a single step before a horrifying thrill spun him again with the energy of a man half his age and his eyes and mouth soundlessly opened in horror.

As it struck.

CHAPTER ONE

I t consumed Angus Staford as it had consumed dead men since the beginning of time, effortlessly crushing bone without removing its scarlet stare from the surrounding night.

A clawed hand grasped its mane.

"Eat," a voice growled, "and soon you will feast."

The monstrous silhouette that towered beside the prehistoric wolf could scent the old man's vivid fear in the blood that flooded over the cobblestones, and his own fangs parted. His eyes glinted, red, as he raised an angry stare at the mansion so protected by bars and ironwood doors. Then a porch light lit at the entrance of the mansion and beast master and beast leaped over the black hedge at their backs.

Instantly they were charging through privet and shadow and as they reached the fence they sailed against the haggard skull of a moon to land without sound on the surrounding tarn. With gigantic strides they were soon lost in the moor's shadow and silence.

* * *

Fairly flying through the forest, master and beast somehow evaded twigs and slivers of moon that could have revealed their presence. Then, as they reached the crest of a hill, they stopped with unnatural grace and lifted faces to see an all but invisible glow rising in the east.

It was time, once more, to hide.

Slouching forward, they reached the far side of the hill soon enough and descended and with each stride the beast master knew every age buried beneath the loam. Moments later, and miles into the night, the master slowed until the wolf reached his side. He once more curled claws in its coarse mane. His blood-red eyes glowed in the dark and, in the surrounding night, the bittern and the tern fell silent.

He whispered, "Soon, old man."

He turned his bestial face to the rising sun.

"*Soon ...*"

CHAPTER TWO

With hands shoved deeply into the pockets of his grey worsted overcoat; it was bitterly cold in the forbidding North York Moor of East England, London Metropolitan Police Commander Winston Blackthorn stood over the ravaged body of the caretaker, Angus Staford.

Blackthorn was a grave, taciturn man of sixty-something with a towering, even formidable, farmer's physique. His shoulders were wide, his heavy chest was deep, and his long arms stretched the voluminous overcoat that would have easily swallowed a lesser man, which almost every man was. His eyes – gray and narrow like gun sights – revealed neither compassion nor weakness as he stared upon the gory remains.

With a frown that would have stilled a riot, Blackthorn turned his squared, prizefighter face toward the manor of Great Britain's most revered multi-billionaire, Major Augustus Milton.

Blackthorn knew that the legendary war hero, big game hunter, and financial giant was aware of the death of his ninety-year-old chauffer and wondered how the old man had taken the blow. But such niceties were not his primary concern; his men were trained for that. His primary charge, communicated to him by no less than Commissioner Nigel Rafferty himself, was to catch this killer with as little fanfare as possible.

A black-coated constable who had loped from the manor stopped before Blackthorn. After catching his breath, the young man stated, "All family members are well, governor. The lord of the house, Major Milton, is shocked, but he declined medical assistance. And we've searched and secured each and every building." He swept out his arm. "We didn't find a thing, sir! It's like the old man was killed by a ghost!"

"Yes," Blackthorn muttered in the quiet tone of a man inured to excitement but never excited. "A ghost with fangs." He paused grimly. "Very well, lad. Return to your duties. And remain close to your mates. All men are to search two by two. No man is to go alone. Be aware that this animal might still be about."

Pembry ran toward his patrol.

As Scotland Yard's most senior homicide investigator, Blackthorn had solved a thousand murders. But he could remember none so gruesome as what he was witnessing. Indeed, before this moment, he had reckoned himself beyond the touch of horror or shock. But this was more than murder. In this surreal, forbidding moor it was almost a witness to the supernatural. Only a supernatural creature could have mutilated a man so savagely in so few seconds and yet no one heard or saw a thing.

Or so they said.

It was the kind of event that gave rise to whispers of werewolves and fiendish creatures of the night roaming the moor – childish fears a rational man would, of course, ignore. But as Blackthorn stood above the darkening blood, he mused that such rumors were not as easily dismissed in this hauntingly lonesome moor as they were in the russet-hued halls of headquarters.

Angus Staford's throat had been ripped out with what appeared to be a single snap of powerful fangs. His torso had been slashed open with what also appeared to be a single blow and the lungs, heart, and liver were cleanly torn away by this unknown creature. And it *must* be an 'unknown creature' for not even a Grizzly or Siberian tiger could inflict such damage on a man in mere seconds. A World War II Webley revolver remained at Mr. Staford's waist. He had been slaughtered before he could fire a shot.

Blackthorn muttered, "At least it was quick, old man."

Although Blackthorn would need a laser-micrometer to verify it, he calculated that the incision marks on the neck matched the incision marks on the torso and amputated appendages. But that only suggested that a single creature had done this. It did not prove there was only one creature. And that was an important thing. If there was one creature, then there could be two. Or three. Or ten. And there was nothing to indicate otherwise.

Yet one conclusion was incontestable; this was a creature of incomprehensible physical might. It was also unnaturally intelligent. Even now, after six of its victims had been discovered along the boundaries of North York Moor, the Metropolitan Police had not managed to locate a single witness or survivor. Five of the world's best hunters had been commissioned to track it, and all had failed. Not that they were without excuse. It was all but impossible to track man or beast through this ever-changing wasteland of moor. Streams appeared and disappeared by the minute and the ubiquitous quicksand swallowed tracks as quickly as men.

Blackthorn recalled a celebrity-survivalist who had ventured into this moor to survive alone for a month. After a week the famous expert radioed for help and by morning rescuers reached his last known location but there was no body. Further, there was no evidence that he had ever ventured beyond his camp. It was if the moor had opened its mouth and swallowed him whole.

Out of his overcoat Blackthorn removed a half-smoked cigar obtained from his favorite tobacconist,

Bradley on Oxford Street, as a presence announced itself, "Commander?"

Blackthorn's spoke over his shoulder, "Yes, Pembry?"

"They found something, sir."

"Take me to it, lad."

Within moments Blackthorn stood like a monument to justice beneath the iron bars of a huge picture window. The heavy black rods were set deep in granite and appeared strong enough to stop a rhinoceros.

Pembry pointed toward the garden beneath the casement with, "It's right there, commander."

Sweeping back the gray wings of his overcoat, Blackthorn knelt. Across the ground lay an enormous track. Blackthorn's eyes narrowed as he stared over four immense claw marks pressed into the soil – claws at least three inches in length. Blackthorn lifted his face, "Is this the only track?"

"Aye, commander. But there's something else. We just don't know what to make of it."

"Show me."

Pembry pointed high on the wall, "It's up there, sir."

Gazing up, Blackthorn saw obvious claw marks ascending along the smooth granite wall to a fourth-floor window. The marks appeared to have been torn by human hands.

"Bring me Crime Scene," Blackthorn said without emotion.

Only a minute passed before Crime Scene technicians arrived and Blackthorn pointed to the wall. "Take pictures of those marks and lift me a plaster of that track in the garden. And I'll have the evidence when you're finished. I'll walk this through myself."

In short order Blackthorn was presented with a plaster cast and film. He deposited both in an armored case bracketed to the inside of the trunk of his Jaguar as Pembry asked, "Is that a bear track, commander?"

"What? Oh, no, son. That's not a bear track. Now go find Inspector Marshal and have him report."

Minutes later the squat, stoutly built Inspector Marshal rushed up, somewhat breathless, as Blackthorn's said, "Bill, I'm off to the lab with this evidence. I'm giving you full authority and command."

With his brushy, exquisitely curled mustache concealing half his ruddy complexion, Inspector Bill Marshal said, "Very well, governor. May I ask, sir, what you make of this so far?"

Blackthorn revealed nothing. "The print in the garden has four claws, mate. But the print climbing the wall reveals five claws so we're dealing with two different creatures. All I know for certain is that you need to be on your best guard until my return."

"Am I to record this as an animal attack, inspector?"

"For the moment, yes, and you are to contact London and conscript thirty additional men to secure that fence on a rotating watch. I'll inform the Detective Chief-Superintendent that you and the lads are to be left alone for the duration of this tour."

"Understood, commander."

"You will also contact Holland and Holland and requisition them to bring out big game rifles for the lads. Elephant guns. We'll need one rifle for each man plus suitable ammunition for a safari." Blackthorn lifted his chin to the moor. "It may not be darkest Africa, old man, but this moor is as dangerous as any jungle ever cursed by God."

"Do you think this animal might be part of someone's illegal menagerie, commander? Perhaps an escaped tiger?"

"No," Blackthorn said curtly. "This was no tiger."

Inspector Marshal's mouth was a grim line as he followed with, "Then is it possible, commander, that this horrible thing was the work of a madman?"

Securing the trunk, Blackthorn straightened. "The bizarre is always possible, old friend. And I have seen men as bloodless as any animal. But this was not the work of a man."

"Then what kind creature are we looking for?"

Blackthorn turned away.

"I don't know, mate. But I know a man who might."

CHAPTER THREE

Waiting for his flight to depart Heathrow, Blackthorn studiously read each of Inspector Marshal's supplemental reports and they clearly explained and corroborated the whereabouts of everyone present at the estate during the hour of Angus Staford's gruesome death.

With the exacting thoroughness of a court reporter, Marshal confirmed that Staford was the longest-serving and most trusted employee of Augustus Milton. He also confirmed that Staford's preparation of the Rolls Royce was a frequent and familiar procedure. Almost as an afterthought the inspector also reported that the major had not even attempted to conceal his deep grief and that he was not in any sense a suspect.

A survivor of World War II and a retired member of MI-6 as well as a former European banker who once chaired the powerful British Foreign Finance Committee, Major Augustus Milton was famous for his self-control, discipline, prescience, and judgment. But when told about the loss of his beloved servant, the old man was brokenhearted to a depth that provoked Marshal, as his report stated, to fear for Milton's already precarious life. With an alert inspector's eye for detail, Marshal wrote that Milton had at last turned to the blazing hearth and said cryptically, "And even heroes die …"

Marshal confirmed that at one hour and four minutes before official sunrise Major Milton had dispatched Mr. Staford according to their prearranged schedule – a schedule of which the entire family was aware – to ready the major's carriage. Milton said that although he had felt an uneasiness in his soul, he possessed no logical explanation for the sensation, therefore he had seen no need for extravagant caution.

A thorough accounting of everyone's whereabouts at the time of the killing was largely a formality because no human could have committed this act. But by procedure and policy, and his own inflexible nature, Marshal verified all alibis.

According to their hand-written statements, each was enjoying breakfast when Mr. Staford was sent to the car. And when he did not immediately return, as he always did, Milton casually sent his son to discover the cause. The son, Richard Milton, found the body and informed the local sheriff, who summoned Blackthorn from a nearby hotel where he had been encamped since these murders across the moor had begun.

That the entire family arose early was not surprising to Blackthorn, who was familiar with the habits of this clan. It was well known that Augustus Milton had not become one of Britain's richest men by folding his hands to rest. Rather, he had lived by an ironclad work ethic all his life – an ethic forged in the crucible of World War II when only the most resolute determination and iron endurance decided a nation's freedom or the most bitter defeat. But they were not only habits that enabled Milton to survive England's darkest hours, they had also lifted him to the pinnacle of United Kingdom banking.

To this day Milton was famous for rising early with a grim inveteracy of purpose that allowed no rest until his herculean efforts in labor and finance were finished. It occurred to Blackthorn that the old man was still very much like an old machine of World War II, strong to this day because his heart had been forged to endure the unendurable.

Augustus Milton was a mythical character in Great Britain and all noteworthy men knew his name and story. He had been barely thirteen years old when the war began but had fought in the French Resistance beside British soldiers. And the mere story of how Milton had ended up in the French underground after his family was killed during the endless Luftwaffe bombings of London was a tale that was often told and retold among the campfires of young soldiers.

Although young and inexperienced, Milton rapidly distinguished himself in battle and was often decorated for fearless and conspicuous gallantry. And in time he rose to the highest ranks of MI6 and executed his country's darkest missions with legendary cunning and courage. Then, upon retirement from Intelligence, he dedicated himself to rebuilding Great Britain's former throne as a financial superpower – a position it held before the Luftwaffe reduced its revered financial houses to rubble.

In his legendary life Milton had married three times yet lost all wives to tragedies unquestioned by police or colored by the most common gossip. Two wives had died in traffic accidents and his third, and last, wife died in Africa from a mysterious hemorrhagic fever. It was a bitter blow to a man who had given so much to the world. But Milton was rumored to have borne his loss as a man accustomed to loss. He quietly removed his family from Africa and relocated them to his family's hereditary estate, a centuries-old castle which he restored with the fortune he'd accumulated.

The youngest of Milton's children, a girl, was sixteen. The oldest was in their forties, but all resided in the manor. Perhaps they remained at the old man's side to alleviate a portion of Milton's loneliness in his waning years. Or perhaps it was merely a matter of convenience. Blackthorn did not know and did not particularly care because their reasons – at this moment – were unimportant to his greater investigation.

The severe, implacable detective checked the Robert Loomes' watch on his left wrist – a sturdy black on black timepiece noticeably out of place among the aristocratic dress of first class. But it was a soldier's watch – a practical tool for a practical man. Then, lifting his diplomatic pouch, he stood.

It was time to board his flight and discover if this American could indeed track this monster in the mist.

CHAPTER FOUR

Nathaniel Hunter laughed loudly.

"Reginald! Are you telling me that you've got over a million dinosaur bones in this basement that you haven't even identified?"

Reginald Tannebalm, assistant senior paleontologist for the Smithsonian Institute's Museum of Natural History, gazed from atop his ladder and replied patiently, "Listen, Hunter, I'm just one guy surrounded by bazillions of dinosaur bones. And just to be perfectly clear, I am not responsible for identifying every damn dinosaur bone in the world. Those English dudes could do some work every now and then instead of hanging out their windows drinking coffee. And why are you harassing me, anyway? Aren't you supposed to be tracking a tiger or something? I thought you were in China."

"It was Taiwan." Hunter picked up a photograph. "They captured it yesterday. What's wrong, Reggie? Don't you like my company?"

"It's the highlight of my day."

Hunter laughed, "Coming down here is a hobby of mine when I'm in town, and you know I love to learn from you." Lifting the photograph higher, he asked, "What's so special about a human footprint?"

"That's a fossilized footprint that destroys every theory ever held by Darwin and his darlings."

"Why does it do that?"

"Because the leading theory of evolution dates the earliest hominids to about two million BC - give or take. But that's a fossilized human footprint that dates Homo Sapiens to at least thirty million BC. Consequently, the fan-favorite theory of evolution has just been blown clean out of the water because now we have proof that mankind, and I'm talking about dudes who look like *us*, have been walking around on this planet for thirty million years." He seemed to consider. "Probably longer."

Hunter laid it down. "Fair enough." He lifted a long, heavy bone as thick as his arm. "What'd this come from?"

Reggie glanced down, "All we know is that the carbon dates it to the Oligocene Period. But that's the only bone we've found, so we don't know what it belongs to."

Hunter stared along its lines. "It looks like a tarsal."

"Yeah. I looked at it for a second. It's a tarsal. But what it belongs to is anybody's guess."

"Whatever it was, it was big."

"Thank you, Mr. Obvious."

Hunter continued mechanically, "This supported about twenty tons and the thing stayed low to the ground. Did you notice how the tendons connect to this lateral section? This bone gave some strong horizontal support." He slowly turned it. "This is reptilian."

"Good grief," laughed Reggie. "Hunter, you've looked at that for a whole five seconds. How can you say it was reptilian?"

"Because this was built for speed, Reggie. But not prolonged speed. And this lateral section where the tendons connect indicate it was as fast as a shark in the water and probably as fast as a wolf on land."

"No way that thing was faster than a wolf. Its bones were too big. It was too heavy."

"A Saltwater crocodile that weighs a ton can hit twenty-two miles an hour on land, Reggie. But this thing was three times the size of the biggest crocodile I've ever seen and that makes it three times faster."

Reggie leaned back, arms dangling. "Are you saying that's the tarsal of *Sarcosuchus imperator*?" He hesitated. "I don't think so, Hunter. *Imperator* didn't get that big."

"You're right. *Imperator* peaked at about forty feet and maybe eight tons. But nothing says *imperator* was the biggest *crocodilian* of that period. It's just the biggest we've found." Hunter peered along the length of the metatarsal. "Until now. But this boy was *crocodilian*. And I guarantee you that he stood at the top of the food chain."

"Why do you say that?"

"Because I don't see anything tangling with a twenty-ton, eighty-foot-long saltwater crocodile."

"What about Megalodon?"

"Not even Megalodon would want a piece of this guy. That fight could go either way." Hunter laid down the bone and lifted his daypack. "All right, Reggie, I'll let you get back to it. See you tomorrow."

Reggie yelled, "Wait a minute! You discovered it so you have to name it! What's its name?"

Hunter looked back. "How about, '*Venaticus crocodilian*.'"

"Hunter crocodile?"

"What do you think?" Hunter smiled.

Throwing his head back, Reggie laughed.

"Perfect!"

CHAPTER FIVE

I t was Investigator William Marshal's second night since the killing of Angus Staford and, as he had done the night before, he made a conspicuous patrol, encouraging and insuring the welfare of his men. As he slowly and resolutely approached the front gates of the estate – gates located a hefty hundred meters from the manor – he had his Holland and Holland elephant rifle borne snugly over his right shoulder.

Four men snapped to attention.

"As you were, lads," directed Marshal. "How do we fare?"

"All is quiet, sir."

"Good," Marshal nodded. "But stay alert. No one saw or heard a thing the morning Mr. Staford was killed, so we know this animal is as stealthy as a Siberian tiger."

After awkward glances, an older constable tentatively stated, "It might help us out a bit, inspector, if you could tell us what manner of creature we're to be looking for."

Marshal's head bent before he raised his face, "I wish I could tell you, mate. But all we know is that it's a large and ferocious beast." He made a fist as if to punch the creature. "But that's good! The fact that it's large gives us the advantage!"

Pembry's eyes widened. "What advantage, governor?"

"Because it's easier to shoot an elephant than a chipmunk, lad! Just remember your orders! Stick together! I want no man wandering off by himself."

"We're keeping it tight, inspector. No man steps off by himself unless he has to take care of business. Then he gets right back."

"Good, good, and be sure to rotate turns at the fire. Some of you are hardier than others, but enough cold can make a coward of any man. You have a good fire going. Keep it hot. But don't look at the light. It'll fester your night vision."

Glancing toward the others, Pembry added, "The lads and I were talking about military reinforcements, sir. Has Commander Blackthorn gone for soldiers?"

"No, lad, he's gone for a man."

"What man, sir?"

With a frown Marshal turned away.

"A man who will give us a fighting chance."

CHAPTER SIX

The creature glided through the night with a grace that scorned its monstrous shape. Moving through the high bush, it encircled the estate, constantly glancing at the frost white fence.

Yes, they were searching for it, but the master had trained it to search for, and avoid, guards and the small black boxes. It had also been trained to hide from the light, to avoid twigs, to hunt outside the tarn and to kill every human it encountered.

A patrol finally walked past its concealment, disappearing around the corner, and it raced across the outside tarn to clear the iron bars of the towering fence in a leap. As it landed inside the manor, it leaped again, clearing the first six-foot-high wall of hedge.

With head down, cloaked in darkness, it froze.

It could hear the heartbeat of a single human approaching along an inside wall, could see his red-yellow heat signature through the bush. The man was walking slowly, and as he drew closer, it dropped in a crouch. It waited until the man emerged into view, tugging at his clothes.

It struck.

The man whirled as it killed him and then it stood over the ravaged form, jaws separated. It spun as it heard a voice and more of the men began walking toward it. With a smothered snarl it closed its jaws around the man's torso and leaped over the hedge, carrying the man in its fangs.

It waited only briefly at the fence for the small group to walk past its place of hiding. Then it ran forward and soared high, carrying the man in its teeth as it cleared the spikes of the fence.

It effortlessly kept the man in its jaws as it landed on the far side and continued moving. Within moments it was again inside the tree line and angled for its lair, where it would hide during the day.

And feast.

* * *

With the claws of a single hand dug into the stone wall of the mansion, the beast master was as motionless as the darkness cloaking his Herculean form.

Talons of his free hand rested lightly on the pane of glass before he flicked a single claw across the mortar, snapping away chips so the panel would fall clear if it were tapped. Then he could reach through the opening, unlock this window, and soundlessly slip inside.

Yet another path into this castle.

He starkly saw three men round the corner of this long wing of the estate. They did not know he was staring upon them, but how could they? They were only human and human senses were blind and deaf and useless. He leaned back, gazing at the moon. It was cut with ribbons of cloud that he could hear as they passed. Then, when he looked again at the corridor, a human was walking towards him, lantern in hand.

The guard turned a corner and was gone.

He lifted his face to gaze through the corporeal darkness separating him from his pet and saw it pacing impatiently inside the protective tree line. Even at this distance it was a pulsating image of red and yellow and green that he could see as brightly as he could have seen a dancing flame.

His transformation was more than complete – it was perfect. Now he had only to finish his plan and he would succeed where *the other* had failed. But the other had only failed because it had not realized that physical strength alone could not conquer this world.

Yes, humans were stupid, but they could also be courageous and resourceful. So he must be strong. He must be intelligent. He must cloak his existence. He must be a ghost that is there and then is gone because they would not send their armies to hunt a ghost. And when the day came when they finally realized their folly, he would be like a god among them. And it would be too late for despair. Too late for regret. Too late for hope.

Yes …

When all was in order, the slaughter would begin.

And would never end.

CHAPTER SEVEN

A tall man wearing a heavy gray overcoat appeared beside Hunter's table at the restaurant of the Washington Hilton. Gazing up, Hunter calculated the grave Puritan expression and posture.

He gestured to a chair. "Have a seat."

"Thank you," the man said with British formality and removed his overcoat to reveal an investigator's practical suit. And yet Hunter knew this man was more than a simple detective.

His lack of expression lent him the gravity of a spy. With a frown he set a blueprint-sized briefcase on the floor and laid wide, obviously powerful hands on the table.

"Hungry?" asked Hunter. "I'm buying."

"Thank you, no. I dined at my hotel." The man turned his square head to the ornate architecture. "My lodgings are a far humbler affair than this baroque extravagance, I dare say."

Hunter laughed, "You can start any time, detective."

The man smiled tightly, "I apologize for interrupting you, Mr. Hunter. I understand you're on hiatus. But I'm an expert with summary so I will make this relatively painless." He raised his chin. "I am Commander Winston Blackthorn of the London Metropolitan Police. Americans still refer to us as Scotland Yard. And I'm here to ask for your help." Blackthorn raised an arm for the waiter. "Chivas Regal, please."

The waiter nodded, "Of course, sir."

"I am here, Mr. Hunter, because a significant number of civilians have been slaughtered by a maneater that no one has been able to kill. And I'm certain the death toll will continue to rise if this animal is not tracked down by a master hunter and destroyed."

Hunter looked up from his meal. "I presume all this has happened in England?"

"In North York Moor, yes."

"Did you ask Jim Redford for help?"

"We did."

"And?"

"And Redford was unable to track it. He returned to London."

"Redford's the best. What kind of animal is it?"

"We don't know."

"Redford didn't tell you?"

"Redford told us he could not identify it. He said that it moved like a wolf, but it was far too large to be a wolf. In truth, it's as large as a Grizzly bear. But he said it's not a Grizzly, either."

Hunter's eyes narrowed and he leaned back. His head tilted as he studied the commander's grim countenance.

"You do know that there haven't been any indigenous maneaters in Great Britain for eight hundred years, don't you?"

"Redford informed me."

The waiter set down the bourbon and Blackthorn acknowledged him before he continued, "After spending a week attempting to track this beast, Redford told us that this hunt was beyond his skills. He recommended that we contact you. He said you were the only man who has ever tracked a creature born out of time."

Hunter revealed nothing as Blackthorn reached down to unsnap the glossy black case. Then he cleared away his plate and utensils and removed a plaster cast, laying it on the table.

"We believe this is an accurate cast of its print," he stated.

Hunter gazed over the cast. He said nothing for a long time, then, "Look, commander, if this thing has set up residence in that moor, why don't you just let nature take its course? It won't live long. Nothing does in that wilderness."

"Mr. Hunter, God is undoubtedly on our side but we cannot be so confident about Nature. In any case, I have been ordered to find someone capable of tracking down and destroying this monster."

"When did Scotland Yard get assigned to animal control?"

"Eight men slaughtered like sheep volunteered me for the duty. And there is an additional factor. For some reason this creature has become obsessed with the estate of Great Britain's richest patron. He is a highly valued friend of both Parliament and royalty, so orders granting myself special jurisdiction have been signed and properly issued."

Hunter resumed eating. "Why is this animal obsessed with this rich man's place?"

"We have no idea. Neither did Redford. We only know that all the deaths have occurred within three kilometers of his home."

"I assume this guy lives in a castle?" asked Hunter. "Big fences? Hedges? Dogs? Guards?"

"Yes. And now that you mention it, I'll say that the ten-foot iron fence surrounding the major's castle can stop a bull elephant. But it does not stop this creature."

"How many have been killed inside the fence?"

"Two. A chauffer and a constable."

"Outside the walls?"

"We have discovered six. Hikers and hunters."

"Do they have guards at the gates of this place?"

"Day and night."

"So how did it get past the fence?"

Blackthorn took a deep breath. "To be truthful, we don't know. But I suspect the creature leaped over it."

Hunter stared again at the cast. "Was this made in mud or dirt?"

"Dirt. In a garden."

"Freshly tilled?"

"Freshly? No."

"Weather?"

"It rained the day this impression was cast. In fact, it's been raining incessantly for weeks. The entire moor is water-logged."

"Temperature?"

"Fahrenheit?"

"Yeah."

"In the mid-forties, but freezing at night."

Hunter hesitated. "Well, commander, you're looking at the print of an animal that weighs about a thousand pounds. It has five unretractable claws that it uses to –"

"I count four claws."

Hunter half-laughed. "Most would. But there's five. One is a toe claw and sometimes it doesn't print. But it's not a wolf. It's too big and the print doesn't fit." He drew a finger across the cast. "This is the left front paw. It was shifting. Moving around. You can tell by the mulling. It also had its head raised like it was watching something."

"How can you tell it was watching something?"

"You can tell from the expanse moves at the tips of the claws that it shifted its weight to the left, so whatever it was looking at was on that side." Hunter stared longer. "I'll give Redford credit. It does look like a wolf, but there's too many inconsistencies."

"I know why Redford recommended you."

Hunter's eyes shifted from blue to steel gray. "What do you think you know, commander?"

"I know about Alaska," said Blackthorn frankly and with a frank expression. "After I told my captain about Redford's referral, he gave me your file and told me you might be our only hope."

Hunter blinked. "*My file*?"

"You look surprised."

"I am."

Blackthorn dismissed it with a wave. "If you have a name, Mr. Hunter, you have a file. And, in any case, it enabled me to understand what Redford was talking about." His frown deepened. "You've tracked something like this before, haven't you? A creature born out of time?"

"I thought detectives worked with facts."

"I don't consider it an assumption, Mr. Hunter. In fact, I'd say it's a deduction based on substantial evidence."

Hunter stared long at the cast before he allowed, "I've never tracked anything to match this. What I tracked in Alaska was … something else." He paused. "Entirely."

"We've considered that, Mr. Hunter, but – ultimately – the most important thing isn't what species it is."

"Yeah? So what's the most important thing?"

"The most important thing is that you've tracked the most dangerous prey, and prevailed. You prevailed even over an apex predator from another age. And it is critical that someone brings this slaughter to an end. And if it takes a specialist like yourself, then no fee is too high. But this animal *must* be destroyed. If it were me, I'd shoot it with a silver bullet, hang it, burn it, drive a stake through its heart and cut off its head."

"Good grief, Blackthorn. It's just an animal."

The detective leaned aggressively forward. "This thing is more than an animal and you know it. Redford is one of the greatest trackers in the world and he couldn't even get close to it." He pointed at nothing. "How does it get inside a ten-foot iron fence? How does it get past security cameras without leaving a single image? How does it even know what a security camera *is*? And we have no idea why it is targeting the residents of this manor. In sum, Mr. Hunter, the Metropolitan Police know *nothing* about this creature! But we all agree – and I include England's very highest authorities in this opinion – that it must be tracked down and destroyed. And if there are more like it, they'll have to be destroyed, as well."

"That's an extinction level event, detective."

"And I'd like to survive the extinction." Blackthorn removed a dozen color photographs from his briefcase. "This is the body of the chauffer from two nights ago."

Hunter gazed at the photograph.

Blackthorn seemed almost defeated as he remarked, "I've been a police officer my entire adult life, Mr. Hunter. I have witnessed every manner of murder that could be conceived and executed by the most malevolent minds. But I have never investigated such monstrous savagery as befell this poor fellow. I will add that he was ably armed, a seasoned soldier, and yet he was killed before he could even draw his weapon."

It didn't take Hunter more than a heartbeat to recognize the frenzied feeding of a large maneater. There was clear evidence of claw and fang and the indication of enormous strength. He asked, "How were the hikers and hunters that had no association with this rich fellow killed?"

"In the same savage manner. As I said, they appeared to be hikers, campers, and hunters. Some even had shotguns, but their guns were not fired. They were killed so quickly they never got off a shot. But this next-to-last victim was an employee of the major and, as I said, he was killed inside the fence. Then, last night, one of my men was apparently killed."

"Apparently?"

"We haven't found his body. But he is missing. And I knew the lad. He would never willingly leave his post."

With a grunt Hunter returned to his meal. "And the whole countryside isn't in an uproar about this?"

"Our official stance has been that the deaths were weather related or caused by the attacks of wild dogs. We didn't want to incite a panic or, far worse, suicidal safaris. We don't have enough body bags."

With an ominous gaze never leaving Hunter's face, Blackthorn handed over yet another photograph that displayed five claw marks etched deeply in a granite wall. "What do you make of this?" he asked.

Hunter gazed at the picture a long time before he sat back and lifted his gaze to the inspector's implacable face.

"They look like claw marks," Hunter said, flat.

"But what manner of creature could leave those claw marks in solid granite?" Hunter said nothing and so the inspector insisted, "Could the same creature have left both sets of prints?"

"No. Have any sheep or cattle been killed?"

"Just men."

"Would you know?"

"Yes. We've solicited every marshal in the parish and they reported no unusual loss of cattle, swine, poultry or sheep."

Hunter gazed curiously, again, over the cast.

The commander lifted his hands. "What amazes me, Hunter, is that this creature, or creatures, have so effortlessly defeated everything we've thrown at them. And we've used the best trackers, the greatest experts in traps, cameras, satellites. We organized three massive hunts and haven't been able to even prove they exist! And while we're doing all this, these animals kill and disappear again and again like ghosts! Some are saying they're not even flesh and blood!"

Hunter smiled, "So it's supernatural?"

Blackthorn reluctantly allowed, "Frankly I can't blame a man for surrendering to superstition when all logic fails to explain something that is truly terrifying."

Hunter sliced his steak as he shook his head, "I can't help you if it's supernatural, Blackthorn. Not my field."

"I don't need an exorcist. I need the greatest tracker in the world."

"This one print is all you've found? Don't you have hairs? What about saliva from the victims?"

"We did lift a few hairs," brooded Blackthorn. "And our lab tested saliva swabbed from the old man's wounds. Both samples came back to *Canis lupus familiaris*. But this is very obviously not the work of a wolf, so we think the crime scene was contaminated by one of the Old English Mastiffs that patrol the grounds."

"Have any of the dogs been attacked?"

"No. In fact it's all we can do to make the brutes go on patrol. They weigh fourteen stone and they're ten times stronger than a man, but they seem even more frightened than we are."

"Then it's not a ghost."

"Why do you say that?"

"Because dogs aren't afraid of ghosts. They're fascinated by them."

"I thought you didn't believe in ghosts."

Hunter laughed, "I didn't say that. I just said ghosts aren't my field. But if these dogs are acting skittish whenever this creature is close, they might come in handy."

"How so?"

"If we can determine what area the dogs are afraid of, then that's where we'll look first."

Blackthorn's gray eyes widened as he leaned sharply forward. "Are you going to help me? I promise you the ministry will pay any price."

"Don't get excited, Blackthorn. It's been a while."

"What are you mean?"

"What I mean is I haven't done this kind of tracking in a long time. I've mostly been doing academic work. My senses are dull. I'm out of shape. I could get us all killed."

Blackthorn's steel teeth gleamed as he grated, "We're going to be killed, anyway, Mr. Hunter, if these creatures aren't stopped. And I don't care if you're out of shape!" He angrily chased away the objection. "Neither of us are in shape for this! I haven't cleared out a pub in fifteen years! But I cleared out a thousand in my day! And I haven't forgotten how!" He nodded fiercely, "And it's the same with you! It's the same with any soldier. When the hour comes, your body remembers. And it does for you what you can't do for yourself. And you won't find that in any book because there isn't any school for it. But your *bones* remember."

Hunter laughed again. "You missed your calling, Blackthorn. You should have been a politician."

"So you'll help me?" Blackthorn asked with the first hint of desperation. "I can have us on the first flight out."

"Not so fast." Hunter turned his face toward the doors. "Let's get some air. Woodley Park is nice this time of night. That is, if we don't get killed before we get there."

CHAPTER EIGHT

The Washington Hilton borders Woodley Park so it's a simple stroll to enter the darkness of the tree line and within minutes they were meandering along an ominously shadowed walkway that any sane man would avoid at night. Hunter removed two cigars from his coat and offered one to Blackthorn, who expressed surprise as he accepted.

"Your file mentioned that you were uncommonly comfortable," he commented. "But Arturo Fuente Opus costs six thousand pounds a box in London."

Hunter lit one and offered a light. "When I come to the city, I indulge myself. And you keep referring to this file, Blackthorn. Who, exactly, gave you this file and what does it say?"

With the atmosphere of a man who has nothing to hide Blackthorn gestured vaguely, "My supervisor suggested that it was from someone in your state department."

"From 'someone?'"

"That's all I know."

"So what does it say?"

"It was just an analysis of your skills, your history, a list of acquaintances and the like. I must say you have a fascinating history. Trapping or disposing of man-eating tigers or capturing the last surviving member of an endangered species so it can be restored to the wild." Blackthorn mused, "It was, however, a bit short on family.

As a matter of fact, I don't remember seeing any. And it was heavily redacted. But it did mention that highly classified piece of business in Alaska. It did not say, exactly, what you were asked to track. But it kept using a peculiar phrase."

"What was that?"

"It kept referring to your prey as 'the creature.'" Blackthorn cast a steady gaze. "It seemed to me that if it had been a bear, they would have simply called it a bear. But they kept calling 'the creature.' Then, of course, there was Redford saying that you were the only man who has ever seen such a beast So I put it all together and deduced that you'd been asked to track down some kind of creature previously thought to be extinct." He didn't blink. "Am I in the ballpark?"

Hunter smiled wryly, "You're close enough. But I thought the moor was a superstitious community. Why aren't the folks staging werewolf hunts with shotguns and lanterns and pitchforks?"

"Indeed, the moor has a rich history of monsters and legends. We even have names for our individual vampires and werewolves and other, bizarre creatures of the night. But the moor is an old and vast place, and some legends are indeed based on fact. Although Exmoor does not lie within the boundaries of the moor, many official persons believe the Black Beast of Exmoor is a very real creature that secretly lives somewhere in that wasteland. And for the past forty or fifty years there have been cattle mutilations that cannot be explained. What are your theories on that?"

Hunter expelled a long stream of smoke as he answered, "On the Beast of Exmoor?"

"Yes."

"It's a jaguar."

"How can you know that?"

"I saw the thing in a security video. It was just for a second, and it was from a distance, but it's not a wolf. And it's not a lion or a tiger."

"How could you tell?"

"By the way it moved."

"What about an American mountain lion?"

"No. It was a jaguar. Or maybe a hybrid that somebody set free back in '76 when you guys outlawed private ownership of big cats, which happened to be a real popular thing at the time. Seems like every bored rich guy in England had a tiger in his bedroom." He drew again on the Arturo Fuente. "My best guess is that someone set all of their big cats free to avoid prosecution and your Beast of Exmoor is one of its descendants."

"Interesting. How long do Jaguars live in the wild?"

"They can live thirty years or better."

Blackthorn hesitated. "England seems like it would be too harsh an environment for such a big cat to survive so long."

"Nah, Blackthorn. England used to be the home of every big cat in the world. You guys once had lions, tigers, leopards, Sabretooths. Up to about ten thousand years ago there were still jaguars in England. You call them panthers, and they were predominately black, but they were all over the country. And the weather hasn't changed all that much. You'd still have them if you hadn't hunted them to extinction."

With a brooding expression Blackthorn continued, "Well, as I said, our official position is that this has been the work of wild dogs."

"How's that workin' for you?"

"Why do you ask?"

"Because a bunch of weekend warriors tromping through the woods in some kind of hillbilly safari is going to make it a lot more difficult for me to track the thing."

Blackthorn shoved hands in the pockets of his overcoat. "To be perfectly honest, it hasn't worked as well as I'd liked. Rumors have risen about a number of wild beasts running loose in the moor and some are predictably talking about goblins and ghouls and all that rot, so there are a few hardy souls making weekend incursions, as you mentioned, with shotguns and pitchforks because it's impossible to cordon off the entire moor. It is five hundred square miles of woodland and pasture. But, then, amateur hunters don't often venture far enough into the woods to cock up any tracks. They're brave enough when the sun is up. They go home in a hurry when it gets dark."

"Where does this old man live?"

"In the Southeast. His castle sits in the middle of the moor's greatest concentration of veteran trees."

"We should get started as soon as possible."

"We can go straight from your hotel to the airport."

"No, I have to go home and pick up some gear. And a friend. And I'll need you to get me a wildlife permit. And, last thing; you'll have to charter a private cargo plane. A big one."

"What kind of wildlife permit?"

"I'll tell you when I call. How do I contact you?"

Blackthorn smoothly delivered a cell phone from his coat. "Just dial one. I'll answer day or night. And I'll obtain any necessary permits through diplomatic channels, so there won't be any delay. Is your friend, by any chance, an exotic animal?"

"You could say that."

"How exotic?"

"Very." Hunter pocketed the phone. "Have you got orders to go out with me?"

"I've been ordered to make certain the job is finished. And if you're unable to continue, I've been ordered to finish it alone."

"This isn't a duck hunt, Blackthorn. You can get killed."

Jutting his chin forward, Blackthorn said, "Death is infinitely preferable to dishonor, Hunter. And better men than me have held that credo."

Hunter smiled and nodded, "All right. But we have to have an understanding or I can't take you with me."

"Of course."

"You may know the city, commander, but this isn't the city. That moor is one of the most inhospitable, dangerous places on earth. So I'll take you with me. But you have to do exactly what I say when I say it."

"I can do that. When should I expect your call?"

"Tomorrow or the next day. And book me a military C-130. What I'm bringing can't be put on a commercial flight. And I will definitely need your help with Customs. I'll have several things your people will like to confiscate."

They resumed their stroll toward the Hilton as Blackthorn said in a more solemn tone, "Although I think you already realize this, I feel somewhat obligated to say it, nevertheless."

"What's that?"

"I do not know what this creature is, Hunter. But I know what it does. And I guarantee you that this brute will fight us to its last drop of blood."

Hunter bowed his head as he took another step.

"Then that's what we'll take."

CHAPTER NINE

R eggie glanced over his shoulder as Hunter closed the door to the back room of the subterranean paleontology laboratory of the Smithsonian, a section that visitors never see. Only supervisors and selected personnel were allowed in this hallowed sanctuary but Hunter had been given supervisory access and didn't hesitate to use it.

"Kinda early, ain't it?" asked Reggie laconically.

"I have to catch a flight," Hunter remarked. "Come over here, Reggie, and take a look at this for me."

Hunter laid the case containing the cast on the counter and Reggie brushed plaster off his hands. "You know, I've never figured out how you got clearance to this place, dude. But I can't say I'm surprised. In fact, it confirms something I've suspected for a long time."

"What's that?"

"Someone upstairs is completely insane."

Hunter smiled, "I did a favor for one of your head honchos, so he gave me the key to the city."

"What'd you do for him?"

"I found his daughter. Good thing, too. She wasn't long for this world."

"Where was she?"

"Down in Borneo. She got separated from her team after they were ambushed by some real unfriendly natives."

"So cannibalism is still alive and well in Borneo?"

"Oh, yeah. Anyway, her father, who's one of your big contributors, called me up when her group failed to make their rendezvous. So I flew down, picked up her trail, found her, brought her out."

"What happened to her team?"

"After I got her out, I went back and tracked down the bushmen. I found her friends. They'd been dead for a while."

"Wow. You shadowed bushmen in their own back yard and they never knew you were there?"

"I have a light step."

"Ghost in the darkness!" he laughed. "Did you see that movie?"

"Yeah," Hunter smiled. "Good movie."

"Does stuff like that happen in real life?"

Hunter shrugged, "I heard from old timers that the story was true. But the original two lions were a lot bigger than taxidermy left them looking. They're on display in Chicago, but the few survivors said that the original lions were gigantic. Not like the bodies at that fair. I guess preservation shrunk them. But I've heard the story is mostly true. The woods are a big place. I run into things all the time that I can't explain."

Staring down, Hunter realized that whoever made this cast was an expert. It was holding up well to the repeated viewings. There wasn't a speck of plaster out of place. Reggie's eyes flared. "Where was this made?"

"England."

Reggie paused. "Well, that's possible. These things could survive anywhere a wolf or bear could survive."

"You've seen a track like this before?"

Reggie gestured for Hunter to follow; "Come on. We've been putting one together for about a year and I wouldn't be surprised if you've never seen one before. Like I say, they were once all over the place. But we don't often dig up a large specimen still intact."

They walked through the vast warehouse as Reggie added, "Yeah, we found this big boy in South Dakota. The Black Hills." He waved, "They've been found in Spain, Germany, Russia, Italy. Even China. But I've never heard of one being found in England."

"Why is that?"

"Well, all we have is theory, but we think they preferred savannahs and warmer climates."

"Again: Why?"

"The prevailing theory is that they were predominately ambush killers. They liked to hang out at water holes and hit something when it came up for a drink, so they preferred dry terrain with only one or two good places for water. It facilitated hunting."

"What'd they look like?"

"Uh," Reggie began, "that's a bit hard to explain. But it was sort of like a super-wolf. Or a super-Grizzly. Some say it was an offshoot of the Short-nosed Bear. Or some kind of hybrid. Who knows? I mean, they did resemble Dire Wolves in a lot of ways. They also resembled Grizzlies in a lot of ways, but they were meaner than both." He shook his head, "These things were savage, man. I ain't lying. These guys make Velociraptors look like chipmunks."

"It was a prehistoric age, Reggie. Everything was vicious."

"Not like these things, dude. You see, wolves kill to save the pack or themselves. They kill for food. They kill for family. They kill for territory. And Grizzlies are pretty much the same. They don't kill without a reason. But these things were psychopaths, dude. If they were human beings, you'd call them homicidal maniacs. They were the Ted Bundys of super-predators. They hunted and killed anything and everything. Even each other. They had no sense of family or even their own kind. With them it was every land shark for himself."

"How big did they get?"

Reggie pushed a cart from their path. "Some think a mature one could go a thousand pounds. And they were loners, too."

"Because they were cannibals?"

"That's just a guess, but it seems logical. We've found them with their heads severed from a single bite. Bam! Like that! And the bite marks perfectly matched incisors of their own species."

"They were carnivorous?"

"That's a better question than you know. Some think they were omnivorous because their molars were perfect for eating plants and their incisors were perfect for eating meat. But I don't agree. I think they were *hyper*carnivorous. I think that all they ate was meat. But they could live off plants in a pinch."

Hunter took a moment to consider the implications of that before asking, "How long were they around?"

"Oh, we think they stood near the top of the food chain during the Burdigalian Epoch until the late Pliocene. It was a top-tier hitter in Amphicyonidae: Subfamily, Amphicyoninae. They were all over North America, Europe, Asia, Australia, Africa, South America. Some paleontologists refer to them as 'bear-dogs.' But we think the largest ones, like the one that left this print, looked more like a wolf. They supposedly changed shape as they aged. They became more wolflike. And they were awesome predators. There was nothing they couldn't kill."

Hunter considered that before, "How would one of them have fared against a Sabretooth?"

Reggie laughed hard. "Dude! If they had both lived at the same time? It would have been no contest. This bruiser would have eaten a Sabretooth for lunch and picked its teeth with its canines."

They rounded the corner and a gigantic skeleton loomed before Hunter. It was six feet at the shoulder and at least twelve feet in length. Its forelegs were long with tremendous bone strength and its hindlegs resembled the legs of a gargantuan wolf. Its neck was set on huge shoulders, and the skull was three feet across. Its fangs were twice the size of a Grizzly's, and the jaws were four feet in length. Hunter didn't even bother to count the incisors; there were enough fangs to rip the head off a wild bull.

"This is the largest specimen we've ever found," said Reggie in something like awe. "X-rays suggest it was about twelve years old."

"The longer they lived, the bigger they got?"

"Yeah. This one weighed about half a ton."

Hunter strolled down the right side studying the close formation of ribs. They were unusually wide and tight – like armor. Its paws were commensurate with its overall stature. They were enormous with claws that vaguely matched the marks captured in the cast.

Hunter asked quietly, "Have you estimated bite strength?"

"Yeah. The computer calculates bite strength at four thousand pounds per square inch. About the same as a Great White Shark. That's why some people call them bone crushers. And its occipital sockets indicate it could see at twenty-five thousand lumen – a lot like a wolf – so I guaranteed you it could read body heat at less than two thousand microns." Reggie lifted a hand as if to honor it. "This thing's infrared and heat vision were more sensitive than what we've got in our best satellites. And the auditory cavity suggests it could hear at five hundred thousand cycles per second. That's bat sonar, dude. I bet this thing could hear a heartbeat at a thousand yards."

Hunter gazed up a long time. "Ultrasonic hearing. Heat vision. Like a sand viper."

"But ten thousand times more accurate. This was the most perfectly designed wolf any paleontologist has ever seen. One of these things could take down a T-Rex all by itself. Eat it for lunch. Eat it for dinner. Eat it 'till it was gone. And, like I said, a Sabretooth would have just been an appetizer." Reggie paused before saying, "Let me put it like this. If you took the strongest wolf and the strongest Grizzly and put them in a blender with Superman's steroids, this is what you'd get. It's like God said, 'I'm gonna make myself the ultimate beast of prey.' So he made this guy."

Hunter carefully studied the skull as he asked, "Are you sure the cast belongs to this thing?"

"That cast is almost a perfect match for what we have on file for this animal," Reggie answered. "And I've seen dozens of prints. The pads have the characteristics of both a wolf and a bear. It's … I don't know how to say it … *unique*."

"If they were such super predators, why'd they die out?"

"Who knows? Like every other dinosaur, they had their time. All I know is the world moved on and they didn't. Some think that other species evolved that could run a helluva lot faster for the long haul. I'm talking about species that could run really, really fast for a *really* long way. And this super-wolf was so big that it couldn't stay in fifth gear that long. So it was fast as greased lightning on a downhill run for … I don't know … two or three hundred yards? Then it had to shift into grandma low. In any case, the world got faster for the long haul and these guys didn't. So they died out."

"You said this print was 'almost' a perfect match," Hunter repeated. "What do you mean by 'almost?'"

"Well, what I mean is that it's *close*. But it's not an exact match for what we've got on file for this thing." Reggie stared, silent for a second. "Why are you asking all this?"

Hunter slowly stepped back, staring up.

"A man should know his enemy."

Reggie gazed from the skeleton to Hunter before raising a hand again to the skull. "Hunter, these guys were the heavyweight champions of the savannah for fourteen million years. But these bad boys are extinct, man."

Hunter stared over the great, distended fangs.
"Are they?"

CHAPTER TEN

B ack in Montana, Hunter parked his beat-up deuce-and-a-half outside the cabin. Dropping to the ground, he saw the wide-open doors beside the wood pile that led downward to the cellar, noted the absence of dead bodies, and figured everything was probably all right.

Hunter descended the steps to the basement and closed the wide double doors. Long ago he had dug out a series of tunnels beneath the cabin because living below ground was warmer in the never-ending winter. And the cavern had, consequently, become a den for his best friend.

Hunter dropped his gear on the floor vaguely noting that everything was in place. His rifles remained untouched. His canned goods were undisturbed. It took him a few minutes to light a half dozen kerosene lanterns stationed strategically throughout the cavern but when he was finished, the shelter was glowing. He spent five minutes building a fire in the hearth. Then a colossal shadow emerged from the gloom at his back.

Without turning, Hunter laughed, "I've been in here long enough to steal us blind and you're just waking up?"

The Grizzly gently nudged Hunter with a grunt.

Once again Hunter was thankful that he'd built the cavern with a ten-foot ceiling as the Grizzly stood to its full height, his broad forehead swaying less than an inch beneath the rafters. Then it dropped again and embraced Hunter with a hug that Hunter knew could snap an oak tree but the grip was gentle and the claws touched lightly as feathers. And that was it. The big hello. Afterwards the Grizzly simply laid out before the fire, staring into the flames.

Hunter removed his coat and sat on his wooden bunk. It wasn't the kind of bed a civilized man would force his dog to use, but Hunter found it comfortable enough. Plus, if his roommate got the impulse to sit on it, destroying it in the process, it was easy to replace.

Out of curiosity Hunter glanced across the floor; no bones were scattered although he wouldn't have been surprised.

Hunter asked, "You hungry?"

The bear rose good-naturedly to amble forward again and Hunter removed the haunch of a wild boar he had killed on his way up the mountain out of a canvas bag. He'd left the rest of the hog with a Cheyenne family that lived further down. He routinely insured that his community was well fed and safe from both the merciless elements of nature and the even less merciful elements of man.

When he stopped at Old Man Tankersley's store to pick up supplies he'd been informed of all the current need-to-know. Without question, when it came to the latest news, gossip, UFO sightings and end-of-the-world premonitions, Tankersley's was the place to go. In five minutes Hunter caught up on the usual as well as something new. It seemed the community hospital was down one sawbones since Doc Hefler had a heart attack last week, nor was it likely the 89-year-old would be 'bouncing back.' Hunter said he'd try to find a physician to fill in until feds appointed a replacement.

When Hunter's single-prop plane, which he flew himself, landed at their small airport, Sheriff Tyrone Cahill, a long-time friend, dragged him aside to say poaching along the river had gotten "entirely out of hand."

Cahill never officially asked Hunter to intervene in matters of law enforcement, but Hunter knew what he *wasn't* asking. So, when this was finished, he'd systematically track down the trophy hunters and make that wilderness a very miserable place to be for anyone who did not reside in Montana.

It had been Hunter's usual homecoming, no better, no worse.

In some ways Hunter was the frontier's most immutable law and he frequently took justice into his own hands to maintain peace on his mountain and the reservation. No one ever asked for it. No one ever spoke of it. But everyone knew of it and *almost* everyone approved. And that was how Hunter wanted it. He didn't want money and he didn't want glory. He just wanted people to live in peace and he wanted to be one of them.

He tossed the haunch so that it landed in front of Ben, who picked it up and walked back to the fireplace. With a grunt the bear laid down, notched the slab between paws as large as hubcaps, and began tearing off strips, chewing slowly. Next, Hunter pulled out Blackthorn's cell phone and hit 'one.'

London's senior homicide detective answered on the first ring.

"It's me," said Hunter. "No, I'm still in Montana. I'll meet you at Dulles tomorrow night. Now, write this down. I need a wildlife permit for a North American Grizzly. Two years old. He weighs a thousand pounds, and we'll need a very large cage, so we'll need a heavy charter. His name is Ben and I'll text you his U. S. Fish and Wildlife number. And we'll have to ride in cargo with him or something might happen. Like what? Like he might get upset, Blackthorn, and no cage is gonna hold him if he does. No, I can arrange a flight to Washington. I have a friend who owns a C-130. Yeah, I'll call you tomorrow and tell you what time we're landing because we'll need to get back into the air right away. I don't want Ben cooling his heels around too many people. Yeah, I'm bringing a Ruger .454, a Marlin 45.70, and a Remington 870. No, I prefer my own load. Later."

As he shut the phone Hunter watched as Ben meditatively devoured the leg. He was in his happy place, close to the fire with a good meal, and cared for little more. Hunter never regretted his decision to remove the Grizzly cub from certain death in the Montana wild. As the last surviving member of a family whose mother had decimated the cattle of ranchers, Hunter found Ben alone but alive after he tracked down and killed the mother.

Hunter suspected that she was already shot and dying, which she was, and that was why she'd resorted to feeding on cattle. But none of that mattered after she killed a professional tracker who'd been hired to dispatch her. Afterwards, Hunter found Ben, who was barely a week old, and knew the cub would die alone, so he brought him home.

The rest was simple enough as Ben adjusted to his new life in Hunter's "den." Ben took to the cabin like he'd been born there, and Montana Fish and Game was proud to add a healthy Grizzly to their roster. After tagging him, they left Ben to Hunter's supervision with no restrictions unless the cub, too, developed bad habits like feeding on the stores of ranchers. But that hadn't been a problem so far. Ben much preferred big game like moose, boar, or bighorn and Hunter's mountain had enough game for a dozen Grizzlies.

For the most part, Ben required no upkeep. When he was hungry, he wandered out and took down a moose. When he was finished, he came home and slept. He had never displayed a hint of ill will toward any human being. He was a giant even for a Grizzly, but he was gentle and possessed an amiable nature. "Thanks for not eating all our cans," muttered Hunter. "I guess you learned your lesson when you opened that pepper, huh?"

Watching the half-ton bear eat, so content, Hunter was again uncertain whether he should take him on this trip. He had never taken Ben on a trip, had never used him on a track, and wasn't sure how he would behave. But there was too much about this that was unsettling and Hunter sensed that he might need Ben's giant strength.

As Hunter pondered the situation, he didn't like the fact that this unknown creature's track was linked to a long extinct species that had been such a legendary predator. Nor did he like the fact that Reggie had said the print was "almost" a perfect match because the "almost' threw a chimera-like enigma into an already-dangerous mix that he knew from experience could be explosively deadly. Also, it was profoundly disturbing that the creature was so obsessed with this old man's estate. It was unnatural, and anything unnatural instantly piqued his suspicion.

But letting Ben run wild in that unforgiving, godless North York Moor was another thing altogether. Hunter had no intentions of releasing Ben in that graveyard of a wilderness. It was unfamiliar territory and the bear could get confused and then he would prey on cattle, revealing his presence, and those farmers would hunt him down. So, instead, Hunter would keep him on a chain – for whatever good it would do. And Hunter had absolutely no intention of letting Ben fight this creature. For certain, it'd be a battle for the ages, but it would probably end with the death of both.

He recalled how Roman emperors had matched full-grown lions against Grizzlies in the coliseum. The bears had won every contest simply by smashing a paw down on the lion's head, crushing its skull. The fights became so predictable that they were eventually discontinued. There was no sport to it. And although this unknown creature surely didn't have the advantages a Grizzly possessed over a lion, it might be the most powerful terrestrial predator this world had ever known. And even Grizzlies can be killed.

It was still early but Hunter felt the need to rest. As he lay back, he heard Ben rise and come to his side and knew the bear would remain at his side while he slept. And he would be at his side when he awoke.

CHAPTER ELEVEN

Blackthorn had met them in Washington when Hunter's plane stopped so Hunter could take another flight and said he'd like to ride along in cargo. Hunter had no objections, and as they flew over the Atlantic, Blackthorn idly studied Ben. The expression on the detective's face was almost comical.

Secured inside a ten-by-twenty-foot cage, Ben lay stretched out, sleeping peacefully. The jet was large enough to carry tanks and helicopters so it was adequate for carrying Ben. Hanging outside the steel bars was a chain that Hunter would use as a leash.

"I was wondering if what they say is true," murmured the detective.

"What do they say?"

"Is a Grizzly really the biggest and most dangerous bear?"

"Nope."

"Why not?"

"Polar bears are bigger and more dangerous. Kodiaks are bigger, more dangerous, and downright insane. Grizzlies, by comparison, are choir boys." He yawned. "A Grizzly will only fight if he's sick, scared, or starving. Otherwise, he'll just wander around eating berries and fish and whatever else he can scavenge. Sometimes he'll take a moose or big game. But they live pretty well off fish and berries."

"How big would you say he is?"

"I haven't measured him for a suit."

"Come on, Hunter. Take a guess."

"Aren't detectives trained to guess someone's weight?"

"I wouldn't call him 'a someone.'"

Hunter replied tiredly, "He's about ten feet and I already told you he weighs a little more than a thousand. But it's not all muscle. He's been eating everything in sight to get ready for winter."

"For hibernation?" Blackthorn shifted toward Hunter. "How can they sleep for three straight months?"

"They don't. They just sleep more than usual. They wake up, look outside, see the snow, and go back to sleep. Bears don't like to walk around in the snow any more than we do. Their feet get cold, too."

With noticeable concern Blackthorn asked, "Just for, uh, *reference* ... how does one survive a Grizzly attack?"

"'One' doesn't."

"What about climbing a tree?"

"He can climb better than you can."

"What about playing dead?"

"They eat the dead, Blackthorn."

Blackthorn took a long moment before his next question. "How, exactly, does a Grizzly kill someone?"

Hunter felt the warmth of sleep closing. "I don't think you're stupid enough to even make him look sideways at you, Blackthorn, much less kill you. But if Ben were defending himself – or defending *me* since he considers me family – he'd probably just whack you."

"Whack me? One whack would hurt me?"

"One whack would kill you graveyard dead, man."

"What! How?" Blackthorn sat back. "Where do bears strike?"

"Where he hits you doesn't matter. You'd be getting hit by a paw as big as a hubcap with four-inch claws at the end of it. He could hit you in the foot and kill you."

"Is that how a Grizzly typically kills people?"

"Grizzlies don't *typically* kill people, Blackthorn. That's a myth. Polar bears are famous for killing people. Kodiaks and Brown bears are famous for killing people. But a Grizzly will usually just paw you. They won't even whack you. And when he's sure you're gonna leave him alone so he can eat in peace, he'll go his way. He doesn't want any trouble. He just wants to eat."

The detective shifted to gaze at the canvas bundle containing his hunting gear. "You brought a shotgun?" he asked finally. "That's not a proper weapon for this animal is it? Don't you need an elephant gun?"

Hunter seriously felt the need for sleep as he replied, "Every weapon has its place. And if you're hunting a proven maneater in thick bush, a pump action with magnum shells is the weapon you want. So is a .454 revolver. I use a Ruger Alaskan with a four-inch barrel. You can swing it at close range without getting it caught on branches. It's the best last-chance weapon against a big predator."

"Why is the shotgun so useful?"

"Because a cut-down shotgun fires a three-inch magnum shell at a thousand feet per second. It makes a three-quarter-inch hole going in and leaves a hole the size of a basketball coming out. The downside is that a shotgun is short-range so you only have time for one or two shots at a very fast-moving bear and, if you miss, you'll be killed at the speed of light."

Blackthorn pressed, "Okay, well, I got that. So tell me this, why is this big fellow coming with us? Does he track with you? Like a bloodhound?"

"I'm not bringing him for nothing, Blackthorn. Yeah, I'll use him on the track. He smells, hears, and senses things that we can't. So if he starts acting strange, you'd better look sharp."

"How will you know if he's acting strange?"

"I'll know. Believe me."

There was a pause as if Blackthorn were considering something of grave importance. Finally he asked, "I only repeat this question because there does happen to be a rather important legal issue here. Is it possible that he might 'accidentally' hurt someone? Perhaps one of my men? Or even – god forbid – one of Milton's family?"

"Good god, Blackthorn, how many times do I have to say it? Ben is a lover, not a fighter." Hunter laid his head back. "For the final time, the only reason Ben would hurt someone is to protect himself or me. Unless he's starving. Then I can't make any promises. Did you make the arrangements?"

Blackthorn nodded, "Yes, yes, that only took a phone call. Apparently, the moor is chock full of sheep herders who are more than willing to sell their stock at black market prices to feed your bear. But why didn't we just buy a cow? They're bigger. They last longer."

"I don't want him to develop a taste for cattle," remarked Hunter sleepily. "But sheep are fine. He preys on bighorn sheep back home. Now try and get some sleep, man. There won't be much time after we land."

"Is he going to keep sleeping?"

"He'll do whatever I do."

"What's he going to do if you get killed?"

Eyes closed, Hunter replied quietly, "Then I guess you'll get a front row seat to the Wrath of God."

CHAPTER TWELVE

Hunter judged Blackthorn's Jaguar to be a somewhat extravagant police vehicle by American standards. As they cruised through North York Moor, he glanced back to insure the truck carrying Ben remained close. By chance he also noticed the ominous mouth of the moor closing upon them like the Sargasso Sea on a doomed ship.

This vast wilderness was a naked, windswept sea of tarn broken by jagged fangs of rock and black islands of forest. Nor did there seem to be any evident life, but for fowl. Gazing at the distant tree lines, Hunter could not see beyond the gloomy surface but he knew how very dangerous this moor could be. It was eternally cold and wet and pitted with ubiquitous bogs and quicksand. It was one of the most dangerous wildernesses in the world.

By late afternoon they arrived at the sprawling manor of Major Augustus Milton. It was almost twilight, and as they exited the Jaguar, a man with a curling black mustache approached holding a double-barrel rifle that Hunter couldn't identify from his angle. It was a side-by-side and had been the preferred weapon of trophy hunters when trophies worthy of such a formidable weapon still roamed the earth.

"Good evening, Inspector Marshal," Blackthorn addressed the man with a commander's air. "How are the lads holding up?"

Inspector Marshal solemnly shook his head, "Not good, governor, not good. I'm afraid we lost Pembry."

"Yes. The commissioner informed me. Do we have any idea what happened?"

Marshal lifted an arm to the gigantic maze of six-foot high hedges decorating seven acres directly in front of the estate. "We've examined the grounds, but we can't determine what happened, sir. We've been hoping Mr. Hunter might be able to help."

"Of course," Blackthorn said as he extended an arm. "Well, then, allow me to introduce Nathaniel Hunter. He is our wilderness expert. Mr. Hunter, this is Inspector William Marshal. He has thirty years in-service with Metropolitan Police. He's my most stalwart man."

"Inspector," nodded Hunter.

Marshal reflected the gesture. "A privilege, Mr. Hunter. The commander relayed your message. The kitchen is prepared."

"Thank you. And it's just Hunter."

"Then it's just Bill, sir."

Hunter lifted his gaze to study the towering home of Augustus Milton. It was the kind of old-world castle one sees in magazines and although Hunter had not expected to be impressed, he was.

Located deep inside hundreds of square miles of England's oldest forests, the estate was built in four wings and covered at least six acres of relatively dry land. Each wing was five stories squared with casements and ramparts built entirely from granite. Only the twin doors were constructed with black iron brackets and wood but they were formidable, wide, and tall. And since each had to weigh a ton, impractical for ordinary use.

"What door do they use to go in and out?" asked Hunter.

Marshal pointed to a drive that ran through an arch attached to the nearest wall. "The family parks between the west and south wings and they use an entry that joins the extensions. No one – in case you're wondering – bothers to use those Frankenstein front doors except for visitors. The major likes to keep guests on formal footing, you know."

"Does the major get a lot of visitors?"

"Oh, yes," Marshal affirmed. "The major retains majority ownership of many, many banks, and frequently entertains partners and financiers. He is also a retired military man of famous patriotism, so his old mates come along. And, naturally, his family receives guests."

Hunter turned. "All right, Blackthorn. First, I want to see those claw marks on the wall."

Three minutes later Hunter was gazing up at five floors of flat, gray exterior granite. The rock was untouched to the second tier. He took a long time putting himself into the mind of whatever had been on this wall and knew there was no denying it. Clearly a man-like creature had ascended this spot using the claws of both hands and feet. The marks were occasionally interrupted by deep pockets dug into the stone as if to gain purchase. The path passed windows of each floor.

Uneasily Blackthorn asked, "What do you make of it?"

Hunter attempted to downplay his own fears by saying, "Well, something climbed this wall. That's pretty obvious."

"Any idea what?"

"It's too early to tell."

"What about that track in the planter?"

The investigator pointed at the garden running alongside the wall and Hunter knelt, studying the print. It was twice as wide as his hand and he'd been right in estimating its weight. It was a thousand pounds – as heavy as Ben. And this creature had paused – or waited – as it had apparently stared at the beast clawing its way up the granite.

"Any idea what that is?" continued Blackthorn.

"It looks like a wolf the size of a Grizzly." Hunter stood. "But it can't be either one. Take me to where the chauffer was killed."

Uncharacteristically, Blackthorn looked surprised. "But what about Pembry's last location? That site is fresher." He stared. "In the most terrible sense of the word, of course."

"First I want to see how it killed the chauffer. Then I'll look at how it killed Pembry. If it did anything different, then it's learning."

"Is that important?"

"Everything's important, Bill."

In a few moments they stood over cold and blackened ground. Hunter walked to the nearest six-foot hedge, examining the leaves. He gently lifted a handful of twigs from the ground; they were smashed flat. Then he gazed along the top of the hedge and saw an unnatural smoothness; it was as if an invisible giant had passed his hand across the leaves.

"Do you see anything?" asked Blackthorn.

Hunter pointed. "It came through this hedge. Like a tiger might do. It was using concealment. But then it leaped over the hedge when it retreated. Exposing itself like a tiger *wouldn't*." He turned to the manor. "So it's either stupid or something spooked it. And I don't think it's stupid."

Blackthorn glanced at the manor before asking incredulously, "You think a *porch light* scared this brute off?"

"Maybe."

"Is that a weakness?"

"It depends."

"What do you mean?"

Hunter studied the ground between the mansion and fence. "It depends on why the light scared it. If it's just scared of light, then that's good. That means it's not too smart. But if it retreated because it won't break a rule, then that's not good."

"What rule?"

"If it has a rule to remain invisible, then it has a game plan. That means that it's smart and disciplined." Hunter paused. "Or well trained."

"Do other predators do that?"

"Do what?"

"Use darkness like a game plan?'"

"Sure. Spiders. Snakes. Jaguars. Wolves. With some it's instinct. With some it's intelligence. They use their best gifts during the most opportune hours for hunting and rarely deviate. Call it instinct. Call it intelligence. Call it whatever you want. But an animal that won't violate its game plan is far more difficult to catch than some careless outlaw."

Walking around the hedge, Hunter understood why they hadn't found more tracks. This half-frozen ground was covered with centuries of loam. A buffalo could walk across this hardtack without leaving a track. But he followed the all-but-invisible, displaced twigs until he reached the fence, which was capped with unusually sharp spikes.

Reaching out, Hunter tried to shake it. The iron posts were deeply set in granite. He would walk the full perimeter before dark, but he knew the creature had leaped this barrier because no animal could knock it down. It was probably a relic from the Middle Ages that had defied human invaders of far greater resolve than wolves. Kneeling, he studied the loam.

Something this big would have left a set of prints when it pushed off to clear the fence but the ground was marred by a thousand tracks and Hunter asked, "Bill? How often do your men come this way?"

"We obbo from dusk to dawn, sir. Men and dogs. No zone remains unmonitored for more than twenty minutes."

"Obbo?"

"Our word for 'observation,'" volunteered Blackthorn. "In America you would call it 'patrol.'"

Hunter glanced in both directions. "I see you've got horses. New shoes. Big. Heavy. Clydesdales?"

The commander affirmed, "Yes, sir. The major was gracious enough to grant us use of his entire stable of Clydesdales. All eight of them."

"Big dogs, big horses, a lot of men, a lot of prints." Hunter brushed off a knee as he rose. "All right. Take me to where Pembry was last seen."

Five minutes later they were standing on the east side of the manor and Hunter knelt over a patch of grass blackened by blood. He removed a lighter and held the flame close to the loam. He lowered his head to gaze along the grass with a ground-level view. Then he said, "It waited for Pembry here. It mulled about like it was studying the building. But it was anxious or maybe … impatient. Like it was expecting someone to be here that wasn't."

He passed a hand over a small impression. "This is where Pembry stopped. This sharp ridge of broken twigs – right there – is where this thing pushed off with its back feet and attacked." He pointed to a blackened patch. "It killed Pembry here. Then it took his body."

Blackthorn recoiled. "Are you saying this animal leaped that fence with a two-hundred-pound man in its teeth?!"

"All I know is what the tracks say." Hunter rose. "Okay, I've seen enough. I need to get Ben out of that truck before he gets antsy."

"Absolutely," agreed Blackthorn. "I don't fancy witnessing the Wrath of God before dinner."

* * *

Ben lazily gazed over the compound and Hunter wondered if this estate was the equivalent of an amusement park in the bear's mind. But then Ben suddenly, sharply turned his head, staring in the direction of the moor. In the next split-second he stood, towering above the roof of the truck, and began swaying, his nose lifted high.

"What does that mean?" nervously asked Blackthorn, backing away.

"He smells something," said Hunter.

"*Smells what?*"

Hunter stared into a mist settling on the moor. "It could be anything. A bear has a better nose than a bloodhound."

Reaching for, but not drawing, the revolver at his waist, Blackthorn angled to the side so he could see around Ben. He lifted his chin, eyes wide, staring in the bear's direction. "I don't see anything," he whispered.

Hunter muttered, "Why are you whispering? And Ben doesn't see it, either. But he can smell it and he doesn't like it."

The inspector's hand slowly fell from his pistol. He began to reach for Ben, as if to comfort him, then apparently thought better of it. "Well," he commented, "it looks like this big lug might come in handy, after all. Does this mean you'll be tracking tonight?"

"No," said Hunter firmly. "I'm not going to track it in the dark. It has too much advantage." He turned toward the mansion. "I need to secure a place for Ben. Then I'm gonna look around inside the house."

Inspector Marshal stepped forward. "There is a large shed out back. I had it filled with a load of fresh straw this morning. It's warm and dry and I think your friend will be comfortable."

"Take me to it."

"As you say, sir."

* * *

One hundred meters from the rear entrance of the manor, Hunter stared over a shed large enough for a half dozen Clydesdales. It had a tin roof and walls of tightly sealed one-inch-thick planks. There were dozens of horse-riding blankets, saddles, harnesses and an empty 55-gallon drum positioned in the center on a pallet of fire bricks. Standing close, Blackthorn didn't flinch as Ben ambled past, casting the detective an unconcerned glance. It seemed to Hunter that each of them had casually accepted the other's existence.

"Get on in there, you bruiser! I'll see if we can't scare you up a flock of sheep!"

Locking the chain around the shed's support beam, Hunter took time to kindle a sizeable fire in the drum. Within minutes the sturdy structure was warming and Ben was sprawled in every direction on an enormous mound of dry straw.

Hunter turned on an overhead light – the place was wired for electricity – and he shouted, "Hey! How about this, boy? We've got electricity! We're moving up in the world!" He nuzzled the bear's head. "Try not to cause any trouble while I'm gone, okay? I'm gonna get you something to eat."

As he walked toward the wide-open doors Hunter saw three red crates stacked against the wall and identified them instantly. He removed the bowie knife from his belt, gently pried off the lid, and stared down to make sure the contents were safe. He counted fifteen sticks of dynamite in the top box, but they appeared to be in good shape. None of them were sweating. Carefully, he secured the lid again to protect them from the humidity.

He looked at Blackthorn, "Did you know this was here?"

"I did not."

Marshall seemed crestfallen, "Forgive me, sir, I reckoned all this was riding equipment. I never expected dynamite. The fault is mine."

"It's no big deal," Hunter said easily. "Ben doesn't have an appetite for dynamite. Just leave it here. I'll feel safer knowing it's out here with him where nobody will bother it."

"Very good, sir."

Ben grunted softly and studied his surroundings as Hunter walked toward the house. A pleasant woman far older than Hunter met him at the back entrance of the manor with an immense platter of raw lamb chops. Hunter bowed his head, "Thank you, ma'am. You're very kind."

Clasping her hands, she smiled, "My name is Zelda, Mr. Hunter, and there's no need to fret. We're well prepared for your friend. The icebox is filled with enough lamp chops for a dozen Grizzly bears."

"And these are all lamb?"

"Absolutely," she nodded. "Inspector Marshal told us that you didn't want your friend to develop a sweet tooth for cows."

"Thank you, Ms. Zelda."

"It's just Zelda, son."

"Thank you."

"At your service."

After depositing the platter, a full bucket of water, and saying a few encouraging words to Ben, Hunter was joined by Blackthorn and Marshal as he returned to the manor. With an uneasy gaze Blackthorn asked, "Why do you want to look around inside?"

Hunter raised his face to the vacant, eye-like windows. "This creature wants someone inside this house, Blackthorn. We'll be one step ahead of the game if we know who it is."

"But what about Pembry and the chauffer?"

"I think they were targets of opportunity. It wasn't here for either of them. They just got in its way."

The inspector seemed more troubled. "Do you have any idea yet what we're dealing with? I mean, what kind of animal could – *or would* – come here hunting a specific person?"

"Tracking a maneater is like putting together a bloody jigsaw puzzle one piece at a time until you figure out what kind of an animal you're dealing with. Then you have to figure out what it wants. And animals are like people. Some have personal reasons for why they do things. Some are just hungry. And as far as this animal goes, I haven't figured out much yet." Hunter studied the steep walls of the manor. "Still, he's got some kind of reason for why he's doing this. Big places like this scare animals away, so this thing must want something inside this place real bad."

Blackthorn seemed wounded. "You're very careful with what you say, Hunter. But I am a veteran homicide detective and, while I cannot say I've seen everything, I'm quite sturdy with bad news. Why won't you just tell me what we're dealing with?"

"Because it's nothing but a theory, Blackthorn. I don't have any evidence. But I've seen something like this before."

"In Alaska?"

"Yeah."

"When are you going to tell me about all that?"

"When it's relevant."

Blackthorn accepted the excuse without expression. "Very well. And just so you know, my men are carrying the heaviest gauge weapons we could procure. Ben should be safe out here with us."

"Ben will be safe, anyway. It's your men I'm worried about." Hunter had to crank his head all the way back to see the top of the ramparts. "Good grief, this place is big."

"Why are you worried about my men?"

"Because the greatest danger is the possibility that this animal wants to get inside this mansion. And, if it does, then this goes from being a safari to a standup fight real fast and I'm not sure you've got the firepower for it."

Blackthorn waved a hand at the edifice. "Come along, Hunter! What are the odds of a wild animal breeching these walls? This castle was built during the French and English wars! These walls are two feet of solid granite taken from this family's own tor."

Hunter stared. "What's a tor?"

"Uh," Blackthorn hesitated, "in America I believe you would call it 'a rock quarry.' Yes, indeed, this family owns an enormous tor east of the manor. It's how the major's ancestors made their fortune. And I've heard it's the finest granite in all of Britain. Perhaps the world."

"Well, that's great. But granite doesn't cover windows and doors. And this place has a ton of them."

"Are you really convinced it wants to get inside?"

Hunter turned to face him. "Look, all I've seen are tracks. But I already know this much. We're not gonna have to go after this animal because he's coming to *us*." He pointed to the granite walls. "It's after someone inside that house. And you'd better prepare them for it because we might have to use them as bait."

"As bait!" The investigator stepped back. "Are you insane!"

"This person is bait whether we're using them or not, Blackthorn. But we might be able to save them if we can figure out who it is."

"That's a risky plan, mate."

"It's better than the alternative."

"What's the alternative?"

"Tracking this beast through that moor." Hunter glanced over his shoulder. "That's death valley out there. That moor is deadly even if you're *not* tracking a super-predator."

Blackthorn strolled, head bent, before he allowed, "I can accept that. But I'm still not convinced with your supposition. Why are you so convinced this infernal creature is after someone inside the house?"

"From the vantage points it picks." Hunter swept out an arm. "It could have watched this place from that tree line. But it didn't do that. It comes close to a specific door like it's waiting for someone to walk out that door. Pembry and the chauffer just happened to bump into it. An accident. But it wasn't here for them. It was waiting for someone else. And until it gets to them, it's gonna keep coming."

With a bitter expression Blackthorn muttered, "I thought tracking this creature would be the easiest way to kill it."

Hunter shook his head, "Tracking it is the *hardest* way to kill it. Tracking puts you on its home ground, where it's strongest. Where it has every advantage. An ambush is the easiest way to kill it. That's how they kill tigers. They wait for a tiger to reach a certain spot, then shoot it from a safe elevation. They don't stalk it through the jungle. That's akin to suicide."

There was a moment as Blackthorn studied the black walls of surrounding moor. "Yes. Well. I see." Glancing toward Ben, he asked, "Is the big fellow going to be all right out here by himself?"

"Why wouldn't he be?"

"I thought he might get lonely."

Hunter smiled, "Grows on you, doesn't he?"

"Much to my surprise," remarked Blackthorn, "he does."

CHAPTER THIRTEEN

Hunter was fairly chagrined that he'd failed to consider the fact that Blackthorn was, of course, already familiar with everyone who lived and worked in the house. The chief investigator had obviously confirmed their identities before verifying alibis from four nights ago.

Introductions to the kitchen staff were polite, perfunctory, and unrevealing. Then Blackthorn led Hunter to the front of the impressive manor to enter a trophy room unlike any Hunter had ever seen.

The enormous chamber was three hundred feet long and resembled nothing so much as a Viking Meeting Hall. It was also a trophy room with gigantic boar, bear, tiger, mountain lion, a full-size bull elephant bearing tusks worthy of a Mastodon and a magnificent Andrea Condor, its twenty-foot wings spread impressively across the ceiling. There were Polar bear and multiple Kodiaks and Grizzlies immortalized in ferocious fighting stances. Upon every wall were innumerable artifacts from distant lands that spoke of vanished civilizations and wars lost to time. And at the far end of the hall sat an old man behind a desk who rose with ramrod military bearing.

Dressed in a three-piece brown suit and tie, the man did not move from behind his desk as Blackthorn led Hunter through the menagerie of the world's greatest beasts and finally stopped.

"Mr. Hunter," Blackthorn announced, "I'd like to introduce you to Major Augustus Milton of Her Majesty's SAS. Retired, of course. Major, this is Nathaniel Hunter."

Coming around the desk, Milton extended a hand. "Of course, commander! It is a privilege to finally meet you, Mr. Hunter! I've read all about your exploits! Please just refer to me as 'major.' Everyone else does." He laughed, "Even my children!"

Hunter shook hands and glanced at the display. "Quite a trophy room you've got here, major."

Accepting the implied invitation, Milton walked forward, gesturing for Hunter to accompany him. "Oh, yes, they were all magnificent, which is why I chose to preserve their magnificence." He stopped, gazing up at a huge Polar bear. "In 1962 I was commissioned by the American Wildlife Preserve to remove this beast from a small fishing village at the fringe of the Arctic Circle. He had killed several villagers and had begun stalking personnel at a nearby naval station." He lowered his chin. "In any case, I tracked him and dispatched him. He topped sixteen feet and weighed nineteen hundred pounds. Surely the last of his kind. It was a terrible thing to destroy him, of course, but he had become a maneater and I needn't tell you that leaves little choice. It's a great evil to destroy such a king of his kind. But, if it must be done, then it should be done quickly and mercifully."

Hunter was familiar with campfire stories recalling bygone times when bears topped twenty feet and weighted more than a ton but he'd always listened with skepticism. Until now.

"You say you've heard of me?" Hunter asked.

"Oh, yes," answered the major. "I've followed your exploits for years, Mr. Hunter. And I must say I possessed similar goals in my youth. But the war and military service sabotaged my personal ambitions. Then, after my government service was complete, I entered banking to help rebuild my country. And, quite to my surprise, I found that I had a knack for it. But don't make the mistake I made, Mr. Hunter. Stick with your passions! I've never seen anyone on their death bed surrounded by pictures of where they were employed."

Hunter felt an unexpected sympathy for the old man. And, at the same time, he felt certain that he knew who this creature was obsessed with killing. He asked, "Do you know why I'm here, major?"

"Indeed," Milton nodded, "I observed the track myself." He stared, clearly expectant. "What did you make of it?"

Implacably holding the gaze, Hunter said, "Four claw marks. Narrow front pads. Large rear pad. But it's too big for a wolf. What did you think?"

Milton frowned, "To tell the truth, my boy, I didn't know what to think, and I have still not made up my mind." He glanced at the Polar bear. "So they have conscripted you to kill it?"

"Yes."

And, with that, the tour ended as Milton strolled back toward the hearth where a wood fire warmed the hall. "Sit with me, gentlemen," he said. "I rarely have the opportunity to share brandy with men such as yourselves." He laughed without humor. "Men such as yourselves are as rare now as these magnificent giants that once ruled this earth."

Hunter acquiesced, "I'll be happy to, major. But I need to check on a friend first."

The major's eyes brightened. "The Grizzly?"

"Yes."

"Are the arrangements adequate?"

"They're fine."

"Yes, well, I saw you unload him from the transport. He's a fine example of a North American Grizzly. I assume you will be staying with him in the shed?"

"Yes."

"Ah," he nodded, "as it should be. I'm too old now for sleeping under the stars, but I did love it so." He poured three brandies. "To tell you the truth, I rarely go outside at all, anymore. All of them begin fussing at me if I venture too far onto the grounds."

Hunter hesitated, eyes narrowing. "I just have one question for you, major."

"Yes?"

"On the morning that your chauffer, Mr. Staford, was killed, did you meet with him first?"

Milton said plainly, "Why, yes. Of course. Angus always came to me before he started the car to make sure I was prepared. We spoke for a moment, and then I gave him my briefcase. That's been our normal routine for decades."

"Thank you. I'll be back in a moment."

"Take your time, Mr. Hunter."

Hunter heard Blackthorn mutter an apology before following Hunter out the back. As they walked toward the shed, Blackthorn whispered, "Are you thinking that this creature is after Milton?"

"Of course," muttered Hunter. "Who else would it be after? Zelda? You're got a murder in progress, Blackthorn. This animal isn't stalking you, your men, or the staff. It's here for that old man. I've only been here an hour but that's already the only thing that makes sense." He stopped, turning into the detective. "Listen, I'll track down this animal but you'll have to find out who wants Milton dead because stopping one without stopping the other ain't gonna work. You have to stop both."

"You're speaking like this creature is some kind of bloodhound."

"It's got the instincts of a bloodhound, yeah, but there's something more to it. I just can't see it yet.

"Look, man, I know it's not a tiger or a wolf. I know it's not a Grizzly. And it's got the hunting instincts of a bloodhound but no bloodhound can leap a ten-foot fence carrying a man in its teeth. But this thing can. Now do *you* know of any animal that can do that?"

"No animal that currently walks the earth, no."

"And neither do I! And I know this animal wasn't born in this moor. It was set loose here by somebody with a plan. So, the two questions you need to ask are, first, who brought the damn thing here and, second, who put it on Milton's scent?" He pointed to the mansion. "And I'm betting it's someone inside that house."

Blackthorn recoiled. "This's the wildest conjecture I've ever heard, Hunter! You're trusting your instincts too much, man! You have no proof!"

"What kind of proof do you want?"

"Why does the major have to be the target?"

Hunter held up a hand, counting off. "One, this took a lot of work to set up and that means the money has to be worth the trouble. Two, Milton is a multi-billionaire and that makes him the most likely suspect. Three, Milton almost never goes outside. That's why this thing hasn't had a chance to kill him and why it keeps coming back. Four, somebody in that house knew Milton was leaving that morning and that's why this animal was waiting beside his car. Five, it ended up killing the chauffer because he was carrying Milton's briefcase and Milton's scent was all over him. Otherwise it would have just passed on the chauffer and waited for Milton – his real target."

"But you said it killed the chauffer because he got in its way!"

Hunter's frustration emerged, "The chauffer *did* get in its way but it was waiting for the major! It got confused by the scent on the briefcase and killed the wrong man!"

"If you were a bit off-base about the chauffer, then could you be wrong about someone in the house controlling this animal?"

"No," Hunter shook his head, "I assumed this thing was a wild animal. Now I think it's more like an attack dog. It responds to commands. And that means whoever is commanding it has to stay close to it. And that puts them in Milton's house."

Without waiting for a retort Hunter entered the shed. Although Ben blinked, he didn't otherwise acknowledge the approach. Nor did he seem to pay any attention to Blackthorn. Without a word Hunter knelt beside the huge Grizzly, unlocking his chain.

"Come on," said Hunter gently. "We've got work to do."

Ben lumbered up and began walking toward the open twin doors. He lifted his nose to Blackthorn for an indifferent sniff and ambled along as if he'd known the detective all his life. With similar indifference Blackthorn walked on the left side of the bear, as close as Hunter.

"Now what?" Blackthorn asked.

"I'm going to find out what I can about this family," Hunter answered grimly. "And I'm putting Ben out front while we talk to Milton. I want Ben where I can see him."

"You think he'll alert us if the creature is close?"

"I know he will."

"How?"

"You saw it at the truck," stated Hunter. "He'll stand up. He'll start sniffing the wind and swaying back and forth. He'll look scared. Then he'll look angry like he's getting psyched up for a fight."

"What are you going to chain him to?"

"One of those columns."

After a moment Blackthorn commented, *"That's optimistic."*

"It won't hold him if he gets mad, but it'll slow him down long enough for me to reach him." Hunter glanced over. "You need to get your hands on one of those elephant guns because that pistol you're carrying will just piss this animal off."

As they rounded the corner of the manor, with Ben sauntering between them, a dozen London police officers scattered with indistinct shouts. Hunter wasted no time chaining him to a column clearly visible from Milton's hearth; the floor to ceiling window allowed a vast view of the front side of the estate. Afterwards Hunter simply dropped the slack chain on the slate and turned his face to the tree line.

He could see nothing, but his instincts assured him that the creature was already closing. Also staring out, Blackthorn beckoned to Inspector Marshal, who rushed up: "Sir!"

"Bill," Blackthorn laid a brawny hand on Marshal's shoulder, "procure me one of those elephant guns with a handful of rounds, would you?"

"Right away, governor!"

In seconds Marshal returned holding a rifle obviously designed for elephant. Extra rounds, each three inches in length, were secured in the leather strap but Hunter knew the extra rounds didn't matter. Blackthorn would have time for one shot and, if he missed, he was dead.

Suddenly Ben raised his nose. He began turning his head from left to right and then he stood to his full height taking all slack from the chain. With paws close to his sides, he swayed ten feet above the porch.

A Grizzly is a subspecies of Brown bear, which is a close relative of the Kodiak, the second largest bear on the planet. But Ben was uncommonly large even for a Grizzly and almost equal in size to a Kodiak. His head was wider than Hunter's chest. His five claws, each four inches in length, curved with perfect menace. And as he swayed against the granite wall, he was a prehistoric image of the purest muscular might.

By reflex Hunter removed the Ruger from his holster and insured that five .454 Magnum rounds were loaded. Then he unslung the 45.70 he'd brought from the shed and eased down the looped lever, checking for the brass glint of a cartridge. The shotgun was slung across his back.

Once more Hunter assessed what he was up against.

If this beast could leap a ten-foot fence carrying a man in its teeth, then it was incredibly strong. It took tremendous power for an animal – even an animal as powerful as a Siberian tiger – to clear that fence. And if it had that kind of strength, then it was also fast.

Blackthorn asked eerily, "Do you see anything?"

"We're not going to see anything this early," Hunter muttered. "Eventually it might get desperate enough to hit us in broad daylight, but not yet."

"Then why is Ben getting anxious?"

Hunter lowered the Marlin. "Don't get me wrong. It's on its way. Ben can sense that. But it's still a few miles off, and it's moving slow." He glanced at the descending sun. "It'll be here around dusk. Then it'll pick a place to study us."

"To study *us*! For what?"

"It'll want to know what it's dealing with."

"Hasn't it already done that?"

"Not with me and Ben. And it knows we're in here. Just like we know it's out there." Hunter gazed over the grounds. "Until it figures us out, it'll just watch unless someone orders it to attack."

The enormous front door of the manor opened and Augustus Milton stepped out staring at the faraway tree line before turning his face toward Hunter. "Your Grizzly senses something!" he shouted. "It seems a little early for this animal! But perhaps it's growing impatient!"

Hunter gently laid a hand on Ben's flank. "Look sharp," he said and stepped toward Milton. "Let's have some of that brandy, major!"

Milton lifted both arms.

"Indeed!"

* * *

Sipping slowly, Hunter recollected that it'd been decades since he'd enjoyed brandy. He'd forgotten the taste, the scent, the sensation. It was more pleasant than he remembered and he found himself gazing with sharper interest across Milton's trophy hall. The old man seemed to notice and pointed to a Kodiak bear that stood in a dynamic stance. The crest of its enormous head almost touched the ceiling.

"He was nineteen feet, ten inches at the crest and twenty-one hundred pounds," Milton stated, raising a toast. "But, unfortunately, he'd been wounded and could no longer catch normal prey. As a result, he became a maneater, so the wildlife ambassadors of Alaska asked me to dispatch him. After I killed him, I saw that his right foreleg was consumed by gangrene. He'd apparently stepped in a beartrap. He'd managed to escape, but it killed him, nonetheless. I don't doubt that the pain drove him insane before I put him out of his misery. It was a tragic end for such an awesome champion."

With a brief pause the major continued, "That is how all true giants die, Mr. Hunter. With an animal, it begins with some small infection. But then the infection spreads until that magnificent creature is just a ghost of its former self. It is a slow and a horrible disintegration of mind and body, and an ignoble death." He frowned. "That is how heroes die, man and beast."

Hunter noted the acceptance in Milton's voice.

"With a man," Milton continued, "it might begin with the loss of a finger. But, then, because of the finger, he loses the hand. And as he is gradually crippled, he loses an eye. Or a leg. And then he will be slowly destroyed piece by piece as he dies the most ignoble death. It is a grueling, ghastly process that can turn the strongest man into what he once pitied. He becomes weak and, eventually, a coward. And when he does finally die after long and useless years, he will die in obscurity and no one will remember how magnificent he once was. They will only remember how he was always weak, always sick, always alone." His pale face shone like bone in the light of the flames as he muttered, "The death of the weak is merciful and quick. The strong die piece by piece. And that is the tragic truth."

Hunter turned his face to the flames.

Then Milton smiled faintly as he added, "You say you've never seen a track like that, Mr. Hunter. But something did make that track, so would you care to hazard a guess?"

After some hesitation Hunter replied, "Right now I don't have enough information to make an educated guess."

"Then would you care for a suggestion?"

"Sure."

Milton nodded, "Well, it's a proper story, so I must begin at the beginning. As it happened, I first saw the beast from a helicopter. But we couldn't land at the time, and so we went back the next day to confirm. But, unfortunately, we were unable to locate it again."

"What did you see?"

"Many years ago in Colombia I thought I glimpsed a great boa constrictor moving through a field," Milton continued. "I had seen many monstrous snakes in the jungle, of course, but I had never seen a boa constrictor forty meters in length. Later, after I reported my sighting, they told me that it sounded like what paleontologists call a *Titanoboa*. But then they told me those great snakes had been extinct since the Paleocene Epoch. They told me I was wrong. They said it must have been a trick caused by the height of the helicopter. But they were the ones who were wrong because I was later commissioned by those same officials to hunt down and kill that great beast after an entire village mysteriously went missing. Of course, the military suppressed the evidence. But I know what I saw and what I killed. And so I ask, Mr. Hunter, do you think this might be a similar creature? Do you think this could be a creature thought to be extinct but does, in fact, still exist? Like that gigantic boa?"

Hunter didn't blink. "That's … unlikely. If it'd been here for any length of time, like years, someone would have seen it. There'd be more than a few witnesses, plaster casts of its tracks. There would be centuries-old legends and rumors and probably a long list of strange, unexplained deaths. But from what I understand, these deaths are all recent."

"Well, yes, but I think it is the only logical explanation," Milton stated with conviction. "And we both know that it's possible, however unlikely."

Casting a glance at Blackthorn, who was holding his brandy as steadily as a marble statue, Hunter said, "It could be a hybrid." He waited for the old man's reaction. When there was none, Hunter continued, "If you haven't heard, major, breeding dangerous hybrids has become a lucrative business in the last twenty years. Rich people don't think twice about paying a fortune for a white tiger. But most of the breeding facilities are illegal. So when a hybrid escapes, the owners don't report it. They can't. And you end up with a situation like this."

"I don't doubt it," stated Milton. "But I don't believe that even outlawed science can breed a creature that is part wolf and part Grizzly, Mr. Hunter, which this creature surely is." His blue eyes gleamed as he asked, "Do you think there's a chance that someone might have just randomly released it into the moor because they could no long afford to keep it?"

Hunter wished he could have formulated a better response, but he simply said, "It's a big investment to raise an apex predator like a lion or bear. It requires a lot of time, food, and medical attention. It's also illegal because English law prohibiting the unsanctioned possession of apex predators hasn't changed in thirty years. I can't see why someone would invest all that money and then bring it here to just release it in the wild." He noted that the major had not blinked as he added, "No, major, I don't think anyone just turned it loose because they couldn't afford it, anymore."

As if unpersuaded, the old man grunted, "But you do agree that the track is a curious thing, am I not right? It is the size of a Grizzly's print, but it has the outline of a wolf. And, then, there are those claw marks ascending the wall. Claw marks in the form of a human hand! Torn into solid granite! What did you make of that?"

Reluctantly Hunter conceded that Milton was not half so daft as some might presume. Perhaps the old man was not the financial Svengali he had been in his prime but he had lost none of his powers for observation.

"That's a good question," Hunter answered finally. "I might need your wisdom on that one, major."

Blackthorn was frowning at Hunter, who didn't need to look. Then Milton, who apparently thought Blackthorn was staring over *him*, laughed, "It's quite all right, commander! No one pays attention to the ramblings of a senile old man! And if you would allow me, gentlemen, I would like to offer something that might prove useful." He rose and beckoned. "This way."

Without hesitation they followed Milton to an overlarge armoire dominating a wall. After removing a brass key from his jacket, the major unlocked it and swung open the doors to reveal a vast arsenal of heavy, double-barrel rifles. At the base were dusty boxes of ammunition.

Milton removed a bolt-action rifle with a heavy stock and forearm. "Although we don't know what this creature is, I believe we can agree that it will be difficult to put down."

He presented the rifle to Hunter. The barrel had been cut down to allow freer movement in heavy bush and it was extraordinarily heavy. As Hunter studied it, he realized it was constructed of cold-forged vault steel. He read, *600 Nitrous Express* on the receiver.

Hunter dimly wondered if he would even be standing after he pulled the trigger. The recoil might break his back or the rifle could go flying from his hands like a twig in a hurricane. Somewhat wistfully, he remarked, "This is quite a rifle, major. Bolt action. Eighteen-inch barrel. Created for elephant. Is this what you used for the Kodiak?"

"And the Polar bear," nodded Milton. "So I hope you'll make good use of it, Mr. Hunter." He removed a second rifle that he handed to Blackthorn as he added, "And this is for you, commander. It is a five hundred caliber Belgium Magnum. It provides twice the velocity and has three times the stopping power of that four-five-eight from Holland and Holland. It is no exaggeration to say that it will drop a river horse in its tracks."

Hunter was impressed. He knew that stopping a hippopotamus with a single round was no small thing. Hippos were gigantically strong and their ferocity was legendary. In Africa they killed more people than crocodiles and were more bullet-resistant than rhinoceros.

Lifting rifle and ammo, Hunter walked to the mantle where he sat and began inserting shells into the leather sling. Hunter had estimated twenty slots and he was right. He finished, left the empty box on the table, and when he hefted the rifle it was considerably heavier. Each round was at least two ounces and the rifle weighed fifteen pounds.

The major also sat, resumed his brandy, and seemed to read Hunter's mind. "Yes," he commented, "it's something of a chore to carry about in the hot sun all day, but the sling helps. And, believe me, you'll be glad to have the extra stopping power when the moment comes."

A woman wearing an informal off-white gown appeared in the room's arched entrance. She inclined her head as if to imply polite acknowledgement, and spoke with a South African accent, "I'm sorry, major. I wanted to check on you. But if I'm interrupting –"

"Nonsense," Milburn graciously stretched out an arm. "These men have been assigned to hunt down the animal that killed Angus, my dear. We must grant them every facility." He gently grasped her hand. "Gentlemen, I'd like to introduce you to my daughter, Bronte."

Blackthorn bowed and beamed. *"Enchante'."*

Hunter nodded and waved. "Hi."

Bronte crossed the room. "It's my pleasure, gentlemen. Are either of you hungry?"

"We're fine, thank you," stated Blackthorn.

Bronte laughed, "I don't see how you can be fine, commander. Mr. Hunter is an American, so you've obviously traveled a long way. I'll have Zelda prepare some hors d'oeuvres."

The major's eyebrows rose as he asked, "Would you gentlemen like some hors d'oeuvres? I personally find them tedious, but some like them." He waved obscurely. "I can only appreciate them with something more bracing than brandy. Would either of you care for a bourbon?"

Blackthorn politely raised a hand, "No, thank you, major. If I get too comfortable, my feet go to sleep."

Hunter said, "The brandy will have to do, major. I'll be going out tomorrow."

"Indeed!" the major exclaimed with a toast. "You must be as sharp as your prey! Which reminds me, Mr. Hunter! Concerning the moor, I must warn you." He sat heavily before the fire, and continued, "As dangerous as this beast is, the moor is no less. Temperatures can drop swiftly. Those who are unprepared die quickly. And, then, there's the Sphagnum moss bogs which can indeed become quicksand with enough rain. And it has rained a great deal in past weeks. The quicksand may not swallow you whole, but you'll be unable to escape, and you'll freeze to death in short order. And paths can change in a matter of hours. The path you took in the morning may even exist in the afternoon." He nodded solemnly, "Yes, the moor is full of death. No man should go into it alone."

Four figures appeared in the entrance and Hunter stood not so much from courtesy as caution before realizing they were the major's remaining children. There were two females and two males and one daughter appeared older than Bronte. They entered the room as the tallest daughter smiled, "Hello again, Commander Blackthorn. And I see you've brought a guest with you. Are we to be introduced?"

"I will do the honor," said Milton. "Gentlemen, this is my oldest daughter, Flora, and my youngest child, Emily. And these are my two lads, Richard and Barron. Just to mention it, Barron and Bronte are fraternal twins. They were born when my wife and I lived in Africa. In fact, you could say they are as much children of Africa as England." He smiled. "And now, children, allow me to introduce to you Nathaniel Hunter. He is a legendary American tracker who has volunteered to assist Commander Blackthorn."

All approached to either bow or shake hands and they seemed normal enough. At least, all but the youngest – the one named Emily. She was something of a thin, shy ghost in a white cotton dress. Her hair was jet black, long, and void of any enhancing ribbons or bows. And Hunter noticed scars on the left side of her face as if she had escaped near death at the rabid fury of some bestial attack. She moved with a slight limp, her face bowed.

As soon as they were introduced, Emily walked away without shaking Hunter's hand. She silently moved to the window and stared out, tilting her head as she watched Ben. Very delicately – everything about her seemed delicate – she placed her small hand on the glass as if to touch him. All of it was a bit unusual, but there was nothing wrong with it. Perhaps she simply preferred the company of animals to people.

Returning his mind to the others and projecting his limited charm, Hunter asked, "So you and Bronte were raised in Africa?"

"Yes," smiled Barron. "As the major says, my sister and I have spent far more time in Africa than England."

"This place must seem strange to you."

Barron chuckled, "Yes, but this is the major's ancestral home. Bronte and I had never seen anything like it – not even in pictures – until we arrived. And I must admit it was initially rather frightening. We'd never imagined a place so remote and lonely and, well, depressing. But we're adjusting."

"Why don't the two of you live in London?" asked Hunter.

"Bronte and I prefer to remain with the family for now. But we do plan to eventually move to the city."

Hunter continued in what he hoped was a casual demeanor, "So what did you do in Africa?"

"I was a cultural attaché to the British State Department in Uganda. In English that means I helped British citizens with local laws and customs." He laughed again, "Basically I was a glorified tour guide. But since I was attached to the ostentatious British Embassy, they had to give me a polysyllabic title."

"Did both of you work with the embassy?"

Bronte laughed, "Oh, no, Mr. Hunter, I obtained a doctorate in English Literature at the University of Nairobi. I'm currently employed with the insurance division of Lloyd's."

"That's interesting," smiled Hunter, gesturing past Emily at the front window. "Would you insure my bear?"

"Believe me, Mr. Hunter, I've insured stranger things."

"Like what?"

Richard Milton, the eldest son, joined their group cupping a glass of bourbon on ice and smiled benignly.

"Well," Bronte continued, "I suppose you've heard that Lloyd's is renowned for insuring the breasts, legs, and butts of oh-so-delicate actresses. And Hollywood men, those metrosexual darlings, are obsessed with insuring their perfectly fake teeth. God forbid one of them should lose his ceramic smile in some world-shattering accident." She rolled her eyes. "At least there's never a need to insure their egos. I doubt they could pay the premium."

"So what, exactly, do you do at Lloyd's?" asked Hunter. "Why do they need an expert in the English language?"

"To put it simply, I specialize in crafting extremely specific language for the more unusual policies. You see, since the most bizarre policies require the most bizarre language, Lloyd's prefers to use English specialists instead of stuffy barristers."

Hunter found Bronte genuinely interesting. "I hate to pry, but what kind of unusual policies have you drawn?"

Oh," she began with a dramatic eyeroll, "I've written policies covering alien invasions, the finger bones of Jesus when he was three years old – forget the fact that Jesus died with all his fingers - and recently there was a nose –"

Hunter laughed, "A nose?"

"Oh, indeed. Last week I wrote a policy for a perfumer because he can discern over a thousand compounds as well as their individual elements with his unique sense of smell. Now, should any tragedy befall his supernatural schnoz, his future is secure."

Bronte turned her face to the window. "So, yes, Mr. Hunter, to insure your bear would be a rather mundane business. We typically insure service animals and endangered species as well as the facilities that maintain them. Some of the facilities are insured for hundreds of millions of pounds. I've even written a policy insuring the offspring of their research because the little ones are ten million-pound investments. And that's not an elaboration, you know. The rarest animals are insured more heavily than satellites."

"What would threaten an animal that's so heavily protected?" asked Hunter.

"Trips," said Bronte quaintly.

"Trips?"

"Yes. There's always the possibility that an animal could be injured or, god forbid, killed on a trip. This is just a small example, of course, but we recently insured animals for another trip to the Antarctic."

"Sled dogs?"

"And every fragment of gear, harness, foot pad, plane ticket and hotel room as well as every can of dog food and the rather exorbitant expense of breeding and training. But we had to insure them all by name because God does not make all sled dogs equal."

"Who pays for all these policies?" asked Hunter.

Bronte's shrug expressed her indifference. "To be honest, Mr. Hunter, I rarely meet the owners. The only exception is when it's a particularly unique type of research facility. Then I request a session with management to better understand how I should draft the policy. I never see their premiums. The only check I've ever seen is my own."

Hunter wondered why the thought of insuring one of his adventures had never occurred to him. Turning toward her fraternal twin, Barron, he asked, "Do you also work in insurance now?"

"Not at all," replied Barron. "I couldn't endure that nonsense for a single moment. No, sir. Now I work at one of the major's banks. Or, rather, at one of the satellites. Richard is president of the main bank. I'm primarily just –"

"A gofer," smiled Richard and turned toward Blackthorn.

"Yes," echoed Barron. "As Americans would say – a gofer."

Hunter revealed nothing. "Is it an investment bank?"

"Good god!" exclaimed Major Milton from his chair. "For god's sake, no, Mr. Hunter! Don't you know that investment banks are one of the worst money pits ever invented? Indeed, one of the reasons I've kept my fortune is because I steered clear of that untidy business from the beginning. I knew men who bought into that nonsense and lost a billion pounds in a single hour when margins were called." He threw a gesture at the wall. "Which was inevitable."

Barron laughed, "The major owns fifty banks and a dozen corporations but there's not an investment bank among them. No, indeed, the major believes that basic commodities and patience are the only worthy investments."

"Slow and steady is the ticket," chimed Bronte.

Hunter was not interested in anything they said but for the fact he needed to understand them. What did catch and capture his interest was Milton's youngest child – Emily. Even while he was engaged in conversation, he remained aware of her. But Emily merely stood in place, her small hand pressed against the window, silently watching Ben.

He also caught how Blackthorn had engaged Richard and Flora in what appeared to be an increasingly strained conversation. And, after a half-hour, the five Milton children began to retire. Bronte walked to Emily and gently turned her toward the door and, one by one, they were gone. Walking to the same window, Hunter saw that Ben was even more alert than before. Then he fixed on Blackthorn with, "It seems like you had a serious conversation going with the older ones."

Blackthorn grumbled, "They're concerned for their father. I can't say I blame them."

CHAPTER FOURTEEN

Milton resumed his chair. "Come, gentlemen, indulge me with a little more discussion before I retire. I rarely get the chance these days to talk about anything but money."

Hunter walked forward and re-took the seat closest to his rifle. "I'm told the moor is renowned for its hunting, major."

"For fowl," muttered Milton. "Yes, grouse hunting is something of a local sport. And we have our share of wildlife, although it's nothing compared to what you'll find in the great wildernesses of Wyoming or Montana. We do have abundant roe deer, badger, and shrew. We have several species of hawk. And we have a rather unique assortment of owls. Indeed, the moor possesses what locals call the Great European Eagle Owl. A gigantic and truly magnificent creature. It's easily the size of an American Golden Eagle, although it's legitimately an owl. Some speculate that it is an immigrant from the upper steppes of Russia." He lifted an arm. "Sometimes you can see one pass across the face of the moon as it screeches. My old friend, Angus, used to say the Eagle Owl was the spirit guide for guardians of the forest. That it was here to guard the creatures of the forest and save them from an unnatural death. And death does come in unnatural forms in the moor. Angus once said that the Eagle Owl will find the greatest hunter and remain at his side if the hunter is stalking a beast that must die so others may live. And, to be sure, we have been seeing quite a lot from this great guardian of the forest recently."

"Why is that?" asked Hunter.

"Well," Milton glanced at the dying light, "in the past several years a horde of hounds have begun roaming the moor. They were once proper hounds, but the owners turned them loose, and now they're savage as dingoes. They do not belong here. This is not their first estate. And they have turned uncommonly and unnaturally vicious, so you should be ready to defend yourself if you stumble into a pack of them." He added grievously, "England was once a sacred land. Now it is a feast for dogs."

More disparate small talk followed until the fire crackled and fell, dying, and the major did not rise to stoke it so Hunter set his brandy on the table and stood. "I've enjoyed this, major," he commented as he lifted the Winchester. "I'll test this in the morning."

"That is wise," responded Milton. "I haven't fired it, myself, in a few years. It has done nothing but gather dust. But I'm sure you brought your own cleaning kit. You know what to do."

Blackthorn shook the major's hand. "Thank you for your hospitality, major. Hunter has elected to sleep with his bear but I've made arrangements to stay at the inn near –"

"I instructed Zelda to prepare a room for you," said Milton forcefully, if not fearfully. "I would consider it a great personal favor, commander, if you would remain in the house until this terrible situation is resolved."

"Of course," Blackthorn acquiesced as Zelda magically appeared in the doorway. He added, "And with that, gentlemen, I'll say good night. Summon me if there is any need whatsoever."

"Thank you, commander. Zelda will show you to your room."

Zelda led Blackthorn up the immense winding staircase as Hunter turned away. But he stopped as the major stared out the window and spoke as if he were quoting, "With what fated steps, Hunter's Moon, do you rise as blood …"

Hunter realized he was speaking of the Hunter's Moon that was to rise in only a few nights. The major's eyes glinted as he looked to Hunter again, and he said, "That rifle I quit-claim to you, Mr. Hunter. And I prophesize that 'ere this evil is done, it shall be yours by blood."

* * *

Lying upon a thick mound of straw in the shed, Hunter gazed through the wide-open double doors. The stars were as uncountable as Hunter had ever seen in the most remote wilderness.

Cold suited this place.

All life, Hunter thought, exists under a death sentence. But life here was a living death sentence. Life here was born in the shadow of death and never truly escaped. Gazing at the back of Ben's enormous head, Hunter knew the Grizzly was wide awake and also staring out the doors. Yes, the great bear knew something was out there. He didn't know what it was and he didn't know where it was. But a scent was in the wind and Ben was fiercely alert.

Since Hunter had coaxed Ben to lie beside him on the straw, the Grizzly had sullenly refused to turn his back to the entrance. He rested, eventually, but continued to search distant shadows.

The night outside the doors was a depthless ocean of black that only reluctantly retreated to the moor's half-dead day before descending again with implacable dominion. Even in the day it was dark as pitch – always dark, always cold, always deathly quiet.

Hunter had walked through the night of a thousand forests so black that he *felt* the darkness separating before him like water and closing upon him as he moved. But the solidness of this darkness contained something even worse. It was as if this darkness were inhabited with a merciless and malignant consciousness that knew exactly what it wanted to claim. It was as if this moor was a living thing hungry to steal the lives of more victims.

Before Hunter realized he had moved, he reached out to lay a hand on Ben, patting the Grizzly's neck and shoulder. He was trying to calm his friend. But Hunter knew Ben would not allow himself to be comforted. No, the bear would not relax, would not cease watching, would not lessen his alertness because he was afraid of what was out there.

In the moment Hunter did regret bringing him – his only friend. He regretted it because he knew Ben would fight to the death when this beast came. He would fight because of instinct. He would fight because of fear. He would fight because he was not willing to die without a fight. But, most of all, he would fight because Hunter would fight.

Not at all thankful for this quiet moment to contemplate, Hunter considered the horror and bloodshed that had engulfed him like a firestorm in Alaska. In that frozen wilderness the scientifically created abomination named Luther had come horrifyingly close to becoming a human tiger that could have effortlessly fulfilled the subconscious desires of the human mind. And Hunter didn't regret taking his head, in the end. If Luther had achieved his ambition to become the perfect predator with the unbridled physical power to satisfy his most obscene desires, no one would have survived.

And now someone had done it again so that there was another prehistoric creature running wild because this animal was not of this age. And it confirmed to him that the federal government didn't fully destroy Luther's work.

Those originally responsible for that catastrophe remained free and had quite probably perfected their experiment.

But why?

Luther had been a biblical disaster that wiped out a dozen research installations, killed countless people, and cost the American government tens of billions, so what were they trying to perfect? The experiment had been a bust. It didn't work. Immortality was beyond the reach of man. So who had resurrected this cursed science?

Regardless of the answers, if Hunter could discover who was responsible for this, he wouldn't trust the government to shut it down this time. That had been a mistake and he should have known better. This time, if he could identify them, he'd spend his life – his *fortune* insuring they could never do it again. And if he had to go outside the law to do it, so be it. Among other things, he considered it a matter of self-preservation. He couldn't keep chasing these things across every wilderness on the planet. The odds of destroying each and every one of them were not in his favor. In fact, they were very much against him.

A black shape blocked out the stars and was gone.

Hunter didn't blink; he knew what he'd seen. He shifted his gaze to the six-foot hedges surrounding the manor searching for something to break the outline. Then Ben turned his brown-black face curiously toward Hunter. Yes, he'd seen it, too, and was waiting for Hunter's reaction.

Hunter knew that, first, a shape *did* cross the field about sixty yards out. It was fast. It was big. Second, Hunter realized that, despite its size, it could move without making a sound.

Wrapping his fingers silently around the Marlin, Hunter curled into a tight crouch on the straw, trying not to rattle the hay. He was angry that it was impossible to reach his feet in absolute silence but wind moving over moist moss would have made more sound.

Before he had laid down, Hunter had ejected every slug from the shotgun only to insert them again. Then he had reassured himself that he'd racked a fresh shell into the chamber for a total of six shots, so he was confident; he didn't need to check the shotgun again. And since he hadn't yet removed the gun belt, the Ruger Alaskan with five .454 rounds rested on the front side of his hip. He ignored the major's rifle. This would be too close a thing for an unproven weapon.

He rose and, placing his boots very carefully heel to toe, rolling along the outer edge, and slowly eased his way through the shed to the wide-open doors. He stopped six inches from the frame, head down, not bothering to search with sight. Rather, he listened.

Nothing …

Hunter gradually realized he wouldn't hear it unless it no longer cared, and he wouldn't see it unless it was directly in front of him, so it could be anywhere. For a split-second he had the vivid image of the beast simply sticking its head through the door, staring him in the face. Then he felt a gigantic Grizzly head at this shoulder and all fears vanished.

Ben slowly swung his face side to side, obviously searching. But it was as if the bear, too, wanted to get a feel for the night before venturing out. Feeling the gigantic strength, Hunter knew he couldn't stop Ben from charging into the night if that's what the Grizzly decided to do.

Nor would Ben give him any warning.

It was a common mistake for people to believe a Grizzly gives a warning before it attacks. In truth a Grizzly normally doesn't give any sign, which is an unusual trait, because most animals *do* give some kind of notice before they commit themselves to a fight.

A wolf will lower its head and stare, and that means you may not be long for this world. A bull will fiercely shake its head and violently paw the ground. But a bear will simply charge and crash into its prey with the force of a freight train with no warning whatsoever.

Although bears may seem ponderous and slow when they're sedately searching for berries, in battle they move faster than the eye can see. So if Ben decided to attack, Hunter knew he'd never be able to hold him back. Ben would move and by the time Hunter even realized what was happening the bear would be gone.

Hunter wondered if this is what the beast did every night – leaping the fence and roaming the grounds without alerting the hypervigilant Clydesdales and dogs. But, even with the thought, he decided that was unlikely. If the creature made this kind of probe each night, there would have been more deaths. So this was a new tactic, and that was curious because animals don't choose new tactics until old tactics fail. If a path has been safe, they keep using it. If a stream is full of fish, they keep using it. So, if something works, they keep doing it. And what it had been doing had been working. It had come in silence, it had killed, and it had disappeared without being wounded. It had never failed to achieve what it wanted to achieve so why would it do something new?

Hunter briefly closed his eyes; the wind was behind him and steady, and that wasn't good. The creature was up wind and would catch his scent. But Hunter had no choice. It was time.

First rule for stalking in the dark …

… Never look for it. You won't see it. The red and green cones of your eyes are far more perceptive to movement than shape …

Second rule …

… Sound travels further in the cold but twigs snap more easily in the cold and the wind will snap a twig every few seconds, so don't over-react to sound … Don't move … Wait for the sound to come closer … If it continues to close, it's not the wind …

This was a game Hunter had played as far back as he could remember and he knew he could wait for minutes, hours, days, weeks, or months before he moved. But he also knew that Ben would not be so patient. In fact, the Grizzly was already nervous and if his fear grew to panic, instinct would compel him to fight or flee and Ben had never fled from a fight in his life.

Hunter had already memorized the lay of the land. The tree line to both the west and the east was a hundred yards out. The manor was a hundred yards straight ahead. A twenty-foot-wide cobblestone drive encircled the building in front of the hedge.

He recalled Reggie's words, "*Its occipital sockets indicate it could see at twenty-five thousand lumen – a lot like a wolf – so I guaranteed you it could read body heat at less than two thousand microns. This thing's infrared and heat vision were more sensitive than what we've got in our best satellites. And the auditory cavity suggests it could hear at five hundred thousand cycles per second. That's bat sonar ... This thing could hear a heartbeat at a thousand yards ...*"

It had every advantage so Hunter had to neutralize its night vision to have any chance. Then an idea dawned and he turned his face, staring at the five thousand-gallon diesel tank. Numerous ten-gallon cans were stacked around it. After slinging the Marlin, he picked up two full cannisters and stood in the door, verifying the beast wasn't close.

He glanced down. "Let's go."

Hunter was out the door, moving to the left. He loped low and more quietly than he thought possible as he stopped and un-capped the first diesel can. Pouring generously, he backed across the tarn to the shed. Then he opened the second can and continued the long stream of diesel far to the right. When he was finished, he'd laid a heavy line of diesel a hundred yards long.

Kneeling, listening for even a twig snapping in the cold, Hunter pushed Ben away from the fuel and removed a Zippo. Since diesel only burns half as long as gasoline, he would have, at best, thirty seconds to identify this beast and hit it with the rifle. It was a half-baked plan and full of holes, but it was the only plan Hunter had time to conceive. With a brief glance at Ben, who actually seemed to know what was happening, Hunter said, "Here we go."

He struck the lighter and touched the diesel.

Flames erupted ten feet into the night and the blazing line raced across the back field casting a bright orange glow across the entire glade. In the same moment Hunter whipped the Marlin into his shoulder.

A roar erupted behind the manor and Hunter twisted to see a titanic shape reared against the wall. Its hulking shadow, cast against the stone, was even more enormous than Hunter expected.

He fired a shot.

The kick of the rifle was unfelt as Hunter fast-worked the lever and raised aim again. He saw the shape running parallel to the wall and fired. He worked the action yet again as it reached the east wing.

It was gone.

"Come on!" Hunter shouted and they charged forward as horrified screams tore through the night. Although Hunter was sprinting full-out, Ben effortlessly surged ahead of him. Hunter shouted but it useless; Ben had seen the creature and made his decision.

Clutching the rifle tight in a hand, Hunter rounded the corner, flying along the wall. He was already out of breath and knew he'd never catch the creature in a flat run so he angled to the right, gaining distance on the building. When he had a good angle, he spun and fell to a single knee to see a massive shadow racing across the barred windows far ahead of him. The shape was partially illuminated by the flame and spotlighted by a three-quarter moon.

Hunter fired and saw the bullet impact the wall. Fast working the action, Hunter fired again and missed. Compensating, he aimed well ahead of it this time and fired his fifth shot; the wall exploded in the face of the beast but Hunter wasn't certain whether he'd hit until it skidded on the frost.

Enraged, it turned into Hunter as if to attack and, in the moment, Hunter felt that it was communicating a personal intent to kill him and him alone. Then it turned and launched itself again into its run, immediately reaching the front hedges. Having lost the angle, Hunter gave chase, surprised he could still throw one foot in front of the other with his legs dying fast.

Instinct made him whirl.

Hunter twisted down and away as a savage image that blocked out the sky and stars sailed past him. With a guttural roar the creature came down where Hunter had stood as he fast-drew the Ruger and fired from the waist. Hunter didn't know what exactly he was shooting but didn't question it as he rapid-fired four more rounds from the .454 Magnum and the creature retreated at each round until the revolver clicked.

They squared off.

The gorilla-size abomination bent forward, long arms descending almost to its knees. The stark white half-moon outlined a monstrous, slouching shape. Red eyes gleamed, and as it snarled, Hunter plainly saw tusks to rival a Sabretooth's. Its hands convulsed, claws clicking.

They stood like two boxers waiting for an opening.

Hunter gasped, "*You're dead*!"

Fangs fiendishly gaped, drooling.

"I killed you!" shouted Hunter.

"*Fool!*" it growled. "*You killed Luther! I am NOT Luther! And I will destroy you for this! Know that I will not leave this place until I feast on your bones!*"

Hunter ripped the shotgun from his back, racking and firing in the same split-second. The blast was blinding and the creature was slammed back against the ground as Hunter racked another shell into the chamber. But before he could fire again, it erupted from the tarn and catapulted past Hunter's face. Only at the last second did Hunter duck as a clawed hand lashed out, narrowly missing his head. Hitting and rolling away, Hunter came up firing the shotgun and wildly searching for …

It was gone.

Like that.

Hunter caught his breath, still searching although instinct confirmed that it was gone and he wouldn't find it no matter how long he stared. Exhausted and breathless, Hunter gazed across the back field, remembering the sight of those razor-sharp claws as they caressed his face.

It can't be!

Hunter had fought this creature once before and almost lost. He couldn't understand it. Not in the moment.

Attempting to wipe sweat from his eyes with a forearm Hunter staggered forward until he reached the face of the manor. Chaotic howls were still rising and he angled in that direction knowing what had happened. In another moment he stood over guards, but there was no time to help the wounded. Shoving rounds into the Marlin, Hunter glimpsed, etched against the moon, a monstrous wolf as it soared over the spikes of the fence and he spun, firing from the hip.

A yelp cut the night.

As Hunter stumbled forward again, he could hear Ben raging at the fence. Hunter was certain the Grizzly couldn't smash through that immovable iron barrier, but he also didn't want one of the guards to shoot Ben by mistake. The elephant guns might not be enough to stop that wolf but they were enough for Ben.

Barely able to see through the fog of exhaustion, Hunter finally reached Ben who was swaying side to side and pushing against the fence. The Grizzly stood on hindlegs with forelegs pressed against the bars as if to smash them from his path. Gasping and moaning, Hunter was still trying to catch his breath. He was vaguely aware that he was clutching Ben's mane before realizing that he was, in fact, leaning on him. Then Ben dropped to all fours and turned as uncountable shapes rushed forward.

"Don't shoot!" Hunter shouted. "It's me and Ben!" As they reached his position without a shot, Hunter pointed, "You've got wounded men over there! They need assistance!"

Step by step, Hunter began to collect himself. His teeth clenched as he bowed his head and deliberately took long, deep breaths until the adrenaline white and dizziness began to fade. After two minutes he was breathing painfully but steadily.

Yeah …

I'm out of shape …

Ben was casting glances between the black forest wall and Hunter. Then more shouts arose and headlights approached and Hunter walked slowly back the way he had come, Ben tight to his side. There was no ambulances, so the wounded constables were hastily loaded into cars.

As if taking substance from the night, Blackthorn appeared. He was holding the rifle that Milton had given him. The detective seemed to instantly understand every turn of what had transpired and defiantly lifted his chin toward the moor as he asked, "Did you get it?"

Hunter again wiped sweat from his face. "I took a few shots," he gasped. "I don't know if I hit it."

"Are you all right?"

"Yeah. What about your men?"

"I don't know." Blackthorn stepped forward and spoke in a low tone to Inspector Marshal. "Bill! See the men to hospital. Report back and let me know their status. I'll take the watch." He angled his flashlight at Hunter's face. "You need to take care of that cut, boyo."

"What cut?"

"Your face."

Hunter lifted his hand and saw it was gleaming a very bright red. It had been impossible to see in the dark, but under the glow of the flashlight Hunter saw that his hand, arm, and chest were soaked in blood.

"*He cut me*," Hunter whispered. "*I didn't even feel it …*"

"The wolf cut you?"

"No," Hunter shook his head. "Not the wolf. It was … something else."

Blackthorn grunted, "This night is full of monsters. In any case, go inside and get that fixed up." He waved at Ben. "And take Ben with you. There's a lot of frightened men out here and frightened men make mistakes. I don't want the big fellow to get shot by accident."

Hunter hesitated.

"Are you sure you're all right, mate?" demanded Blackthorn. "Hunter! Can you hear me, man?"

Hunter had been staring toward the rear of the manor, his mind reliving the brief battle with the *Homo Scimitar*.

But now was not the time to contemplate that nightmare.

"Yeah," Hunter replied hoarsely, "I hear you."

"The library on the first floor is big enough to hold Ben," added Blackthorn. "Put him in there and lock the door. He'll be all right. Then get yourself fixed up. You're losing blood and I don't need you in an infirmary. I need you here."

Hunter glanced down, "Come on, Ben."

Ben was at his side and didn't hesitate at the front doors so Hunter led him without incident into the library. As luck would have it, there was a key in the lock and Hunter secured the massive wood slabs after the bear lumbered to a long window, staring toward the moor.

Hunter walked to the brightly illuminated trophy room where Milton was standing with rifle in hand. At Hunter's arrival the old man asked, "Did you get a clear shot?"

"No," Hunter answered and collapsed into a chair beside the expansive hearth. Milton casually sat the stock of the rifle on the floor, leaning it against a cabinet. "Did you wound it?"

"It didn't jump that fence like it was wounded."

"Pity." Milton addressed Zelda as she entered. "Zelda, please retrieve the medical kit and help Mr. Hunter with his wound. And summon the others, if you would, to assist the officers."

After a quick shout toward the kitchen, Zelda came calmly forward. She leaned over Hunter, lifting his chin and peering at his face before straightening. "You've got yourself a sharp cut, Mr. Hunter. And you look a bit pale. How about a pint while I fetch the first aid?"

What Hunter needed was water but he was too tired to object. He nodded, "That's fine. And I locked Ben in the library. He'll be less apt to tear something up if you throw him some lamb chops."

As others rushed into the room in various stages of dress Zelda gave terse instructions and they ran outside. A moment later Zelda returned with a first aid kit and a pint of English ale. Hunter took a long swallow before setting the pewter flagon aside. Afterwards he opened the medical kit and managed, "Thank you, but I'll take it from here. I've got a bit of experience."

"I'm sure you do," Zelda smiled. "Inform me if you need anything more, Mr. Hunter. I'll see to Ben."

"Ben isn't tamed," said Hunter as he doused a bandage with alcohol. "Make some noise to let him know you're coming. You don't want to surprise him."

Zelda removed a large keyring from her apron. "I'll make plenty of noise to let the big lug know I'm coming.

And I'll lock him up safely when I'm done. He'll be all right with a plate and warm fire."

Hunter generously cleaned the long cut with alcohol. Then he pulled a bandana from his vest and wrapped it around his forehead, and it was enough. He took a longer sip of the dark ale and gazed upon Milton's solemn aspect. The old man had once more taken his seat with both hands flat on the desk. He was staring in the direction of the unseen front doors and Hunter continued to watch until Milton asked, "Did you get a good look at it?"

Hunter decided to quit evasive answers.

"Yeah."

"It's not a bear, is it?"

"No. It's not a bear."

"And, so, what do we have?"

"It's a prehistoric species," said Hunter wearily, a deeper breath. "I've never seen anything like it."

"A prehistoric wolf?"

"Not … really."

"What do you mean?"

Hunter leaned back, "It has aspects of a wolf but it's more than a wolf. It's not like anything I've ever seen. And it's fast. Faster than a wolf. Faster than a bear." He shook his head. "I don't know. It might be the result of an experiment. Like I said earlier, it could be a hybrid. Or it could be what paleontologist call an Amphicyon – a relative of the Dire Wolf."

Hunter's adrenaline had burned out, the depths of exhaustion had come, and he didn't care to fully explain the terrifying realization that was inexorably enveloping his mind and soul. Conversely, Milton seemed to have no difficulty accepting the lack of description and said, "Do you think now that it has existed in this moor all its life?"

"No," Hunter shook his head. "Even if it's the last of its kind, it had to come from a pack. And this moor isn't big enough to hide a pack of those things." He raised a dead stare. "I don't know how it got here."

Abruptly, Milton appeared perilously exhausted as if some long-dreaded despair had finally seized his soul, annihilating his will to live. It was almost as if this was the last challenge in a long life of challenges, and whatever stalwart will had carried him this far was fading fast.

Hunter wanted to know what was in the old man's mind. He was still gazing, unblinking, when Zelda re-entered the hall. "I've seen to the big fellow," she said politely. "You were right, Mr. Hunter. He was a bit nervy. But when he saw the lamb chops, he lumbered forward quite the gentleman. I'm sure he'll be happy until you get back to him."

"Thank you."

"Don't hesitate to call if you need anything more," Again Zelda was simply gone, no formalities. She fulfilled her duties quietly and dismissed herself humbly, a ghost tending to the living.

Milton's entire family rushed into the room congregating around the old man. They laid hands on his shoulders or grasped his hands. As one, except for the mysterious Emily, they began asking questions but Hunter cared nothing for their concern. He was convinced that one of them was guilty of this plot to kill the old man. No other theory made sense.

Finally Bronte turned toward Hunter and took long strides to his chair. "Mr. Hunter? What happened?"

Hunter said without finesse, "It got inside the fence."

"Did you kill it?"

"No."

"Why not?"

"Because I missed."

Flora leaned over Milton. "Major! These people are not equal to this challenge! Please call someone else!"

"There will be no one else!" declared Blackthorn as his heavy steps arrived in the entrance of the room. His gaze settled on Hunter as he stated, "We searched for blood outside the fence."

"And?"

"Nothing." Blackthorn turned to the family. "And no one else will be summoned. We must deal with this ourselves."

Richard Milton, his father's replacement in the banking empire, stepped forward. "So we are to be massacred one by one? I disagree, commander! No law forbids me from hiring my own bodyguards!" He pointed. "As well as additional bodyguards for the major and the rest of my family!"

"Why didn't you do that a few weeks ago?" asked Hunter, watching closely. "You might have saved Mr. Staford's life."

Tilting his long face forward, Richard Milton said with barely restrained spite, "Until now I had faith in the Metropolitan Police Department, Mr. Hunter, as well as your famous skills. I believed the two of you were quite capable of dealing with this threat. But I was obviously mistaken. So now I'm going to do whatever it takes to protect my family."

Blackthorn displayed no offense. "This creature has killed every man it has encountered, civilian or otherwise, Mr. Milton, so the competence of my men is of no relevance. And you will not be hiring additional security as long as my officers are on the grounds."

Richard Milton retorted, "You can't nick me just because I'm trying to save my family!"

Blackthorn crossed heavy arms and his granite face was a monument to English fortitude as he leaned forward, "You are correct, Mr. Milton. I can't nick a man for trying to save his own life. That is a god given right. But I can throw you in the catacombs for endangering my men, which is exactly what you'll be doing if you solicit private security."

Flora said bitterly, "Why don't you throw him beneath Whitehall, anyway, commander? And why don't you arrest the rest of us, as well? I'm sure we would all prefer jail to a cemetery."

"Hush, Flora," said Milton with obvious irritation. "These men are doing all that can be done." He focused on Hunter. "Do you think it will attack us again tonight, Mr. Hunter?"

Hesitating a long time, Hunter finally said, "I think it's wounded, so it shouldn't be back tonight."

Stiffly, Milton stood. "Then I am going to retire. This has been a bit too exhilarating." He grasped his cane and began rounding the desk. "Good luck, Mr. Hunter. Good luck, commander."

Ushered by Bronte and Richard, the old man shuffled down the immense hall, where he disappeared. Suddenly Blackthorn loomed over Hunter, frowning stoically, "How's the cut?"

"It's all right."

"I think you've had enough for one night, mate. You need some rest. Are you going back to the shed?"

Hunter stood. "No. I'll be staying in the house. I want to be in here if it comes back."

"I don't think the wolf is coming back."

"I'm not talking about the wolf."

Blackthorn's sharply lifted his chin. "What's that?"

"I'll tell you later. I'm too tired right now. Getting punchy. I have to lay down."

Milton's children were speaking closely and fearfully as Hunter walked down the hall and into the library. As he shut the door, Ben lifted his head. The big Grizzly had discovered the luxurious rug before the fireplace and completely covered it with his thousand-pound frame.

There was a long, wide couch, and Hunter sat wearily.

He hauled the shotgun from his back and set it on the floor. Then he laboriously removed the gun belt and pulled the Ruger from the holster, dropping the rest. He methodically reloaded the rifle, slid it beneath a pillow, and stretched out.

Ben was already snoring.

Hunter could do nothing until morning and he was being enveloped by exhaustion like a man sinking into a warm ocean. But sleep didn't come as image after image shocked his mind – frightening images of fire and blood and a final fight to the death with a nightmare from his past.

It's out there …

Hunter's teeth came together.

It's out there!

Hunter had only seen it for a moment but that was all he needed because he vividly remembered the sight of it from his first deadly encounter and there was no mistaking the predatory face overshadowing the ape-man chest and gorilla-heavy arms and legs.

It was a creature designed for landing atop its prey, bearing it to the ground, and ripping it to shreds with fang and claw. And, despite its heavy muscularity, it was well adapted for moving at high speeds over long distances – a quality that separated it from every other ambush-killer of the prehistoric world. Even today Hunter was stunned that he had killed the first Scimitar in Alaska. And he *had* killed it. That was the one thing Hunter *was* certain of. So this one had to be a clone.

He'd thought that the renegade science used to create the Scimitar in Alaska had been outlawed by the American government. But he was obviously wrong because there was no mistaking what had been out there tonight. Hunter knew by the way it moved, the way it attacked. And there was no doubt. It was the same creature.

It was *Homo Scimitar*. Someone had repeated the experiment and created another human tiger.

Hunter closed his eyes.

It was no coincidence that both species he'd encountered tonight – the Homo Scimitar and Amphicyon – were prehistoric super-predators. It was no coincidence that they were both in this moor. And it was no coincidence that Hunter was here, too. In fact, if these creatures were here by the mysterious design of an unknown agency, then that's why Hunter was here, too, and that realization raised a graveyard of questions.

Hunter couldn't conceive of how something like this could happen twice. For that matter, he'd never understood how it happened in the first place.

In Alaska, the last time Hunter encountered this beast, a rogue CIA scientist had injected himself with a combination of human DNA and the unbuffered DNA of what researchers called a *Homo Scimitar* and the horrendous result had been an abomination that slaughtered an entire team of elite Special Forces soldiers before Hunter finally managed to kill it in the most agonizing, deadliest battle of his life. Hunter felt a chill as he remembered the final fight to kill Luther because the conflict had cost Hunter everything he loved.

It had taken him a year to recover from the wounds he gained in that battle and now he faced another one? In this moor?

What was it doing here?

Hunter opened his eyes, staring at the ceiling.

The answer had something to do with Milton.

It occurred to Hunter that maybe the only reason the old man was still alive was because this creature was waiting for something else to fall into place. But only an intelligent creature could weight those factors and make that decision, so this creature was, without question, intelligent. And that meant this one was different from the first. It meant this one had a realization of what Luther had only *hoped* to achieve. And if this Scimitar was the fulfillment of what Luther never managed to grasp in order to make his dream live, everyone here was going to drown in blood.

Hunter had gotten a good enough look at the Amphicyon to know that, unlike the skeleton in the Smithsonian, this creature was far more wolf than bear. Despite its bulk, the body was elongated and clearly built for speed. It was the perfect creature for tracking and cornering the most dynamic or difficult prey and the Scimitar was using it like an attack dog.

Nothing was fast enough to escape it. Nothing was strong enough to defy it. It was the perfect killer, and the Homo Scimitar was perhaps the *only* creature that could master it.

Hunter grimaced when he remembered the image of the Scimitar as it had growled to him, *"I will feast on your bones ..."*

Luther, the original Scimitar, had been far more beast than man but this one seemed an equal measure of both. It was only in the area of speed and strength and sheer appearance that it resembled the Scimitar that Hunter had faced in Alaska because this Scimitar was infinitely more intelligent. And although Hunter did not want to believe both creatures were created by the same renegade experiment, he was forced to accept it. It was the only possible explanation.

Hunter was certain that John Chaney, who befriended him in the first ordeal, had completely destroyed the laboratory where the original Scimitar had been spawned.

Chaney, who initially began his long law enforcement career in the FBI, had risen through the ranks to such a level that he was also sworn in and qualified as a U. S. Marshal with special privileges from the State Department and Homeland Security. Chaney could do whatever he wanted within the halls of federal government, making Hunter wish Chaney was here because this was a murder mystery that desperately needed solving.

In the bloody aftermath of Alaska, Chaney had mobilized National Guard Units at his own discretion to make sure the Scimitar never again walked the earth. But he had obviously missed something because someone had preserved and resurrected this outlawed science. And if an agency was willing to duplicate the abomination that had been Luther, why not create the wolves, as well? Why not create even more creatures from prehistoric remnants that would execute this Scimitar's commands? But what were these creatures doing in this godforsaken place?

Hunter closed his eyes again. His reasoning was circular. He wouldn't – *couldn't* – reach any conclusions until he rested. He didn't have enough information. Then a single thought caused his heart to skip as he surrendered to sleep … *I'll have to track it tomorrow … No other way … I can't let it think I'm afraid …*

Laying a hand on his rifle for comfort, Hunter slowed his breathing. He tried to relax but the image of the Scimitar kept returning to his mind.

Red eyes gleamed as it stared over him, fangs distended …

"*I will feast on your bones!*"

"Tomorrow," Hunter whispered.

And knew nothing.

"*Tomorrow …*"

CHAPTER FIFTEEN

G rowling, he stumbled through the forest and collapsed far outside the irritating white lights of the estate, a hand across his stomach. Hefting his hulking frame upon a small mound of oozing slime, he propped himself on an elbow and removed his palm, staring down. Even in the pitch black he could see blood dripping from his fingers.

He had not expected to be wounded. It had come as a surprise, and when he rose up to finish the kill, an abysmal pain had exploded in strange ways so that even his legs and back convulsed at the agony of it, so he had chosen to retreat until he understood. He inhaled a long time as the wolves gathered round him, nervous and uncertain.

This was not supposed to happen. He was supposed to be invulnerable to their weapons. But there was no denying that he was not so strong as *the other one* had been.

In his altered state he could not re-calculate the process he had used to modify the original serum that Luther had used, but he would do so as soon as he reached his liar. At the moment, his greatest concern was surviving. So he breathed heavily, slowly, knowing they would not chase him into the night. They feared him far too much to pursue him through the dark. And, in that, he was fortunate, for they would have caught him in this wounded state.

Hunter ... was his name.

He had attacked his enemy on sight. If he had been in control of the rage coursing through his heart and mind, he would have simply faded into the mist. But he had covered the distance to Hunter in seconds knowing nothing but the lust, the purpose, the mind of killing.

Even when he stood face to face with the man who had so hatefully killed Luther, he did not anticipate a fight. He had thought that he would kill the tracker mercilessly and quickly decimate the soldiers ...

No, his mind whispered, *these are not soldiers ...*

These are police ...

But, then, the tracker had reacted with a speed almost matching his own and he'd missed the opportunity. Then he had wasted a precious second vainly voicing his intentions, giving the man time to strike. He would not make such a mistake again. The next time he met the tracker, and he knew it would be soon, he would not lose a split-second with meaningless words. He would take his head and feast. Then he would slaughter the rest ...

He laid in silence, breathing steadily, until pain faded and strength returned, and he stood. He needed time to fully recover from his wounds. He needed to return to his lair and re-examine his calculations and modify the process because this transformation was not yet perfect.

If it were perfect, he would not be wounded.

He felt his fangs grinding in the remaining pangs of agony as he stood. But he knew he was becoming stronger by the moment. Just as he knew he would reach his lair long before sunrise. There he would be safe to feed, to sleep, and to finish his work.

He crept through the black moor into the face of the white skull of a moon, a slouching hulk with arms descending to his knees led by an instinct that read the darkness of the night with the darkness of his heart.

* * *

It was no surprise that Hunter met Milton on the expansive steps of the manor in the morning. Casting a brief glance at Ben, the major smiled. In the crook of his right arm lay a double-barrel rifle.

Hunter carried the Winchester and shotgun as well as the gun belt with the holstered Ruger and bowie knife. The 45.70 Marlin was also slung across his back. A thin rope was looped from his right shoulder to his left hip; a collapsible grappling hook was tied to the end of it. A satchel included a poncho, four ounces of pemmican, water purification tablets, leather twine, a spare knife, a medical kit with morphine and adrenaline syringes, matches and a tin jar of phosphorous rock in alcohol. The satchel also held spare rounds for the Ruger and shotgun. Around his neck hung a binocular case. He wore heavy wool pants, a thick wool shirt and a thigh-length quilt-jacket sheathed in sealskin.

"Yes," murmured Milton, "traveling light. As I expected. Do you have everything you might require?"

Hunter insured that rounds were chambered in the Winchester. "I'm good. I'll test the rifle when I reach the tree line. If I don't like the feel of it, I'll leave it at the gate and take the Marlin."

"Very good. Do you think it knows you're coming?"

"Oh, yeah."

Ben was possessively close to Hunter's side as if the bear sensed that Hunter would need his protection. But Hunter had no intention of taking Ben with him because the Grizzly would attack the Scimitar on sight and he didn't need the bear in front of him while he was trying to take a shot. And there were other, unknown factors, as well. Right now Hunter knew there was one Scimitar and one Amphicyon. But what if there was more than one Amphicyon and more than one Scimitar?

Logically, if some madman was willing to reconstitute one prehistoric wolf, why not reconstitute a dozen? And while Ben might hold his own against one of the gigantic predators, a pack would inexorably bring him down. Even a normal pack of gray wolves could bring down a Grizzly. A pack of super-wolves would kill him inside ten seconds.

"What will you do first?" asked the major.

Hunter took a moment to scan the forest. "Circle the estate," he remarked tiredly. "Look for sign."

Milton stomped as if to warm his feet. "If the tracks take you east, be mindful of an isolated grove of cypress circled by tall black stones. It appears harmless. But it is three acres of quicksand. In my youth it was greatly feared by the locals. And for good reason. More than one hunter has imprudently ventured into that flat and never returned."

"I'll keep an eye out for it," muttered Hunter and looped the bear-chain around his fist. "Have Zelda feed Ben in a few hours. I'm gonna chain him up at the gate so he can stand guard with them." He paused. "After I'm gone, lock this place up. It's probably going to get lively out there, and I don't want anybody to get shot."

"Do you think it will be rash enough to attack in the daylight?"

"It will eventually."

"Why do you say that?"

"Because I think it's here to get its hands on something. And it knows it can't wait forever."

Adjusting the Marlin, Hunter stepped forward as he consciously gave himself over to instinct and reflex. He was hunting now, and hunting was sight, sense, smell and something unknown.

Inside five minutes he was staring at white frost topping the spikes. The black iron was sheathed in microscopic crystal and the ground directly outside the barrier was a frozen sea. Hunter searched for the scent of ammonia, but detected nothing. Then he walked along the tracks of horses, dogs, and guards who had circled the estate through the night. When he reached the gate, he found Blackthorn standing with his rifle at port arms.

The commander was wearing paneled hunting pants, a thick wool shirt covered by a Hemingway-style sweater and a dark green parka. A strap across his right shoulder supported a shiny leather case at his left hip. His hunting boots were laced with military precision. Unable to conceal his amusement, Hunter said, "Did you clear out the Big and Tall Department at William Powell?"

The sarcasm was not missed as Blackthorn replied, "Although it was once a great passion of mine, I've not hunted in many years. So while I was waiting for your call in New York I took advantage of the opportunity to patronize a Manhattan outdoors establishment which, by good fortune, happened to be of an English proprietor. I'm afraid this was all they had in their Big and Tall division." Indifferently he brushed a hand across the coat. "I admit it's a bit dandy. But I'm sure it'll be seasoned by the end of the day."

Hunter laughed, "Maybe I should go alone on this one."

"I agree. Unfortunately, after filing my report to the Detective Chief-Superintendent, I was again ordered to accompany you." Blackthorn's mouth pressed in a bitter line. "I don't know what he expects me to do should you be killed, but I'll do my best to die like an Englishman."

Hunter gestured to the rifle, "You any good with that?"

"Three years Special Air Service," Blackthorn stated as if that was all that needed to be said.

"All right, then. Remember what I told you."

"Do what you say when you say. I remember."

Hunter stepped to the large iron post that supported one side of the gate and wrapped Ben's chain around it before padlocking. Then he addressed the guards, "I'm leaving Ben here. If he starts acting nervous, it's because that wolf is close. If that happens, unchain him and get out of the way."

A guard nervously asked, "W-W-What will he do?"

"He's not going to hurt you, boy. But get out of his way just the same. The last place you want to get is between him and that wolf."

"But how will we know if he's getting nervous?"

"He'll stand up on his back legs. He'll raise his nose. Then he'll start grunting and swaying." Hunter leaned close to Ben, a casual hug of his gigantic head. "Don't kill any of these boys."

They looked wide-eyed at Blackthorn, who said, "Mr. Hunter's the wilderness expert, lads. We can trust him."

Leaving the gate, Hunter walked toward the spot where he was certain the creature had landed. Two minutes later he was kneeling twenty feet from the bars as Blackthorn glanced incredulously at the fence. The detective asked, "Do you really think that thing could have leaped this far? Didn't you say it weighted half a ton?"

"That was just a guess. But now, looking at this, I'd say he probably weighs more like seven … eight hundred. He's not as big as I thought."

"Well, that's good. But could he have really made this jump?"

"A Siberian tiger weighs eight hundred pounds and could easily make that jump, so it's possible. In fact, it's more than possible. It's likely." Hunter stood, pointing down. "It's bleeding."

"Where?"

Hunter pointed to a few specks of black on the yellow tarn. Frowning over the miniscule droplets, Blackthorn muttered, "That doesn't look too bad."

"We'll see." Hunter turned his face to the forest wall. "It angled for those trees, and that makes sense. It'd want to get out of sight as fast as possible. Especially from cameras."

Blackthorn straightened. "Are you serious! Are you telling me this thing really does know what a camera is? I mean, I know it's evaded cameras until now but how can it even know what a camera *is*!"

"Do you have it on camera?"

"As I told you, no."

"Then I guess it does."

"But how?"

"It doesn't understand cameras like you do, Blackthorn. It just knows to look for anything unusual. And cameras are not a natural part of the forest, so it avoids them."

Hunter lifted the .600 Nitrous Express and fired into a tree. He instantly worked the bolt to slam in another three-inch round and pushed an extra cartridge into the magazine as Blackthorn came down from a leap. "Bloody hell, Hunter! Why'd you do that!"

"Never go into battle with an unproven weapon, old son. And if I was you, I'd test that rifle before staking my life on it."

For a moment Blackthorn stared. Then he leveled at a tree and fired both barrels. He leaned forward, peering. "Right," he said. "Dead-on." He cracked open the breech to replace both shells. He snapped it shut as he added, "Let's get on with it. I'll stay well behind you so I don't cock up any tracks."

They moved close to the tree line before Hunter knelt again. Finally he said, "This print wasn't made by the one I hit."

After staring as if he didn't quite comprehend, Blackthorn suddenly exclaimed, "You're telling me there's *two of them*?"

"Yeah."

"Well," the detective asked, more nervous, "do you think there might be *more* than two?'

"It's possible," Hunter muttered, subdued. "And these two are working together."

"Is that normal?"

Hunter stood. "It's normal for wolves. Wolves work together. They always have. It's instinct. And I don't think prehistoric wolves are gonna be any different. Instincts don't change."

"So that's what this is? A prehistoric wolf?"

"It looks like it. But I don't know. It could be a hybrid. We'll know by the end of the day."

"How will we know?"

"Because we'll get a good look at 'em."

Blackthorn's face twisted as he quietly asked, "Why do I feel you're not telling me everything?"

"Because I don't know everything, Blackthorn. I'm just *assuming*. But we'll know soon enough. Let's go."

Blackthorn muttered an indistinct curse as Hunter picked a silent path over black water and moss. Three hours later Hunter stopped and knelt again. He stared for a long time.

"What is it?" whispered Blackthorn.

"It looks like three individual wolves."

Blackthorn's eyes flared. "There's three of them?"

"Looks like it."

"I guess he's the runt of the group." Blackthorn declared as if mustering his courage. "They probably left the little one as a lookout. That's always how it works."

"Not with wolves, it's not."

"What are you saying?"

"I'm saying the one that waited here is the Alpha – the leader of the pack. He's commanding the others and … he's big."

Blackthorn paused. "How big?"

"*Big.*"

"Bloody hell, Hunter! *How big*!"

Hunter lifted his face. "He's as big as Ben. Maybe bigger. At least a thousand pounds. Or you could say he's half a ton of muscle and bone with a real vicious set of fangs that have the bite strength of a Great White Shark."

Blackthorn angrily exclaimed, "Look! Maybe we should go back and come up with a better plan! This was dangerous when there was just one of them! And now there's *three*? This is not good, mate!"

Hunter's lips barely moved, "It's too late."

"What do you mean?"

"We're five miles inside the tree line. They know we're here. If we turn around, they'll come after us. And if we're doomed to run into them one way or another, I'd rather have them in front of me."

Setting his steps on submerged roots and moss, avoiding leaves and twigs, Hunter bent beneath limbs without disturbing them as he moved forward. The forest flowed around them in a depthless dark only pierced by the distant screech of fowl. Streams meandering through the morass began to thicken and tighten like tendrils of a wet, brackish spiderweb.

A great shadow darkened where Hunter stood and he looked up to see a truly gigantic Eagle Owl descending. The magnificent brown bird – it was as large as a condor – landed on a branch to Hunter's side and Hunter simply stared into its eyes. Then he remembered Milton's words, "*Some say the Eagle Owl watches over those who protect the forest …*"

Hunter sighed, then pointed with his rifle at the ground. "Quicksand, Blackthorn. Step exactly where I step."

Blackthorn glared at the smooth glaze of mud. "How do you know that's quicksand?"

"Wanna step in it and find out?"

Following Hunter to the right, Blackthorn repeated, "I hate riddles, Hunter. It goes against my grain as an investigator. How did you know that was quicksand?"

"Because nothing's growing on it."

"That's how you can tell?"

"It's one way. It's also a lot wetter than the surrounding ground, but it's not lower. And there's no animal tracks across it."

"That stuff will suck you down, mate."

Hunter smoothly slipped beneath a limb. "That's a myth."

"What? That people get sucked down in quicksand? That's a myth? Are you saying people *don't* die in quicksand?"

"Sure they do. They sink down to their waist. But that's about as far as they go. They don't get sucked under the surface. That part's a myth. In reality, after sinking down to their waist, people just can't get out of it, and they end up freezing to death. Or they die of thirst. Whichever. But the quicksand isn't really what kills them. It's the cold, the lack of water. Other stuff. Truth is, Blackthorn, I've found plenty of skeletons still stuck in quicksand years after they died there."

"Why don't they sink all the way down?"

"Because quicksand is heavier than your body. You don't see leaves sinking into quicksand, do you? The only people who sink out of sight are the people who keep fighting it, kicking mud out of the way. They panic and dig their own grave until they're gone. If you just lay over on it and spread out your weight, you'll be okay. It's thicker than you are. Just move slow and roll out of it."

"You know this from experience?"

"Yeah. When I was young."

"Who taught you to get out of it?"

"Nobody. I had to figure it out or die."

"You've lived a hard life, mate."

"You could say that."

Hunter abruptly raised a hand, staring down. His head tilted as he stared, unblinking, on a long black alley of mud clearly marked by tracks. Kneeling, he said nothing until Blackthorn whispered, "What is it?"

It was as if Hunter were speaking to someone who was not there as he whispered, "So you're their master, huh?"

Blackthorn shifted. "Hunter! What is it, man!"

"Same prints I saw in Alaska."

"You're just now seeing them?"

"We're just now reaching them." Hunter stared down a long time. "He took another route from the estate and hooked up with the wolves here."

"Huh," Blackthorn considered, "who is 'he.'"

"It's what I faced in Alaska. It's called a Homo Scimitar." Hunter raised his face. "I don't have time to tell you what he is. For now, just be on guard against anything that looks like a werewolf."

"Are the wolves hunting him, too?"

"No. If they were hunting him, one would have circled ahead to wait while the other two chased him into the trap. But they're not doing that. They're following him in a straight line, so this guy controls all three of them. He's their master."

Blackthorn's alertness increased dramatically. "It's hard to believe they're following a human being."

"He's not a human being."

After a long stare Blackthorn asked, "What, exactly, was the beast you faced in Alaska?"

"I'll tell you later."

Blackthorn glared in various directions. "Very well. Then tell me something else."

"What's that?"

"Why couldn't Redford track this thing?"

"I think Redford did before he decided he didn't want any part of this."

That answer made Blackthorn lower his chin, staring over Hunter. "So why did Redford tell us that he couldn't find it?"

"Because he didn't want you to think him a coward."

Clearly the detective didn't like the reply but now wasn't the time. His hands twisted on the rifle as he searched the surrounding forest. Then he looked at his wristwatch and punched in a command.

Hunter glanced up. "What you got there?"

"A GPS locator. So we don't get lost."

"I thought you SAS guys were experts at navigating."

"A little help from science never hurts, mate."

Smiling, Hunter rose. "Don't worry, Blackthorn. I'll get you back in time for supper."

"I trust you will. Now what?"

"Straight ahead. But we need to be quiet from here. The tracks show they're slowing down, and we don't want to accidentally walk up on them." Hunter hesitated, as if calculating. "Things are about to get serious. Make sure you do exactly what I do."

"Things are *about* to get serious?"

"Do you understand, Blackthorn?"

"Yes! I understand!"

Hunter was searching high, low, always slow. He moved for a long time without comment. Then he pointed and whispered, "The one that went over the fence is still bleeding. And it looks like I wounded the Scimitar, too. There's two trails of blood."

"How can you possibly see blood in this muck?"

"Practice. Now, listen; they went up this way about an hour ago. We're about to come up on them. When we do, stay close to me. I can't be worried about where you're at."

"I won't be wandering off, bucko. You can trust me on *that.*"

After a dozen stops and starts Hunter emerged from a stand of chestnut and stared over what could only be classified as huts. Each structure was constructed from meticulously cut granite stones, all of them entwined in vine. Overall it presented the impression of an abandoned Viking village re-claimed by the jungle. And although it'd surely been centuries since anybody inhabited this place, Hunter detected the faint outline of a road.

Four flat lanes of stone spread from a distinct intersection.

"Who lived here?" Hunter asked absently.

Blackthorn rumbled, "People say it was some kind of civilization that existed as far back as biblical times, but nobody knows for sure. Then they just vanished. Some say they were killed off by Caesar. Some say the Vikings killed them. And some say they just died out." His gaze scanned the harsh, surrounding swamp. "It's amazing to me that they survived here at all."

"It wasn't always like this," Hunter murmured. "This was a jungle once. It was beautiful. It had fruit, game, good ground for crops. They were probably real happy here."

"What changed all that?"

"The same thing that changes everything else."

"What's that?"

"Nature changes. And that's what changes people." Hunter pointed to the barely visible wall of a hut. "Are all these places built from granite?"

"I believe so," Blackthorn answered. "Tors are plentiful in the moors. Especially at Dartmoor and here. Why?"

"Because these walls are good for concealing heat signatures." Hunter brushed aside leaves, staring down. "Did your people search all the huts?"

"They searched all the ones they knew about, but there's dozens of these old villages and I don't know if each of them is mapped." Blackthorn gazed to the left, right. "They say human life began in Africa. But I think these places are older than that. I wouldn't be surprised if life began right here."

"I wouldn't doubt it." Hunter was silent a long time, studying the tracks and the huts before as he said, "They could be hiding in these ruins."

Blackthorn pointed the rifle. "*These ruins*?"

"Maybe." Hunter looked up. "This leader is smart."

"This madman with the wolves?"

"Yeah. He's their leader. He tells them when to attack. When to retreat. So I'm sure he's telling them where to hide."

"What makes you think he's smart?"

"First, because he hasn't broken into that house and killed every one of you. That means he's waiting for something. He's patient. And it takes intelligence to be patient. It takes discipline and strength." Hunter remained as he was, head bowed. "And it takes a *reason*."

The investigator was relentlessly searching. "Do you think they're somewhere around here?"

"They're moving east along this grade."

"How long ago?"

"A couple of hours."

"So they're close?"

"If they've stopped moving, yeah." After staring down another moment, Hunter added, "Remember what I told you. No shooting unless I shoot first. And look sharp."

Instantly every tree erupted with wings as hundreds of small bats took flight. Blackthorn had whirled, rifle leveled. Hunter didn't move but remained on a knee, gazing at the ground as the sky vanished behind spectral shapes that blocked out the sun.

Blackthorn gasped, "Are those *bats*?!"

"You've never seen a bat, Blackthorn?"

"I've never seen ten thousand of them at the same time! What kind of bats are they?"

"Daubenton bats. Medium size. Dark when they're young. Brown when they're old. They're carnivores."

"Meat eaters?"

"Yeah. But they don't normally feed or fly during the day."

"They sure look like they're flying to me!"

"Something spooked them."

"Us?"

Hunter paused. "I don't think so." He moved his hand, shifting windblown leaves before added, "Men died here."

Blackthorn pointed. "Here? Where?"

Hunter pointed along the tracks. "It started here and went up that way." Blackthorn was close as Hunter threaded a soundless path through the mossy black stones. Then he stopped.

Upon the ground were the bodies of four men in bloody, shredded English hunting gear. Heavy rifles had been smashed to splinters and the fragments were lying across stone and tarn. Blood was frozen in deep, gaping wounds where organs had been savagely ripped from their chests. Every muscle group had been ravaged. After studying the wounds, Hunter quietly commented, "Well, there's some good news."

"What's that?"

"There's still just three wolves."

"*That's* good news?"

"Better than four, ain't it?"

"Not as good as one. Who are these poor buggers?"

"Looks like a local safari. They came in yesterday from the north. They were attacked back there but made it this far before they went down." He stared up the slope in front of them. "The wolves went over that hill a few minutes ago. Water is still pooling in their tracks. But they stopped here to feed on leftovers. They're probably getting tired."

Straightening, Blackthorn raised a keen gaze to the slope. "Let's stay on top of them, then."

"You've got courage, Blackthorn, I'll give you that. A lot of men would be wanting to turn back right about now."

"I'm one of them. But we have a job to do." He straightened, a nod. "'Tis an evil deed. Let it be done quickly. And you said it yourself. I'd rather keep them in front of me."

Hunter's head snapped up. Eyes wide, he stared unblinking at the slope. The forest fell deathly still as he said quietly, "Blackthorn? Do exactly what I do." He stopped breathing. "*Exactly.*"

"What is it?" he grunted.

A monstrous black shape rose from the far side of the mound like a colossus rising from a hungry grave. Gigantic with incisive, separated fangs. It was as heavy as a bear, but it wasn't a bear. Rather, its wedged jaws and elongated body was the image of a misshapen, prehistoric wolf.

"Dear god!" gasped Blackthorn.

Another form emerged from a hut to their right, staring with eyes glowing red in the gathering gloom. It was not so large as the monstrosity that stood on the hill but it was the size of a wild bull. Then, not truly needing to confirm it, Hunter slowly turned his head left and saw a third beast emerging from the gray slabs, boldly displaying itself. As Hunter held its gaze, it began to dip its head like a wolf will do before it attacks. It, too, was smaller than the gargantuan Alpha that stood upon the hill, but it was also the size of a bull; it was bleeding from its shoulder.

Blackthorn began to step back.

"*Don't move!*" Hunter rasped.

The Alpha lowered its head with a subterranean growl and leaped forward to viciously strike the ground.

"Hunter!"

"Don't shoot!"

"It's going to attack!"

"*Do not raise that rifle!*"

Very slowly Hunter glanced to the left, the right, and saw the smaller two hadn't yet advanced. Then the Alpha roared and lashed out to strike a huge stone that lay between Hunter and itself; the blow sent the rock spinning a hundred feet across the moor where it smashed into a wall and shattered in an explosion of white dust. As the beast squared off again, it was the purest image of prehistoric might and unquenchable rage.

CHAPTER SIXTEEN

Hunter's finger settled – subtly – on the trigger of the rifle. He had two shots in the Winchester before he tossed it and ripped the Marlin from his shoulder because it had five more. But he wasn't sure if even that much ordinance was enough to put down this Alpha. For certain, it wasn't enough to put down all three of them. Without a glance Hunter knew that Blackthorn wouldn't be restrained much longer, so there were no good moves. There was no defense, nowhere to hide, nowhere to run.

The Alpha was on the verge of charging.

Hunter's only chance was to scare them with something they'd never seen before and didn't understand. It would only buy them thirty seconds – at best – but that'd be enough to retreat into the trees and hit these animals with a few rifle rounds to slow them down. Fighting adrenaline, Hunter slowly slipped a hand into his pouch and, even more slowly, removed the tin of phosphorous.

Hunter whispered, "Get ready to run."

Blackthorn stiffened.

Four things happened simultaneously.

Hunter tossed the tin of phosphorous as the Alpha charged and at its first step Hunter raised the Winchester and fired. The bullet hit the container as it descended in the face of the beast and the explosion was even more violent and shocking than Hunter anticipated.

Upon contact with the air, the phosphorous detonated like napalm creating a twenty-foot-wide cloud of mushrooming white fire. And although Hunter couldn't see beyond the flames, he heard the Alpha screaming and raging. The monstrous beast came down – somewhere – with a roar that would have been deafening if Hunter had been facing it, but he was already running. He blasted a path through the forest in a dead run tearing a hole through briars that shredded his arms unfelt and unseen.

Chestnuts flashed past Hunter in a gray-purple blur as he searched frantically for high ground. Then, with the visual acuity that only comes with adrenaline-fueled fear, Hunter sighted a slope to the left and quickly reached the top, turning and kneeling as he pulled the stock of the rifle hard into his shoulder. Blackthorn came down beside him and duplicated the stance, rifle level.

Three ferocious forms tore from the forest wall.

Hunter coldly targeted the Alpha and fired two shots. He didn't hear the reports and didn't feel the recoil. Then the Winchester was out of rounds and Hunter tossed it ripping up the Marlin from his shoulder. He levered it and centered on the Alpha as it leaped back and to the side. Before it landed, Hunter fired again, hitting it somewhere in the chest.

Realizing he had to fire faster than he could lever the rifle, Hunter ripped out the Ruger and fired five rounds from the .454, hitting the Alpha with each round. Then, with a commanding bellow, the Alpha twisted and was lost in the trees like a runaway freight train. The others spun and within seconds were also gone leaving the air rumbling with gunshots and roars.

Without hesitation Hunter ran down the far side of the slope, Blackthorn descending in his steps.

Hunter reloaded the Ruger and Winchester as he moved, spinning and searching. As they reached a ravine, he realized Blackthorn had been cursing since the first shot was fired. Then they reached a wide, level stretch of yellow tarn and

Hunter turned again, every instinct keen to catch sight or sound of what was behind them. "Blackthorn!" he shouted. "Are you okay?"

Face drawn, Blackthorn didn't reply or take his wide, white eyes from the wood line.

"*BLACKTHORN*!"

Blackthorn whirled, clearly shocked.

"Look at yourself!" demanded Hunter. "*Are you hurt*?"

"No!"

"Watch our backs! I'll watch the front! Let's go!"

"What's the plan?"

"The plan is to get back to the estate alive! We're going back the same way we came! Shoot anything you see!"

"I hit one of them! I know I did!"

"You're not gonna put any of them down with one round!" With a vicious effort, Hunter calmed himself. "Just stay alert. They'll be moving ahead to flank us."

"I thought you said they'd chase us!"

"They're not stupid, Blackthorn! They're not going to chase us because they know where we're going! But they'll still look for a place to ambush us."

"Can they outflank us?"

"If we get close to something they can use for cover," Hunter muttered angrily. "We just have to stay away from anything they can use. Come on. Keep your eyes on that tree line. That's where they'll be. But they won't charge if they see you watching them. They're not going to expose themselves to gun fire in the open field. Not while the sun's out."

"Jesus!"

"Calm down, man."

The detective released a tense breath.

"All right," he nodded. "Let's go."

It would take five hours to reach the compound and Hunter tried not to think about anything beyond that. Searching constantly, he saw every waving leaf and every shadow moved by the leaves. He didn't see the creatures but he wasn't looking for them. He was looking for movement because, like any creature, they couldn't walk through brush without shifting whatever lay beside or before them. They were stealthy, yeah, but they weren't ghosts.

They were as real as any maneater could be.

Together Hunter and Blackthorn marched, uncaring of stealth, through one field after another until Hunter saw the gray mossy outline of the estate rising beyond skeletal trees. They had no choice but to move through the chestnut and birch to reach the manor, but it was a risk Hunter was willing to take. He knew what they needed to stage an ambush and he was careful to avoid large rocks that might conceal them.

A half-hour later guards at the gate shouted and ran forward to meet them at the edge of the tarn. Then they were inside the compound and Hunter turned to Blackthorn.

The commander's face was flushed. Sweating profusely, he swiped his brow with the forearm of his heavy coat as he took a series of painful breaths. Then, with an agonized expression, he shouted, "Hunter! I need you to tell me what the hell we're dealing with!"

Hunter searched the tree line as he slowed his breathing. "It's hard to believe they did it again," he said.

"No more riddles!" roared Blackthorn, stepping into Hunter's face. He pointed viciously at the wood line. "You know what those things are! You've always known! And don't tell me it's *just a wolf* because I've *never* seen a wolf that weighed a hundred stone!"

Hunter wearily swept a hand down his face. "I'll tell you what I think. But not here. Let's go inside."

As they walked toward the house, Blackthorn asked, "I'm correct, aren't I?"

"About what?"

"You've known all along."

"I suspected."

"How in the blazes could you suspect *this*?"

Hunter's frown deepened.

"I told you, Blackthorn. I've seen one before."

"Where?"

Hunter paused.

"In a grave."

* * *

"What in the name of Jesus Christ of Nazareth is an Amphicyon?" asked Blackthorn.

The homicide detective poured himself a glass of scotch, no ice, and unceremoniously threw it back with a single gulp. His question went unanswered as he made himself another and Major Milton commented mildly, "I thought it was against regulations to drink on duty, commander."

"Blast regulations," muttered Blackthorn and swallowed. He slammed the glass on the bar and turned. "I'm not an imbecile, Hunter. Was that the same creature you faced in Alaska?"

"No," said Hunter, refilling empty loops in his gun belt. "What I faced in Alaska was worse. And he's dead. But one of them is out there, too. I went up against him last night."

"You're not talking about the wolves?"

"No. I'm talking about what I killed in Alaska. One of them is out there, too. And he's more dangerous than all those wolves put together."

"You're certain of this?"

"I know what I saw," Hunter said, loosening his shoulder. "But it's not the same creature I tracked in Alaska. That one's dead. I killed him. Took his head, in the end. But it's the same species. And I can promise you that he *is* here to kill one or all of you. Killing is all he does."

"What *possible reason* could –"

"I don't know, Blackthorn!" Hunter came to his feet. "But those wolves are prehistoric and this Scimitar is controlling them! They're like attack dogs for him! He sends them out like a hunter sends out hunting dogs. They tree or kill the prey. And if you think those wolves are dangerous, they're *nothing* compared to the Scimitar!"

Half-turning away before whirling back, Blackthorn exclaimed, "Damn it, Hunter! Why didn't you kill the thing last night?"

"Believe me, Blackthorn, he ain't easy to kill. He wasn't easy to kill the first time and I bet he's gonna be twice as hard this time."

Hunter knew his response was inadequate but, with an effort, the experienced homicide investigator seemed to shelve the matter. Blackthorn sniffed, frowning, before he said with remarkable equity, "So you say this Scimitar is controlling the wolves?"

"Yeah."

"How?"

Hunter hesitated as his gaze moved left to right along the floor. "I don't know how. Maybe he raised them. Maybe he beat them down until they submitted. But I know that Scimitar is the leader of that pack. It explains why they haven't killed everybody in here. Maybe our suspicions are wrong. Maybe the Scimitar *meant* to kill your chauffer. Maybe he was always the target! I don't know. But the Scimitar is holding them back right now from killing every one of us." A pause. "He's waiting for something."

Blackthorn cut a suspicious glance at Major Milton. "Major? Did you know about any of this?"

"Absolutely not!" denied Milton.

Blackthorn stared out the front window before gazing back. "I'm a bit confused, Hunter. I thought of us as mates. Why didn't you tell me all this last night?"

"Because I didn't believe it myself," answered Hunter wearily. "It just seemed impossible. But you're right. I should have told you what I suspected."

From Blackthorn's stoic countenance, no apology was needed. After a time he said, "Well, an error in judgment is inevitable in this madness. God grant it's the only mistake we make."

"My judgment's been off since last night," Hunter muttered, his face twisting in regret. "The Scimitar threw me off. He threw me off my whole game. I didn't expect *him*. God Almighty, he was the *last* thing I expected."

"What does this Scimitar look like?"

Hunter paused. "He looks vaguely like a cross between a Sabretooth tiger and a human being. He's big like a man, but he's stronger and faster. Like a tiger. And the one I faced in Alaska was no more intelligent than any other animal. But this one is … not the same."

"How do you mean?"

"He's smarter. He's got all the advantages of this animal – the strength, the speed, the fangs and claws – but he's got an intelligence that is *way* beyond what I faced in Alaska."

Blackthorn stared. "I've never heard of anything like this in my life. And I consider myself an educated man."

Hunter's teeth were bared as he began, "A few years ago some scientists in Alaska found an unknown species in a glacier. It was pretty well preserved and it looked like a cross between a Smilodon and Homo Erectus. For lack of a better description, they called it *Homo Scimitar* – half man, half tiger." He paused. "Anyway, subsequent analysis revealed that it was immune to viruses and bacteria. Then they discovered that it had an incredible ability to heal, which also gave it an extended life span. I mean, compared to us, it was immortal. And its physical superiority was obvious because they found it on top of a Sabretooth tiger that it'd killed with its bare hands. So they isolated segments of its DNA, synthesized a serum, and that's how all this got started."

"A serum?" grunted Blackthorn. "For what?"

"For what they considered to be immortality," Hunter commented as if the bizarre was now become routine to him. "They wanted to extend human life and they thought an isolated element of this thing's DNA was the secret formula for it. But then one of those idiot-scientists jumped the gun and injected himself with the stuff before it was tested, and it changed him."

"Changed him?"

"Physically."

"It changed him into that creature out there?"

"Sort of."

"What do you mean?"

"I mean that the creature I faced last night is more human than the creature that hunted me in Alaska. The one I faced in Alaska was a lot more animal than man. But this one is the opposite. It moves the same. It has the same speed. Same strength. Same lust for killing. But it seems somehow smarter. Like it retains some vestige of human consciousness."

"How did you kill the one in Alaska?"

Hunter rested back in the chair. "I used a snare. Caught it by the neck. Choked it out. Killed it like anything else gets killed by a snare." A pause, and he gestured, "Well, then I set it on fire. Then I cut its head off."

Blackthorn nodded with approval. "Did that do the job?"

"Yeah."

"Do you think you can do it again?"

"No," Hunter said with conviction. "That was a last-chance suicide move that I made because I had no choice. There's no way I could pull it off again. Half of it was skill, and half was guts but *all* of it luck. And I don't wanna play that hand again."

Blackthorn's aspect was stoic. "So how do we kill this one?"

Finally Hunter answered, "Well, one thing is certain. We can't beat it with brute strength. It *is* brute strength." His jaw tightened. "The one in Alaska was like a rhino. It was practically bulletproof. But this one doesn't seem to have that same level of resistance. It was hurt last night when I hit it with the shotgun, so it might be vulnerable to rifle fire." He rose and walked to the fire. "I need time to think. But I know we can kill it."

"How do you know that?"

"I told you. Because I hurt it."

"So?"

Hunter stared into the flames, raging and consuming. "If we can hurt it a little," he said stoically, "we can hurt it all the way to the grave."

The detective cupped his chin and strolled a few steps before he muttered, "We do have one advantage."

"What's that?"

"It's just an animal."

Hunter sadly shook his head. "That's what I've been trying to tell you, Blackthorn. It's not just an animal. It's got the body of the most efficient killing machine that ever existed, yeah, but it's also got the subconscious mind of a human being."

"Subconscious?" Blackthorn seemed perplexed. "What's so dangerous about the subconscious?"

Hunter had analyzed his ordeal in Alaska so many times that his next statement felt rehearsed as he said calmly, "Think of it like this, Blackthorn. This Scimitar is the embodiment of what science calls the *ID*. That's the most primeval, most repressed part of the human mind. It's the seat of our most violent instincts. It's the home of all the thoughts and desires that we won't even admit to ourselves. But that's exactly what drives this creature. That's its power because it carries out the slightest impulse with no restraint. No hesitation. And, believe me, the subconscious mind is *not* an enemy you want to face. It is absolutely merciless and efficient." Hunter shook his head, "The only reason everybody on this planet isn't dead is because nobody has the physical power to execute every homicidal thought that crosses their subconscious mind. But this creature *does* have that power. And when it finally gets what it wants and turns that power loose on whoever is still alive? It's going to kill anything and everything that gets in its way unless we kill it first."

Blackthorn didn't miss a beat. "You said it's waiting for something. Waiting for what?"

There was a moment. Then Hunter answered, "I think the human side of its mind is holding it back for a reason. But I don't know what it could be. All I know is that he hasn't completely surrendered to his subconscious just yet. That's why he's being so patient. He's waiting for something. It's the only thing that makes sense."

Flora, the eldest daughter, spoke, "For a man who knew nothing yesterday, Mr. Hunter, you seem to know a great deal today. Are you certain that you're right?"

Hunter turned his face to her. "I'm certain."

Blackthorn stepped forward, "Then we are in a more perilous situation than I thought. Yes. Perhaps, when I inform the superintendent, we'll receive reinforcements."

"More men are just more dead bodies," Hunter commented. "This thing will absolutely kill whatever gets between him and what he wants. And it wants something in this house. So we're gonna have to use this house. Lure it in here. Kill it in here."

The youngest son, Barron, stepped forward. "Has it escaped everyone's attention that we could just *leave*?"

"You can't escape it," said Hunter. "He'll follow you. He'll find you. And he'll kill you."

Flora interjected, "I do not mean to speak unduly of my own accomplishments, Mr. hunter, but I have an extensive background in biology and psychology. In fact, I was in my second year of medical school when the major decided to re-locate to the United Kingdom, and I feel that much of what you're saying is merely conjecture. You have no physical samples of this beast. You have not had sufficient time to test it in a controlled laboratory setting. How can you be so certain?"

Unaffected, Hunter stated, "Because I've tracked and killed one. I know how it thinks. I know how it moves. I know how it kills and I know why it kills. And that beats any lab test you've got. So I know he's going to keep coming until he gets what he wants. And if any of you leave, and you've got what he wants, it will follow you like a hound out of Hell."

Barron objected, "I'll hire an army of bodyguards!"

Hunter pointed toward the window. "You've *already* got an army of bodyguards, boy! Hiring more bodyguards won't help. You can't run from this creature. You have to kill him or he *will* hunt you down and kill you like a dog! He's a hunter. It's what he's born to do. It's what he lives to do, He hunts and kills and if he has to leave a trail of dead bodies halfway around the world to kill you, he'll do it."

Major Milton spoke, "I've never been one to run, children. Run if you wish, but I'll see this through." He picked up the phone. "Commander? May I receive a visitor before dark? It is a matter of the most pressing importance."

Blackthorn hesitated. "If you must, Major."

"Thank you." Milton picked up the phone, dialed, and waited. Then, "Trevor? Yes, it's Augustus. Please come to the house immediately and bring my final papers. Yes, it's quite safe as long as it's daylight. The police are still on the grounds."

Flora bent, hands on Milton's arm. Her voice was concerned. "Why do you need Trevor, Major?"

"I'm going to amend my will," stated Milton, resolute.

His children exchanged glances.

"An enemy has done this," angrily muttered Milton as he stood. "I'm going to amend my will so that only my immediate family will profit from my death. None of those corporate leeches will garner a cent." He began breathing more harshly. "So, the estate will pass to all of you and together you shall decide expenditures. And a trust will be assigned to care for Emily all her life. Even more, this land and house shall be held in that trust as Emily's permanent home with whatever financial provisions shall be required to care for her forever. And it shall be inviolable."

After a moment Blackthorn said, "Very well, Major. We shall receive your visitor. I need to inform the lads. If you would excuse me."

He exited the front doors.

Hunter knew he could have simply alerted the guards over the radio but Blackthorn obviously had another reason to remove himself from the room. For a moment Hunter wondered what it was, then dismissed it. He didn't have time to ponder what the detective might be doing behind the scenes. There were already too many unknowns in this.

Only Barron Milton had the bad form to ask, "But what if none of us survive?"

"Then it will be given to charity!" surged Milton as he snatched up his cane. "This isn't about money, boy! It's about dying like a soldier and not like a goat tied to a stake! And since I can't discover who's responsible for this, I'll blame every one of those corporate jackals!"

With a sharp gasp Emily spun at the window, staring. Just as quickly, Bronte stepped to her side. "No," she whispered, "they're not here, Emily. *They are not here.*"

Devastated, Milton bowed his head, "Forgive me, dear Emily, I ... forgot myself. Forgive me, my dear child."

Hunter acutely caught every word and gesture but revealed nothing. He never lifted his head or turned his gaze to the exchange, but he remembered every detail because he realized this mystery was important. But at this point it was wiser to conceal than reveal.

With rapidly spiraling anger Milton came around the desk exuding remarkable energy and stood against the flames of the hearth. Then he inexorably turned toward his children as he declared, "It is possible that not all of us shall survive this event, and that is why I intend to revise my will. And I want to remind all of you that there are far worse fates than a brave death. To live in fear is a fate far worse. To watch everyone that you love pass long before your time is far more terrible. So, I encourage you to be brave. Those of us that survive shall have the means to enjoy a long and productive life. I am going to leave my entire fortune to my eldest surviving child, and he or she will ensure that the rest of you are prudently cared for even if you have been gravely wounded. I have accumulated enough wealth to care for you all." He stared upon Hunter. "I do not believe I shall be needing it."

Hunter said, "It might not be after you."

"Of course it is," laughed Milton. "And it's not like I didn't expect this one day, Mr. Hunter. Yes … I knew this day would come. You can't make a fortune of eighty billion pounds without making enough enemies to sink the Bismark." He paused a long time, then said, "Wealthy men and assassins live by the same rule, Mr. Hunter."

"What's that?"

"Never turn your back to a friend."

CHAPTER SEVENTEEN

B lackthorn found all was in order as he walked the perimeter. Although the men were obviously shaken, they seemed stalwart enough. Mounted patrols were preparing for their shifts and dogs were roaming the grounds. But even though the gory scene of last night's attack had been sanitized with lime and gasoline, the mastiffs shied away from the area.

Apparently, Milton's barrister lived close because he arrived within a half-hour. Blackthorn watched impassively as a long black Rolls passed without delay through the front gate and an hour later the Rolls exited, similarly without fanfare. Blackthorn could only presume that the old man had finalized his will, as he implied. But such civilized processes were not among Blackthorn's concerns because he could not dismiss the horrific images of the day from his mind. And he was becoming increasingly anxious about the horrors that were sure to come with full night.

Sensing an approach, Blackthorn bent his head to see Inspector Marshal stoutly striding forward, his heavy rifle – a weapon almost as tall as Marshal himself – slung over his bulldog shoulder.

Blackthorn asked, "How are you holding up, old man?"

Inspector Marshal's head bobbed once. "Very good, governor. I take it you weren't injured today?"

"It was a close thing but, no, we escaped intact. And how are the lads holding up?"

Marshal's head made a quick cut to the left before he noted, "I just received a report from hospital, sir. They lost Jameson, O'Reilly, and Placard. Thompson and Atkins are disabled but expected to survive. They've been airlifted to London. I haven't notified the Deputy Assistant-Commissioner of the event, sir."

"I'll inform him," stated Blackthorn.

"Very well." With noticeable anxiety the stout investigator added, "Did you happen to get a good look at the beast today, commander? Could you inform me what manner of creature it is, sir?"

"There are three of them, mate. Mr. Hunter tells me they're prehistoric wolves and must have been illegally spawned in some outlawed genetic experiment. They're as big as Grizzly bears, but faster. And there's a last creature that's more dangerous than all them together. Mr. Hunter calls it a *Scimitar*."

Inspector Marshall's eyes widened. "Really, governor. And did Mr. Hunter tell you what this Scimitar looks like?"

"He informed me that it looks like an unholy union between a Sabretooth tiger and a man – strange as that may sound. But he's faced one of these creatures before, so he's the expert. He said it's not so large as the wolves but make no mistake; Mr. Hunter told me that it is the most dangerous creature he has ever faced." Blackthorn clapped a hand on Marshall's shoulder. "Take no chances with it, man. This beast is the devil himself. Shoot it straightaway. And pass that along to the men. But be mindful. Do it quietly. I don't want the lads more nervous than they are."

"Understood, commander." Marshall promptly turned to leave before he hesitated. He turned back with, "Just for my own readiness, sir, do you happen to know whether these creatures will be attacking again tonight?"

Blackthorn's countenance darkened.

"Yes, old friend, I believe they will."

* * *

As Hunter reached the library doors, they were open. Curious, he walked silently forward until he heard soft singing and gently pushed against the door, gazing over the room.

Seated on the floor was Milton's youngest daughter, Emily, and Ben was sleeping soundly on the rug with his nose pointed at the crackling embers of the fireplace. Emily was softly rubbing his enormous head as if he were a puppy, and Ben obviously loved the attention. With no expression Hunter entered, walked to a chair, and began removing his gear.

Emily turned her head to gaze at him as he dropped his pack in a chair and sat the rifle against the arm. Hunter chose to leave the gun belt around his waist but lifted the shotgun over his head and also rested it in the chair. Then he turned, walked to the couch, and laid down.

If Emily wanted to speak, it was fine with him. If she didn't, then that was all right, too. Whatever she wanted to do.

Hunter understood her all too well; she felt closer to animals than people and had a love for them. And they sensed her love and returned it. The fact that she could even approach Ben in what had already become a combat situation was testimony to that.

Hunter had always considered such encounters a spiritual thing, a phenomenon that not all the training in the world could produce, and he had no power to grant it any more than he had a right to interrupt it. Without another thought he dismissed whatever questions he'd harbored about Emily's condition. If Ben saw good in her, that was enough for Hunter to scratch her off any 'list of suspects.'

Closing his eyes, Hunter took a deep breath. He slowed his mind so he could begin thinking about what was coming tonight. He knew, by morning, someone would be counting the dead on one side or the other – or both. What happened today had thrown this situation into a higher dimension because now the wolves and the Scimitar knew they were being hunted by something they should consider a powerful enemy.

The world of a predator was hunting, always hunting. It was instinct and senses and experience. But the experience of living only to hunt established a mind that knew nothing else. And once that mind was set, a predator would never be less than a predator. It would rarely run. If it sensed that it was being hunted, it would turn the game around on whatever was hunting it. It would do what it knew best. It would kill.

In Montana, if one listened to campfire talk by trappers, all the stories would eventually come around to the prey that once turned the tables on them and began hunting the trapper. Almost always the trapper would name a Grizzly or a Brown bear. In Manchuria one could hear similar tales, but it would involve tigers. And in South America it was always a jaguar. But the story was always the same, for when an apex predator realizes that something had chosen them for prey, they turn and hunt what is hunting them.

Up to now the wolves had stalked Milton because he was prey. Now they would be stalking Blackthorn and himself because they were the enemy. And both of them had to be killed, as well.

"What his name?"

Emily's quiet voice brought Hunter from his thoughts and he glanced at her. She had barely moved since he entered.

"Ben," he said with inflection.

"How old is he?"

"He's four years old. How old are you?"

"Sixteen."

"What's your name?"

"Emily."

"That's a beautiful name."

"Thank you. What's your name?"

"Hunter."

"Hunter," she repeated. "That's pretty."

Hunter smiled and noticed that she was still humming her song between words. Then she continued, "I read a book about a bear named Ben."

He laughed, "Yeah? What was the book?"

"'The Adventures of Grizzly Adams.' His bear was named Ben, too. It was short for Benjamin Franklin. Is that where you got his name?"

Hunter smiled, "Yeah. That's where I got it."

"Ben is a nice name."

As if he were approaching a wounded animal, Hunter knew not to spook her. He would let her talk, and he'd answer. He was curious about the claw marks on her face, and her limp, but he wouldn't ask. And, somehow, he knew it wasn't important. But what he was watching was important. In the five minutes that had passed since he entered the library, he felt he'd come to know her as solidly as he knew himself.

She looked directly at Hunter, "Does he watch over you? Like … does he protect you when you're asleep?"

With a slight pause Hunter said, "If Ben loves you, he always watches over you to make sure you're safe. Even when you're asleep."

"Will you take him home when you leave?"

Although he didn't scowl, the question revealed so much about Emily that Hunter was moved. Without another word, Hunter knew that she was just like him. Clearly she was highly intelligent and knew the hearts of both man and beast, and she preferred the friendship of beasts. He was much the same when he was her age and longed for those days often enough. When he didn't answer, she added, "If you don't take him home, I think Ben would be happy with me. He likes my singing."

"Yes," Hunter said quietly, "he does."

He rose and walked forward and picked up a stick, tossing it into the fire, half-anticipating her to leave the room. But she merely turned her attention to Ben, petting and singing softly.

Hunter continued to needlessly poke the fire. He felt like she needed a friend, and he was more than willing to be one. And, of a sudden, this entire thing inspired him with a new purpose. Whereas he had approached this as yet another hunt for a dangerous predator, it unexpectantly became personal.

Even knowing that the wolves were now targeting both Blackthorn and himself hadn't provoked this impression. But, then, he was accustomed to being hunted by apex predators. And those who hired him were normally no more than clients. It's not that Hunter made it a point to never become personally involved, he simply didn't care.

"You hurt him last night," said Emily, still bent over Ben, rubbing the wide patch between his ears.

Her words fired a jolt down Hunter's spine, and he quietly set the poker aside and turned in his seat, forearms on his knees. He said, "Yeah, well, he hurt me, too."

Whatever gift she possessed was rare and Hunter knew knew that he didn't possess it himself, didn't understand it, and didn't want it. After she was silent, Hunter asked, "Can you sense him out there?"

"Sometimes."

"You have a gift."

She smiled wanly. "Is it a gift?"

"Yeah," Hunter nodded, "it's a very special gift."

"I scare my family."

"That's because they don't understand," said Hunter. "But they will one day. And if they don't, it doesn't change the fact that you're a very special young lady with an amazing gift."

She said even more quietly, "The monster scares me."

"I know," Hunter said firmly. "He scares me, too. But Ben's here. And Ben will protect you."

She smiled over the bear, "Ben's my friend."

Hunter hesitated but something compelled him to say, "I'm not going to let that creature hurt you, Emily."

Her gaze rose to him. "My father says you're the best there is."

"Your father's a good man," Hunter smiled. "But there's a lot of good trackers. You could say they're all the best."

"He meant you're the best there is at killing monsters." Emily's gaze froze on Hunter's. "Are you the best?"

It was the longest moment of Hunter's life. And he didn't want to answer the question but he felt like he should. It was the least he could do to quiet her fears. He sighed, "Yeah. I'm the best there is."

With a start Emily sharply looked toward the interior of the mansion. She quickly rose to her feet, brushing off her dress. With a glance she said, "The other man is coming. Thank you."

She was out another door leaving Hunter in awe. He knew he could trust what she'd said so he just took a chair and waited. And in two minutes Blackthorn swept through the door. The commander ignored Ben as he took a chair opposite Hunter before the blazing hearth. Then, without preamble, he stated, "I need to know everything you know."

In a dead tone Hunter answered, "I've already told you everything, Blackthorn. What else do you want to know?"

"You said those scientists in Alaska created this serum so they could become immortal. Is that right?"

"That's what they told me."

"Did they succeed?"

Hunter grunted, "Hell if I know. I killed him. You might even say he died young."

With a groan Blackthorn stretched out heavy arms on the chair. "I contacted the commissioner about today's events. I told him this is a military matter now."

"And he told you there would be no military."

Blackthorn didn't bother to hide his surprise as he asked, "How did you know?"

Hunter's laugh was cynical. "Because it's the same thing they told us in Alaska after half my team got wiped out by that Scimitar. We called for help and they told us we were on our own."

"What was their contingency plan if you failed?"

Hunter picked up a stick, tossed it in the fire. "Chaney told me they were going to let it slip through the perimeter and pick up its trail with another team."

"Chaney?"

"He's an FBI agent with close association to the U. S. Marshals. Chaney's got credentials for both, plus a Homeland Security shield. He helped me in that stunt up north and probably saved my life. 'Cause the truth is, they never wanted us to kill the thing in the first place. They just wanted me to find it so they could capture it and keep on going. I'm the one, in the end, who chose to kill it. Against all orders, of course. And they've never forgiven me."

Blackthorn expressed confusion. "Then why would they let you participate in this hunt? You killed the first one. You ruined their whole plan. Wouldn't they be afraid you'd kill this one, too?"

"Sometimes I wonder whether you're really a detective, Blackthorn."

"Why is that?"

"Who gave you my file?"

"The Deputy Assistant-Commissioner."

"How did he get it?"

Blackthorn reclined deeper into the chair. "Perceptive of you to ask. In fact, I asked him the same thing. He told me that it was on his desk when he arrived Monday morning. He didn't know who left it. But there was a note that said you'd dealt with this type of situation before. So the commissioner told me to contact you and, well, you know the rest."

"The chauffer was killed Tuesday night?"

"Early Wednesday morning, yes."

"But my file showed up on your boss's desk a day earlier?"

"Yes. We presumed someone left your file on Monday because of the six previous unexplained deaths in the moor. Pembry wasn't killed until after I'd read it. Redford had already mentioned your name, so I wasn't exactly shocked to see a file on you, as well. In any case, I was convinced you were the only man who might be able to help us, so traveling to America to ask you was the simplest decision I've made in this whole bloody affair."

"Then whoever gave your boss this file on me was off the books. The United States government would never want me participating in another one of these monster hunts. And I don't think your government would, either." Hunter bent his head, then laughed lightly, "I guess Chaney's keeping his hand on this thing. I don't blame him. He knows what's at stake."

Blackthorn was silent, then, "Just what is it about this Scimitar that makes it so bloody hard to kill?"

Hunter felt more morose as he said, "In its original form the Scimitar was the most efficient predator of its age. Maybe of any age. Still, it didn't have the benefit of a conscious mind. So it was limited. But with this merging of animal and man, it gains a measure of human intelligence. And what's even worse than that – human intelligence and human motivations."

"How much human intelligence?"

Hunter shrugged, "I don't know exactly. I know this one seems a lot smarter than the one I faced in Alaska. That one was just an animal. This one has a level of intelligence that

I never saw in the first one. Not even at the end. And that's what's gonna make this one twice as hard to kill."

"Explain."

"Because I managed to trap the first one. Trapped it the same way you'd trap a rabbit or anything else. It was a simple trick, I just used it in a unique way. But I'm not sure this one can be trapped. At least, not as easily."

Blackthorn leaned forward. "You said you only encountered it for a moment. How can you be certain?"

"Well, for one thing, he's not trying to do this alone. He brought hunters to do what he doesn't want to do for himself and to cut down on his exposure. So he's already executing a level of control that is hell and gone from the creature I confronted in Alaska. That one had no control at all. And it was easy to trap at the last of it. But this one is on a different level altogether. Its intelligence gives it an edge the first one didn't have."

"You said this one was vulnerable."

Hunter's eyes narrowed on the flames. "Yeah," he said slowly, "he does seem to be."

"How do you mean? Exactly."

Hunter's face reflected confusion winding in on itself. "All I can say is that it seemed like he wasn't as resistant to injury. I know because I hurt him with the shotgun even though I didn't blow a hole through him. So he can feel pain a lot easier than the first one. But choosing which one you'd rather face is like choosing between facing a lion or a tiger. It doesn't matter. You don't wanna face either one."

Moments passed as a clock ticked on the mantle.

Gruffly Blackthorn stated, "Very well. I'll make quick arrangements for your return to America. Thank you for your best efforts. And thank you for saving my life. Ask any boon you crave and, if honor permits, I will fulfill it. I remain in your debt. But this is obviously a doomed situation and I cannot expect you to continue. The lads and I will sort this out."

"I'm not leaving," stated Hunter.

Blackthorn raised both hands. "Why not? If you stay, you're as good as dead. Along with the rest of us."

"Blackthorn," Hunter turned his gaze, "if these animals escape from this moor, who do you think they're gonna call to hunt them down?" He tapped his chest. "And if I refuse to do it, someone will *force* me to do it. Or I'll be compelled to do it because innocent people will be getting killed left and right all over the planet. So, bottom line, if I'm gonna have to kill this thing here or somewhere else, I'd prefer to do it here."

"Why not somewhere else?"

"Because we have an advantage here that I might not have somewhere else."

"What advantage?"

"I keep telling you, Blackthorn, that it *wants* something in this house. That means we know where it's going to be."

"In this house?"

"Yes!"

"Are you suggested we can use this house like a, uh … a mousetrap?"

"That's exactly what I'm saying."

Blackthorn paused in confusion or concentration. "Are you talking about trapping this so-called leader or the wolves?"

"Just the leader. Don't worry about the wolves."

"Why not?"

"If we kill the Scimitar, the wolves will scatter. We can hunt them from helicopters. But we *have to* kill the Scimitar. He's the leader. They'll do whatever he commands. And as long as he's in charge, the wolves are dangerous off the charts. But when he's gone, they'll be confused. Then we'll hunt 'em from the air and pick 'em off one by one. They won't get far. They won't even leave this moor. It's the only ground they know."

Hunter and Blackthorn surged to their feet as the library doors were thrown open and Barron Milton rushed inside gesticulating wildly. Raising hands as if to frame some alarming situation he gasped, "Mr. Hunter! Commander! Something's in the house! I swear it! I tell you I swear it!"

Hunter snatched up the Marlin and walked forward knowing Blackthorn had done the same with the elephant gun. He calmly faced the young Milton before saying, "Calm down, boy. What did you hear?"

"It's in the attic!" Barron whispered as if the creature could hear his horror through the walls. "I'll take you to the door! I know I heard something!"

Blackthorn asked, "Could it be one of the staff?"

"No! Father keeps his important papers up there! No one is allowed up there! And I know I heard something! I swear to you!"

"All right, all right," said Hunter. "Can you take me to this door without making a sound?"

"*Yes!*"

As Barron moved away, motioning, Hunter turned into Blackthorn with, "I doubt the Scimitar would make a mistake like this. If the boy heard something, maybe the Scimitar wanted him to."

"It's trying to lure us in?" muttered Blackthorn.

"Maybe. You loaded?"

Blackthorn snapped open the rifle to insure two rounds were chambered, snapped it shut, and lifted the radio. "Inspector Marshall," he said evenly.

"*Yes, commander?*"

"Close the men in a tight perimeter on the house. We believe one of the creatures is inside. If it gets outside, shoot it on sight. But don't get in its path. I repeat: *Do not get in its path.*"

"*Understood.*"

It took almost a minute to follow Barron's faltering, hesitating approach to the base of a stairway that led upward to a closed door. Holding the Marlin low, Hunter placed a foot on the extreme left of the first step because the plank was less likely to creak at the edge. He didn't look but knew Blackthorn was duplicating his approach. Keenly attuned to any sound, Hunter rose until he was facing a door.

Hunter softly laid the tips of his fingers against the panel and began to reach for the knob. But at the last moment an impression of something *close* caused him to stop. It was the same impression he'd often felt when hunting a dangerous predator and realized that the beast had circled to come up behind him. Then he realized his shadow would be visible at the base of the door and very slowly raised a flat hand to Blackthorn. He motioned for the detective to back silently down the stairs –

A phantom at the threshold closed fast.

Hunter didn't have time to shout before the panel disintegrated in the thunder of obliterated wooden splinters.

The beast was in the air, descending, as Hunter spun and fired a shot only inches wide of Blackthorn's head but before he could work the lever for a second shot the creature crashed into the fourth-floor landing and leaped to the left, disappearing.

Enraged, Blackthorn shouted something as he gained his feet and swung the rifle, firing twice into the swirling dust. Then he hastily reloaded, cursing, and recklessly descended the stairs. At the last few steps he fiercely leaped to the landing, rifle raised.

"Hold it!" shouted Hunter as he landed beside the commander. "He wants you to chase him!"

Blackthorn raged, "Then let's go after him!" He violently scattered sweat from his face. "Let's kill this thing!"

Grabbing the detective's arm, Hunter jerked him back. "Stay behind me!"

Frowning, Blackthorn obviously didn't like it, but nodded. For a moment Hunter knelt, staring down the corridor. If the Scimitar had already descended to a lower level, there would be sounds of alarm. But there was only silence. It was as if the entire household had flung themselves into hiding.

Six connecting halls ran off the corridor, so the creature could be hiding in any of them. Or none. Hunter would have to search every room, every cubby. Slinging the rifle, he drew the Ruger and thumbed back the hammer. It would be easier to swing and fire the handgun inside the narrow confines.

Blackthorn hissed, "How do you hunt something like this?"

"The same way you hunt a tiger."

"How do you do that?"

"You drive it."

"What does that mean?"

"You've got rifles outside, don't you?"

"Absolutely."

"Then we drive it toward the rifles."

"Yes! Capital!"

Hunter smashed the pistol against the first door. The move made Blackthorn leap. When he recovered, he shouted, "How are we going to sneak up on it if you're crashing on the doors?"

"Stay with me, Blackthorn! We're not trying to sneak up on it! We're trying to drive it!"

"By banging on the doors?"

"Yes!"

"Then to hell with this stalking!" Blackthorn smashed the butt of his rifle against a wall. "*We're coming*!"

CHAPTER EIGHTEEN

Hunter fell flat as the door beside him exploded in splinters and felt the concussion of Blackthorn's rifle. The next moment was a mingling of howls and roars as Blackthorn was smashed into a wall. Not bothering to gain his feet, Hunter rolled and fired past Blackthorn yet again but even as he pulled the trigger, he recognized there was nothing in the opposite door.

The shot blasted out a window.

Hunter's last glimpse of it indicated that it had fled into the adjoining room through a connecting door. Then he sensed Blackthorn at his back; the detective was certainly not one to shrink from a fight.

With a glance Hunter confirmed that the creature had already fled the second room, as well. A quick check affirmed that all the chambers connected by interior doors. That was not a good thing; the passages would allow the beast to easily double back and forth as they went from room to room and that was a game Hunter knew he would eventually lose. There was simply no way to secure so many doors and, sooner or later, Hunter would simply be too slow or fail to make the right move and the beast would hit him and it would be over that fast. Harshly swiping sweat from his face and unconsciously glancing at his palm to insure there was no blood, he glanced back to see Blackthorn's chest bright red between the folds of his coat.

"Blackthorn?" he asked. "Are you all right?"

"I'm fine." Blackthorn shook sweat from his face. "Come on, man! We can't let him get away!"

A series of rapid crashing sounds in the hallway caused them to whirl. As they charged back into the corridor, Hunter barely glimpsed a tawny shape disappearing into the most distant room and got off a shot with the revolver. He didn't know whether he hit it but the last vanishing shade twisted violently as it was gone.

Hunter reached the door in seconds, disregarding whether Blackthorn managed to keep up but at the last second felt a presence close to the wall and frantically leaped away as an attack erupted from the wall itself in a white explosion of dust and wood. Even in the chaos Hunter got a clear look at the beast in the full light of the corridor and saw blood. Then the Scimitar lashed out and struck the pistol aside and, grabbing Hunter by the throat, lifted him from the floor.

The hallway exploded.

The beast yelped and flung Hunter violently into Blackthorn. Hunter was first to reach his feet and barely glimpsed the beast as it vaulted the railing and dropped from sight. Not caring for wounds, Hunter reached the rail and glanced down. He saw the creature leaping from landing to landing and rushed after it. But he hadn't taken two steps before he heard Blackthorn pounding down the stairs in his wake, hatefully reloading the rifle.

"What is it doing!" shouted the detective.

"It's getting away!"

In seconds they passed every landing to reach what Hunter recognized as some kind of basement; a huge wooden door held together with iron bands stood open, framing in the darkness within.

"What the hell!" exclaimed Blackthorn. "It can't escape from a storage! Maybe it's not so smart after all!"

Hunter unlocked the Ruger and quickly removed three spent rounds, reloading three more. He peered cautiously toward each side of the doorway to check for an ambush.

This was a prime place for an attack. It was a blind spot, cloaked in darkness. Hunter could be standing directly beside the Scimitar and would never see the blow that killed him. Finally, after he was satisfied that the door, at least, was clear, Hunter stepped over the threshold.

They cleared what could be visually cleared. Then they began moving aside barrels, furniture, crates in what Blackthorn referred to as the "storage." Finally Hunter slid a container to the side, exposing a square of darkness. Kneeling, he lifted a sweat-soaked hand to feel wind coldly rushing past him into the opening. The passage was drawing the air.

"It's a tunnel," he said. "There's no claw marks coming in but there's some good scratch marks going out. It looks like he didn't change until he was inside."

At the offhand remark Blackthorn stared hard before, "Change?" He paused. "Are you saying this thing can make a conscious decision to change from one form to another? From a human being into … *into this?*"

"Yeah," muttered Hunter, "that's exactly what I'm saying."

* * *

"How could it possibly know about that old tunnel?" asked Milton, brow hard in concentration. He stared aside before muttering, "Perhaps we underestimated this creature, Mr. Hunter. It seems to be far more cunning than we presumed."

Hunter lowered his face, not even glancing at Blackthorn as the detective's radio crackled, "*SP Thirteen to Command. Someone is requesting permission to enter the grounds, commander.*"

Blackthorn lifted the mic. "Who is it, six-two-one?"

"*It's a scientist, commander. He says he's from London and that he's here on a critical matter. He also has an assistant.*"

"Two of you escort them to the house. Be sure they do not wander onto the grounds."

"*Confirm, commander. We're bringing them to the house.*"

Flora, standing beside her father, glared at Blackthorn, at the major, and at Blackthorn again before she exclaimed, "I can't believe that you two have let this monster escape you twice!"

Blackthorn frowned, "He cannot escape us, madam."

A knock.

Blackthorn walked to the foyer and Hunter angled away to appraise whoever had arrived. As the door swung open, he saw a tall, austere man in a black two-piece suit and tie enter. He was followed by a woman bearing a stainless-steel briefcase.

Blackthorn spoke to his men with an authority not to be disregarded. "Return to your posts, mates. And stay sharp. Tonight is likely to be lively."

"Sir!"

They were gone.

The man introduced himself as Dr. Felix Brosnan of the Bristol Genetics Laboratory in London. But after five minutes of conversation the woman had not been recognized and Hunter grew curious. Finally, when dialogue ebbed, Milton asked, "And who is your companion, Dr. Brosnan?"

The woman stepped forward. "Allow me to introduce myself, Major Milton. I am Dr. Eve Cathcart. And with your permission I'd like to show you something."

Milton lifted both hands. "Of course."

Cathcart laid the briefcase on the desk. After running through combinations she opened it and removed an eight-by-ten color photograph that she raised before Milton.

"Have you seen this creature?" she asked.

Consternation hardened Milton's face before he slowly shook his head. "No. I can't say that I've ever seen such a creature."

"I have," stated Hunter.

Cathcart turned. "I presumed."

"Is this where we need to speak in private?"

"I believe so." Dr. Cathcart nodded to Milton. "Would you excuse me, Major?"

"Of course," Milton bent his head. "Any help you can provide will be greatly appreciated." He looked away. "We need all the help we can get."

* * *

Hunter was leaning against the mantle when Cathcart entered the library and shut the doors. As she turned, she was facing Ben, who was already agitated. Recoiling and screaming, she slid along the wall, hand clutching her chest before Hunter said, "Come over here, Ben."

After one last, great sniff the Grizzly ponderously turned and ambled to Hunter, who led him to the rug. "Lay down." Ben had no objections and sprawled out as Hunter turned to the room.

Still breathing wildly, Cathcart gasped, "What the hell is a Grizzly doing in here?!"

"I thought the CIA knew everything."

"I'm not CIA!"

It took Cathcart another moment to wipe sweat from her face, brush back her hair, and approach the fireplace. When she reached Hunter, her face was still flushed. "I'm not the enemy, Hunter."

Hunter smiled with grim amusement. "If you've got something useful to say, doctor, why don't you say it?"

"Are we in a hurry?"

"They'll be here when it's full dark. We don't have much time."

"Don't you want to know who I'm with?"

"I'm more interested in what you have to say."

"Okay." Cathcart straightened her suit, gathering. "I want you to know, Hunter, that I'm very aware of everything that happened in Alaska with Luther and I'm pretty sure I know what's happening here."

"And how would you know all that?"

"Last weekend a Homeland Security agent named Chaney arrived out of nowhere in my office. I believe you know him. Chaney gave me a highly classified file that detailed everything that happened in Alaska."

"And why would my old friend do that?"

"Because Chaney knew I was part of the original Scimitar Project. Just like he somehow knew I was part of *this* mess. Now, listen to me because I want to be perfectly clear; the rest of us at the Corona Institute never knew what happened to Luther after he escaped from the lab. I mean, you know, we heard rumors. But that's about it. Then I read Chaney's file and I saw that it was *much* worse than I was afraid of. I had no idea that so many innocent people had been killed. Then, of course, there was information about your participation. Chaney told me that he was very aware of what was happening here, and that he had known for a while, and that I should call you before this turned into the same fiasco that went down in Alaska." Her lips tightened. "He said you might be able to stop it before it gets completely out of control."

"That was gracious of him."

"He has faith in you."

"I'm flattered."

"I know what's out there, Hunter."

"I'll bet you do."

"I helped clone the Amphicyon."

Hunter bowed his head with a laugh, then looked up. "What is it about you mad scientists that always causes you to lose control over what you create?"

Cathcart stepped up. "I didn't 'lose control' of the Amphicyon! They were stolen from my lab where they were perfectly secure!"

"Not secure enough."

Lifting a hand to her forehead, Cathcart walked to a chair and sat. "After you killed Luther in Alaska – and, yeah, I knew Luther personally – the government shut down the Scimitar Project." She threw out a hand. "Believe me, buster, Chaney saw to that with a vengeance. I'm surprised he didn't take a flame thrower to the place. But Chaney was never told that Luther was only one of six clinicians and physicists on the staff of Dr. Raymond Vang. He never saw files that would have informed him that the Corona Institute had satellite installations in a dozen countries and one of them was here in England. Those were classified beyond his 'need to know.' Or something like that. Do you see where I'm going with this?"

With no expression Hunter simply said, "Yep."

"Luther was just a second-rate scientist who went off-protocol with an untested version of the Scimitar serum. But Vang was the genius who *built* the Scimitar Project. He conceived it, secured the funding, the classification, the whole nine yards. It was his baby from day one. And despite that big investigation and all those congressional shakedowns, Vang continued to pursue the project in his private lab with private funding."

Hunter scowled, "Didn't you eggheads learn anything from what happened with Luther?"

Cathcart's eyes widened. "Of course we did! But Vang isn't a fool, Hunter! Vang knew better than anyone that Luther used an imperfect version of the serum. He said the only reason you were able to hunt Luther down and kill him was because Luther's transformation was never complete!

Luther was nothing more than an animal and that's why he died like an animal. He was stupid. But Vang saw how the serum could be synthesized to achieve what he wanted! He saw how it could be altered to promote its full physical effects while avoiding the rabid lust to kill. Vang believed he could harness the Scimitar's full physical potential without sacrificing his human consciousness."

"How did Vang know his version would work?"

"Because he tested it on three subjects before he used it on himself and they were transformed into Scimitars with a human consciousness."

Hunter's eyes blazed.

"Where are these test subjects now?"

"They're dead! Vang kept them in an airtight quarantine chamber. And after he saw the test serum was successful, he just shut off the air to the chamber. They used up all the oxygen and suffocated. They may be strong but they die from a lack of oxygen like anything else."

"Must have been a strong chamber."

"It was."

"So what are you doing here, doctor?"

"I guess you've already realized that Vang is here."

"We've met each other."

"Did you see how Vang seemed different from Luther?"

"He's more human."

"Exactly!" Cathcart walked forward. "That's what I've come to make sure you know! I'm here to tell you that Luther was just a dark reflection of the real thing! You see, when Luther changed, he lost every shred of emotional and mental control. But Vang refined the serum so that he can make the transition and not lose his human mind, his human competence. He doesn't sacrifice any shred of his intelligence so he's twice as dangerous as Luther!"

"What else do you know about Vang?"

"About Vang?" Cathcart had been on a roll, but now she faltered. "About him personally? Why?"

"I have my reasons."

She strolled for a few steps before turning back. "Okay, well, Vang was obsessed with perfecting the serum. It's all he ever talked about. He wouldn't shut up about how great it'd be to get immunized against every disease known to mankind. How great it would be to live for a thousand years. To get smarter and smarter with each century until he'd be like a god. I couldn't believe I was hearing all this from a sane human being – much less a respected scientist. But he also knew that the version of the serum that Luther used was horribly imperfect on *so many levels*. So Vang worked relentlessly to synthesize a version that promoted the physical elements of the Scimitar – the resistance to bacteria, the immunity to disease, the strength and speed, even the ferocity, but only to a level that it didn't affect the host subject's cerebral locus. In other words, Vang developed a version of the serum that would grant him all the Scimitar's physical superiority without destroying his humanity. And I think he did it. That's the only explanation for why he's here."

Hunter's teeth gleamed as he said, "You've told me all that, Cathcart. That's not what I'm asking."

"Then *what* are you asking!"

"What would Vang be *here*?" Hunter stared. "Why here and not somewhere else? Does this place hold some kind of personal interest for him? Is it family? Does he know Milton? What is it about this place?"

"This place?"

"This moor! This family! This house! All of it! Try and think of why Vang would come *here*."

After casting glances to either side, Cathcart finally said, "It's got to have something to do with his long-term survivability." She raised a finger. "Vang is always thinking long-term. So I think he's come here to secure his future. It's the only thing that explains why he doesn't just disappear."

Hunter laughed out loud. "How could he just disappear? I don't see how he can blend in with the crowd!"

"You quite obviously don't understand."

"I quite obviously don't."

"If Vang used this enhanced version of the serum on himself, then he *already* has the Scimitar's genetic resistance to disease and aging. Even in human form, Vang has all of that. But transforming himself into the Scimitar gives him superhuman strength and speed. And since he's doing that, he must be here to gain more than immortality. That's why he's risking his life."

"How is he risking his life?"

"Because every time Vang transforms into the Scimitar it gets more difficult for him to change back to his human form." Cathcart was carefully separating each word. "Hear me very carefully. At this moment, Vang is using the physical power of the Scimitar to get what he wants. But once he gets it, he's going to change back to human form and live out the rest of his life as a human being with all the immunity powers of the Scimitar. And then he'll be able to blend in. To disappear forever in a crowd. He will, for all practical purposes, be immortal, indestructible, and invulnerable. But he'll look just like everybody else. He'll look human and he'll live for a thousand years like a human being."

Hunter muttered, "Vang's a fool."

"What? Why do you say that?"

"Vang thinks he can control the Scimitar? Think again. This creature is getting stronger every day. It evolves. It adapts. It keeps mutating until it finds a way to overcome. That's all it does. Whatever narrow measure of conscious control Vang has right now over that Scimitar is fading fast. And soon enough there won't be any Vang. There'll just be the Scimitar. The brute, unthinking, murdering mind of the Scimitar." He sighed, pausing. "All right. How does Vang control the wolves?"

Cathcart took a moment. "Uh … I don't know. I mean, the wolves had strict obedience training when we raised them in the lab. They're not stupid, you know. The truth is that they're actually pretty smart. They're as smart as any wolf. But they always had a special relationship with Dr. Vang. It's like they looked at him as some kind of father figure. So I guess he has as much control over them as any owner over his dog. No more, no less. It's a classic relationship between pet and master."

"When did all this happen?"

"The wolves were stolen three months ago. And, to be honest, I didn't know about anything happening here until Chaney showed up in my office."

"When was that?"

"Five days ago. He said the British government had asked Homeland Security for help because the marshals had experience dealing with this kind of strange encounter. Then Chaney traced this whole fiasco back to Vang. And, boy, let me tell you: He! Was! *Pissed*!"

Hunter laughed, "I'll bet."

"He said that I was partially responsible for all this and that if I didn't do something *biblical* to help you he was going crucify me in molasses – or something like that. I can't remember the exact words but I got the point. Then he told me he was going to get you involved and that, if anything bad happened to you, I was going to an MI-6-controlled sanitorium where I'd be locked away for the rest of my natural life. Or jail. Or Hell. I can't remember which one but none of it was good."

"How'd someone like you get my file on a desk at Scotland Yard?"

"Chaney did that. I got the impression that he's done all this cloak and dagger stuff before."

Hunter's eyes never left her face. "How much did you tell Chaney about Vang?"

Her eyes opened wider. "Are you kidding? I told him everything that I'm telling you! I told him Vang isn't making any of the mistakes Luther made and that he has to be stopped! You have to understand! Vang is here for a *very* specific reason that is critical to his long-term survival! I mean, if you thought Luther was the ultimate predator in his half-baked masquerade of a Scimitar you should take a moment to realize that Vang is already ten times what Luther ever dreamed of becoming!"

She grew animated, "Vang is the full-blown ideal of a super predator that literally has no equal in tens of billions of years of evolution. He is truly the first of his kind! A human being – no, a *genius* with the physical strength and speed of a tiger who is completely immune to any disease or bacteria or virus. He can heal up overnight from any injury and – by any 'normal' yard stick – *is* immortal! And if he gets what he came here for he might actually become a god! And he's going to be a *merciless* god with a taste for human flesh!"

Hunter knew all this. Perhaps not in this detail, but he had known. Head bent, he said firmly, "You need to get out of here, doctor. It's about to get bad around here."

"I'm not going anywhere."

"You got a death wish, Cathcart?"

She stepped forward again. "Listen! I'm *not* going to my grave with buckets of blood on my hands! Especially when I know that I could have done something to stop it!" She paused. "And as far as I go, don't make any mistake. I'm not ashamed of the work I've done. We were trying to isolate genomes to cure cancer and a thousand other diseases. But *this* …" She shook her head with evident horror, "*This is evil*!"

Hunter remembered how his battle with Luther forced him to the edge of all he was, and he honestly didn't know if he could go there again. It had been the narrowest of fights, the kind of fight you don't think you can win even once, much less twice. But all that was irrelevant now. He was in this and there was no getting out of it without forfeiting whatever it was that kept him on his feet – his heart, his soul.

"All right," he said "Tell me about what you did to the Amphicyon. They're not the same as their cousins, are they?"

"Is that important?"

"Yes."

Cathcart began pacing. "Well, modern wolves and Amphicyon share eighty percent of their DNA. All we did was substitute segments from gray wolf DNA into what we assumed were missing sections of damaged Amphicyon DNA. We didn't expect it to change them that much, but it did. It made them even more like wolves than they originally were. It basically made them into wolves as big as Grizzlies. And, believe me, we were as shocked as you were."

"I seriously doubt that."

"Do you really think they'll attack tonight?"

"Oh, yeah." Taking a second to swipe grime from his face, Hunter added, "And we need to get ready."

"*Then let's get on with it*!" Blackthorn walked forward from the doors. "Why don't we start setting up some kind of a trap? That'd be a change of pace around here! *Us* trapping *them*!"

"We won't be catching them by surprise," muttered Hunter. "They can hear your heartbeat at a thousand feet. They can read your body heat behind a stone wall. But we can set up a trap, anyway, and hope for the best."

"A trap needs bait. Have something in mind?"

Hunter stared long before he commented. "One of us." He paused. "All of us ... *None of us*."

Blackthorn appeared angry. "I'm not following."

Hunter walked past him.

"We'll need Milton."

CHAPTER NINETEEN

Not surprisingly, Milton understood the dynamics of the plan long before the others. Perhaps it was because the old man had trapped a thousand maneaters as a big game hunter. With bowed head he muttered, "We will use both ourselves and the horses as bait. We will lure the wolves into the stables. Then we'll lock the doors and burn it down with the wolves inside it. If that doesn't kill them, nothing will."

Hunter focused on Blackthorn. "There's only two ways in and out of that stable. Once we close the door, we'll have them in a barrel."

The detective frowned, "And are *we* going to be in this barrel when we set it on fire?"

Hunter turned to Milton. "Is there another way out of that stable besides the two doors?"

"Yes," Milton answered immediately. "In the back of the sixth stall there is a small blacksmith shop. If you remove the vent, a man can escape through the wall."

"So we trap them in the stable and set it on fire," said Hunter, straightening. "I doubt that we'll get all of them. But we might get one or two and that's a start."

"Right," Blackthorn lifted his rifle, "then let's get on with it. I don't much fancy setting this up with them demons watching. I'm already nervous as a whore in church."

* * *

With a curse Hunter finally succeeded in wrenching the ventilation fan from the blacksmith shop; the man-size opening revealed the field outside. With half his body inside the vent he shouted, "Blackthorn! Make sure this spot doesn't get doused with gasoline! If we step out of this hole into a lake of fire, it's not gonna be pretty!"

"I'll see to it myself!" shouted Blackthorn from a distant corner outside the barn. He lifted a five-gallon cannister and began splashing gasoline along the wall. Hunter brought his head into the barn as Milton stated, "In Africa we used to smoke elements of a trap in order to hide the human scent. Will the smell of gasoline not warn them?"

"No," said Hunter, "these wolves were raised in a lab. They're used to all kinds of chemical smells, so the scent of gas won't make them any more alert than they already are."

After a half-hour Blackthorn re-entered the shop wiping sweat from his face. "*That's* a man's work! Give the lads a few minutes and they'll have the whole building soaked with petrol."

"Except for the escape tunnel," Hunter confirmed. "Right?"

"Affirmative."

"Fresh blood is the best bait," stated Milton ominously. He removed a handgun from his belt and led a stallion into the middle of the stable. Then he raised the pistol to the head of the Clydesdale and shot it between the eyes.

It collapsed to the floor. With no expression the major simply tucked the pistol into his belt and re-entered the stall. "These beasts won't pass up the prospect of fresh meat. Not if they're anything like real wolves. And I suspect they are."

Hunter pointed. "Major, turn on all the lights. They're gonna know we're here, anyway. We might as well advertise it. Blackthorn! Do your men know they have to chain the doors *before* they set fire to this place?"

"I believe I've made that clear enough," answered the detective.

"Good. Then have your guys splash gas along the inside of these walls, too." Hunter rotated slowly, staring at the vastness of the stable. "It'll be better if both sides go up like a match. They'll be less prone to break through the walls."

Blackthorn exited and within moments returned with ten men carrying five-gallon cans. They began splashing along the walls, soaking everything they could reach, as Blackthorn nervously commented, "This place is going to go up in a bonfire, Hunter."

"If we're lucky."

Gazing across millions of dollars in high-quality saddle gear hung along the walls and stalls, Hunter commented, "This is going to be a huge loss for you, Major. I'm sorry about that."

Milton waved, "Trinkets, Mr. Hunter. All of it is vanity. And all of it is meaningless … in the end."

* * *

Hunter had never tracked in this part of the world but felt the sun would vanish in a blink and tonight's moon would rise as a pale sphere. But tomorrow night everything would change because, if weather cooperated, because it would be a Hunter's Moon, as some called it. The moon would be as bright as a blood-red sun.

The scientific explanation for it was simple. It was caused by a lunar eclipse – a time when the earth passed between the moon and the sun to leave the moon illuminated only by indirect light through space dust which often reflected red after filtering through the atmosphere of the earth. It was rare, and Hunter had always found it beautiful.

"This moor feels cursed," muttered Blackthorn from his position beside the east doors.

The detective had chosen a post where he could see the rear half of the estate. Milton was positioned at the west doors and Hunter had been walking between them for the past hour weaving half-inch bridles he'd pulled from the wall. He had tirelessly braided the straps into three-strand ropes and now he was attaching a long chain to the contraption.

With a skeptical aspect Blackthorn asked, "Do you really think that net is going to hold any of those beasts while this place burns down?"

"I just want to slow them down."

Blackthorn released a heavy breath. "You really believe dropping this barn on their heads will kill them?"

"Every little bit helps."

"How long before they come in?"

"When they're sure."

"Of what?"

Hunter shrugged, "Well, you've changed your men's routine, and they'll notice that, so they'll make sure they locate every one of them before they come in. But after they've accounted for everybody, they'll come."

"The lads are hiding."

"And they'll find every one of them. They can see in the dark better than a bat. And they're gonna count heads."

"Are you suggesting they can *count*?"

"They remember *scents*, and they know the scent of everyone that's been here. Once they're fairly certain that there's nothing new to the situation, they'll circle a few times to make sure no one new is hiding in the trees. Then they'll approach. I told you before. They're not stupid and they don't like surprises. In some ways they're smarter than human beings. But, then, that's not saying a whole lot."

Moments passed as Hunter continued to work and Blackthorn's head steadily turned left to right. Finally, the detective asked, "How long do you plan to stay in here after we light the fire?"

"Just long enough to get one of them tangled in this net."

"If you wait one second too long, this will be your funeral pyre."

Hunter glanced along the gasoline-soaked walls. "Yeah, it's gonna get real hot real fast. But we've only got one shot at this. We have to make the most of it." He climbed a ladder that led to a ledge filled with barley and hauled up the net. A rope connected the webbing to pipes set in cement.

"Won't it be suspicious of that contraption?" asked Blackthorn.

Hunter dropped to the floor. "There's a million ropes in here. They're accustomed to ropes just like they're accustomed to gasoline. None of that will spook them."

For the longest time they simply stood in the doorway staring at the night. Then, as if he had been meaning to ask it for a long time, Blackthorn said, "Was it this close a thing in Alaska?"

"No," Hunter admitted, "this is much, much worse."

"How is that even possible?"

Hunter laughed harshly, "Because there was only one of them in Alaska, buddy. And we've got four of them here. That's what makes it more dangerous. Plus that, this Scimitar is a lot smarter than the one I faced in Alaska and, believe me, that one was smart enough to almost put me in the dirt. So, on balance, I'd say this is a helluva lot worse."

From Blackthorn's frown he didn't appear to like the answer. He gazed along the walls so heavy with the stench of gasoline before he commented wistfully, "I always thought 'going out in a blaze of glory' was just an expression. I was wrong."

"Hunter!" shouted the major.

In seconds they reached the front end of the stable where Milton was pointing.

"Look!"

Hunter saw a large Mastiff backing away from the iron fence as if it sensed a tiger. Although the constable was pulling at its leash, the two-hundred-pound mastiff would go no closer.

"Yeah," Hunter said quietly, "they're here." He turned his head. "Blackthorn! Remind Marshal to wait until they're inside before they lock the doors!"

Blackthorn backed away from the doors, speaking into his radio. Hunter, with the major beside him, also backed away from the entrance to leave it empty and inviting. Then, as they reached the blacksmith stall, a monstrous shape leaped into the front gates.

It was the smallest of the three Amphicyon but it loomed large enough in the open doors of the stable to block out the night. Then it lowered its head, glaring balefully at Milton.

Hunter whispered to Milton, *"Get out …"*

Blackthorn grabbed Milton's arm, pulling him into the blacksmith stall as the beast slowly advanced searching above its head and to each side as Hunter cautiously backed toward the ladder that he knew was somewhere to his right. He didn't wonder whether he could step up to it. He knew that if he *didn't* step up to it, he was dead because that thing could bridge this gap with a single quick leap. Then Hunter felt the wall at his back and, without removing his eyes from the beast, reached up with his left hand to subtly grab the ladder. Now he'd only have to swing around, take two quick steps, and he'd be in the loft.

Doors slammed behind the beast and it leaped into the air whirling. Then doors to Hunter's right were slammed shut.

Hunter heard the flames before he saw them and the entire structure went up like an inferno. And in the same split-second Hunter spun, hit the ladder, and vaulted into the loft. He didn't look back to see how the beast had reacted as he grabbed the net. He simply whirled and threw; the net enveloped the beast as it descended toward the loft and it attempted to lash out before it crashed into the wall, entangled in the straps.

A colossal crash at the far end of the stable sent shards flying the length of the walk and Hunter knew the Alpha had witnessed the trap as it had closed. Hunter also knew the great beast was analyzing the situation with preternatural instincts and speed.

With two leaps Hunter cleared the last wall to land in the blacksmith stall. Then he twisted through the ventilation duck to see Blackthorn crouching ten feet away, a forearm across his face.

The detective screamed, "*Get out of there, you fool!*"

Hunter fell outside the wall and leaped up. He was instantly running as the atmosphere behind him blazed too hot to endure. When they had enough distance on the inferno Hunter turned to see the gigantic black shape of the Alpha running from the front of the barn. Shots were fired and it howled once before it disappeared. Seconds later there were panicked shouts of men, then cries of agony and horror and, finally, silence but for the roaring of the crucible that was fast reducing the stable to ashes. And then in a slow-motion death, the stable collapsed into a volcanic mound.

Blackthorn raised a fist. "We got him!"

Hunter didn't bother to search for the Alpha or the men that had been killed. There would be time enough to assess the damage after they dug this creature's charred carcass from–

An eruption tore from the middle of the burning wreckage and Hunter watched as a flaming black shape reached the apex of a leap and began to descend. Hunter knew what it was, had almost anticipated it, just as he knew that it would be twice as dangerous now.

"Run!" shouted Hunter as he grabbed Blackthorn and hauled the detective toward a tree; the trunk was thirty feet away and Hunter reached it in two seconds. "Climb!"

Blackthorn hurled his rifle over his shoulder and leaped up to grab a limb, climbing fast. He was only two feet behind Hunter, who was also climbing. Then the entire tree shook with an impact that almost knocked Hunter from his hold. With a frantic glance Hunter saw the creature had backed off a step, shaking insanely as if it could extinguish the flames by sheer will. Then, apparently realizing that it couldn't knock them from the tree, the creature stared up, face fully aflame, red eyes blazing.

It leaped and sank claws into the trunk.

"*It can climb!*" roared Blackthorn.

The beast blasted a limb from the trunk and leaped higher in the same split-second. It was already close enough for Hunter to recoil from the heat and as it leaped again Hunter jumped and didn't have to confirm whether Blackthorn followed.

Hunter hit the ground hard and rolled, trying to swing his rifle around for a shot but Blackthorn had also leaped and reoriented even faster. The detective fired two shots into the beast; the creature twisted, howling, before it fell, smashing into the ground in flaming flesh. Then it twisted again, regaining its feet, and stalked toward Hunter as if it knew who was truly responsible for its pain.

The only reason Hunter didn't immediately fire was because he feared anything but a shot directly into its forehead would be deflected. But at six feet Hunter had no choice. The bullet hit it squarely between the eyes and it bent. But it was an even more horrifying image as it raised its charred face. It took another step as Hunter fired again to hit it between the eyes and, as if struck by lightning, it dropped to the ground.

In a burning mass, it lay. Sheets of skin lifted, rising, still flaming to float like fiery kites before slowly settling in spirals of orange thread. Then a gruesome crackling erupted as muscles peeled away revealing white bone that blackened as Hunter watched.

Uniformed shapes ran forward – a dozen constables with rifles – and together they unleashed a furious fuselage into the fallen form. Firing and re-loading, they poured bullets into it at a minigun rate until, as if by some unspoken command, they stopped.

Hunter stoically stared as the beast was consumed. He felt no relief because his mind had already accepted the fact that this had been the weakest of the three and it had almost killed them together.

The ubiquitous Marshal appeared at Blackthorn's side and then Milton eased up beside Hunter and silently watched as the last flames curled into the night. In the end there was only a smoking black carcass motionless on smoking black tarn. Then a slight movement on the third floor of the mansion caught Hunter's attention and he turned his face to see a silhouette in a window. The silhouette turned away, dropping the curtain.

Sweeping a hand over his face, Blackthorn gasped, "By god, that was a close one! And that was the runt of them! We'll need a howitzer for the other two!"

Hunter lifted his eyes. "Choppers."

"What?"

"Choppers." Hunter pointed to the night sky. "It's probably your boss. And he's got help."

The sound of rotors descended and Hunter didn't even bother to look because he knew who it was. This thing had been a secret in life and it would remain a secret.

Three gigantic Sea King helicopters with no evident markings settled. One put down inside the fence and, as the door opened, Blackthorn asked with a bitter edge, "Who recovered the creature's body in Alaska?"

"These guys," said Hunter. "Different uniforms. Same job."

Five men boldly approached. Four were wearing military battle dress uniforms but the foremost was tall, even elegant, and arrayed in an obviously expensive civilian suit. He knew Blackthorn because he asked, "Are you injured, Winston?"

"Commissioner," responded Blackthorn, glancing at the soldiers who seemed to appear from every behind every wall. Blackthorn focused again on the soldiers. "Who are these men, sir?"

"I'm afraid they've been dispatched to secure this specimen, Commander."

"By whose authority, sir?"

"By royal authority."

Blackthorn stiffened. "Commissioner! We have six dead civilians and five dead police officers! And this creature is the only evidence we have of who might have committed this crime!"

"It has to be this way, Winston. I can't expatiate on it." The newcomer focused singly on Hunter. "Mr. Hunter, I am Commissioner Nigel Rafferty with London Metropolitan Police. We appreciate your participation in this most highly sensitive matter. Are you willing to finish your mission? England is prepared to make it worth your time."

Hunter thought of the consequences that would surely befall Blackthorn if he *didn't* finish it.

"Sure," he said.

"You do understand that I'm referring to all of the remaining creatures?"

"Yeah," Hunter allowed. "I understand completely."

"Then you should also understand that a non-disclosure agreement will be ready for your signature when this assignment is complete."

Hunter almost laughed. "Of course."

"You're familiar with the procedure?"

"Quite familiar."

"Do you know what it means?"

"Yes."

With ramrod bearing Rafferty turned again to Blackthorn. "I assume you've already concluded that we've been outranked on this matter, Winston." He shook his head.

"Believe me, old man, I don't like it any more than you. But we all have our orders."

Soldiers began to lock wide canvas straps and heavy chains around the creature's shoulders and hips. Finally a soldier shouted, "We're ready, commissioner!"

"Get that bloody thing back to the base!"

The helicopter roared and ascended, slowly taking up slack. In five seconds the lines tightened and the creature was lifted from the ground as if it were weightless. For a moment Hunter thought liquid fire was pouring from the corpse, then realized it was melted flesh falling in a slow, steady stream.

With an air of finality Rafferty stated, "I doubt that we shall meet again, Mr. Hunter, and so I wish you success. Commander Blackthorn, it's my privilege to inform you that your promotion to Deputy Assistant Commissioner in Charge of Special Operations has been approved. Congratulations, Winston. We'll formalize it after you've tidied this up. Very well?"

Blackthorn was grim. "Very well, commissioner."

"Good man." Rafferty walked toward the gate surrounded by a dozen black-clad soldiers and was lost in the crowd. Blackthorn sighed, "A dishonorable thing to accept a promotion in exchange for silence."

Hunter tilted his head back, feeling exhausted now that his last stores of adrenaline were exhausted. "Let me give you some advice, Blackthorn."

"What?"

"When this is finished, just take the promotion and forget it." Hunter gazed over Blackthorn's bitter expression. "I wasn't here. You weren't here. And none of this ever happened."

CHAPTER TWENTY

Hunter didn't expect a victory party when they got back to the mansion and was glad his powers of anticipation did not disappoint. Leaning against the wall, he listened to the hushed silence in the trophy room. The entire family was present and had become pale and motionless as Major Milton explained the night's events.

Still sweating, Hunter drew a forearm across his eyes. Then he ran a hand through his hair, smearing it back with the gritty feel of charcoal and soot. He tried to ignore the wrenching pain in his shoulder that he'd gained throwing himself up the ladder. He tried to ignore the bruised leg gained from his fall. He was alive. It was enough. And whether he was in shape for this or not didn't make any difference. He was in this now. Up to his neck.

Robert Milton, the eldest son, angrily rose from his chair and approached Hunter. "Are you certain these creatures were set free to hunt down and kill our father, Mr. Hunter?"

Hunter's stare was dead. "No," he answered. "They could be here to kill every one of you. The only thing I know for sure is that they didn't originally come here to kill me or Blackthorn. But we've managed to volunteer ourselves for the list."

Hunter's attention was abruptly arrested by a rising conversation between Blackthorn and Flora, the oldest daughter. From the tone, Hunter knew Flora was fast approaching an anger she didn't care to modulate.

"Who were those men!" Flora demanded. "They took that monster's body like it belonged to them! And that body was *evidence* that someone is trying to kill everybody in this family!"

Blackthorn appeared unaffected. "They were soldiers, madam. They came here to secure property that belongs to the crown because this matter no longer lies within the jurisdiction of London Metropolitan Police." He walked to pour himself a scotch before adding, "Special Branch has taken responsibility for the situation."

Flora stepped into the detective. "That's illegal!"

"That's irrelevant. And, what's more, Ms. Milton, if you ever speak of this matter you will be immediately and irrevocably interred in a state-controlled sanitorium. You will never know freedom again."

Flora took three imperious steps to stand before Hunter. "Mr. Hunter! You must convince my father to leave this house! He respects you! Surely you can talk sense into him."

Milton said gruffly, "No, Flora. When death comes for you in your own home, there's no place to run. You have retreated as far as you can retreat. So when your own camp is overrun, you fight. It's all you have left."

"Your father is right," muttered Hunter. "He has to make a stand here. Live or die."

Barron Milton nervously asked, "But what about the rest of us, Mr. Hunter? Commander Blackthorn? I mean, I know that you're supposed to protect the major but what are your orders concerning the rest of us?"

"I believe Mr. Hunter's deductions are correct," answered Blackthorn. "If these creatures are hunting one of you instead of your father, they'll follow you. And they'll find you."

Bronte walked forward. "I can't speak for the others. But I, for one, am staying."

Hunter focused on Bronte; it seemed strange that she should volunteer to stay beside her father so readily.

"Then I'm staying, as well," stated Flora. "I will not leave as long as the major remains in this frightful situation."

Eve Cathcart turned into her assistant, firmly placing a hand on his shoulder. "I need you to return to the office, Peter. And be mindful that you do not speak to anyone."

Dr. Peter Brosnan hesitantly asked, "But what about you, doctor?"

"I'm staying."

He hesitated. "But you'll be *killed.*"

"We're under the protection of Scotland Yard's best man, Peter, and that's more than anyone can ask. But I need you to go back to the office and do something for me." She reached into her briefcase, scribbled, and tore off a sheet that she stuffed into his coat. "This is the password to my computer. Copy everything personal and every work-related file and hide the flash drive in one of the gaming machines at your father's casino. Don't keep it on you. Don't keep it at home. Don't keep it in your box. Hide it in one of your father's games and tell no one. Do you understand?"

Brosnan nodded.

"Good." Eve ushered him toward Blackthorn. "Does my colleague have your permission to leave, commander? You heard what I said. And you should carefully consider your words because, when this is over, you might very well find my files to be of great use."

Blackthorn asked, "Insurance?"

"If that's what it takes to guarantee our lives, yes."

It was as if Blackthorn were weighing a dozen equally unwanted courses of action and Hunter couldn't guess what his answer would be until he said, "What you ask is no simple matter. And what you are asking your man to do is exceedingly dangerous."

Eve said nothing until Blackthorn stated, "Very well. Your man can return to London. But I insist on sending a plain clothes detective with him for his own safety. Then we'll stable him until this situation is resolved. If he is agreeable to that, I have no objections."

"Of course he's agreeable," said Eve.

Blackthorn raised his radio. "Inspector Marshal, report to the house."

"Right away, sir."

Blackthorn continued, "Inspector Marshal is my best man. He is also, as it happens, the only plain clothes officer I have on premises. He will accompany your man to the lab where he may secure your files. Then the inspector will fortify him in a secure hotel where he'll be guarded by uniformed constables until this situation is resolved." He stared over Brosnan. "You have the right to refuse police protection, doctor, but I strongly advise you to accept it."

Not surprising to Hunter, Dr. Brosnan seemed more shaken than Cathcart even though he had remained in the house. Placing a hand on his chest, Brosnan asked, "Am I in danger?"

Blackthorn sternness softened. "It's best to be cautious, lad."

With no fanfare Inspector Marshal materialized in the doorway of the trophy room. "Yes, commander!"

Blackthorn turned and, after concise instructions, Marshal closely escorted Dr. Brosnan out the doors. Inside a minute Hunter heard one of the Jaguars moving toward the gate before the sound faded into the night. As silence again dominated the room it seemed as if the same cloud of distraction enveloped them.

Hunter raised his face, staring at the ceiling. He felt that whoever he'd glimpsed standing in the window was critically important. He tried to recall details of the shape but it could have been any of them. He stood to walk from the room when Cathcart grabbed his arm.

"Where are you going?" she asked.

"Upstairs."

"Why?"

"To look around."

"I'm going with you."

Hunter didn't care to argue. If she wanted to come, so be it. He doubted that they'd have another encounter tonight, anyway. It was obvious that the beast had brought three wolves for a reason. For a plan. And now that plan was moot. He had to recover from his wounds and rethink his next move.

Suddenly a prolonged crash thundered in the room and Hunter leaped from the stairs to the front doors, ripping one open. He charged onto the porch, staring in the way of the front gate, and saw an orange glow burning at the edge of the moor. Already men were running toward the chaos. Either the wolves or the Scimitar had attacked Marshal's car.

Cathcart shouted, "What is it!?"

"They attacked the car," said Hunter as he swept past her to snatch up the Marlin. "Stay here with Ben. He won't let anything hurt you." He yelled in the direction of the library. "Ben!"

Ben charged through the open door swinging his gigantic head side to side, sizing up the crowd, the room, the trophies. He didn't seem confused or excited and Hunter was certain the family would be temporarily safe with Ben guarding both entrances, front and rear. He walked forward and laid a hand on the bear's head.

"*Stay!*"

Hunter hit the front door and launched himself into a run with the Marlin tight in his fist. He passed half the constables as he closed on a fire which was burning at the point where the driveway merged with the hardtop. When he arrived at the site, he saw Blackthorn crouching and holding a body tightly in his arms and Hunter knew it was Inspector Marshal. There was also enough visible blood in the light of the flames for Hunter to know he was dead. On the far side of the Jaguar, constables were struggling to extract another body.

Hunter had survived far too many disasters to lose a split-second to grief. He knew time was critical, so he ran past the wreck to the edge of the road and knelt. He confirmed fresh tracks of the Alpha and the Scimitar. He also confirmed their direction; the wolves were moving away from the crash site. But Hunter lost the direction of the Scimitar almost immediately.

He was tempted to go after it. To at least determine its direction. But to track the Scimitar at night was suicide.

He walked to the car.

Marshal lay in a widening pool of blood. Hunter knelt and gently moved the shredded remnants of his coat to study the wound. Then he raised his face to Blackthorn. "The Scimitar did this."

Blackthorn stared down like an angry captain from the crow's nest of a ship. "You're certain?"

"Yeah."

Rising, Hunter walked to the body of Dr. Brosnan. He knelt, studying his wounds. As he rose, one of the guards gasped, "This is balls up, mate! We're doomed! We're not going home!"

Hunter turned to gaze into a constable's eyes and the pale young man whispered, "We're going to die, aren't we?"

"No," Hunter said. "You'll live if you stay together. You have enough guns to drive it back. But any man that goes out alone is dead."

Hunter swiftly rounded the car to where Blackthorn still knelt with Marshal's body. He said, "The wolves stopped the car, but Vang killed them both."

Blackthorn growled, "Where is the Scimitar now?"

"He's gone."

"Did he retreat into the moor?"

Hunter squinted and, after a moment, turned his face toward the manor. "We need to get back," he said. "Something's not right."

* * *

Standing forlorn and alone in the vast trophy room of the mansion, Eve Cathcart wrapped her arms about her shoulders. She didn't know when Hunter would return and felt distinctly unwelcome. Without making a show of it she subtly moved to a place beside Ben; she felt safer with the bear than she did with anyone in the room.

For a time she simply stared into the fire wondering if she was making the right decision and attempted to estimate her chances of survival before she ceased trying. She had no idea whether she could survive this but there was something tightening around her that felt deathly cold.

As if from nowhere, Emily appeared beside Cathcart and silently sat on the floor beside Ben. She didn't hesitate as she lifted a hand to his mane and Ben gently turned his face, gazing steadily over her as Emily began singing softly. It was a surreal, eerie moment, and Cathcart was so captivated that she almost forget her fears.

She wondered at the strangeness of this little girl that had no fear of a gigantic Grizzly that could be a thousand times more dangerous than any wolf that ever lived. Glancing over the room, Cathcart saw that no one else seemed to take notice. It was as if they had witnessed Emily's fearless approach to wildlife many times before, perhaps even expected it.

A deep growl horrified Cathcart and she leaped to her feet, spinning with an arm fully extended as if to push it away.

The Scimitar stood in the rear entrance of the trophy room.

It was monstrous with huge swells of hulking muscle beneath its white coat of fur. Its crimson eyes glowed and separated jaws revealed jagged fangs. Its gorilla chest seemed hard as iron and its arms hung almost to its knees. With its stare locked on Augustus Milton, it walked forward.

Ben roared and surged up and collided with the Scimitar before the gigantic trophies of the dead. Instantly Ben twisted, taking the battle to the floor in a crushing embrace, paws flashing in repeated blows and then the Scimitar grabbed the gigantic bear and flung it into a corner.

As the Scimitar stalked forward again, a man standing near Cathcart raised a rifle and fired two shots before the Scimitar was upon him. It struck once and with a short cry the man fell back, his rifle clattering across the floor.

Milton raised a rifle and fired as Ben landed solidly on the Scimitar's back, taking the battle to the floor once more. The Grizzly's fangs sank into Vang's neck, rending ferociously with a rage Cathcart had never witnessed in another living thing, and Vang shrieked, rising up.

* * *

Gunshots erupted inside the mansion and Hunter was instantly running. He flew past every constable as he closed on the gates with long, leaping strides. When he cleared the open portal, Hunter cut violently to the right as roars and screams collided in the night.

* * *

Twisting violently, Vang grabbed Ben's foreleg and, with a prehistoric strength that seemed impossible, hurled the Grizzly far into the long chamber where Ben rolled and crashed.

As the Scimitar turned back again it seemed to be struggling for breath and Eve saw that it was bleeding badly from a deep and ragged neck wound. Then Milton fired both barrels from the elephant rifle that hit it point blank in the face and it howled.

With a roar Ben charged again, sweeping shattered furniture from his path like leaves and Vang leaped cleanly beyond Milton's desk to crash through the window and into the night.

* * *

Hunter was almost at the mansion when the Scimitar erupted through the front window of the structure trailed by spiraling white shards. Hunter quick-fired from the hip and knew his shot was true because the beast roared and twisted in the air, grasping its chest. Then it crashed awkwardly across the cobblestones and was up again.

It bounded toward the nearest part of the maze as Hunter fired again but there was no cry and he knew he'd missed. Then Ben crashed through the broken window and blasted a path into the maze in pursuit. There was no stopping the Grizzly now and Hunter didn't try. He reached the mansion and rushed into a storm of screams.

Poised in the door, Hunter saw Richard Milton sprawled motionless on the floor. His chest was a deep cavern of blood and his heart lay beside him on the rug. Then he saw Augustus Milton as he collapsed into his chair, simultaneously dropping a smoking rifle. The rest of the children were lying across the rugs or the hardwood floor and a quick glance assured Hunter that Cathcart was unharmed. There was no time for anything else.

Hunter was out the door in pursuit of Ben. He could hear the bear in the distance, roaring in rage. It took him a full minute to find Ben viciously slamming front paws against the fence that would not yield even to his great strength.

The Scimitar had leaped the barrier and was gone.

"Ben!" Hunter shouted and the bear whirled with gaping jaws. But at the sight of Hunter he immediately ceased snarling and descended. He did cast a resentful look at the moor, then rose up on his hind legs to wrap front legs around Hunter's shoulders. The Grizzly pulled Hunter close in a hug, as if to confirm that he was unharmed, before dropping again.

"It's okay," Hunter said quietly. "Come on."

The mansion hummed like a hive of angry wasps as Hunter approached the front doors. With Ben beside him, he stoically moved inside and saw Blackthorn kneeling over the body of Major Augustus Milton's eldest son. The investigator tiredly turned his face as Hunter stopped and stared. He shook his head once. Then the commander focused on a young constable that had entered behind Hunter and said with calm deliberation, "Assemble the men in front of the porch."

From a chair against the front wall, Flora, bloodied and pale, shouted, "*What are you doing*! These animals are going to kill every one of us! I thought you were here to protect us!"

She rose and rushed to Hunter and slapped him – hard – in the face. Her rage was palpable as she screamed, "We trusted you!" She viciously pointed to Richard Milton's body. "He was my brother and *he* trusted you! And now he's dead!"

Hunter stared at nothing. His rising rage was something he could not contain and knew it. With sunrise the final hunt would begin. This had gone on long enough and he was so deep in blood that there was no turning back. And if he were to be the next victim of this thing, then he would be its last. He would make sure of that.

Blackthorn moved past him as the constables congregated in front of the porch. Knowing there was nothing else he could do in the room, Hunter followed him outside. On the porch Blackthorn fixed Hunter with a stare. "Is it safe for them to make a run for a village?"

"Yeah," said Hunter "Vang is gone for a while."

"How do you know that?"

"He's wounded pretty bad. But don't waste time. If they're gonna leave, they need to do it now."

Blackthorn stood over them as he stated, "Three of you will remove the body of Major Milton's eldest son. He is in the trophy room. You will place the bodies of Inspector Marshal, the doctor, and the major's son into vehicles with no more than one victim per vehicle. The rest of you will collect every member of the major's house staff. The staff will ride with you. Divide them up with no less than four officers per vehicle. Each officer is to remain fully armed with weapons ready since we do not know if you'll be able to pass through the moor unmolested. Now get cracking."

A constable asked, "The family, commander?"

"They're staying."

"Where are we to go, sir?"

"You'll report to the local magistrate," answered Blackthorn, all business. "Then you will return to London. Do not come back here. I'm formally relieving you of this detail."

"Should we let the home office know what happened here tonight, commander?"

Blackthorn's face was bitter. "They already know, lad. Now go inside and help your mates. We can't leave anyone behind." He cut a gesture to the entrance. "Crack it up."

The youth hurried into the house. In a moment three constables descended the porch carrying the body of Richard Milton and respectfully placed him in a car. Inspector Marshal and Doctor Brosnan were placed in still more vehicles and within two minutes the staff piled into other cars with rifles protruding from every window. Then, without formality, they sped from the mansion and were out the gate. In another thirty seconds they were swallowed by the gloom of the moor, red tail lights disappearing into depthless black.

Staring into the darkness, Blackthorn was a monument to concentration. Hunter knew they were both listening for gunshots, but there was nothing. Then, after a time, Blackthorn walked into the house, Hunter remaining close.

What Hunter saw was a portrait in grief with each surviving child of Augustus Milton holding or consoling another in turns. Bronte had settled on the floor near her father's chair, holding his hand, and Milton was the very image of sorrow. His gaze was vacant, like a dying man, and a single arm stretched across the desk.

Barron asked weakly, "Are we leaving, too?"

"No," stated Blackthorn with open compassion. "As Mr. Hunter told you, lad, if you leave, it will follow. You cannot escape it. The only choice you have is to kill it. Or it will most certainly kill you."

"Are you and Mr. Hunter leaving?"

"No, son, we're not leaving."

Barron glanced from one to the other before he continued, "But if the two of you are going to stay, why did you send away your men?"

For the first time, Hunter saw something like despondence in Blackthorn's remorseless face. "Because they cannot protect you," he said. "And I won't sacrifice their lives in a fight they cannot win. But Mr. Hunter and I are in charge of this detail, and we'll see it through."

Hunter knelt beside Ben. The Grizzly had very obviously engaged the Scimitar in a ferocious fight and was wounded. Soon Blackthorn stood over them and asked gravely, "How's my mate?"

Hunter glanced up. "Ah, he's got some cuts, but he'll be all right." He stood, still resting a hand on Ben's head. "It's no worse than he'd get tangling with a bunch of wolves."

"Does he need anything?"

"No," Hunter shook his head. "His paws are okay. His mouth is okay. The rest are just battle scars."

Blackthorn addressed Flora, "What happened, Ms. Milton?"

All of them pointed toward the kitchen and responded in an excited cacophony, "It came from the kitchen! It killed Richard and then the bear attacked it! Then the major shot it! He shot it twice! No! He shot it four times! It jumped through the window!"

Hunter was two steps ahead of Blackthorn, both of them holding rifles low as they crept along the gloomy passage to the kitchen. The back door of the mansion stood open and Blackthorn walked forward to slam it. With restrained rage he rasped, "This door isn't broken and it was locked! Someone opened this thing for it!"

Hunter's face was blank.

Blackthorn loudly slammed down the rifle on the kitchen's island. He glanced from side to side, shaking his head, before he asked, "Why would any of them help this beast?"

Hunter set the stock of the rifle on his hip. "I don't know, man. But if you don't find out who it is, our chances of getting any of these people out of here alive are less than zero."

"We can't make any formal accusations. There are no clues. Nothing. It could be any of them."

"So we treat all of them as if they're innocent?'"

"No!" Blackthorn angrily raised his face. "We treat all of them as if they're guilty! They'll have to *prove* their innocence!"

"I thought it was innocent until proven guilty."

"Not when you're trapped in a house with a homicidal monster! In this situation everyone is guilty until proven otherwise! We can trust no one! And you can go nowhere in this house without me." He leaned on a single arm, staring to the side. "So what's the plan?"

Hunter hesitated. "In the morning I'll pick up the trail at the road and track 'em. And I'm going by myself."

"That is unwise."

"I'll be moving fast. You can't keep up."

"You can't kill all three, mate."

Walking up, Hunter continued, "Right now there's two wolves and a Scimitar squaring off against you and me and Ben. And the three of us don't stand a chance against the three of them in a standup fight and you know it. I'm gonna have to improve the odds."

"How are you going to do that?"

"By killing at least one of them."

Blackthorn's frown seemed a frozen fixture before he muttered, "I won't try to stop you from doing what I brought you here to do. But won't they attack in the morning? Shouldn't we be ready for a fight? I might need you here."

"No. The Scimitar won't expose himself to rifle fire in the open field during the daylight. Not even a tiger would do that. He'll wait until dark. Then he'll sneak in here and hit us with some kind of blitzkrieg attack – him and the wolves, all at the same time." Hunter frowned, lowering his chin. "I hate to say it but we won't win that one. Not without room to maneuver and retreat. And we don't have that."

Blackthorn slammed both hands on the marble island. "Why did that blasted thing choose to attack us inside the house tonight? Why tonight? Was this its plan all along?"

"I'm not sure it still has a plan."

The detective's eyes flared. "The scientist! The woman! It attacked the house hours after she arrived! Perhaps she opened the door!"

Hunter blinked. "Are you serious?"

"Of course I'm serious! Why wouldn't she help it? She helped create the thing!"

"Maybe the door wasn't even locked," Hunter said more calmly. "There was a lot of staff in here, man. Someone could have inadvertently left the door unlocked. And we did kill one of his wolves, Blackthorn. He's not gonna take that lying down. He didn't bring three wolves by accident. He brought three for a reason. And now that reason is probably floating face down in the creek and it's enraged."

"I don't accept that," the detective muttered. "That beast wouldn't risk a carefully laid plan for something as petty as rage. You said yourself that it was patient. You even said it was smart."

"Yeah, well, I think the 'patient' part just got overruled by something more primitive."

Blackthorn's eyes narrowed like gunsights. "That's the second time you've said something like that. What do you mean?"

A voice emerged from the entry.

"What Mr. Hunter is trying to say, inspector, is that Vang is evolving." Eve Cathcart was poised in the archway. "Pardon me, gentlemen," she added, "but I was getting worried. And there are four of us, Mr. Hunter. Not three. I think you know you can trust me."

Blackthorn asked, "How long have you been standing there, doctor?"

"Long enough to know you're both scared." Her smile was tight. "And so am I."

Blackthorn's face was glacial.

Cathcart continued, "What's out there is the first of its kind, detective. And it might be the last. The Scimitar was the deadliest predator of its age. But when Vang altered its DNA he managed to disassemble and then reconstruct the genomes to accept human intelligence. So now – as you know – Vang has the Scimitar's strengths controlled by a human mind. And that change makes Vang ten thousand times more dangerous than it ever was even in its own prehistoric age. To be more exact, that one change makes Vang more dangerous than any predator that has ever walked the face of this planet since God created light. So, if you're sane, you *should* be afraid."

No one moved or spoke.

"But the Scimitar serum is like a living thing," she continued. "It's evolving. It's adapting. It's overcoming what Vang did to allow human consciousness. So it's rapidly reclaiming its innate savagery. But even if it does that, it will still retain a shred …" She half-turned, hands raised, "a *memory* of intelligence. It will never become the wild beast that Luther became. It'll be far worse. It will be just as ruthless, just as savage, just as murderous as Luther, but it will still have a shadow of Vang's intelligence that will make it literally unstoppable. It will be able to understand, on an intellectual level, all your methods. And you won't understand any of his."

Blackthorn stared long before he said, "Yes. Well. None of that is welcome news. But to get back to the point, doctor, do you think your arrival might have provoked Vang to attack the house?"

Cathcart seemed reluctant to speak. Then, "It's possible. If Vang saw me arrive, then he would naturally assume that I'm here to help you kill him."

Blackthorn sighed, "I should have sent you off with the lads."

"It wouldn't make any difference," Hunter interjected. He focused on Cathcart. "That's like taking your boots off after you've crossed a stream. It's too late. Does Vang's serum have any weaknesses, doctor? Think hard. Your life depends on it."

Cathcart answered, "Frankly, I can't think of anything. But I'm just a medical doctor and molecular biologist. My job is not that hard and you don't have to be that smart. But Vang is a theoretical physicist. His whole life revolves around complex subatomic theorems and equations. Some of them are too complex to even describe. All I can tell you for certain is that Vang used a ridiculously powerful electromagnetic matrix so that he could manipulate the DNA, and it worked."

Hunter said wearily, "You're almost right, Eve. But you're wrong about one thing."

"What?"

He leaned on both arms. "When the Scimitar DNA is full blown there won't be anything left of Vang at all. Not even a shadow of his intelligence. I've hunted this animal. I know it. It has no mind. It is the purest evil. With each second, there's less Vang and more Scimitar. And soon there won't be any Vang. It'll just be the Scimitar. But that doesn't make it less dangerous. It makes it more dangerous because it's had time to *learn* what we're about. He'll understand humans like he's never understood them before. He'll know our instincts, our habits, our *fears*. And that knowledge will make it ten thousand times more dangerous. He won't retain the 'intelligence' to actually 'think.' The Scimitar's nature will vanish all that from the planet. But he'll have *knowledge*. And that knowledge will make all the difference in the world. The Scimitar will use what he knows to beat us at every turn. So when I say the Scimitar is mutating beyond whatever controls Vang established in the DNA, you can take that to the bank. All of Vang's fail safes are falling one by one. My guess is that within a very short time there won't be any of Vang left. He'll just be the Scimitar with absolutely no thread of intelligence, as you wrongly assume. Vang will be death walking, and no one of the face of this earth will be able to hide from him."

CHAPTER TWENTY-ONE

W ith a fearful grimace Cathcart asked, "How long, do you think, before the Scimitar is full blown?"

Hunter hesitated. "I don't know. A week, maybe."

"Do you think that's why Vang attacked the house? Because he's no longer in control?"

"There's another possibility."

"What?"

"Maybe Vang has decided that it's time for him to grab what he's come here to grab."

Cathcart crossed arms and walked away from the island before turning back. "So what do we do?"

Blackthorn spoke like an executioner throwing the switch. "We kill it, doctor. But there's a wrinkle."

"Oh, god," groaned Cathcart. "Now what?"

"Someone in this house is in league with that devil," said Blackthorn plainly. "They've allowed the Scimitar to get inside these walls twice. And until we find out whoever it is, there's no safety inside *or* outside."

Eve stared a long moment before asking, "Do you have any idea who it is?"

He responded heavily, "First I'm going to search the entirety of this house and make certain we're secure."

Hunter stressed, "*It's gone.*"

Straightening his long overcoat, the detective stated, "You may have the luxury of being able to trust your instincts, Hunter. But I'm a police officer. I have to rely on my training."

Hunter lifted his rifle. "I'll do it."

"We'll both do it."

"No. You need to stay with the family. You'll have Ben with you. And I'll take Cathcart with me. Then none of us will be alone."

"You're not trained to do a house search."

"And you're not trained to hunt a tiger." Hunter checked the Marlin, levering a round. "Trust me, Blackthorn, if he's in the house, I'll find him. And the family will be better off with you guarding them, anyway. That's something you *are* trained to do."

* * *

It only took one moment for Cathcart to prepare herself. She put her hair in a quick tail with some kind of pin she picked from her shirt pocket, retied her shoes, and cinched her belt.

Hunter gave her a shogun. It was an elaborately ornamented double-barrel over and under choked for geese hunting.

Cathcart didn't seem to mind the length or weight. In fact, she handled it like a professional. After stuffing a flashlight in her belt and shoving a handful of shells into her right coat pocket she turned to Hunter with a surprisingly comfortable, "Okay. I'm ready."

Hunter led her up the spiral staircase to the third floor. He'd search the rest of the house later. Right now he wanted to examine that window where he'd seen the shadow. As they ascended stairs, he remarked, "You seem pretty comfortable with a shotgun, Cathcart."

Searching the stairs above them, she answered, "Uh huh. I was born in Minnesota. Skeet shooting was a big sport with my family. I've been shooting since I was twelve. I even won a couple of trophies."

"Makes sense. I thought your accent was a little strange."

"I've lived in London fifteen years. I lost my Minnesota accent a long time ago. Now I've got some kind of muddled Minnesota-English accent that makes people think I'm from the Philippines." She shrugged as Hunter glanced. "Don't ask me. I've never been to the Philippines."

"Have you ever shot an animal?"

"Nope."

"You think you can?"

"Why?"

They paused on the second-floor landing and Hunter turned to her, "Because some people can't. They freeze up. Some call it buck fever. You know what I'm talking about?"

Her expression was unafraid. "You mean they have it in their sights and they can't pull the trigger?"

"Yeah."

She chuckled, "Don't worry. I know who Vang is and I know what he is. I *will* pull the trigger."

"Determination is just part of it," Hunter clarified. "Expect to be afraid. He'll try and terrify you. And he will." He paused, searching her gaze, then he sighed, "Cathcart, you can do this. Believe me, I'll be afraid, too. Just stay focused. Get it in your mind: You have one reason for existing. To put a bullet exactly where you mean to put it. Forget your life before this or after this. There is nothing but *this*. Don't expect to live. Don't expect to die. You have one reason for existing and that is to put a bullet exactly where you intend to put that bullet. *That* is your life."

She hefted the shotgun. "Got it."

"Stay close to me."

"I'm your shadow." She was indeed close as they climbed. "Tell me again why we're going to look at this floor first?"

"Because I saw someone at the window when we killed the wolf. It was … strange. I just wanna look around and see what's up here."

Upon reaching the floor Hunter stalked soundlessly along the corridor to a small hall that cut to the left; a window stood at the end. Always cautious, Hunter counted six rooms, three on each side. The doors were closed with no hint of what lay within. Hunter choose the first door on the left simply because it was closest. He tried the doorknob; it was locked. He slammed his shoulder into it and it smashed into the wall. Without entering Hunter stared over the chamber.

It was a room replete with a couch and an elaborate makeup table bracketed by lamps. Half a dozen clothes racks were loaded with what appeared to be a woman's wardrobe.

"It's a dressing room," said Cathcart. "You know, I might be more useful if you'd tell me what we're looking for. Besides a monster, of course."

"I don't know yet, myself."

Cathcart angled past him to the nearest clothes rack. She ran a hand across the garments and softly rubbed fingertips. "These haven't been worn in a long time." She glanced over. "I bet these belonged to Milton's wife and he hasn't been in here since she died."

It was disturbing, in a way, that Milton would keep a tribute like this to his dead wife. In Hunter's opinion you were supposed to box all these things up when your spouse died, but then he'd never been married. He could be as wrong as the next bachelor.

As he was pondering, Eve opened the door of a walk-in closet and vanished. When she emerged, she said, "It's a nice bathroom, and about what you'd expect in a woman's closet – shoes, boots, pants, blouses. Riding clothes, mostly. Nothing formal. I guess she kept her fancy stuff somewhere else."

Hunter turned. "Let's try another one."

As they stepped across the corridor to the first room on the right, Hunter kicked the door open. He was fast running out of patience and didn't care if it was unlocked. Inside was a massive assortment of cardboard boxes. Hunter walked into it and swept out the bowie. He slashed the tape; it contained more boxes. Two additional rooms offered more of the same and then Hunter paused before the door beside the window. He kicked hard but it didn't crash open like the others. Then he noticed the deadbolt lock atop the doorknob. He kicked again and split the panel in half.

Cathcart poked her head inside. "Looks like an ordinary sitting room," she commented. She cautiously walked to a couch and lifted a book. "Wow," she continued, "*Titus Andronicus*. What kind of person reads this for entertainment? I had to read this in college and it made wanna vomit."

Hunter moved to the closet. He knew it would be locked so he lifted the heavy rifle and smashed it in half. Then he shouldered his way past the shattered fragments and what he saw stopped him with one foot inside, one outside. Beside him, Cathcart turned on the light. After a moment she whispered, "What is god's name is this?"

Strips of white rope had been nailed to the ceiling and were tied to claws with the skulls of vultures and bats. A water buffalo skull was solemnly placed on a black altar. The skull was ringed by red and black candles half-burned. Upon the floor was an enormous leopard skin, the head and open fangs raised in a warning. Along the left-side wall was a waist-high table varnished black and topped with a hundred vials, mortars, leather bags, small cups with tiny plants and flowers that Hunter didn't recognize. The walls and ceiling were painted red with symbols elegantly etched in black. There were no chairs.

Cathcart quietly asked, "Have you ever seen anything like this?"

Hunter shook his head, "No."

She stepped to the long table and lifted half a dozen vials. She held one to the light. "You know, Hunter, I'm a chemist. And this little collection of compounds doesn't look very savory to me. They have solid particles in them. They're unfiltered. I bet that if you secretly dropped this into someone's meal, or maybe their drink, it'd be lights out. What do you think?"

"It looks like an altar," Hunter said after a moment. "Maybe this is something Milton set up. He spent a lot of time in Africa." He paused. "Well, whatever somebody does in their private life is none of my business. This isn't important to me."

Cathcart grabbed his arm as he stepped away. "Woah! I think you're wrong, bwana! This *is* important. I can feel it. Whoever would build something like this is the same kind of person who would work with a homicidal maniac like Vang!" She pointed as she added, "Look at this! This isn't some kind of harmless hobby! This means something! *This is dark*!"

Kneeling, Hunter saw a faint trail leading across the leopard skin. He saw faint scratches on the floor and knew the Scimitar had been in this room. Then he saw something that stood in what seemed a place of honor.

It was a waist-high glass vase enamored with red etchings and filled with the bones of animals not indigenous to this continent. There were gazelle antlers and hyena skulls along with the fangs and claws of lion and leopard and crocodile. Hunter tried to imagine the patience and dedication required to create this temple and knew this was the very soul of whoever created it.

Hunter walked back to the door where Cathcart had retreated. He eased back the drape at the spot where he'd seen the silhouette.

Yeah, from this vantage point they'd enjoyed an unobstructed view of the battle. Maybe the Scimitar had stood here, too. But this view would be common knowledge to both family and staff, and all of them had reason to be concerned about the outcome of the fight. That someone had stood here revealed nothing; it was only Hunter's instincts that made him so suspicious.

Cathcart shifted. "Now what?"

"Hell if I know," muttered Hunter. "Would Vang build something like this for himself?"

"Oh, hell, no. Vang doesn't have a religious bone in his body. Not for black magic or white magic or God or Satan or whatever the hell kind of Haitian Voodoo this mess is. He's a stone-cold nonbeliever in anything but himself." Cathcart stepped closer. "What do you say we get out of here, huh? Fight another day? Isn't that the better part of valor? I mean, I don't want to seem unreasonably alarmed, but this is clearly proof that we're trapped in here with a homicidal maniac. Two of them, in fact. One outside and one inside."

Hunter responded morosely, "They're just waiting for us to try some idiotic move like that. Expose ourselves outside." He took a moment. "I need you to tell me everything that happened when the Scimitar attacked blow by blow. Don't give me the Reader's Digest version."

Like someone describing a bomb blast they had witnessed up close but remained too shocked to remember in detail, she said, "Well, uh, it was *fast*. Vang came down that hallway leading from the kitchen but Ben must have sensed him because he was up in a flash and attacked Vang on sight. They tied up big-time in the middle of the room like wrestlers. They were knocking stuff over and destroying all those trophies and furniture and everything else and, for a second, I thought Ben was gonna get the best of him. Even kill him. Then Vang literally picked Ben up like he was some kind of rag doll and threw him halfway across the room. Then that one guy–"

"Richard."

"Yeah. Richard. He snatched up a rifle and shot Vang at close range. I mean, he shot Vang point blank! Shot him twice! And when he did that, Vang jumped on him. It looked like Vang hit him, and that was it. Then Milton shot Vang with both barrels from that elephant rifle and Vang howled like he was hurt. Then Ben charged forward and smashed into Vang like a freight train and they went down again. There were a bunch of blows that I couldn't follow. I don't know who hit who. It was too fast. Finally Vang threw Ben away again and the major shot him two more times. And that … I don't know how to say it … that was like it really did hurt Vang bad. Finally. He howled and ran past the major and jumped out the window. Then you shot him when he was in the air. I saw him twist like he was hurt. Then he hit the driveway and jumped up and ran off. That was it. The whole thing didn't last thirty seconds."

"Vang never said anything?"

Cathcart gaped. "*He can talk?*"

"I didn't tell you?"

"*No!*"

"Yeah, he can talk."

"That's impossible!"

"Everything happening here is impossible, Cathcart." Hunter cast a final glance at the closet. "Okay, I'm done. How about you?"

"Overdone."

"Let's go downstairs. I have to tell Blackthorn about this."

"What about the search?"

"Later. Blackthorn needs to know this."

"Why now?"

"Because those vials probably contain stuff that can kill him if they drop it on his food or in his scotch. Blackthorn needs to know what kind of psychopath is in the room with him."

"But he won't know which one it is."

"It doesn't matter. If I know Blackthorn, he'll just peg all of them as witch doctors and put them in chains."

"He's not big on proof, huh?"

"He's big on surviving."

* * *

As they entered the trophy room Hunter immediately saw that Zelda, apparently as a departing gift, had put out large platters of food; it was curious that he hadn't noticed it before.

The family was seated at the table eating silently and solemnly but Hunter merely glanced at a plate before passing it up; he wouldn't be eating anything more in this house. He reached Milton, who was seated in a despondent posture. Staring down, Hunter asked quietly, "Do you know anything about an altar on the third floor of this place, Major?"

Milton appeared confused. "What? An altar? No. Most certainly. What are you talking about? What kind of altar?"

"Bones. Skin of a leopard. The skull of a water buffalo. A lot of vials filled with some unsavory looking elements."

"Are you sure they're not souvenirs? Several rooms are devoted to my collections."

"This isn't a collection."

Milton stood. "Take me to it."

Slinging his rifle, Hunter mounted the stairs. They reached the third floor and he led them down the short hallway. "It's in there," he said.

Milton entered, followed closely by Blackthorn, and Hunter saw that although Blackthorn held his rifle in a fist, he'd drawn his pistol. They remained in the chamber for a long time and Hunter heard brushes of conversation. He couldn't make out the words but he determined Milton was explaining the contents. After several moments they emerged and Blackthorn's face was strained and pale. The big investigator said nothing as he took a stand before the window, staring into the seemingly corporeal darkness. Then Milton stepped into the hall with a troubled expression.

Hunter asked, "Do you recognize any of it?"

The question seemed to drag Milton from a faraway place. "What? Oh. Yes. It's an altar. Much like one that I saw in Western Uganda."

"An altar to what?"

Milton's eyebrows rose. "I can't say." His gaze roamed the gloomy corridor. "I found it when I was with a United Nations emergency response team. It was in a cave."

Cathcart asked, "Why were you in a cave?"

"Because legend held that a young boy had entered a cave on a mountain somewhere in Western Uganda, and when the boy emerged, he was infected with the Marburg Virus. So we were searching for a cave where we might find the source of the virus, and a possible cure. We suspected it would be in a cave littered with the bones of animals and, more than likely, men. And then we found it just where we thought it would be." He hesitated. "It was, of course, prehistoric. And it held a sea of bones from bats, vultures, jackals, lions, rhino, elephant – all manner of beasts. We also found the petrified skull of a water buffalo prominently set on a large altar. The place was obviously the seat of some ancient cult and, just as obviously, an obscenely bloody one. It was ... a disturbing sight."

Cathcart was closely eying the major. "Certainly you'd seen such things before. What was so frightening about that one?"

As if to himself, Milton answered, "That is somewhat difficult to describe. But it was as if you could sense the souls of all those who died there. As if their spirits were still imprisoned within those walls." He gestured, "The guides in their Luganda dialect called it '*Mayemba*.' And they were very frightened of it. They refused to go further once they saw the petroglyphs which, in my judgment, pre-dated Uganda by a hundred thousand years." He took several faltering steps, head bowed, before turning. "The carvings were atavistic and spoke of the worship to some horrific, slouching, manlike thing that greatly resembled the beast that attacked us tonight. And there was an unknown form of writing. But when I asked the guides if they could translate it, they only repeated the word – *Mayemba*." He gestured, "None of the guides would stay near the cave. They retreated to the base of the mountain. But it was just as well. Considering the depths of their horror, we were probably lucky they remained with us at all."

"Was it a place of sacrifice?" asked Blackthorn.

Milton grimaced, "The best we could determine, it was built to pay homage to the beast depicted in the pictographs. Apparently, the beast was their god. The early hominids who inhabited that area must have worshipped him as we worship our Christian god. But he was a god in the flesh. And I can't say when the cult ceased to exist. But it must have continued for many centuries after the creatures died out."

The detective followed, "How do you know it's extinct?"

"Well," Milton began with a searching stare, "the cave did not appear to be recently used, detective. In fact, it looked as if it'd been abandoned for many, many thousands of years. So we naturally assumed that after the last of the creatures died, the cult was disbanded. It may have been centuries later, but it died as all beliefs die – reluctantly but inevitably."

Hunter stepped up. "How closely did the pictographs resemble the creature that attacked us in the house tonight?"

The mere reminder of the attack appeared to cast a cloud of depression upon Milton. It was as if this brief interlude had momentarily distracted him from the death of his eldest son, but mentioning the attack reminded him anew of all he had lost in the last moments.

'It was not an identical depiction," he answered weakly. "But it was a reasonable representation. Yes, it was clearly the same creature, although features varied. And I cannot imagine any age containing more than one such primate. There is no question that what killed Richard was the same beast depicted on those walls."

"Could you determine whether this cult was afraid of this creature?" asked Hunter.

"Oh, yes, indeed they were. There were drawings that depicted the beast killing enormous numbers of human beings – presumably members of that very cult. So even if it was their god, it was also their enemy." Milton gestured to the wallpaper as if he could still see the pictographs. "But that is nothing unusual. Many ancient cultures worshipped creatures that preyed upon them. The Hindus worshiped lions. The Kenyans worshiped snakes. The Waghoba worshiped leopards. In our own religion we are taught to fear god, as well. It seems we are compelled to worship what we fear. And if we do not fear it in the beginning, we will fear it in the end."

"So someone in this house worships the thing that killed your son," said Cathcart without even a hint of mercy. "Who might do that, Major?"

Milton was abruptly motionless. "I cannot believe such a thing. It is unthinkable. This was a derelict religion abandoned by base savages in an obscene age. I saw nothing to indicate that it continued to exist anywhere in Uganda or any other nation."

Blackthorn stated sternly, "It's not a derelict religion anymore, Major. Someone in this house duplicated that altar. Which of your children knew about it?"

"All of them knew of it! I have thoroughly documented my journeys and discoveries in my annals all my life. And my children have always had access to them. But do you realize what you're suggesting? It's madness!"

"I realize that," muttered Blackthorn.

In the first glimmer of anger Hunter had observed in the old man, Milton turned squarely into the investigator. He stamped his cane once as he grated, "What you are suggesting is heresy, commander! It is impossible that one of my children would have been subjugated by that demon! And it *was* a demon! Such a monstrous thing cannot exist without the devil's hand! And if one of my children were involved in this terrible thing then that means one of my children murdered their own brother! That is unthinkable!"

Blackthorn's unflinching composure revealed no satisfaction that he was beginning to unravel this mystery, but neither did it reveal any compassion for Milton's suffering. It was as if the homicide investigator were a bloodhound closing fast on his prey and would not allow himself to be distracted by anything so trifling as human emotion.

"Take the major downstairs," Hunter said to Blackthorn. "And take Dr. Cathcart with you. I'm gonna finish searching."

The commander stepped up. "What are you saying?"

Hunter's teeth gleamed, "I'm telling you to take them downstairs, Blackthorn. I haven't finished searching." He slung the rifle and took the double-barrel shogun from Cathcart as he muttered, "I'll do this alone."

Cathcart began, "Wha –"

"I'll need the shells, too."

Fumbling in her jacket, Cathcart handed him half a dozen shells that Hunter dropped in his coat. As he turned to leave, Cathcart reached out as if to again grab his arm.

Hunter turned and muttered, "If this room is really a temple, then Vang has been coming to it ever since we've been here. So he's probably somewhere in this house right now and I can't kill him while I'm worried about you shooting me in the back. So go downstairs."

Without waiting for any words of agreement or disagreement Hunter walked down the passageway and into the main corridor, turning left for a path deeper into the manor.

He didn't want Blackthorn close, either, if he found Vang hiding within these walls. Whoever died was going to die quickly and violently. It would be over in seconds and the last thing Hunter needed was an amateur hunter in the mix. If that happened, Hunter would have to deal with killing this all-but-unkillable Scimitar and not getting shot by his companion at the same time. And even though Blackthorn was a professional homicide detective, hunting an apex predator required a different skill set.

When Milton recalled what they had discovered in that cave, Hunter knew what he was dealing with because that cave had not merely been a temple to some mythical being. It had been the lair of this predator.

Yes, the natives worshipped it there because that's where it feasted and rested. And the bones of so many various species were not sacrifices. They were victims. That's why there were human skeletons beside the bones of lions and buffalo. This creature didn't care what it slaughtered. It killed those who worshipped it as quickly as it killed anything else.

Those early humans had probably sought to appease the Scimitar's endless hunger and rage with human sacrifices, all of them making the mistake of thinking like men and failing to understand they were dealing with a creature that lived only to kill. They had been trying to appease a beast that would be the end of the world, and that mistake cost them their lives. If they had been wise, they would have realized the futility of trying to satisfy an insatiable god that only craved blood. They would have abandoned their god, set the forest on fire, and fled the area. Yet, as it is with the worship of any god, man often sets reason aside and just hopes he is right. But they hadn't been right, and it cost them their lives. Probably to the last man.

Animals are scavengers – all of them.

Some say eagles don't feast on the dead, but Hunter knew they did. Some say snakes don't kill and eat their young. But they do. And some might have said that this beast was selective in its prey, that it wouldn't feast on those who held it up to the moon in glory and worship, but Hunter knew it wasn't selective in its prey. It killed anything, everything. And it killed for the pleasure.

And – in the moment – Hunter was certain that it was somewhere in this house.

Cracking the shotgun open, Hunter insured that there were two big ten-gauge rounds chambered. Minutes later he stopped before a large window at the end of the passageway. He stared at the aperture; it was locked. But there was something amiss. He could see something not quite right in the caulking that held one of the panes in place. Hunter raised a hand and flicked the pane with a finger and it fell away.

Hunter turned his head, gazing narrowly down the corridor. Vang had probably done the same with a hundred windows so that he could make silent entry any time he wanted. There were hundreds of rooms. So why did Vang visit the altar room? What was in that room that …

Hunter stopped.

So Vang could speak with whoever was working with him inside this house! That room is where they met! To Vang it was just a convenient place for him to coordinate his plan. But to whoever met him, it was an altar to what they worshipped in their degenerate fantasy. Ten thousand years had passed between the earliest proto-humans and modern man and they were still the same when it came to superstition.

Vang would not hesitate to indulge this fool's romantic and obsessive passion to worship him as a living god. He was using their stupidity to every advantage. That's why scratches marked the floor before that skull. It's where Vang stood when they convened.

He was manipulating their greed, their superstition, their resentment and hate and whatever other twisted motivations inclined them to murder their entire family. Vang was controlling them with their darkest desires because once he grasped what he was here to gain, they would be the first to die. And whatever promises he had made would be as useless as the blood that would flow from their gaping throats.

But what did he want?

Hunter began to lose focus as he concentrated on what was truly happening inside this cursed house. The fact that Vang had chosen to kill Inspector Marshal and Dr. Dobson before they cleared the estate indicated he was afraid of something leaving this place. Then Vang had doubled back and entered the manor through the nearby kitchen door because he was pressed for time and had to finish it quick. He had probably planned to kill Milton and retreat into the moor before the wolves became unmanageable, but Ben interfered.

What happened that caused him to attack tonight?

Hunter paused and – entirely in his mind – he again saw Milton signing his newly altered will before committing it to his lawyer.

That's it …

Milton had altered his will. He had left the entirety of his fortune to his eldest surviving child.

Of course.

And now Vang had no more reason to wait. Now he could kill Milton, and the entire family, save the one child that served him. That's why he had attacked. The opera was finished. It was time to end this blood-soaked masquerade.

So the game was up. Vang had come to secure Milton's money and now he had.

Some part of Vang realized that living forever like a hunted animal would be a living hell. That's why he needed Milton's enormous fortune. This had been Vang's plan all along. It's why he'd staged so many false attacks. He'd been goading Milton to fear the physical horror overhanging his house. He had been provoking the old man with the gruesome deaths of those closest to him. He had struck Milton with a terror so real and close that Milton could trust no one but his family. He had horrified the old hunter into a panic so that he would leave his entire fortune to whatever child might survive this terrible ordeal – the one who worshipped him.

It was a masterful plan but one of the children – or all of them – had to be coaching and guiding their father, inspiring him to move in the right direction. And it had to be someone who knew Vang before his transformation. Someone who knew him before he became the Scimitar. Someone who might have even presented the plan to him in exchange for their own immortality.

Hunter spun and fired.

The white blast of the shotgun was blinding in the long, window-lined corridor and the impact demolished the plaster wall at the connecting hallway and Hunter knew that he'd missed. But he'd glimpsed a shadow that flitted across the intersection moving fast. Instantly Hunter was running. He broke stride for a split-second to tear out the spent shell and slam in another. Then he went around the corner faster than prudence allowed.

He sensed that Vang wouldn't stop moving now that he'd been found. He would be in a full flight mode to get clear fast, so Hunter had to stay on top of him and that meant throwing caution aside and charging through doors to close the distance before Vang could escape.

With the thought Hunter broke into a run.

A roar reverberated in the castle and Hunter sprinted toward one of the ubiquitous staircases. He reached it and knelt, searching. He saw the faint, curving white lines where Vang had spun to his right. Beyond the marks was a twisting stairwell that rose to the fifth and final floor.

The attic.

That was a dead end.

Staring down, Hunter's eyes narrowed.

... No ... Vang won't go to the attic because he knows he'd be cornered. He knows there's only one way out. It's a –

TRAP!

CHAPTER TWENTY-TWO

Hunter whirled and fired the shotgun into Vang who stood one step away with his arm upraised to deliver a blow that would have torn Hunter's head from his neck and Vang screamed in rage. He twisted as Hunter fired again, hitting him point blank in the spine to blast him into the wall where stone shattered like glass.

Two rounds and the shotgun was empty and Hunter had no time to reload as Vang came off the wall roaring, "*DAMN YOU!*"

In the purest rage Vang lashed out with a curving left hand and Hunter ducked. He sensed the ungodly power of the blow as it passed over his back and leaped to his right as Vang spun into him matching or even surpassing his speed as Hunter threw the shogun. Vang swatted the weapon from the air and snarled viciously to reveal Sabretooth fangs as Hunter whirled the Marlin down and up and fired in the same breath.

At close range the impact of a 45.70 will knock down a Grizzly and Vang did feel the round because he staggered back. By instinct or reflex he threw a hulking forearm over his face as Hunter fast-worked the action on the Marlin and fired again point-blank. There was no time for thought but some part of Hunter's mind did register the eruption of blood and Vang's spiraling howl soared to the heights of the threshold.

Count!

Hunter had three more rounds in the Marlin as he fired again knowing he would have no time to reload. He had five big cartridges in the Ruger at his waist and then he would be empty and at the mercy of Vang unless Hunter hurt the Scimitar enough to make him retreat; there was no running from this. There was no place to run. Hunter would make the Scimitar retreat or he would die here and now.

Those were Hunter's thoughts as he worked the action of the Marlin, firing the final three rounds and he instantly dropped the rifle to draw the Ruger to fire just as quickly. And with each round Hunter saw an eruption of blood exploding black in the moonlight as the Scimitar bent, twisted, was backed away and finally swung an arm as if to strike but Hunter remained out of reach firing and firing and firing. Then Hunter fired the last round from the Ruger and the pistol was empty.

Vang staggered and threw out both arms to the side as he bent with a bellow of agony and rage. In absolute shock, Hunter saw that he was horribly wounded.

Hunter raised the empty Ruger at Vang's face as he gasped, "Take one step! See what happens!"

Vang rasped, "*Now you die …*"

"Let's see who dies!"

Vang bent forward as a thick drought of blood erupted from the gaping red fangs. "*You have no idea what I am!*"

"You're insane, Vang!"

"*You think you can kill me with a gun?*"

Hunter thumbed back the hammer on the Ruger and nodded curtly, "Let's find out."

Vang's head swung side to side as if measuring the length of an uncertain leap before he raised his gaze. "*I am forever!*"

"You're a relic, Vang!"

Rising to his full height, Vang roared, "*You are the relic! You're a stone-age hunter lost in time! Before I was trapped,*

I killed your kind until there was no one left to kill! *And I'll do it again*!"

Hunter shouted, "Vang! Listen to me! You can't control the Scimitar! It's too strong! Come with me and I'll take you in! You're already immortal! What more do you want?"

"*I want what it wants*!"

"What does it want!"

"*To kill*!"

Vang took a lightning-fast step and launched himself into a leap over Hunter who twisting down and away to avoid the herculean arm that lashed out at the last second and then Vang crashed through the window at the end of the passage, dropping instantly.

Hunter rushed to the window in time to see Vang hit the ground where he rebounded like a tiger and charged from the mansion. With gigantic strides he reached the maze in a heartbeat and was lost in the darkness. But Hunter continued to stare, searching the distant tips of the iron fence barely visible in the moonlight. Within seconds he saw a black shape etched against the stars, soaring over the barrier.

All was silence.

Falling to his knees, Hunter swept a forearm down his face. He spent a split-second in relief before he snatched up the Marlin; he began shoving shells in it as fast as his shaking hands allowed. It took him far longer than he liked but it was done, and he stood.

Trembling, Hunter moved to the shattered window and leaned against the frame, head down and breathing hard as the corridor behind him was shaken by a stampeding host of footsteps and chaotic shouts. In another moment Blackthorn stood beside him, rifle high, staring out the window. The investigator's face was that of a man eager for battle. But he saw nothing – as Hunter knew – and reached out to grasp his shoulder.

"Hunter! Are you all right, man?"

Eyes closed, Hunter whispered, "Yeah." He paused as he concentrated on breathing. "I'm okay … I think."

"Was it the Scimitar or the wolf?"

"It was Vang …"

"Bloody hell!" Blackthorn spun from the emptiness of the window and his entire body stiffened as he turned back and shouted, "How did the blasted thing get in here this time?"

"He's always been in here."

Blackthorn's anger was a physical force. "What did you say?"

"I said he's been inside this house since we got here."

It seemed the news was either totally unacceptable or incomprehensible to the investigator. He turned, staring in every direction. Hunter already knew that Ben stood in the hall, ready for anything. Then he noticed young Barron Milton standing there armed with a rifle. And Cathcart was there, as well, but she was unarmed. Hunter knew that Milton would have been present but the old man couldn't have made the climb so quickly.

Hunter searched Cathcart's face; she was in shock.

All right.

It was enough.

Hunter pushed off the wall. "He won't be back until tonight," he said as he moved back into the passage.

"How do you know that?" demanded Blackthorn.

"Because he always has to retreat for a while when he's wounded." Hunter blinked, trying to focus. "And he's seriously wounded this time. Another minute and I might have killed him."

"Then why didn't you finish him?"

"I ran out of bullets."

Blackthorn blinked. "Did *he* know you ran out of bullets?"

"I'm pretty sure he didn't."

Blackthorn blew out a wistful breath and shook his head. "That's the luck of the devil, mate."

"*For me.*"

Cathcart fell in beside him as Blackthorn backed away from the window as if he were holding a rear guard. Hunter was too tired to care. Let the detective worry all the way to the trophy room.

Ben was close to Hunter as they stepped forward and Hunter ignored the walls and floor, all painted with blood. It seemed impossible that a creature could be so gravely wounded and continue to fight. But not only had it continued, it had almost overcome. It had almost killed him after he'd hit it with enough ordinance to drop a dozen Grizzlies.

'Hard to kill' just didn't say it.

Immortal …

Yeah …

That was the word.

* * *

After returning to the trophy room Hunter was overwhelmed by a combination of pain, fatigue, and emotional exhaustion and all he remembered was lying down on a sofa to rest. When he awoke, the morning had already come though it was barely distinguishable from night.

Cathcart was seated close, asleep in a chair.

"Hey," said Hunter, and she awoke slowly. It took her a minute before she groaned, "What time is it?"

"It's looks like noon."

Hunter could barely remember being this thirsty and was surprised to find a bottle of water on the floor beside him. He drank all of it and saw Cathcart doing the same with her own bottle. Finally she shook her head and said weakly, "I don't see how you guys do it."

Hunter croaked, "Me, either."

"How do you feel?"

"I'll be all right. How about you?"

She yawned, "I'm just tired." A long pause. "At least I haven't been beat up yet. Not like you, anyway. That's a relief." Her gaze roamed the ceiling. "You think he stayed gone last night?"

"Yeah. He stayed gone."

"How do you know?"

"If he'd been able to slip back into the house, he probably would have attacked us when we were at our most vulnerable. But he wasn't up to it himself. He was barely alive when he went out that window. So he's been resting somewhere. But not here."

At that moment Blackthorn walked up holding two cups of coffee and from the look of the squared away detective Hunter would not have been surprised if he hadn't slept a wink all night. In fact, on second thought, Hunter was certain of it. Blackthorn had stood guard all night long with rifle in hand and appeared none the lesser for it.

"How are you two feeling today?" he asked and offered a cup of coffee to Cathcart. "Thank you," she murmured. "I'm fine."

"I'm all right," Hunter answered. "Anything happening?"

"All is quiet on the front. And I think you were right. Vang retreated to the moor to heal up."

"He's probably staying in one of those huts," groaned Hunter. "He's got one of them set up with camping gear. And once he gets inside it, he changes to human and lays down. His healing does the rest."

"Why is he staying in human form as much as possible?"

Cathcart said drearily, "Because he's nearing the end of his rope. He's probably realized that he won't be able to change again more than once or twice. At that point the Scimitar transformation will be permanent and that's the last thing he wants. It is like he's designed this entire scenario so that he can live forever in human form with an untouchable fortune to secure his safety. But getting trapped in the form of a Scimitar would ruin that."

After a thoughtful pause Blackthorn rumbled, "Yes. I can agree with that premise." He set his gaze on Hunter. "Did you learn anything else last night?"

"Nothing we didn't already know. He said he was going to kill every one of us. Then he jumped out the window." He expelled a hard breath. "I got lucky on that one."

Blackthorn stared. "Are you absolutely certain he didn't know you were out of bullets?"

"Why do you keep asking?"

"Because maybe you hurt him worse than you thought."

"I said that if I'd had *one more minute* with him, I might have killed him." Hunter began breathing more regularly. "But I wouldn't have survived for five more seconds."

Blackthorn accepted it with, "So he did not know."

"If he had known I was empty, I'd be dead. That's the only thing I *am* sure of."

There was a long pause.

"Well, you're a better man than me, Gunga Din," allowed the detective, a sip of coffee. "I can't say that I could have bluffed that hand without quaking in my boots."

"I didn't say I wasn't."

Cathcart walked over and stared out the shattered window at the storm shrouded day. Suddenly Hunter noticed that someone had recently tossed half a dozen sticks in the hearth so that the enormous trophy room had not discernably dipped in temperature. Noticing her stance against the gray light, Blackthorn asked, "Are you quite all right, doctor?"

Cathcart turned to stare. Her lips tightened momentarily before she stated, "I thought I'd lived a good life until this moment. I thought I'd never have any sincere regrets. But I was wrong. I wonder if everybody feels like this at the end."

Hunter reached down, lifted another log in a single hand, and tossed it into the hearth to an explosion of sparks.

As he reclined again into the chair his face was as grim as his words.

"We're not dead yet," he said, and stared into the flames. "We're not even close."

* * *

A gray sun distantly burned in a sky of somber cloud. An oppressive darkness of day smothered the moor, refusing to release the night. A windless, soundless stillness smothered the wilderness.

Standing beside Blackthorn, Hunter cast a gaze at the surviving members of Milton's family. The old man sat nearby, head down, breathing heavily and haltingly. Though it was day, it was as if the long night would not release them from its skeletal grip.

Obviously, Hunter's discovery of that nightmarish altar had planted agonizing seeds of doubt in Milton's mind and he was uncertain, now, whom he could trust. Although the old man had angrily denied the possibility that he might have been betrayed, a doubt had taken root in his soul. And it seemed to have extinguished the defiant fire that had so stubbornly burned within him. His face was haggard and pale. It was obvious that his confidence had been broken with the thought, consequently leaving him as his noblest trophies – a sad relic of the greatness he had been.

"There's no question that one of them is working with Vang," Hunter quietly told Blackthorn, both of them in conference near the kitchen wall at the rear of the trophy room. Cathcart, seated nearby and nursing a coffee, glanced up at the words but said nothing as Hunter added, "I don't know how you do that detective stuff but you're running out of time, partner. This will be our last night. If we live through it."

"Why is it so important we know who Vang is working with in this house?" asked Cathcart. "Let's just kill Vang and get out of here."

Hunter stared at her with graveyard eyes. "First, because killing Vang ain't no piece of cake. Second, and I've already told you, we *can't* get out. There's too many of them. And third, whoever Vang is working with won't let us leave because they can't let the truth behind this go public. There can't let any of us live to tell the tale."

Cathcart appeared amazed. "What can one of them do to us if we decide to get out of here? One of them is *the last thing* I'm worried about. I just don't wanna end up as dog food."

"I think you're underestimating the damage an untrained adult can do with a loaded weapon," offered Blackthorn. "You're certainly underestimating the damage they can do if they're all in this together. So Hunter is right. Vang is certainly no criminal genius. He's probably laid a trail of clues as wide as the channel that I will put together when we are out of this. And that track will lead directly to someone in this house. Then they will be disowned by their father and they know it. So they're in this, now, and can't let any of us survive. Even if Vang is dead, they have to make sure no one gets out of here alive."

"So disarm them!" demanded Cathcart. "Why does Barron have a rifle?

Blackthorn shook his head, "Ordinarily you would be correct and I would disarm him. But at this disastrous intersection I will not deprive any person of a chance to defend their life against this monster. I would not do that to a convicted murderer who deserved the hangman. And I have no reason to believe all of them are involved. But one of them certainly is."

Without blinking Cathcart said, "Why do you always sound like Winston Churchill?"

"A great and noble man," Blackthorn intoned. "He reminds me of me."

Cathcart bent over, elbows on knees, before she said, "All right. But which one could be working with Vang? None of them are likely suspects to me."

"They are all suspects. Especially the little one."

"Who are you talking about?

"Emily."

Cathcart retorted, "That's nuts, Blackthorn! In the first place, don't you remember what Milton said? He said he can't leave any of his fortune to Emily. It would destroy her. She has to be cared for with a trust fund." She motioned to the window. "She was in some kind of terrible accident or something. She's not able to take care of herself. And she's certainly not able to orchestrate this kind of conspiracy."

The detective was unshaken. "Yes, but someone must manage that trust fund. And he might be in league with Vang. The trust fund manager could know Vang in a thousand ways. And Emily is easily manipulated. She might have been persuaded to plant the first seeds of horror in her father's heart, consequently causing him to rewrite his will. It is not impossible. So it must be considered." A pause. "Everyone is a suspect until they are not."

Hunter commented, "It's *vaguely* possible in the most outrageous sense of the word. But I don't think that kid had anything to do with this. The others, sure. It could be any of them. But not Emily."

"Why not?" countered Blackthorn. "Emily does not speak to any of us. Or, for that matter, any of *them*. But who knows whom she speaks to in private?"

"Because I understand her," Hunter replied morosely. "She's just a lost, lonely kid. She's been injured. She's had a hard life. She's not comfortable with people so she prefers the company of animals. She's at home with animals because they don't scare her." He paused. "Sometimes when I look at her, I feel like I'm looking at myself when I was her age. She's quiet, keeps to herself, doesn't care much for people, and has a way with animals. They comfort her and she comforts them. All she really needs is a friend, and I don't blame her for choosing animals over people. I do, too, most of the time. Even now. And I can't see her betraying her father. Especially not for money. She doesn't care about money any more than I do."

Cathcart was silent for a long time, arms crossed on upraised knees. "Okay, so what about the others?"

Hunter's jaw tightened, "It has to be whoever knew Vang possessed the serum before any of this got started. I'm convinced this was set up *before* Vang used the serum on himself. I don't think he would have ever done it if he couldn't guarantee his long-term survival. And that takes a ton of money. Vang knew exactly what happened to Luther. He wasn't going to let himself get taken out like some wild dog. So achieving immortality was only half of this. The other half was making sure he'd live long enough to enjoy it."

"That is not perfectly logical," pondered Blackthorn. "Vang could have maintained his human form forever. Why did he not simply remain in human form as a professor? He could have manufactured a fake death certificate in his supposed old age, changed identities, and moved to an even more prestigious post with a new identity. Perhaps a post he created for himself and prepared for decades. He could have lived forever as a rich and powerful scientist. Why all this carnage?"

Cathcart insisted, "*Maybe* he could have remained in human form, Blackthorn. You still don't get the power of this serum. There was *always* a chance the change might have been permanent, so Vang needed a backup plan. That's why he set this up. But whoever is working with him wanted something in exchange for their help and I bet it was to be immortal, too. Just like him. And now we've complicated, if not destroyed, his 'perfect plan.' I can understand why he's enraged. He probably wants to kill us now more than he even wants to grab the money."

"It could be worse," suggested Hunter.

"How could this *possibly* be worse?" muttered Cathcart.

"I think Vang considers all of us to be low-brow Neanderthals who have no right to even be in the same room with him, much less hunting him. Vang isn't afraid of us. He's *insulted*. He's genuinely offended that the same fools that killed Luther would dare to come after him."

Blackthorn growled, "You're saying this is personal to him?"

"Yeah."

Blackthorn mused, "I must say I'm taking the matter rather personally, myself. I always take attempts on my life personally. But why is that important?"

"Because it makes Vang unstable."

"Unstable!" laughed Cathcart. "So the rest of this is the work of a *stable* Scimitar?"

Hunter emphasized, "What I'm saying is that Vang had a plan. And he was sticking to that plan – more or less. But now we've set his plan off-kilter and he's seriously insulted that peons like us would do that to him. Which means that he could do something completely off the charts that we're not prepared for because he wants *revenge*. So that inserts a wild card into this mix. We can't sit back and think we've got this figured out."

After a pause Cathcart agreed, "Yeah. That would be him. The only person Vang ever respected – or even considered – was Vang. He bulldozed over everyone else in the lab or in the business end of things." She looked at Hunter. "Are you still going after him today?"

Hunter turned his head to the sky. "The sun's going to have to break through a little more. It's still too dark." He stared at Blackthorn. "We have a little time. Why don't you see what you can get out of the kids? Do some of that detective stuff."

Blackthorn glanced at them gathered at the table. "Yes," he muttered, "it's all we have."

With commanding strides Blackthorn moved to the front of the room. Hunter studied Cathcart's dismal posture before he said, "You look awfully depressed for somebody who's saving the world."

Cathcart managed a weak smile, "Is that what we're doing?"

"Of course."

"Coulda' fooled me."

"Tell me what you know about Vang personally."

Cathcart raised her face. "Look, dude, I want to help. But I've already told you everything I know."

"Tell me what kind of person he is."

"He's a pig."

"Yeah, well, we know that. Was he an outdoorsman?"

After a long pause Cathcart asked incredulously, "How in god's name would I know if an insane doctor with a god complex was an outdoorsman? I wasn't married to the guy. I hated his guts. But he was a genius and I needed him so I just sucked it up and shut up and did my job. Believe me, I tried not to talk to him. At all."

"Fair enough. Well, does he *seem* like an outdoorsman?"

"How does an outdoorsman 'seem?'"

"What did he wear?"

"*What*?"

"What kind of clothes did he wear?"

An empty stare.

"Cathcart," Hunter proceeded, "work with me, okay? Did he wear wingtip shoes or hiking boots?"

"Wingtips."

"Did he dress like a hiker or a banker?"

"A banker."

"Did he smoke?"

"Yes."

"Cigars or pipes?"

"Some weird-looking pipe. Looked expensive to me. Everything about Vang was expensive. I don't why his pipe would be any different."

"What did he drive?"

"A Bentley." Cathcart stared expectantly. "What does that tell you?"

"It tells me he's not an outdoorsman."

"The Scimitar is!"

"Not really."

"How can you say that? The DNA of the Scimitar is prehistoric and it's a proven fact that DNA contains cellular memory! It's also one of the meanest predators that's ever lived and I guarantee you it remembers that!" She waved into the air. "It probably knows these woods better than you do! Where are you going with this?"

"Instinct and knowledge are two different things," Hunter said with conviction. "Right now the Scimitar is like a lion that's been raised in captivity. If you raise a lion in captivity, then turn it loose in the wild, that lion will be dead in a week. If the Scimitar survives long enough, then sure, it'll learn what it needs to do to survive. But learning how to survive in the wild is a tricky thing for any creature and a Scimitar is no different. As a Scimitar, Vang might be the toughest animal in that moor. But tough will only get you so far. You have to have knowledge to survive. You have to have experience. And Vang doesn't have either. And that's his weakness."

Cathcart answered his argument with, "I don't see how a lack of experience is going to help you bring down a homicidal freak of nature that has the strength of fifty gorillas. So what if he doesn't know which way is north?"

"Because Vang is a smart man, but it's just book smarts. And the Scimitar's senses are perfect, but senses are limited. Young tigers don't live to be old tigers because they have a good nose. They get old because they get smart. And if they don't get smart, they get dead. The trick in the jungle is staying alive long enough to learn how to *keep* staying alive. And it doesn't matter how strong you are or how great your senses are. If you make a mistake because you don't know what dangers to avoid, you're as good as dead. I've seen eight hundred-pound tigers walk over a deadfall because they didn't know any better, and that was it."

"What's a deadfall?"

"It's a hole in the ground with stakes sticking up at the base. If you fall in it, you're dead."

"Yeah. Saw that in a movie. So what's your point?"

"My point is that a tiger has the brute strength to tear an elephant apart. But because it doesn't know any better, it steps into a hole dug by some ninety-year old geezer who can barely lift his chopsticks and now it's dead. So strength isn't enough. It never has been."

Cathcart was staring aside like she was watching a rattlesnake. Then she asked, "Are you seriously talking about setting a trap? How are you going to do that? Vang isn't as stupid as those wolves, you know. He's not going to step into a beartrap. I said he was a pig. Not a moron."

Hunter's gaze seemed far away as he continued, "I grew up in the wild, Cathcart. Spent my whole life in the wilderness. And people think nature is kind. But nature isn't kind. Not to anyone. Nature destroys everything, in the end. It destroys the young, the old, the weak, the strong. It doesn't matter. All it takes is a single mistake. And nature will consume the strongest of us like it consumes everything else."

Cathcart turned her face to the shattered window. "You think there's something in that moor that can destroy Vang? Some kind of trap?"

"Yeah," said Hunter, and turned his head to the window, staring at the darkness. "I do."

CHAPTER TWENTY-THREE

Seated at the table, surrounded by the nervous and dejected family, Blackthorn began ponderously, "And so, young people, I would like to ask you a few questions. I trust you will be cooperative."

No one spoke.

Blackthorn began, "Needless to say, this is a tragic situation for all of you that –"

"Not as tragic as it is for Richard," said Flora quietly.

"My condolences for your brother," Blackthorn continued. "I understand he was a banker?"

"Richard was president of the major's corporate bank in London. We only got to see him on weekends."

"I understand." Blackthorn focused on Barron Milton. "And you are the major's youngest son? Do you also work at the bank?"

"I'm vice-president of a branch office. The major doesn't believe I'm ready to pilot a full bank."

"Would you have any idea why the creature might have singled out your brother in an attack?"

"I have none," Baron said despondently. "I presumed it was because Richard shot it. I think he wounded it … if such a thing … can be done." He looked away. "I have no idea. Who knows what's in the mind of a monster like that?"

Blackthorn paused. "They are all like that, young Milton. Let's just say it attacked your brother because he was a brave man, and he wounded it. And you, Madam Bronte, you also work at this bank?"

"Uh, no," Bronte replied, "I work at Lloyd's of London. I craft the more eccentric insurance policies. Some of the policies have to be written from scratch and Lloyd's prefers to use someone like me."

"Someone like you?"

"I have a doctorate in English Literature and I'm fluent in five contemporary languages. I'm also proficient, of course, in Greek and Latin. And, at Lloyd's, some of the required language must be precise beyond the abilities of your routine solicitor. A solicitor is not an artist with language. They're not even a noteworthy editor."

"Of course," agreed Blackthorn. "But if I may say, a mastery of language hardly seems a sufficient qualification for writing complex insurance policies. Did they also provide you with policy training?"

"Yes. Before we came home, I spent two years absorbing legal phraseology. But all the legal training in the world is of no use if your command of language is insufficient for the rhetorical challenges of precisely protecting unique elements of complex properties. You see," Bronte added in a humbler tone, "solicitors, or even advocates, are trained in a specific use of language. Their knowledge is insufficient to resolve the more challenging lexical difficulties for which the French would probably use an *avoues*."

Gloom masked Blackthorn's face as he said, "You say you relocated to Britain. Am I correct in understanding that you and your brother, Barron, were born in Africa?"

"We all resided in Africa for years while the major established his banking network," Flora intervened. "But we are all British citizens, commander, and we've always considered Great Britain our home."

"If I might ask, in what countries did you establish residence?"

Flora re-entered the dialogue with a scowl, "Everywhere, commander. We lived in Kenya, Nigeria, South Africa, Uganda, Nairobi. We spent six months in the Congo and I, for one, have no fond memories of that bloody land."

"Why is that?"

"Because the Congo is cursed," Flora answered bitterly. "It was my most unfortunate time on that continent. Bronte and Barron hadn't been born, so they have no memory of it. But it was nothing but communists and cannibals and rapists and murderers and poachers who would kill a human being as quickly as they'd kill a dog. I was overjoyed when we left."

Blackthorn focused once more on Barron. "May I ask in what nation were you and your sister born, Barron?"

"In Uganda, where the major kept his main residence. And Emily was born there, as well."

The one child of Milton's that never spoke sat invisibly at the distant end of the table and Blackthorn finally turned his attention toward her. Emily was yet to speak a word not only to him but to anyone at all – as far as he knew.

She had been silent since Blackthorn and Hunter had arrived and even now sat with head bowed, hands hidden beneath the table. If Emily Milton were not wearing a pretty cotton dress she would have not been out of place in a cloister. And she was thin, almost emaciated. She was little more than a waif in a mist. Her dark hair was her most prominent feature but it was simple, long, and lifeless as it lay about her face and shoulders. Yet there was also something impenetrable about the youngest child that seemed to conceal an almost supernatural power of awareness. It was as if she did not need for another to speak in order to know their mind. Nor was she quick to reveal her own.

"Madam Emily," Blackthorn said in his gentlest tone, "I would like to ask you some questions – if you please."

Emily's eyes cut upward to fix on him. Her eyes were a startling blue. Blackthorn held the unblinking, icy gaze as he asked, "Madam Emily? I mean you no harm. Are you quite all right?"

"She's a bit reserved," offered Flora. Then, "Emily? Darling? Would you please answer the commander's questions?"

Another frozen moment of an ice-blue gaze before Emily said, "Thank you for asking, commander. I'm fine."

Blackthorn reminded himself that nothing in this house was what it seemed. His face tilted back as if he were addressing someone who's guilt was as certain as the Colossus of Rhodes.

"Madam Emily," he continued, "please let me offer my condolences for your brother."

"That is quite benevolent of you, commander. Thank you."

The unusual elevation of her language actually startled Blackthorn somewhat although he revealed nothing. He continued, "Madam Emily, before tonight, have you ever seen the beast that attacked your brother?"

"How could I have beheld it before tonight?"

Again – such formality.

"Perhaps from the window of your room?" Blackthorn concluded that searching her gaze was like searching the surface of a frozen lake. "As you are probably aware, this creature has been circling your father's estate for some time. There is every chance that you – or any of you – might have glimpsed it at twilight. Perhaps while you were watching a beautiful sunset from your widow, you saw it moving in the trees?"

Emily's tone was abruptly empty. "I am not so inclined."

"Inclined?"

"To watching horrible things."

Seated beside her, Flora reached out gently, resting her hand on the table, "Emily," she whispered, "hold my hand."

Emily mechanically grasped her hand as Bronte continued, "Emily, please cooperate with the investigator. He's just trying to help."

Blackthorn felt that Emily's gaze shifted from ice to lasers. Her lips became a thin line. Then she said, "May I assist you with anything else, commander?"

There was no simple way of dealing with this one. She was an enigma in full. Her eyes were even colder than ice because ice, at least, can be measured. But whatever existed beneath that blue gaze was utterly unknowable. Still, this was not Blackthorn's first attempt at attempting to crack a recalcitrant witness. He persisted, "Are you afraid, Emily?"

"Yes."

"For yourself?"

"For my father."

Father.

The word struck Blackthorn like a battleax. Of all Milton's children, this one, alone, referred to Major Milton as "father." The rest referred to him as Major as if they had never heard of another term. But Emily was the exact opposite of that. It was as if she had never heard of another term with which to address her dear father. None of this was proof of anything, of course, but it was a curious thing.

"Emily has always been quiet," Flora said. "She lived with nannies at the major's estate in Uganda while we traveled with him."

"Why did Emily not travel with you?"

They exchanged uneasy glances. Finally Flora said, "We don't talk about that, commander."

Blackthorn hesitated. "I see. Then might I talk to you alone for a moment?"

Rising fluidly, Flora spoke with authority over the others, "I'll return in a moment. Don't wander off."

When they were safely outside the hearing of the remaining children, Blackthorn said quietly to Flora, "What's all this about?"

Milton's oldest daughter seemed to gather herself before she said, "When we were living in Uganda, Emily was having a picnic in the back yard with one of our nannies and the nanny never saw a hyena that came up to them. By the time the nanny saw it, it attacked. It killed the nanny and turned on Emily. But Emily – and god only knows how she had the courage or the presence of mind to do it – grabbed the bread knife and stabbed it in the neck. And she killed it. Incredibly. But she was still badly mauled and spent years in hospital while the rest of us traveled with the major."

"Who stayed with Emily?"

"Nannies and nurses. And when she was finally able to travel with us again, she had changed in many, many profound – and even frightening – ways. She was no longer the Emily we knew."

"How so?"

Flora hesitated. "Well, years alone had led her to find life in her books. She had spent all those years in books of every kind, every age, every genre. She's actually a little encyclopedia. She's very smart. But in her most progressive years – years where her personality was formed – she was utterly alone in her own mind. And that's where she still is almost all the time – in her own mind. In her mind, she's with her books, and that makes her feel safe. And I don't think that will ever change."

Blackthorn grunted, "That is perfectly normal. But you said she had changed in frightening ways. What do you mean?"

As if reluctantly surrendering a family secret, Flora said, "The Ugandan physicians told us that something happened to her brain while she was in coma. They said that, when she was unconscious, her brain somehow rewired itself. And they were right because, when she woke up, she had incredibly sensitive hearing. It was superhuman. She could hear a pin drop at a hundred meters. And there was something else about her that was more disturbing."

Blackthorn merely stared until Flora continued with, "It was like a form of extra sensory perception." She turned her face to gaze softly upon Emily. "My dear sister has this frightening ability to simply know things. We cannot reason how she does it, but she can tell us if one of the horses is sick, and no one else will know. Not even the trainers. She can tell us if someone is coming up the drive long before you can see them. I mean, we've asked multiple doctors for answers. Even here in England, we've taken her to the best doctors, but they all tell us the same thing. They tell us that her brain physically rewired itself while she was in coma so it would continue to function. So it would continue to live. And they said this … this *process* … was irreversible. It's permanent. And that's the reason Emily is at home nowhere but inside this house. The outside world assaults her with too much information. She hears too much. She sees and senses too much. But we've all accepted this and we do the best we can. The poor thing must remain in this house for the rest of her life and we try to make it as pleasant as possible. But it's often difficult. For all of us." She raised a hand to her throat and choked, "Those bloody hyenas!"

"They still frighten her?" confirmed Blackthorn.

"She's terrified of them! We never mention them! We don't speak of them at all! No one in this house is allowed to speak of them! The only one who ever speaks of them is Emily."

"What? Why is that?"

Flora hesitated. From what, Blackthorn couldn't determine. Finally she answered with, "Well … sometimes it seems … when she's very, very disturbed, we'll find Emily staring out her bedroom window in the dark and whispering to herself."

"What was she saying?"

"She was saying, '*Ekibe*.'"

Blackthorn's brow hardened. "Ekibe?"

"It means 'hyena' in Ugandan. We don't know how she learned it. She must have heard it from the nanny before she was killed. It was probably the last word she said before she died."

"How did Emily manage to kill such an animal?"

"We have no idea. But she did. We found the beast with a huge knife stuck in its throat and Emily was bleeding to death beside it."

"What were her injuries?"

Flora gestured haplessly, "How much time do you have, inspector? She was in a coma for eight months. When she woke up, she couldn't speak or walk or eat by herself. We had to spoon feed her. It was two years before she could walk again. And I know I've already told you this but she began reading long before that. She began reading almost as soon as she could hold a book. And so books became her entire life – the only life she's ever known, really. And," she lifted a hand to the walls, "this house. This is the only place where she's ever truly felt safe. We all believe it's because this house is built like a vault and it protects her from sensing too much. But it's also built like a castle and she fell in love with castles in her romance novels. And that's just fine with us. If Emily wants to believe this is her castle, then it's her castle. None of us will taint that for her. And we don't walk on eggshells but we do love her and try not to scare her or, uh, disturb her. She's been through quite enough. And that's why we do not speak of certain things. Ever. Not even to you."

"She seems devoted to her father," suggested Blackthorn.

"Oh, yes," Flora said, "she dearly loves the major."

"Emily was not bitter that her father left her for seven years while she recuperated from her injuries?"

Flora appeared confused. "Not at all. Why would she be?"

"And the rest of you did not resent your father for his long absences?"

"Commander, the major would have been forced to travel in order to consolidate his banking empire regardless of Emily's condition and we all understood that. Even Emily understood that. So we never blamed him for his absences. We knew he was doing it for *us*. And, when he was home, he would spend his every waking moment with Emily. He loves her dearly. And she has always known that, as well."

It took Blackthorn a moment to process the implications of this child spending so much time alone in Uganda but for the care of the local people who would have surely known about this ancient cult. Then he said, "Very well. I can say the rest in front of the others. Thank you for explaining this to me."

Flora walked to the table. "Of course."

Once again standing before them, Blackthorn said, "You are aware that your lives are in danger. The time has come to tell you the nature of that danger. In short, there is a madman outside this estate who means to kill at least one member of this family. He is a scientist who has altered himself into a type of Dr. Jekyll and Mr. Hyde. He is completely insane. And he has two wolves with him that are also exceedingly dangerous. One of these creatures killed your chauffer, Mr. Staford. This man's name is Dr. Ashera Vang and I intend to discover whether any of you know him, or have known him, as well as the nature of that relationship."

None of them volunteered any information until Flora said, "You are referring to Dr. Ashera Vang of the Corona Institute?" All eyes focused on her as she added, "Yes, commander, I'm aware of Dr. Vang's research. I have been for many years. I would estimate that most of the medical community is aware of his breakthroughs in virology."

"And I am aware of him," commented Bronte. "Lloyd's has a policy with the Corona Institute."

"Have either of you met Dr. Vang?" asked Blackthorn.

"I have not personally met him, no," answered Flora.

"I'm only aware of the institute because I had to rework their insurance policy," Bronte contributed.

"Why did you need to do that?"

She gestured, "Expansions. Additions. It was actually somewhat intriguing. Some of their equipment is insured for hundreds of millions of pounds. I've never amended a more expensive policy."

"And you, Baron?" Blackthorn asked with an expectant gaze.

"Yes, of course I know of the institute," nodded Baron. "The major's mothership was one of its premier financiers. I'm not intimately familiar with their research work, but I'm familiar with their finances. I've attended several meetings with their board."

"But none of you have ever met or spoken with Doctor Vang?"

Denials.

"And what about Ms. Emily?" Blackthorn pressed. "Would she have had an opportunity to meet the good doctor?"

Emily spoke for herself. "I don't know him."

Before he was aware of it, Blackthorn addressed his next question to Bronte. "Emily's room is on the first floor of the manor?"

"We all live downstairs, commander. No one ever ventures upstairs. There's nothing upstairs but the major's collections. And, in any case, we prefer to remain close."

"But your brother discovered the Scimitar upstairs."

"Only because the major sent him there to deposit his new will in the safe. Otherwise, we stay downstairs. Where it's warmer."

Blackthorn lowered his chin. "I see." A moment. "Well, then, I suppose those are enough questions. I will only add that Mr. Hunter and I intend to resolve this situation."

Flora sat forward, "How?"

"By determining which one of you is working with Dr. Vang in a degenerate plot to murder your father," stated Blackthorn plainly.

All but Emily erupted to their feet and Flora was first to speak.

"How dare you!"

"That's impossible!" objected Bronte.

Baron required a moment before he simply blurted, "*What!*"

"The bear," said Emily, surprising Blackthorn. He all but scowled over her, curious that she would speak at all and far more curious that she did not display offense at his accusation. Then Emily quietly asked, "Would you excuse me so I can go to Ben?"

Flora bent forward, leaning on the table, "Emily, darling, now is not the time to –"

Blackthorn said, "I don't see why not. He's a gentle giant. Why don't you ask Mr. Hunter?"

Emily bowed her face.

Blackthorn walked to where Hunter knelt on the floor taping together five sticks of dynamite. His rifle and pack lay close. Obviously, he was going out. For a moment Blackthorn frowned over the device. Then, "I see you retrieved dynamite from the shed."

Hunter glanced up. "Yeah."

"Where are you storing the rest of it?"

"I locked it up in the cabinet. But some of it was missing from the shed." He glanced at the family. "Somebody moved it."

"How much?"

"Enough to blow us all to hell."

"Who has the key to the cabinet?"

"I gave it back to the major." Hunter cast the old man, sleeping on the couch, a glance. "I'm not taking over this place. This is his house. That should be respected."

"I agree. So how are you going to detonate this contraption?"

"I'll have to use the rifle."

Blackthorn's forehead drew taunt as his gaze narrowed. "I wouldn't exactly call it a suicide move, mate, but —"

Hunter raised his face. "It's the only move I've got. I need something that will take one of them out hard and disorient the rest so I can make it back to this house alive."

The commander turned his stern gaze to the dark sky beyond the window. "It's going to be pitch black inside those trees. Think you can get close enough to them?"

"I can't stalk them. They'll know I'm coming a mile off, so I've got to get them to stalk me." He placed the improvised explosive in the pack and jerked it shut. "I'm leaving Ben with you. He can't beat all three of them, but he can slow them down so you can get off a few good shots. Just make sure you and the major keep rifles close. And you, too, Cathcart. If you can pull a trigger, you can shoot skeet, you can shoot a tiger. You don't have to be Bill Hickock."

Cathcart asked, "How far are you going?"

Hoisting the pack onto his shoulder, Hunter stood. "Not far. They're out there right now circling this place. Making sure we don't try and escape. They're probably just inside the tree line."

"Just the wolves?"

"No. Vang will be with them. He'll be healed up by now. And he'll be watching to make sure I don't lure the wolves into a trap."

"But that's exactly what you're doing."

"Yeah, but Vang doesn't know that. He may be a genius in the lab but he doesn't know Jack about the woods. He won't know what I'm doing until it's done." Hunter took a moment. "Hopefully."

Cathcart continued, "But the smell of dynamite, or gunpowder, won't give you away?"

"I smell like gunpowder all the time, and they know it. A little more isn't gonna make any difference." Hunter bowed his head. "I have to lure one of them close enough to blow it to kingdom come. Then I'll be coming back here fast and I guarantee you I'll have company, so be ready to throw down on them. I will probably need help." He paused. "In fact, I know I will."

Blackthorn revealed rare discomfort. "How are you going to trap one of them?"

"I'll just have to wing it. What do they say? *Carpe Diem*?"

"Seize the day?"

"I reckon this is it."

"That child," Blackthorn threw a gesture. "The small one?"

Hunter glanced at the table. "Emily? What about her?"

"She wants to sit with Ben."

"Bring her up here."

Emily followed Blackthorn to Hunter's side and they both smiled at one another. Then Hunter offered her his hand, and she grasped it. Emily fearlessly followed him to stand beside Ben's head. The bear looked up as Hunter put his hand on Emily's shoulder and emphasized, "Ben! This is Emily! Emily, he knows about two hundred words, so he'll understand most of what you say if you keep it simple."

She smiled, "House trained."

Hunter laughed, "Yeah. Just talk to him like he's a real smart dog. He'll understand. And he likes you, so you'll be safe with him. In fact, you'll be the safest person in the house. You good?"

"Yeah. Thank you."

Hunter paused and, for a moment, his mind was back to a time when he played with bears and wolves deep in the forest, all alone, and no one knew his name. He saw himself in her, and it touched him with a remembrance of a true peace he had once known – a peace that was his life before his skills led the civilized world to use him for darker things. It was a place he wished he could return to, though he knew he never could.

"Yeah," Hunter said quietly, "you're welcome."

Hunter moved back to Blackthorn who watched with some amusement as Emily lowered herself to her knees and reached out with no trepidation or hesitation whatsoever to lay her hand on Bend's head – a Grizzly head twice as wide as her body. She gently began singing to him and stroking his neck and Ben blinked. Blackthorn thought he heard a rough moan.

Hunter picked up the Marlin and levered a round. He took a moment to stare at the darkening clouds. "Give me three hours. If I'm not back, get off this land."

"What are the odds of making the road?"

"Better than the odds of surviving another night."

"How will I know if you're dead?"

"If I'm not back in three hours, I'm dead."

"What about Ben?"

"He can take care of himself." Hunter slid out the Ruger and rotated the cylinder, checking rounds. "After you get these people to London, you can send somebody back for him."

"Somebody? Like who?"

Hunter gazed at how Ben had lifted his head to press his nose against Emily's face, nudging and sniffing. And Emily laughed, hugging his head.

"Bring her with you," he said, and smiled. "He'll follow her anywhere she goes."

CHAPTER TWENTY-FOUR

N orth York Moor was not the poorest ground for tracking Hunter had ever seen but it was a cellar battle. Ground water absorbed prints faster than they could age. Edges collapsed under the soaked weight of the soil leaving nothing to indicate direction. Mulling, that might indicate five minutes of hesitation, was so spread that it could mean five hours.

During Hunter's first foray into the moor the Amphicyon had steadily climbed a long, gradual grade. The ground had grown firmer and dryer until sign became obvious. But that was an exception to the rule. Tracking across the rest of this moor was like tracking across the surface of the ocean. It was always moving, always changing.

Kneeling outside the fence, staring at where the Scimitar landed, Hunter saw that the track had almost already vanished. Blood was plentiful but that didn't indicate much. He already knew it was wounded.

He raised his face to the forest expecting to see red eyes staring back at him. But there was nothing. Still, they were close. They would be watching. So he would give them the impression that he was easy prey, that he was unaware of their presence. Then they might become overconfident and careless.

He calculated options for the best place to ambush one of the wolves. The manor was no place to detonate five sticks of dynamite. The stable was a ruin, the shed was too small and there was only one way in and out. Hunter might lead one of them inside but there would be no escape. So, by process of elimination, only the moor remained.

Hunter scanned the vast tree line to his left. Yeah, they were in there. It was time to get them moving.

Holding the rifle at port arms as if he expected an attack at any moment, Hunter moved soundlessly forward until he entered the forest. The darkness immediately enveloped him as if he'd stepped into night. He thought of revealing the sound of his steps but decided against it; they expected him to be moving in silence, that's what he'd do.

Two hundred feet inside the trees, Hunter stopped with head bowed. He trusted his instincts as much as his senses and he could feel something moving through the trees long before he heard it. But there was nothing close and he was glad of it. He needed time to find the right site.

One direction was the same as another so Hunter moved alongside a stream that wound like a black snake into deeper shadow. He followed the dead water across a wide and empty field to an obscure oasis of trees.

He need a rock formation that would channel the force of the blast but he also needed a shield strong enough to deflect it away from his own body. Then, if he succeeded in destroying one of them and – far less likely – survived the blast, he'd have to outrun the survivors back to the relative security of the manor.

Searching, always searching, Hunter finally saw a narrow cleft between two house-sized boulders inside the oasis. The very stream he had been following ran through them and he knew the blocks were solid enough to contain the force of the dynamite. The would channel the concussion along the length of the crevice and upward. If one of the wolves were inside it, the beast would be maimed if not killed outright.

Glancing over his shoulder, he saw that the patch of moss-covered trees surrounding him stood like an island enclosed by a ring of dual-canopy forest impenetrable to light. They would be coming from some edge of that forest, but he didn't know what angle. All he knew was that there would be no time to redeem a mistake.

Hunter froze as he sensed something.

He heard nothing, but he knew. They were closing. He could feel it the same way a man can feel the air thickening and condensing before a heavy cold descends. And it gave urgency to how he was going to detonate the dynamite with a rifle shot and survive the blast. As they drew closer, they would pick up the pace even more. Already the fowl had fallen silent.

You're out of time …

It wouldn't work to simply leave his scent through this cleft, along with the dynamite, and hope they stepped into it. The mere sight of something unfamiliar would provoke them to avoid this cut altogether. They needed some incentive to enter the kill box.

They needed to see *him* in it.

Hunter unslung the rope looped around his shoulder and snapped open the grappling hook. On the west side of the crevice stood a tall cypress. He hurled the hook high and it dug into a limb only seconds before he ran out of rope. Then he took the dynamite and tied it to the distended rope. Now the dynamite hung from something like a pendulum from the higher rock.

He took twenty steps to the slab he could use to shield himself. The boulder rested on the far side of a slight depression leaving yet another creek between the rocks. On the steep grade beyond the dead water Hunter tested the strength of the hook's hold; it was solid. Calculating, he drew back his arm, clenching the dynamite, and mentally rehearsed what he would do and whether it would work or not was irrelevant. If it didn't work, he was dead. There was no time for anything else.

Now he had to wait in plain sight.

To them, humans were easy prey. And to see a human in the open provoked an instantaneous response. So when they saw him, they'd forget traps and simply charge. Hunter turned his head, again measuring the distance to the boulder which might save his life. It was no more than forty feet from where he stood. But whether he could cover forty feet before they raced three hundred feet from the trees was impossible to know.

Grimly Hunter set his eyes on the tree line. All of this land was swamp and forest but at two hundred feet the old forest goliaths thickened to create a triple canopy that defied the day. It was always night within that stand and the dampness of the ground would prevent Hunter from hearing their approach. He would have been able to determine their location from the calls of fowl but all the fowl had fled.

Hunter lifted the Marlin to ensure a shell was chambered. He had already made certain that four more cartridges were loaded for a total of five shots. But all he'd be able to use was one because, if he missed, he wouldn't have time for another. He also wouldn't have time to run. They'd be on top of him in a heartbeat and finish him fast. At least, he hoped they'd finish him fast. It was distressing to think they might eat him alive.

Carefully descending from the protective slab of granite, Hunter moved to the fringe of the island. He waited for two minutes, but nothing emerged from the tree line, and he began to question his instincts. He backed up slightly to increase his field of vision, half-suspecting they might have suspected this trap and were moving to outflank him, but he saw nothing. Out of sheer nervousness he again checked to make sure a cartridge was in the –

Two shapes materialized outside the distant wall. Their eyes instantly locked on Hunter but – to his surprise – they didn't charge, and so he decided to give them some incentive. He raised the rifle, picked the one to the left, and fired three quick shots. Even before the smoke cleared Hunter knew he must have shot true because it had leaped aside to come down with a roar. Then they launched themselves into an explosive run straight toward him.

Without bothering to sling the rifle, Hunter spun. In three quick steps he snatched the dynamite, never missing a stride, and leaped across the depression, scrambling up the boulder. He risked a single glance to judge their location; they were less than fifty feet from the granite and closing fast.

With the alarming sight Hunter released the dynamite from his grip. It swung on the rope in a perfect arch to intercept the charging Amphicyon and, in the same split-second, Hunter set the Marlin hard into his shoulder. He followed the dynamite and as the first wolf entered the cleft, so did the dynamite.

Hunter fired.

Hearing nothing, Hunter barely knew he had been thrown off the back of the rock by the concussion and he couldn't find the Marlin but it didn't matter as he rolled tight to the rock and covered his head. In the same instant, fire rolled over the boulder and he held his breath until it passed. Debris rained for a long moment – a mixture of wood, rock, and water – and Hunter frantically drew the Ruger at his waist. He was too disoriented to walk and so he rolled to the edge of the bounder and leveled.

Smoke and flame hid whatever might be within the cleft and Hunter was forced to wait patiently until he saw a red and black mass within the gray slabs. After ten seconds the smoke dispersed so that he beheld the mangled, bloody body of an Amphicyon. As Hunter stared, he managed to stand. He holstered the pistol and picked up the Marlin, shoving in rounds. Then, rifle level, he cautiously approached the body and saw that it wasn't the Alpha.

The blast had apparently gone off in its face because there was no head or shoulders. There were only the remnants of front legs, a torso, and two back legs. The blast had done the job. Hunter suddenly came to life with an alarming thought and spun looking for the second Amphicyon. But the big one, the Alpha, was nowhere to be seen.

It had survived.

Only Hunter's eyes shifted as he began scanning all that could be seen but the Alpha had obviously retreated. Perhaps it had even retreated to die, but that was doubtful. If the gigantic wolf had not been standing directly in the face of that blast, it had survived. Wounded – *maybe* – but it'd return soon enough to pick up the hunt.

Hunter needed at least a half hour to reach the safety of the manor, so he began moving. It took him a hundred yards to find his balance, then he picked up the pace until he was fairly running through the trees. He wasn't worried now about coming up on the Alpha by mistake. If that happened, he'd die, rifle or no rifle. His only chance lay in reaching the manor before it tracked him down.

Within a mile trees were flying past Hunter so that he couldn't determine what they even were. But he wasn't truly reading them; his eyes were focused on the twenty feet of ground in front of his feet and nothing more. He was well aware that if he made a single misstep – if he twisted his ankle or knee – the wolf would catch up to him easily enough.

Soon he reached a long layer of mud and slowed down to creep across it. One slip here would be the end. He knew it wasn't quicksand but it was still treacherous terrain. Then he bulled his way through thick brush, uncaring of the thorns and limbs that tore his clothes and skin. He was only careful to keep his face low; he couldn't afford to lose an eye. Finally, thirty minutes later, he staggered from the wall of trees surrounding the estate. The manor loomed large and inviting in the lesser gloom of the glade and Hunter loped forward until he reached the fence. He had no intention of climbing this formidable barrier. He'd run alongside it until he reached the gate.

Leaning on the bars of the fence, fingers slick with mud and sweat, Hunter paused. He was drenched in perspiration and the blood of a hundred cuts. For the first time he noticed a deep incision along the back of his hand. He was distressed and inhaled painfully, struggling to remain conscious.

A horrifying roar spun Hunter and he saw the massive black and red body of the Alpha as it tore free from the trees. It leaped forward, closing with surreal speed.

Hunter flung off his pack and slung it into the spikes of the fence. The pack snagged and he leaped high, furiously hauling on the strap. He slammed a hand down on the crest and, pulling up with all the strength he had left and threw himself over the barrier like a man escaping a fire. In a blur he landed on the far side and only then did it occur to him that the fence wouldn't stop this beast. It would simply leap over it.

A foreleg exploded out through the bars and curled, claws digging deeply into Hunter's right shoulder. Then he was jerked back with stunning force into the fence. The Marlin went flying in the attack and Hunter didn't waste a second considering the loss as he fast-drew the Ruger and fired blindly into the primeval force that was tearing him limb from limb.

He knew he couldn't fight this beast off. He couldn't breathe. He couldn't see. He was losing all feeling in his arms and legs. Hunter knew he was roaring in agony and the realization made him fight even harder.

For some reason this animal was intent on ripping his arm free, but that wouldn't be the end of it. Then it would leap over this barrier and snap his head off with a single bite. Hunter was beginning to lose consciousness and dimly sensed a haze engulfing his mind. In a pathetic attempt to keep fighting, he drew his bowie. He knew it was futile but —

A *mountain* descended upon Hunter with a deafening roar. It blocked out the sky and then a tree – it *must* have been a tree – smashed down with blinding speed to blast away the leg imprisoning him and by instinct Hunter staggered forward. In shock he turned and saw Ben lash out to strike the Amphicyon across its wedged head. Then a shot exploded, stunning Hunter by its closeness, and the Alpha howled, tearing away from the fence.

Hunter glimpsed Blackthorn grimly standing in front of him with a smoking rifle, his chin uplifted, his eyes on fire and a terrible frown on his face. Quick stepping to the side, his gaze darting, Blackthorn seemed to find the object of his search and sharply lifted the rifle and fired again. He stared a moment more before he angrily cracked the rifle open, throwing out two shells. He quickly reloaded from his jacket and snapped it shut.

"Blast!" he gasped. "I missed the second shot!"

Blinking slowly, Hunter realized he couldn't talk, so he didn't try. Unconsciously holding his wounded shoulder, he staggered forward. But within seconds Blackthorn lifted his uninjured arm and supported him and they walked slowly to the manor, the detective attempting to move no faster than Hunter could place one foot before the other. Then Ben surged ahead and stalked the path as if to clear the way.

They staggered under an agonizing, forbidding sky of storm as they entered the broken manor together, leaving a torrent of blood on the stone. Shouts of alarm greeted them but Hunter couldn't feel the hands that removed him from Blackthorn's grip because all he felt was agony.

* * *

An hour later Hunter grimaced as he rolled his left shoulder trying to determine how badly he was injured. He could move his arm within normal range forward and back and to the side but only with knifing pains from the wounds that Blackthorn had sewn shut.

Until the detective took charge of the first aid kit, it never occurred to Hunter that a former Special Air Service commando like the investigator would, of course, also be a trained combat medic. And Blackthorn did his former service proud; he cleaned, sewed, and bandaged Hunter's shoulder with the skill of an emergency room surgeon. At a point Hunter remarked, "Seems like you've done this before."

Intent upon his work, Blackthorn's lips barely moved as he murmured, "I've done this work on five men in a crashed chopper with my hair and fingers on fire, boyo."

"You don't have any hair."

"Exactly. But I still have my fingers."

Cathcart knelt to examine the bandages covering his torso and shoulder. "You did a good job, Blackthorn," she remarked. "Not too tight. Not too loose. Just about right."

She lifted a small flashlight and peered into each eye; Hunter gave her no trouble. He didn't know, himself, how badly he was hurt. Then Cathcart leaned back, saying confidently, "You're in light shock. But that's to be expected. Blood loss will do that."

"How much blood loss?"

"Not too much. You'll feel like yourself in a few hours if you eat something. Right now you need some fruit. I'll get a bowl from the kitchen." Cathcart placed an open bottle of water in his hand. "Try sipping this. Don't drink too fast. You know the drill."

As she disappeared in the direction of the kitchen, Hunter blinked, trying to fully regain focus. He was not in shock so much from blood loss as he was from having experienced the incomprehensible strength, the sheer prehistoric might that had pulled him into those bars. There was no doubt that he would have been torn to pieces if Ben had not intervened.

Now Hunter understood in a much more detailed way why these things were so hard to kill. They were unimaginably strong, yes, but that was just part of it. They also had the hide of a rhinoceros. The skin wasn't just tough. It was thick and heavy like Kevlar. And in his mind Hunter saw again the skeleton at the Smithsonian. Even its bones were designed like armor with the ribs wide and flat and closely set.

In that faint, flashing split-second when Hunter turned and saw Ben, a giant of a Grizzly, raging against the Alpha with only iron bars separating them, he had the impression that they were almost exactly equal in size. The enormous wolf was at least half a ton of pure muscle – the same as Ben – and with each standing on hind legs, both touched ten feet. But there was no way Hunter could have determined which was faster. The human mind can't register movement at that speed. By the time the eye perceives and the brain comprehends that one had moved, the blow was finished and a dozen more have been throw, each equally unseen.

The remembrance provoked Hunter to consider how Vang, in his form as a Scimitar, ever mastered the Amphicyon in the first place. It couldn't be the same mastery a man can hold over a bear or lion. The Amphicyon was too incommensurate a force to submit to anything weaker than itself. So the only alternative was that the Scimitar was superior in strength, and that was how Vang had mastered it. He could have beaten it down in a dozen ways, but however it was done, it was successful. And it implied that Vang in Scimitar form was literally a force of nature. The thought, in total, was vividly alarming because Hunter sensed that, in the end, his personal battle with Vang would come down to flesh and blood and bone.

"Yeah," Hunter said hoarsely, "it figures …"

"What's that, mate?" Blackthorn came away from the window where he'd been standing like the Rock of Gibraltar. "Try and rest, Hunter. It's still an hour until full dark. Would you care for a pint?"

At the question Cathcart stepped up with a platter of sliced fruit, laying it on a table beside Hunter. "That's not what he needs right now, commander," she said pleasantly enough. "I'm sure you gentlemen can't wait to diminish the major's very impressive bar, but right he needs fruit and water. Then both of you should eat a full meal. And if you want a pint, I'll serve it up myself. After all, you two will be fighting off demons in a few hours."

"Make no mistake," said Blackthorn. "You'll be armed, as well." He seemed to be preparing for death as he added, "Mr. Hunter is a capable man. More than capable. And I am no milksop, myself. But what will come at nightfall does not belong to this earth. And certainly not to this age." He grew pensive. "But this is what happens when man believes so arrogantly that he can be like god. Anarchy follows and, always, death. What happens then is beyond the law, and beyond the abilities of the law to address. It must be met on its own terms if there is to be any peace."

Cathcart's head tilted. "What are its own terms?"

"Savagery and brute force." Blackthorn swept back his coat to insure that his revolver remained at his waist. "All they understand is what they would do unto others. You can't reason with them. They respect nothing. All they understand is violence. And violence is the only thing that will stop them."

Slowly chewing on fruit, Hunter raised his gaze when Cathcart asked, "What about you, Hunter? Are you to be as efficient as the commander?" One corner of her mouth lifted in a smile. "Perhaps Dr. Vang and his pet have met their match?"

Hunter spat seeds into the fire. "Vang is the greatest danger. He's ten times more dangerous than the wolf."

"Why is that?"

"You can say that wolf is vicious because it kills for food. But men do far worse. Men don't just kill for food. They'll kill you for your shoes, for a bigger piece of grass or some trinket. And some kill just so they can celebrate the good old-fashioned joy of killing. And that's what makes Vang more dangerous than the wolf. Vang's doing it for the pleasure."

"So what's our play?" she asked.

"Strike first."

"That's it?"

Hunter's efforts to keep his shoulder from stiffening were not having the desired result. He groaned, "Yeah. Pretty much. It's too late to track them. It's pointless, anyway. They'll be here around dark. All we can do is be ready when they get here and hit them before they hit us."

Cathcart cast a gaze. "What about the family?"

"There's no safe place to put them. They might as well stay in here with us. But they're welcome to have a gun if they want."

Blackthorn lifted his rifle from a chair. "Again, don't forget to include yourself in that, Dr. Cathcart. I don't expect you'll be too apt to die like a butchered sheep when they get to you."

Cathcart muttered, "Believe me, commander, I have no intentions of going down without a fight. And I *can* shoot."

As if to drive home a point, Blackthorn solemnly added, "I understand you've devoted your life to saving others, doctor. To mercy. But make no mistake. In this, you must have no mercy. When you see that you have the chance, you must strike as savagely as you can. And strike to kill. Because they'll do the same to you."

Milton, for the first time since the conference upstairs, spoke in a ghastly, coarse voice. "Commander?"

Blackthorn half-turned. "Yes, Major?"

Milton pointed along a hall with a trembling hand. "Behind the third door to your right is a small workshop where my maintenance man keeps his tools. There is a vice grip in there. I suggest that you take an adequate number of rifles and shorten the barrels with a hacksaw so they are more manageable in close quarters. And I would appreciate you doing the same with my personal rifle. It shouldn't require more than a few minutes."

"Well done," stated Blackthorn after glanced at the closet. "Well done, indeed. Hunter? Your rifle? Would you like for me to take your –"

"Not on your life."

"Come now, old man. It might save your life."

Hunter's gaze was sullen. "I'll take my chances."

Turning, Blackthorn said, "Young Milton! Come here, lad! You're an able-bodied man!"

Barron Milton met Blackthorn at the gun cabinet where the investigator knelt, mumbling, "Yes, there seems ample ammunition for ..." He began picking out rifles and laying them across Barron Milton's outstretched arms. Finally he was finished and stood, "There. We'll need to shorten up these rifles in the tool room. Follow me."

Without carrying any rifle but his own and followed by "Young Milton" staggering under the weight of seven, Blackthorn disappeared down the hall. As they were gone, Cathcart laughed, "I think he just wants to give that kid something to do. Get his mind off things." She paused. "Actually, that's a good idea. I wish somebody would take *my* mind off things."

Hunter asked, "How are you feeling?"

"I've been better. So what happened out there?"

Hunter's expression was dismissive. "I got one of the wolves. But not the Alpha. I don't know how he survived the explosion, but he did." He sighed. 'He's tough. I've already hit him a dozen times and Blackthorn hit him at least once. He's got plenty of bullets in him and he hasn't even slowed down."

Cathcart leaned back in her adjacent chair drawing up a single leg. "Wasn't Luther, after his transformation, basically bullet proof? I think I got that from Chaney."

"Basically, yeah."

"But Vang isn't?"

"Well," Hunter deliberated with a pause, "he *wasn't* at the beginning of this but he seems to be evolving on a physical level. He can still be wounded but bullets are less effective every time I go up against him." He grunted, "Not that it matters too much. The wolves aren't bullet resistant either and that Alpha is still running around."

He hesitated, staring off. "The only way to kill Vang is to overload that healing ability of his by inflicting an ungodly level of damage in a very short period of time. It can be done. The trick will be keeping him close long enough to finish the job because if Vang senses he's in trouble, he'll escape. And there's not much that can stop him."

"Did you see him out there today?"

"No. But he'll be here tonight. I guarantee it."

She turned her face to the moor and wrapped arms around her knees, staring before she asked, "Why is it so hard to track out there?"

Hunter answered lazily. "It's just the terrain. In some parts of the world, tracking him down would be a good move. Like in the Sahara. Or Death Valley. But tracking in this mess is like tracking something across quicksand. Tracks only last a couple of hours. If that long."

"Was tracking ever a challenge for you?"

Hunter laughed, "It's always a challenge. It's never gets easier. You just get used to it." He realized he'd needed that laugh as he continued, "Every track has its own set of problems. It's hard to track in the Appalachians because of ground cover."

"What's that?"

"Leaves and loam and debris. You've got centuries of that mess and it won't hardly take a track. You step on it and make an impression but as soon as you take your foot off, it bounces back to whatever shape it's had for a hundred years. You can still read broken blades of grass, or twigs. Leaves that are moved out of place. Mud that's lifted and carried. That's what tracking in the woods is like. Deserts give you a whole different set of problems."

"Like what?"

From her attentiveness Hunter sensed that Cathcart needed this conversation as a distraction from her fear, and there was nothing wrong with that, so he continued, "Wind, mostly. If the wind is blowing steady, it can move tracks inch by inch. Then the prints you're following are half a mile from where they began. So you could be dead on the tracks and he's miles from where you think he is. You're tracking the wind."

"How do you deal with that?"

"Well, the wind is what's moving them, so you move against the wind and hope to pick up the original tracks."

"Hope?"

Hunter stared. "Yeah. What about it?"

"I thought tracking was a skill."

"Tracking is a combination of qualities," Hunter said easily. "It's good eyesight, concentration, determination. You have to know a lot about animals. How they live, what they eat – their habits. A lot of times I can just look at a track and tell you where it came from and where it's going. And then, sometimes, there's a lot of guesswork. I mean, you know a beaver isn't going to wander too far from water. So when you lose his track, you keep moving along the water's edge. You'll pick him up sooner or later."

"Unless he swam off."

"He doesn't sleep in the water. He comes out to eat. To cut down a tree. To chew something up just for the sake of chewing something up. And he'll stay close to his den. So you just keep moving up and down the stream and you'll eventually come across him. It takes patience."

"Patience and time," Cathcart smiled. "How sophisticated. And I thought you were some sort of wilderness wildman. But you're actually quite sophisticated, aren't you?"

"Sure. Wanna tango?"

She smiled, "I'd love to."

Hunter gazed at Milton who seemed to be fading badly under the stress. He looked a lifetime older. "Major?" he asked.

Milton lifted his head. "Yes?"

"Anyone ever call you Yoda when you were on safari?"

The question inspired a weak smile, and Milton said, "Even in those years when I was pretending to be Tarzan, I wasn't any good at it, Mr. Hunter."

Cathcart gave Milton her undivided attention. "What was Africa like in those days, Major?"

"Oh," he gestured weakly, "those days are gone, child."

"But not the men who lived them. You're one of the few who remember it. Tell us. What it was like?"

Milton's pale blue eyes seemed to suddenly stare far away. "Well, young lady, I can tell you about the most remarkable thing I ever witnessed in nature. And it was not in Africa. It was in Montana many years ago. You see, I traveled to America in search of escaped Nazis who fled to New York City after the Armistice. And many did, you know."

"Did the Americans know?"

"Oh, yes, certainly. The FBI interviewed them and left them alone. And we, meaning agents of MI-6, were told that the Nazis were not to be touched for war crimes. Consequently, I asked for a vacation so that I could see a little bit of America, and I was given two weeks. But it was not New York that I wanted to see. I wanted to see the old west. And so, three days later, I was in Montana where I met a friend of mine from the war. He was an American soldier and took me up a mountain where he said he had been watching an event of great interest unfold."

At the remembrance he chuckled, "As it happened, we camped near a den of wolves. There were at least a dozen of them, and a leader. Yes, you can always identify the leader by how he watches over the others. He sits on a rock high above the rest and stares over his pack and the forest, always on guard. But, in any case, my friend told me that a large Grizzly had attacked this very pack three years ago and killed the parents of that particular wolf – the leader. And now that bear had returned to the forest. My friend told me he wanted to see if the wolf would remember. He wanted to know if wolves remembered events like human beings – if they have emotions and feelings like human beings. And it was not more than a day before that great wolf descended from his rock and gathered all the males into something like … I don't know how to describe it … *like a lynch mob*!" He laughed, "You know what I mean, doctor? Like in those old western movies where the mob comes down the street with shotguns and torches and hauls some poor bloke out of jail and hangs him?"

Cathcart asked, "So you're saying wolves take things personally? Like human beings?"

"He's right," said Hunter. "Animals take things personally just like people. Bears, too."

Milton continued, "So the leader took these wolves – it was exactly seven of them – into the woods. And on the first night we heard the sounds of a terrible battle somewhere close. But, of course, we were not going to venture too far from the fire. However, on the next day, we followed the tracks until we came across the body of that Grizzly. Wolf prints were everywhere. Blood marked the entire glade. And the bear bore a thousand wounds that had finally brought him down." He shook his head, "I was astonished because I did not think wolves preyed on bears. And my mate told me, 'They didn't kill him for food.' I said, 'Why did they kill him?' And he said, 'The leader killed him to avenge his parents. He killed him for hate. For love. Like a human being might do.'"

Milton lifted a finger, "You see, animals are more human than many human beings. They have similar thoughts and emotions. And that gave me a new appreciation for nature. An appreciation I had never imagined. In fact, it was that experience that inspired me to become a conservationist and, ultimately, the philanthropist I came to be."

"But you're a famous hunter," observed Cathcart.

Milton nodded wearily before saying, "Yes, most only know me as a hunter. But it's been my life's work to preserve these great species, not harm them. And the specimens I have killed, I killed because they were dying a horrible, lingering death, and then some were killing people. And I preferred that the Wildlife people use me instead of some stampcrab who would have butchered them with all the skill of a broken blunderbuss. So I gave them a quick and merciful death with the dignity they deserved." His eyes narrowed as if in agreement within himself. "Yes. I've given ten billion pounds to conservation and preservation to restore all manner of species and habitats, so this room is not a trophy hall, doctor. It is a shrine to remember those great beasts that should be remembered because they were, in the end, as great as Churchill or Eisenhower or any other hero that men revere. Among their own kind they were champions of a great age. And we will not see their like again."

CHAPTER TWENTY-FIVE

B lackthorn re-entered the great hall holding a rifle in each hand. Trailing him was a much-belabored Barron Milton holding six heavy elephant rifles in his arms. The detective handed Milton his weapon with, "There you are, Major. It's cut down to manageable length for close quarters battle, I should think." He took another rifle from Baron and delivered it to Cathcart. "Do you know how to use a rifle like this?" he asked.

She cracked it open and loaded it. "I'm from Minnesota, commander."

"I thought you were from London."

"I just work in London. I grew up in Minnesota. So, yes, I know how to shoot. Although I don't know what I can hit with this cutdown thing."

Milton eased himself to his feet and took a fighting stance with the stock close to his hip and his left hand firmly over the top of the barrels. "This is how you do it, lass. You fire from the hip, not the shoulder. And be sure to firmly hold your hand over the top of the barrel and aim low because it will rise much more than you expect."

Cathcart stood and duplicated the stance, then said easily, "Okay. I think I've got it."

"We'll practice in a bit," Blackthorn said to her. "Two or three shots and I'm sure you'll master it." He turned toward the family. "Come, young Milton, let's see who cares to defend themselves."

Barron followed the commander to the far end of the room as Milton slowly examined his expensive, ornate rifle so emasculated by Blackthorn's thoroughness. "The most necessary things always seem to be the most regrettable," he muttered. Then he turned a foreboding stare upon Hunter, his old hands tightening on the steel.

"But this is a kill I will not regret."

* * *

A large syringe filled with the amber-colored serum remained and he stared over it calculating the risk of using so much. While still in the laboratory he had not run an analysis of what transformation might be triggered by such an immense infusion, and he did not have the equipment to do so now. But he knew it would be cataclysmic. And perhaps fatal. But he had come too far. There was only one means by which he could survive this now.

He had to finish this hunter. But in order to kill the hunter he would also have to kill the bear because it would defend his master. He did not doubt that he could kill them all – including the bear – but he would need to be far more powerful to take more punishment than he'd suffered until now. And that would require more serum.

Gazing down at his naked chest he saw swollen red splotches where the bullets had wounded him. Blood continued to drip from his mouth and nose and he knew any other human being would be dead. Although the terrible tears in his flesh had closed, the agony remained. And the pain and swelling inspired him to end this tonight because he knew there was no reversing any of this. He was in too deep, so he had to finish them.

Or he would die.

If he had known that he could have survived yet another bullet from the hunter's weapons, he would have slaughtered his enemy last night on the stairs. But he had not known. He had not even been certain that he would survive the fall. But he had hit the ground and was running from the mansion before he even realized he'd landed. As he wiped blood from his mouth again he recognized that this magnificent strength was saving him from the weakness that reduced the rest of them to delicious human morsels he would consume as he pleased.

Yes, the serum had saved him so far.

And it would save him now.

He lifted the syringe, injecting the full portion into his arm. Then he leaned his head back, knowing the white, thrilling, ascending strength flooding through his veins like lava heating his heart and soul and brain making him the god he wanted to be. No, he knew was not god. But it made no difference.

He was the same as god.

It was enough.

He didn't glance again at the walls of the hut where he had been forced to rest since the bear entered the mansion. He had been hiding in the wings of the castle, but that changed where his most hated enemy arrived – the enemy that killed Luther.

Since that day he had hidden within these granite slabs. But this was his last night in these hated ruins. After the Hunter's Moon faded from the sky, he would take the limitless fortune that would remain and live forever with nothing but the blood and the feast. He would live in a castle with walls, and he would hire an army to protect himself, and he would consume all who were brought to him.

As his vision began to explode and blur before changing to that kaleidoscope that could read light and heat and darkness in infinite shades, he blinked, focusing, and saw the last message on the cell phone – a message that read, "IT'S TIME. KILL THEM ALL."

The transformation was so powerful that it took him to his knees and he felt the agony that erupted from his jaws as every fiber in his body remorselessly exploded. He could feel the molten, liquid fire of the Scimitar recreating him into the image he saw Luther embody before he leaped through the window, escaping into that frozen wilderness where the hunter killed him.

His eyes bulged as his spine was arched in anguish as fangs opened with the rage …

He roared.

* * *

Hunter threw up his head.

In the blackness of the moor, something had changed. He couldn't hear it, but he felt it. "Yeah," Hunter hefted his rifle, "I know. You're coming." He stared into the night longer, listening, but there was nothing.

Come on ...

It was still miles away, and it'd be moving slowly. He would take no chances tonight. He would close the distance carefully and silently, staying in the shadows, letting his last wolf move ahead of him, searching for traps. In a few hours he would be here. And then this long night would end for all of them one way or another.

Milton was sleeping soundlessly on a couch in the trophy room and Blackthorn was mingling with various family, no doubt continuing his investigation, while Hunter continued to rest with Cathcart close. She had become disturbingly quiet, so Hunter asked, "What's on your mind?"

"Hmm?" She turned her face to him. "Oh, I was just thinking."

"Want to talk about it?"

Cathcart chuckled, "You a psychiatrist now?"

He shrugged, "I've spent so much time alone in the wild, I've become my own psychiatrist. Yeah, I'm always asking myself if I'm going crazy, which is the only way I know I'm not."

"Because only crazy people think they're perfectly sane?" she smiled. "Yeah, I've heard that. Actually, I think it's true."

Hunter shook his head, "How did someone as smart as you ever get involved in this mess, Cathcart?"

"You know, you could call me 'Eve.'"

"All right. Eve."

Cathcart relaxed deeper into the chair. "I joined because I thought this thing's DNA could be a miracle cure for a thousand diseases."

"As a snake oil salesman might say."

"I'm not joking."

Waiting patiently, Hunter said nothing.

Cathcart leaned into it. "Listen, Hunter, I'm not crazy. This is not the only animal that has offered a cure for human disease. Did you know that Zebrafish produce a protein that might be able to regulate Type Two Diabetes? Or that there's a compound in sharks called squalamine that destroys infections in the human liver? And do you know where angiotensin comes from? It regulates blood pressure."

"Surprise me."

"From snake venom."

Hunter laughed, "How did they discover that?"

She gestured blandly, "It's obvious when you think about it. Doctors have known forever that pit viper venom lowers human blood pressure. Lowers it to the point of death, in fact. So somebody had a 'Eureka' moment and said, 'Hey! Let's use the venom of a pit viper to medicate people with high blood pressure!' And now it's one of the most commonly used high blood pressure medicines in the world. So using this Scimitar to constitute a cure for human diseases is not exactly an earth-shattering concept. In fact, that's how Vang justified the funding for this in the first place. He said it was 'for the good of all mankind.' Ha! What a crock! That was *my* agenda. It wasn't *his* agenda. His agenda was to become immortal and take the secret with him to his grave. And if he had to become a monster to do, he'd do it." A pause. "Well, that's not exactly right. He was always a monster. But now he looks like one."

Hunter blinked slowly before he asked even more slowly, "So that's what got you into all this? To cure people?"

"Yeah," she nodded. "The Scimitar offered endless possibilities if we could only isolate specific amino acids and proteins. In my mind it was something like the Holy Grail." Her lips came together. "I was betting everything I had on it. I was betting my career that proteins unique to this animal – proteins that we can't synthesize – would cure unending human illnesses. And that's why I took the risk of working with Vang."

Hunter didn't have the heart to tell her the parable about 'the best intentions.' Her sincerity was evident in her earnestness, her voice, her face, and it was, in a way, how he'd made his own fortune.

Years ago he discovered a plant in South America that the natives had been using for centuries to cure blood infections. Actually, to say he 'discovered' it was misleading. He'd 'learned about it.' Then he found it, convinced a pharmaceutical company to perfect it for human trials, and consequently made a fortune. The residuals he'd already made were enough for him to live in any style he chose for the next three hundred years.

"Somebody once said that the greatest pharmacy on earth belongs to God," continued Cathcart. "And they were right. Nature is the greatest pharmacy and God is the greatest physician. All we have to do is discover his secrets." She straightened her arms between her knees and turned her face to the fire as she asked, "Is there any chance I might be able to get my hands on Vang's body? That is, if we survive this and he doesn't?"

"Not a chance," Hunter shook his head. "Blackthorn's boss will collect Vang just like they collected Luther up in Alaska." He looked toward the moor. "There won't be any evidence about what happened here. No bodies. Nothing."

"Do you think Blackthorn's people are watching us?"

"Yeah." He became pensive. "Probably with drones since I haven't heard any helicopters. But it doesn't matter. They know what's happening. And when we kill it –"

"*If* we kill it …"

"*When* we kill it, they'll come for the body. Then they'll take it to a lab and continue Vang's work for him."

Cathcart paled. "Are you saying you might have to track one of these things *again*?"

"It looks like my new career."

She sat sharply forward. "Well you can count me out of the next one! I am not built for fighting monsters!"

"I understand, Eve. *Believe me*. But that reminds me; I've been meaning to ask you something even if it sounds stupid."

She laughed without humor, "Finding something stupider than us being trapped in a castle by a demon is hard to beat."

"Is there any chance Vang will just die from this?"

"Why do you ask?"

Hunter's response was flat. "Because I'd rather Vang just dropped dead. It'd be a lot less trouble."

"I understand. But the answer is no. He won't die. Not on his own. Not for a long time."

"Can the effects of the serum be reversed?"

"Nope."

"Why?"

Her face revealed consternation before she said, "Okay. Look of it this way. People think that this serum 'clones' something. Like, it's 'clones' the Scimitar. But that is not what is happening. This serum is like a rabies virus. I mean, you're a wildlife expert. You know that there's no cure for rabies. Not in an animal or human being. So, once rabies takes hold in a creature's nervous system, it's irreversible." She waved, "Yeah, if they can catch rabies within the first six days of infection, they can counteract the virus. But the inoculation that prevents rabies from going full-blown doesn't actually get rid of the virus. It just neutralizes it. And right now – just like rabies – the Scimitar serum is reformatting Vang's brain, his nervous system, his skin and bones and everything else in him, to fit its new matrix. But *unlike* rabies, the Scimitar serum can't be neutralized because it changes the human DNA. It's part of Vang's nervous system now. It can't be taken 'out' of him because it *is* him." Cathcart stared closely. "Do you get it?"

"Yeah," said Hunter. "I get it. The serum has already rewired his nervous system. But that sounds purely physical. How can he … I don't know … override this new hard-wiring and change shape at will?"

"Again, think of it like rabies. That's the best analogy I can come up with." She framed her explanation with both hands. "When someone gets infected with rabies they begin to lose control of their breathing, their ability to control their muscles, their ability to concentrate. But in the early stages of rabies, a person can control all that to a degree. But later, once rabies has infecting enough neurons, they can't control it at all. The virus has their entire nervous system in its grip. The virus is making the decisions. And despite all Vang's testing, he knew that could happen to him. Forget the test subjects. Vang was still afraid the Scimitar serum would instantly take over and there would be no more Vang. But that's not what happened. Instead, Vang is *slowly* losing control of his synapses, his thoughts, his entire neural network. And that's why he can still control it to a degree. Why he can change back and forth. He's not completely 'gone' yet. He still has neurons that haven't been completely rewired.

"Now, the final effect of rabies is death because it shuts down the cerebellum. It destroys the body's ability to control our temperature, our breathing, our perspiration and heartbeat. All the unconscious things our brains do to keep us alive. But the Scimitar serum has the opposite effect when it's full blown. When the virus has completely overridden his human nervous system, when it achieves a threshold effect, the result will be a *superhuman* nervous system and a God-like immunity to every virus and disease known to mankind. And an extremely long life."

"You compare this to rabies," Hunter pondered. "But rabies is incredibly contagious and it's the most dangerous virus in the world. Could Vang infect anybody else with this?"

"You mean like if he attacked someone and by some bizarre act of God they actually live? Would they catch the effects of the Scimitar serum?"

"Yeah."

"No. That would take a massive infusion of the serum created in an electromagnetic matrix that Vang designed for it. It won't work in the earth's normal electromagnetic sphere. It requires a very delicate combination of factors to synthesize the initial serum." A pause. "After initial exposure, of course, all Vang needs are boosters to change. In that aspect it's very much *unlike* rabies that – as you know – can infect anybody, anywhere, anytime."

"How long does Vang have?" Hunter asked, squinting.

"Nobody lives forever."

Cathcart blew out a long breath. "That's anybody's guess because nobody knows how Vang modified the DNA, so he might live a thousand years. He might live even longer. I mean, he'll be immune to every virus, bacteria, and disease known to man. He'll have that Scimitar's iron-clad constitution, so he's not gonna drop dead from a heart attack or stroke." She leaned closer and lowered her tone. "Look, I know Vang sounds invincible. But you need to remember one thing because this is the heart of it. Vang may be immune to everything known to mankind. He may be able to heal up overnight from anything that doesn't kill him. But all that doesn't matter because he can always be killed by superior force. You can always just beat him to death."

Hunter laughed harshly, "I knew you'd say that."

Blackthorn arrived at their quiet tryst appearing a bit distressed if not perplexed. He sat heavily in a lush, brown leather recliner and leaned back, staring vacantly at the ceiling before he said, "I may need your help on this one, doctor."

Cathcart answered, "For what?"

He glanced at where Major Milton appeared to be sleeping soundly on the couch before he said, "Have you taken notice of the major's youngest daughter? The one who looks like a ghost?"

"Emily? Yes, I have. Why?"

"What are your thoughts?"

Casting a glance at Emily Milton, she answered, "Well, she's withdrawn. Scared. But as far as I can tell, she's acting perfectly normally for anyone in this miserable situation. Why? What are you looking for?"

"Do you think she could be working with Vang?"

Cathcart's eyes opened wide and remained that way. "Haven't we already gone over this, inspector? Why do you keep focusing on her?"

"I am quite serious."

"Oh, please, Blackthorn, I thought you were some kind of Grade-A Scotland Yard Sherlock Holmes dude." Cathcart stood and stared for a long moment over Emily, who appeared asleep on Ben's mountainous shoulder. "No, she's not involved. That's impossible."

"Why do you say that?"

"Because I know Vang, commander. He considers people like Emily to be meaningless and expendable." She added with contempt, "Vang holds to some kind of bloodless Darwinian philosophy. Survival of the fittest. If that child were dying of influenza, Vang wouldn't even treat her. He'd say she's weak and stupid and ugly and not worth saving."

Blackthorn's aspect was resolute. "What if he needed her?"

"Needed her for *what*?"

"To plant seeds in the mind of her father to leave all his assets to the oldest surviving child. To keep Vang appraised of her father's schedule. And, most critically, to provoke an atmosphere of fear within this home that would inevitably take her father where she was leading him to go." The detective hesitated. "Are you aware of what this family has discovered Emily doing as of late?"

Cathcart asked with a dead aspect, "No. What have they found her 'doing as of late?'"

"They've found her standing in the dark in her room talking to herself about a hyena. Perhaps she is remembering the trauma of her childhood when she was attacked by a hyena. Or perhaps she is doing it to encourage the others to fear the hyena outside this very door. The hyena that is stalking this family. The hyena that threatens them all – particularly their father. And, doubtless, the others would speak of their fears with the major – I do not believe for one moment that they have not – and he would, of course, contract their fear like some insidious disease and consequently alter his will. It would be a most malignant and effective way to affect the mind of a vulnerable old man."

"Good grief, Blackthorn!" Cathcart exclaimed. "You're ascribing an awful lot of cleverness to a little girl." She pointed to Emily. "The only safety that child has ever known has been living in this castle with her father. Do you seriously think she would sacrifice that just to work with a stranger like Vang? Or money that she'll never see? You do remember that she's going to be cared for by a trust fund, don't you? And do you think she could execute such a cold-blooded plan without making at least one of her siblings suspicious? You deal in probabilities, don't you?"

No answer.

"So do I," Cathcart continued, "and I'd estimate the probability of that timid little girl being in league with the devil to be exactly zero-point-zero. Squared."

Blackthorn did not seem moved. He turned his face to the fire as he asked moodily, "Hunter? What do your instincts tell you?"

Hunter didn't need to glance at Emily Milton. He'd already summed her up and simply said, "She's not part of it."

"How do you know?"

"I didn't say I knew, Blackthorn. You asked me what my instincts tell me and that's what they tell me."

"I am not convinced," Blackthorn disagreed. "She's too secretive. It's as if she's waiting for something."

"Maybe she is," offered Hunter. "But she ain't waitin' for that Scimitar any more than I am."

"Then what is she waiting for?"

"How would I know?" Hunter rose and knelt beside the hearth. He stoked the fire, then tossed in sticks before he set the poker aside. "I've met a lot of people who simply sit on the porch and stare off into space. I've done it myself often enough. I don't know what they're staring at. Or waiting for. Or remembering. But they were no more dangerous than that little girl. So she might be waiting for something – the same as the rest of us. But I bet she doesn't know what it is. And neither do they." He bent his head. "Neither do I."

Almost indignant, Cathcart asked, "Why do you suspect Emily and not the others?"

Blackthorn answered pedantically, "She perfectly fits the typical criteria for a serial killer. She's alone even when surrounded. Not even her own family knows her mind.

And she has every reason to be bitter. The others left her in Uganda when she was crippled. She spent most of her life isolated from her father and the others, so her entire world is herself. It is perfectly logical that she would do anything to protect her world."

"To protect her world from what?"

"The others took her world when she was a young child. She would naturally want to make sure they can never do it again."

"By killing all of them and taking her father's money?"

"Exactly. And when they are gone, her revenge is complete and she will make for herself a new world that no one can take away from her. She will finally be safe." Blackthorn brooded before he observed, "It would be perfectly natural that she would do this."

Cathcart leaned forward, "Did I miss something? Emily's not in danger of losing her home. And the others obviously love her and she knows that. If you're going to suspect someone, why don't you suspect Flora? She's been angry with us since we got here."

"I've given them all consideration," was the grim reply. "Even you, Dr. Cathcart. But developments make your guilt unlikely."

Cathcart laughed, "What Scotland Yard profile do I fit?"

"You're beautiful, smart, and accustomed to winning scientific and bureaucratic wars. Also, I can see you harboring ambitions of living a long and healthy life where you could clothe yourself in all the graces of eternal bliss." Blackthorn set a hard gaze on her. "And in saying that, doctor, I also condemn myself because everyone has a hope to live forever in whatever fashion they desire. Who would not be motivated to murder for such a reward? And that is why everyone in this house is suspect. But that child is the only one I cannot place. Trying to get answers out of her is like trying to grasp a shadow. She reveals nothing. No one understands her. She —"

"That's not true," Hunter objected. "That kid sat with Ben all morning and he accepted her like she was his own. And animals can read people a lot better than humans. An animal can tell right off if someone is good or bad. Maybe it's pheromones. Maybe it's the way they look. Maybe it's just instinct. But they can tell. And Ben was still beside her when we got back, happy as a clam. Remember that?"

"I remember," Blackthorn growled, and looked away as if Hunter had ruined his plan. "It's … puzzling."

Hunter stated, "This isn't her hat size, Blackthorn."

"An American idiom which means?"

"It means that Emily doesn't have it in her to betray her father," said Cathcart plainly and – Hunter thought – convincingly. "Commander, you say that that little girl fits your 'Scotland Yard Holy Profile' for a serial killer. Have you considered that your so-called perfect profile fits most young girls?" She conceded, "Okay, so she's quiet. So are most girls. She's trying to figure things out. To find her way. And she does lack confidence and social skills but *that's* not unusual. A lot of girls are so shy they're afraid to open their mouth. And so what if she doesn't tell everybody what she's thinking? I didn't talk to my brothers and sisters much either. I was always reading a book. Basically, it's perfectly normal for young girls to be weird and incomprehensible. Your problem is you've never raised a girl."

"Have you?" asked Blackthorn.

Cathcart nodded, "Yes, sir, I have a four-year-old and even her teacher thinks she isolates herself too much. But the fact is that she's just a little smarter than the others so she prefers the company of books to people. But she'll grow out of it. They all do. Being secretive, smart, and quiet does not make someone a likely successor to Jack the Ripper."

Hunter muttered, "You haven't picked up anything else?"

"No," Blackthorn shook his head with emerging anger. "They were all associated with Vang's institute in some obtuse way. And yet they all deny knowing him. Which is another reason why I suspect Emily.”

“Are you kidding me?” Cathcart gaped. “Emily knows Vang?”

“No,” Blackthorn frowned. “She is the *only one* who says she does not know Vang or his institute. And *that* is suspicious.”

“Oh, my god.” Cathcart covering her face with her hands before dropping them to her lap. “All right. Whatever. I think you’re wrong. In fact I think Emily might be the only one who *is* telling the truth. But you’re running out of time for your big Perry Mason moment. That sun’s getting real low.”

Hunter asked, “What about Cathcart’s idea?”

The detective turned. “What idea?”

“Her idea about Flora. I mean, Cathcart’s right. Flora is obviously in charge around here.” Hunter shrugged, “I’m no detective but if anybody could organize something like this, it seems like it’d be the one who organizes everything else.”

“She admits that she knows about Vang,” Blackthorn allowed. “But it would be natural for her to know of Vang’s research. Half the world knows of it. And there’s nothing that ties her to him.”

Cathcart: “Like there’s something that ties *Emily* to him?”

Blackthorn’s conviction was Puritanical. “It is always wise to suspect the one who appears most innocent. It is usually the one who claims to know nothing that knows everything. And Emily has repeatedly inspired the others to fear and panic. Everything points to her.”

“Isn’t one of them part of some kind of huge insurance company?” asked Cathcart.

“Yes. Why do you ask?”

"Because Dr. Vang's institute was insured for billions." Cathcart pursed her lips. "Don't detectives say there's no such thing as a coincidence?"

"Lesser detectives. But young Barron had a hefty hand in funding Vang's institute. And Flora, as I've mentioned, freely confesses that she's intimately familiar with his work. But they all deny knowing him and there is no evidence to the contrary. If it is a mask, it's a most cunning one."

"Why?"

"Because if you are associated with a criminal, Dr. Cathcart, the best defense is to reveal all that up front. It gives a detective nowhere to go. Nothing to discover. And you cannot condemn someone merely because they were associated with a ruffian. That might condemn his mother and father, as well. His grandmother. His entire family. But three reasons demand someone inside this house *must* be involved."

Cathcart blinked. "And those are?"

"First, the major has been agitated to a sufficient degree of alarm that he has enacted a new will. That would mean someone who has his confidence and trust has provoked him to that state of mind."

"Maybe it was his own idea," she objected.

"That is doubtful," Blackthorn disagreed. "The major is a seasoned big game hunter. A highly decorated soldier with combat experience. A former operator with MI-6. Such men are not easily intimidated – if at all. It would take someone close to his heart – even someone he desperately loves – to initiate such terror. And even that would not have been possible in his youth. But he is elderly, now, and his nerves, no doubt, are diminished."

Cathcart nodded, "And the second reason?"

"Secondly, only someone intimately familiar with this mansion could have revealed to Vang the location of that tunnel. And, finally, someone had to keep Vang appraised of their father's movements. His schedule. And only someone inside this home would have known he had an appointment four days ago. Only someone in this house could have known that the chauffer would be outside and vulnerable at that very hour."

"So Vang didn't intend to kill the major four days ago?"

Hunter joined the analysis. "No. That's what seemed logical at the time but considering everything's that's happened since then, it doesn't fit. Now I think the chauffer was killed because he was Milton's closest friend and his death would traumatize him the most."

"What about the police officer?"

"More of the same. Still, it wouldn't work if there weren't someone in this house scaring everybody to death."

"That would put me at the top of the list," muttered Cathcart.

Blackthorn stated, "As much as it pains me, I've stricken you from the list of suspects."

"Yeah, I'm pretty broke up about it, myself," Cathcart said dully. "Hell, Blackthorn, why not Barron?"

"Young Barron is too frightened."

Cathcart lifted a hand toward the family, "Well, Flora's been openly hostile to us since we got here. Wouldn't that make her a suspect? And Bronte has been nothing but helpful. And wouldn't that make her a suspect? I mean, if you're going to hide, hide in plain sight. It's the last place anybody is gonna look." She spun to Hunter. "Hunter! What do your instincts tell you?"

Hunter grunted, "They tell me to be careful with everybody in this house except for Emily."

Cathcart slapped a hand on her chest. "*Even me?*"

"Except for you and Emily."

"I won't take that personally," growled Blackthorn.

Gunshots brought them to their feet and they whirled as screams exploded from the kitchen. Hunter, with Blackthorn and Cathcart behind him, charged forward. Hunter entered the hall to the kitchen and didn't slow as he reached chaos raging at the rear entrance – the entrance the Scimitar had used. He identified Bronte and Barron standing in the door holding smoking rifles. He snatched Barron's coat and ripped the youth from the entrance as he shouldered into it, raising the Marlin.

"See anything?" Blackthorn asked nervously.

Hunter peered along the tree line, searching every shadow. Finally he shook his head, "No."

Bronte was straightening and dipping on knees that seemed to be giving way despite her efforts to remain standing. Then Cathcart was behind her, hands on her shoulders, and led her deeper into the kitchen. Stepping back, Blackthorn forcefully slammed and locked the door as Hunter spun into Barron Milton, who was visibly trembling.

"What did you see!" demanded Hunter.

"I saw it!"

"*You saw what!*"

"*IT!*"

"*Where!*"

Barron pointed out the door. "It was running across the back! It was, like … like it was running toward *me* and it was all slouched over and staring at me and it was reaching out for me and … and –"

Blackthorn stormed forward. "Why did you open the door!"

"Emily asked me to look outside!"

Turning into Hunter, Blackthorn demanded, "It's not even night! Would he really try to get in here this early?"

Hunter shook his head, "I don't know."

Enraged, Blackthorn snarled, "What drove it away? Barron has no experience with guns!"

"No," Hunter agreed, "but he alerted the rest of us, and Vang didn't want that." He took a deeper breath. "He lost the element of surprise. But he'll be back soon enough."

"How soon?"

"He'll wait until he thinks we've lowered our guard. Then he'll try some other way of getting inside."

"He won't use this door?"

"Not next time."

"Why not?"

"Because once an animal's den or path has been discovered, that animal won't use it again. And Vang is becoming more animal every minute. Next time, he'll pick another way."

Blackthorn stormed from the kitchen toward the great hall where Emily had been sitting with Ben. But when they reached it, she was gone. Then a small voice emerged from the front of the room. With no hesitation they walked forward and gazed over her. She was sitting contentedly on the floor beside Ben, an arm around a small portion of his neck.

In a voice of barely restrained anger Blackthorn asked, "Did you instruct your brother to open the door and look outside, Emily?"

"No," Emily innocently shook her head, "I just asked him to look outside. I meant for him to look through the window."

"Why?"

She turned her face toward Ben, stroking his neck. "Ben was acting scared. And I felt like something was outside. So I got scared."

"What was Ben doing?" asked Hunter.

"He was staring off into space like he saw a ghost."

"Why did that scare you?"

"If Ben's scared, I'm scared."

Hunter knew it wouldn't be unusual for him to miss something like Ben simply staring off into space. He tended to do that, anyway. He raised his face to Blackthorn. "She's telling the truth."

"How do you know?"

"Because something *was* out there, Blackthorn, and Ben sensed it. Then this girl saw him staring off and got worried. So it's natural that she'd ask her brother to take a look around. She *shouldn't* have, but she doesn't know that. And it's not her fault he opened the door. She expected him to look out the window. It makes sense."

"Then why didn't the boy use a window?"

"Because that boy is scared to death and not thinking straight."

Blackthorn gloomily studied Emily as she laid her head into Ben's shoulder and, after a moment, said, "Ms. Emily, please understand me. I do not want you asking your brother to look outside again. All your lives are in danger. And what's outside that door *is* the danger. Please stay away from windows and doors." He turned his head to the rest. "I would ask the rest of you to do likewise. Please avoid all windows and doors."

"Why didn't Bronte stop her brother from opening the door?" asked Cathcart with clinical precision. "Like Hunter said, Barron is terrified and not thinking straight. But Bronte isn't anywhere near as frightened. She should have known better."

A moment later Bronte was surrounded by the three of them. She had remained at the back door, rifle ready.

Blackthorn growled, "Why did you allow your brother to open the back door? He's frightened. He's prone to errors of judgment. But you are nowhere near as frightened. You should have had your wits about you."

"I didn't see him do it!" quickly answered Bronte. "I turned away for one second and he opened the door! If I'd see him go over to it, I would have asked what he was doing! But it was over –" She snapped her fingers, "– like that! Then he started screaming and shooting and I just ran up and did the same thing he was doing."

"Shooting at *what*?" Blackthorn persisted.

"I didn't see anything! The door was filled with smoke and gunfire so I just started shooting! I don't know if I hit anything! I don't even know if anything was out there!"

"Aren't you in the insurance business?" asked Cathcart abruptly.

A confused stare. "Why do you ask?"

"Does your company insure large corporations?"

Bronte gazed briefly to the side before looking back. "Well, yes, sometimes. Why?"

"What about hospitals?"

"Of course."

"Laboratories?"

Bronte's face tilted back. "Oh," she said, lips parted, "I see where you're going with this. Because I insured Dr. Vang's laboratory, you think I'm working with him. Right?"

"Are you?" Cathcart pressed.

"No," Bronte said frankly. "I only know what corporations own the labs and the equipment that I'm insuring. I don't know the personnel because we don't insure personnel."

Cathcart's face was blank.

Blackthorn appeared to be judging whether to allow a harmless drunk to walk home or arrest him because being drunk in public was, unfortunately, illegal. "Hmmm," he allowed, "well, then, perhaps this is fortuitous. I was worried your rifle might not operate properly after my modifications. How did it function?"

Bronte seemed taken aback. "Uh … it did fine. I guess. How's it supposed to work?"

"Let me see it."

Taking the rifle from her hand, Blackthorn lifted it to the light, aiming. He broke open the breech, snapped it shut again, and gave it back. "It's functioning properly," he nodded. "Very well, then. Do not open this door again. Do you understand?"

"I do."

"Carry on." Blackthorn turned. "Mr. Hunter? Doctor?"

They walked into the great hall and towards Barron Milton, who was in heated conversation with Flora. The confrontation was abrupt and dramatic as the commander demanded, "Young Milton, I have questions that you will answer. Why did you open the back door?"

The youth seemed speechless before he pointed to Emily Milton seated beside Ben. "Emily asked me to take a look outside."

"We know that. But why didn't you look out the window? Why would you open the door when you knew the beast was outside?"

"It was only for a moment! Bronte was there!"

"What do you mean?"

"Bronte was right beside me!"

Bronte said, "He's confused, commander."

Blackthorn turned to confront Bronte, who had obviously followed them from the kitchen and approached without notice. Hunter was curious that he had not heard her steps.

"Explain this contradiction!" demanded Blackthorn.

Bronte gestured widely as she said, "Yes, I was with him! But I wasn't *directly* beside him when he –"

Barron objected, "But you were, Bronte!"

Bronte stepped forcefully into her brother. "No, Barron! I'd walked across the room!" She stared. "Barron? Don't you remember? I stepped away just before you opened the door!"

Confusion etched Barron Milton's face as he glanced frantically left to right. It was as if he were desperately searching for a truth that was directly in front of him, but he couldn't find it. "I …" he hesitated, "I guess you're right. I can't remember. Everything happened so fast."

Milton, who had been awakened by the commotion, was sitting in evident confusion, gazing from one to the other. Blackthorn, to his credit, said in a comforting tone, "All is well, Major. We had a little confusion in the ranks. You know how that happens."

Milton managed, "Oh, yes. Certainly. These things happen."

Hunter, with Cathcart close, followed Blackthorn to the furthest end of the long table and sat. Leaning back, Blackthorn quietly stated, "Only one seems like a proper suspect."

Cathcart muttered, "Is there a difference between a proper suspect and an improper one?"

"A proper suspect is almost certainly guilty," allowed Blackthorn. "Otherwise, one suspect is the same as another."

"Their stories don't agree!"

"That is typical for people caught in frightening situations, Dr. Cathcart. One eyewitness remembers four men wearing Winston Churchill masks. Another remembers six men not wearing any masks at all. None of them are lying. They are simply mistaken. The fact that they have different memories of the same event proves nothing."

Cathcart's eyes narrowed. "Are you still stuck on Emily being the prime suspect?"

"Emily is a mystery," Blackthorn muttered, and fell to brooding. "I'm not sure what to think, anymore."

Cathcart turned, "What do you say, Hunter?"

Hunter laughed as he shook his head, "You guys are like two dogs chasing their tails. What you need to be doing is concentrating on what's about to happen. Not on Emily."

"What's about to happen?"

After a pause Hunter explained, "When I'm tracking a tiger, I'm not primarily looking for the tiger. I'm looking for sign that lets me know whether it's safe to keep moving forward." He gazed across the room. "Vang is like that. He doesn't want to walk into a trap, so he's looking for a sign that will let him know if it's safe to attack. And I think somebody in this room is gonna have to give it to him. So —

at this particular moment – I'm not really looking for Vang. I'm watching everyone else."

"You think Vang is scared of *us*?" asked Cathcart.

"No, he's not scared of us. That's a little strong. But Vang knows we're capable of trapping him because we've trapped and killed two of his wolves. And this is the most dangerous part of the game for him. This is where he puts us all in the dirt and rides off with his money." Hunter glanced at the family. "This fight is why Vang brought the wolves in the first place. He wanted the wolves to do all the killing while he hung back in the shadows and collected the loot. He never wanted to expose himself at all. But now he doesn't have any choice. He has to kill us now, and he has to do it himself, so he'll be waiting for a sign that tells him when it's safe."

After a moment Cathcart asked emptily, "Do we have any more dynamite?"

"Some."

"Why don't we use it to set a trap?"

"If we knew how he was going to attack, we could do it. But we don't know that." Hunter hesitated. "I think it was just dumb luck that the kid opened that back door and saw Vang. Vang was probably moving for one of the windows. Truth is, he's probably in the house right now just waiting for a signal that lets him know it's safe to kill every one of us."

"I think Bronte went back there to signal him," muttered Cathcart sullenly.

Blackthorn stated, "That's an unsubstantiated theory based on nothing but baseless presuppositions."

"Good grief, Blackthorn, you need to renew your human card."

The detective spoke over her, "Think about what you're saying, doctor. You propose that Bronte went to the kitchen for the secret purpose of signaling Vang. But it was Flora who ordered Bronte to the kitchen to secure the door. Also, it was Emily who asked Baron to look outside and that's why he went to the kitchen. And so, since they each participated in the regrettable event, then all four of them would have to be involved. But since you have been, so far, very insistent that neither Emily nor Barron are involved in any nefarious plot to kill their father, then your theory is not logical."

Cathcart rolled a gaze. "Fine. I never claimed to be a detective. So why isn't Vang afraid of military intervention? He's not exactly superhuman. He *can* be killed."

Hunter responded dully, "Because Vang knows the military isn't going to do anything. He knows exactly what happened with Luther. He probably followed every minute of it. The military threw us in a meat grinder and wrote us off. So the only thing he's worried about is getting blown up or walking into some kind of trap."

As if her emotions were all but exhausted Cathcart said, "Tell me again why we just can't make a run for it?" She held up a hand. "Don't get me wrong. I admire you guys' gung-ho attitude to 'finish the fight,' but that *clearly* isn't working out. We might not be down for the count, but we're definitely down. Can't we just get out of here and fight another day?"

CHAPTER TWENTY-SIX

"We'll be slaughtered before we get halfway to the cars," muttered Blackthorn miserably.

"Then why don't we move the cars closer?"

"You miss the point."

"Relax, Blackthorn. It's a joke."

"I don't do jokes."

"I believe you!"

The detective hesitated for a very long time and then he stated ponderously, "If you were trying to create the ultimate beast of prey, Dr. Cathcart, then congratulations. You succeeded. This remaining wolf is capable of killing every one of us in the open field."

"It's an Amphicyon."

"It's a maneater from the pits of hell."

"What about our rifles?" Cathcart fixed a stare on the weapon which was laid on the table. "Are they, like, *useless*?"

"Flesh is flesh," offered Hunter. "This last wolf can be killed, sure, but it'll take a hundred rounds to bring it down. And I have no idea how much damage Vang can take, but trust me, it's gonna be *a lot*. So rifles aren't useless, and you might get Vang with a lucky shot, but you won't live to see it. One second after you hit him, you'll be dead. Because I guarantee he'll live long enough to finish you off. It might be the last thing he does, but unless you blow his head off, he'll get to you."

Cathcart stiffened, staring away.

"Where did Emily go?" she asked.

Blackthorn was up and moving forward, rifle in hand. He swept past Ben and confronted the others. "Where did Madam Emily go?"

"To her room," answered Bronte. "I told her to try and get some sleep. Why? What's wrong?"

"Fool of a child!" snapped Blackthorn as he turned to Cathcart. "I may need your help, doctor. I believe I frightened the girl, but she's not afraid of you. We need to bring her back to this room as quickly and quietly as possible." He turned to the others with, "I told you to remain in this room! A mistake like this can get you killed!"

They were gone leaving Hunter alone in the great hall with two sisters and the last brother. Milton slowly rose from the couch and walked over to settle behind his desk. He gazed numbly about the cluttered desk before he raised a gaze with, "Mr. Hunter? Might I have a word with you?"

Hunter stepped forward and took a chair in front of the desk, laying his rifle across his lap. "Yes, Major?"

"It's about Emily."

Hunter waited but when the old man didn't continue, he said, "They'll bring her back, Major. She just doesn't understand how important it is to stay together."

The major's breathing was staggered. "She's been acting strangely of late. She's been … more distant … than usual. I don't understand it. But I've been worried about her for months." He bowed his head, silent, before adding, "I have heard snatches of your conversation. I know what you suspect. Do you really think my most precious child could be involved?"

Hunter hadn't expected Milton to ask him point-blank and wasn't sure what to say. He knew the others were standing close, and since they had stopped talking, they were obviously listening. With his most persuasive appearance of indifference, Hunter gestured, "She's young, Major, so she's got some strange angles to her. But if someone had held a mirror up to any of us at that age, I'm sure we'd have all looked pretty strange. Plus, she knows she's in danger, and she's scared. And you know how people are. They do funny things when they're scared. But Blackthorn and Eve will bring her back."

Milton lifted a hand to his children. "Flora, tell Mr. Hunter how strangely Emily has been acting of late."

Flora looked at Milton. "Major, I don't think now is —"

"Please, Flora. I am very concerned."

With evident exasperation Flora walked to Milton's side and laid a hand on his shoulder. She fixed a gaze on Hunter, "It's just that Emily has been even more uncommunicative lately than usual. We don't know why. We've tried to bring her out of her shell but … well … she's been in her own world. We've been quite worried."

"Has she done anything out of the ordinary?" asked Hunter. "Besides not talking?"

"Not really, no."

Bronte stepped forward. "Flora! Tell him the truth!"

"For god's sake tell him the truth!" exclaimed Barron.

"Why not tell me?" Hunter asked. "To be honest, I don't think this can get any stranger."

* * *

Although he held his rifle in a hand, Blackthorn drew his pistol with the other as they reached Emily's bedroom door. He knocked once and called, "Ms. Emily? It's Commander Blackthorn. I am coming in. Please don't be afraid. I do not mean to frighten you."

The door was unlocked and Blackthorn entered with Cathcart following close to see a white spectral silhouette standing before the picture window. Framed by the thin, gauzy curtains, Emily seemed more angel than human. And then she turned.

She held a long butcher knife.

Inured to the abrupt appearance of deadly threats, Blackthorn stood stone-still without expression. He did not approach her, nor did he intend to. But he could not allow her to retain possession of that weapon. In a calm voice he asked gently, "Ms. Emily? Are you all right?"

Emily's lips did not seem to move although a hoarse, rasping word emerged. "*Ekibe* …"

Cathcart glanced nervously at the detective.

"Emily," he said gently, "do you know where you're at?"

Her eyes were wide and staring.

"*Ekibe* …"

With no expression Blackthorn slowly holstered his pistol, set down his rifle against the door jam, and lifted hands. "Emily," he said soothingly, "I want you to put the knife on the bed. It is directly to your right."

Emily didn't move.

Very slowly Cathcart eased forward, a single hand upraised, "Emily?" she began, "I know you're frightened, honey. We're all frightened. But don't you think you'd be safer with the rest of us? And you don't want to leave your father alone, do you? He's just as scared as you are." She took a bolder step. "Emily? I want you to lay down the knife on the bed, okay? Can you do that?"

Emily's hand visibly tightened around the hilt. "He's here," she said again. "*Ekibe.*"

Blackthorn stepped out to glance down the hall. When he moved forward again his voice was more commanding. "Ms. Emily," he said, "I must insist that you lay down that knife. Please do it now."

Still, Emily did not move.

Blackthorn shifted as if he were about to walk forward and take the blade by force when Cathcart stepped in front of him. If the girl suddenly stabbed out, Cathcart couldn't avoid it. But without the faintest shade of fear she held Emily's gaze. Then she said quietly but firmly, "Emily? If you don't do what the inspector is telling you to do, he will take that knife away from you, so put it on the bed." Cathcart waited until she sternly added, "*Now!*"

As if she'd made up her mind without prompting, Emily casually laid the knife on the bed. Blackthorn quickly walked forward and searched her white cotton dress but she had no more weapons. The detective gestured to Cathcart as he said, "Dr. Cathcart will take you to your father and the rest of your family. They are very frightened for you."

With an arm wrapped lightly around Emily's shoulders, Cathcart led her down the corridor. When they were gone, Blackthorn turned and lifted one side of the gossamer curtain.

Emily had a good view of the east side of the estate. There was nothing between this window and the whitening tarn and, beyond that, the forest wall of depthless black. In the moment it occurred to Blackthorn that, although the day was not yet gone, it made little difference.

Night had come.

* * *

Hunter was intrigued. He glanced over their faces and waited until Flora finally gestured toward the kitchen and listlessly admitted, "Over the past several weeks we've noticed … things … missing from the kitchen."

"Tell him what happened the night before Mr. Hunter arrived!" pleaded Baron.

Flora snapped, "I'm doing it, Barron! Be patient!" She gathered, then, "Very well. Two nights ago I found Emily walking back to her room holding a butcher knife. And let me be clear, it was a *big* knife. So I asked Emily what she was doing and she, ah, she just repeated a word that she often repeats when she's … disturbed."

"Ekibe," said Barron, a nod.

Hunter waited. "Which means?"

Flora gestured to the wall. "It means 'hyena' in Ugandan. Emily was attacked by a hyena when she was a child and she's still a bit … unhinged … by that awful experience. So sometimes, even now, we'll find her standing by herself repeating that terrible word over and over."

"Yeah," commented Hunter, "Blackthorn told us about that. But I don't think that word means hyena to her anymore."

"What do you think it means?"

"It means she's afraid of something."

"Afraid of what's outside the house?"

Hunter searched Flora's stare.

"Or inside it."

* * *

Emily Milton sat demurely with both hands wrapped around a steaming mug of hot chocolate that Bronte had fixed for her.

As she stared into the flames, Hunter judged her to be the most harmless looking person he'd ever seen. She seemed totally incapable of violence, which would have been encouraging but for the fact that she had been standing alone in a dark room holding a butcher knife.

After ensuring that Emily was calm and relatively content, Blackthorn had shared further details of Flora's story to Hunter and Cathcart taking no pains to conceal the strangeness of what happened to the child after she recovered from her coma. Hunter found it both frightening and confusing, but Cathcart seemed to be taking it in stride as she explained how patients who emerge from coma often display mental faculties they had not previously possessed.

"It's actually a well-known phenomenon in medical circles," Cathcart remarked. "Some people emerge from coma with radically altered personalities. Some return with an almost supernatural ability to anticipate the actions of others. There was a well-documented case in Spain where a man came out of a year-long coma able to predict the future." She looked at Hunter. "Literally. Like some kind of fortune teller. It was weird."

"I'll bet," muttered Hunter.

"How can such a thing be explained?" asked Blackthorn.

"It can't," Cathcart remarked. "Although it's a pretty well-documented phenomenon with psychiatrists and doctors, nobody can explain how or why."

After the detective wandered away to continue his questioning of the others, Cathcart stood and moved to sit beside Hunter, arms crossed, staring across the room at Emily.

"I think she's just scared," she said. "Good grief, Hunter, who isn't? And she's the youngest, so she's probably more scared than any of us. I don't blame her for taking a knife to her room to protect herself from that monster. That's what kids do."

"I know," said Hunter, "but that's not what I'm thinking."

"What are you thinking?"

"I'm thinking she took it protect herself from someone in this house." Hunter laid his rifle to the side and walked forward. He sat on the floor beside Emily, who was gently stroking Ben's neck. "Are you and Ben getting along all right?" he asked quietly.

She smiled, "Yeah. I love Ben."

Despite his rising anxiety, Hunter laughed, "He's a chore to put up with sometimes. He eats everything in sight."

"I would feed him all the time. He's my friend."

Hunter studied her a long moment. "You don't have many friends, do you, kid?"

"No. But Ben's my friend. I love Ben."

"Yeah. I think he loves you, too."

"You can tell?"

"Oh, yeah. He doesn't like a lot of folks."

"Why not?"

Hunter faintly shook his head. "I don't know. Animals just have a sixth sense about people. They like some. And they don't like some. And I take that as a sign."

Emily's ice-blue eyes lifted. "A sign of what?"

"Well, if Ben doesn't like somebody, I figure he's got a good reason. Something I can't see. But it's a good reason. And that's good enough for me. So if he doesn't trust somebody, I don't trust them, either."

"Me, either."

"So what book are you reading now?"

"King Lear. It's a play."

"You like it?"

"It's sad. It's a story about a great king who gets betrayed by his family and dies a really sad death. Have you ever read it?"

Hunter laughed, "No."

Emily turned to Ben, smoothing his coarse fur, as she continued, "I've loved reading ever since my accident. If Ben were here with me, I'd read to him all the time. He'd never be alone. Not like I am." She was silent. "Do you ever get lonely?"

Hunter remembered a life lived in the wilderness with only the moon for a companion in the coldest nights. And he had pondered, often enough, whether loneliness was just his lot in life. Some called it destiny. Some called it the will of God. Hunter didn't call it anything at all, and he didn't complain about it anymore than he complained about the weather. Since he couldn't change either of them, what was the point?

"Sometimes," he said.

"I know what you're thinking," Emily murmured as she continued petting Ben. "But you're not alone. You've got me. I'm your friend." She smiled widely. "Me and Ben!"

Hunter laughed, "Yeah. You and Ben."

Emily caught her breath.

She gasped, "He here!"

After a moment Hunter asked, "The creature that killed your brother is in the house?"

"No! He's outside!"

"Is he alone?"

"The wolf is with him!" she whispered. "He's at the edge of the woods!" She lifted a hand. "They're just standing there. They're not doing anything."

Hunter rose and reached down to settle a firm hand on her shoulder. He spoke directly to Ben. "*Guard*! Stay right beside Ben, Emily! Do *not* move unless I say so!"

A tight nod.

Hunter walked back to Cathcart who was calmly cradling her rifle in hands, staring at the deepening dark.

"Game time!" he said.

She erupted to her feet, rifle in hand.

Then, as if on cue, Blackthorn swept in like some Puritan Evangelical of Old descending the pulpit to announce the Hour of Judgment had come and said, "Prepare yourselves!"

With a dead gaze Cathcart cast him a glance. "Could you *possibly* be more pompous, Blackthorn?"

He remarked, "I don't believe so, no."

Hunter grabbed Blackthorn and turned him He pointed to the shattered front window. "Listen up, chief, it's game time. The wolf will come through that window. I'll be in the hallway. If Vang is coming at us from anywhere inside this place, which he will, Ben will know it before I do and I'll deal with it. And the wolf won't attack until Vang does. That's probably the signal they've always used. The wolf is waiting for all hell to break loose and then it'll come through that window like an avalanche."

Blackthorn turned toward the long room. "I'll place the major in the center of the room. And the others?"

"Just keep them together." Hunter squared off, "Listen, Blackthorn, you've seen this wolf in action. He's fast and he won't go down easy, so you're going to have put a shot directly into its head at point-blank. If you don't hit it point-blank, the bullet will glance off its skull. And you have to hit it *dead-direct in the forehead* where there's the least chance of deflection! Do you understand? You'll only have one shot at this."

"And you'll be in the hall?"

"Yeah. But I'm sure I'll be busy so you're gonna have to hold your own. Cathcart and the kids can shoot, but don't count on them hitting anything. If anyone is gonna put it down, it's gonna be you. So just relax. The best time to shoot is when it's in the air coming down from a jump. Once it's in the air, it can't change direction. It's committed."

Blackthorn expressed uncharacteristic anxiety. "This is nothing like clearing out a pub. Is it always like this?"

"Yeah." Hunter's eyes widened. "So just concentrate on what's in front of you. Don't worry about what's behind you. And remember, it's coming for Milton. But once you get in its way, you'll be the sole focus of what it wants to kill. It won't go for Milton until it kills you."

"How do you know that?"

"Because when Vang attacked the house he could have killed all of them but he ignored them to get to the major. The only one he killed was the oldest boy because he shot it. So once you engage it, you'll be all it cares about."

Cathcart lifted a hand to her face. "Using that old man as bait is such a terrible thing."

With an angry stare Blackthorn said testily, "Yes, doctor, it is. But we will do it because we have no choice."

Hunter walked to Emily and knelt, where he said, "Okay, Emily. I need you to get to the back of the room beside your father, all right? You can take Ben with you."

Emily raised a gaze.

"The wolf is at the door."

* * *

Clinging with savage strength that ground stone beneath his claws, the Scimitar leaned back, his face painted red by the light of a hunter's moon. Eyes glaring, he blinked, trying to focus.

He was hurt and he was no longer healing as before. The seemingly endless strength that had powered him through one raging, mortal conflict after another surged within his hulking arms and chest and legs – yes, he could still crush a stone in his hand as effortlessly as they would crush a flower – but the prehistoric might was not rising to the battle half so swiftly, nor was it lasting so long. It was as if a vaporous circle of a gathering weakness had surrounded and infected his might.

He inhaled deeply, staring up a moment more before he pulled himself into the castle's rampart. He did not attempt to soundlessly remove the loose pane of glass from the window but merely smashed his arm through the aperture and opened the iron lock. Then he curled a hand around the frame and leaned back again as he pulled it open.

Suppressing a groan at the knifing pains that had begun to tear at his chest and ribs, he was inside the house. Then he stood in the dark of the chamber, only his glare visible. Fangs separated as froth speckling the wood beneath his feet. Then he took a single step, an abomination in blood slouching toward Jerusalem.

He must wait for the signal; he had no choice.

In the deepest part of his animal mind he knew he had to kill the hunter to escape from this wilderness of pain. If he did not kill the hunter, the hunter would follow him. He would find him. And he would kill him like he had killed Luther in that frozen desolation of the north.

"It will come," his mind whispered.

The signal …

It will come …

Breathing heavily through gaping fangs, he waited.

* * *

"Emily?" whispered Hunter. "Are you sure?"

Emily pointed to the ceiling. "The monster is upstairs. He's waiting for something."

Adrenaline erupted in Hunter's heart, almost taking his breath. He gently lifted Emily from the floor and told her, "I want you to go over there and stay with your father."

"Okay," she said and walked to the major.

Everyone but Emily was armed and stood close to Milton's chair. Blackthorn took a position in front of the major and his jutting chin, fixed frown and ready gaze was pure British.

Ben lifted his head as Hunter walked to the entrance of the hall. Hunter didn't need to look to know that Ben rose and was following. He lifted his head, staring at the winding dark staircase that ascended into a black hole at the crest. He could not see the fifth and final floor and so he stood staring and listening. He glanced at Ben.

The Grizzly stood with his head raised, angrily searching the darkness. But whatever he could hear was faint and uncertain or he would have charged with or without Hunter's permission. The bear's blood was still heated from his fight with the Amphicyon and Hunter knew he was eager to finish it – to destroy what threatened him.

Hunter squinted. He didn't know if he'd heard anything. But he knew that he sensed something.

The Scimitar was close.

Hunter's teeth came together in a snarl.

"Come on ..."

* * *

Blackthorn herded the family until they were gathered at Milton's chair. Then he said, "None of you are to leave this room no matter what happens or what you see." But even as he finished speaking, Emily turned and began walking toward the kitchen.

"Emily!" Blackthorn demanded as he stepped forward. He grabbed her arm with enough force to signal his resolve as he asked, "Did you not understand what I just said, child?"

Emily pointed upward as if she knew the exact location of a terrible secret. "He's in the bedroom," she said quietly. "He's waiting."

Blackthorn's brow smoothed. His tone was ominous as he asked, "Waiting for what?"

An explosion high in the house shook the floor. Portraits placed upon the walls crashed to the floor. Blackthorn had instinctively ducked at the concussion but even in the supercharged moment he saw that Emily alone failed to react with alarm. It was as if she had been expecting it.

Roars and gunshots erupted in the hall.

* * *

The Scimitar came from the darkness with the speed of a tiger. It hit the third-floor threshold only once before a titanic leap took it into a wall and it was descending directly at Hunter.

Reflex and instinct moved Hunter and he was firing as fast as he could work the lever on the Marlin and the Scimitar roared as every shot found its mark. At the last second Hunter leaped to the side and the beast crashed face-first into the unforgiving stone floor. But it was up in a split second and spun into Hunter as Ben also whirled, lashing out.

Ben's massive paw smashed into the Scimitar's head, blasting it into the wall. The Scimitar staggered as it rose, a hand to its face. But any injury, if there had been any, did nothing to delay Ben's attack because he launched himself forward and grappled with the creature, his great forelegs closing around its torso with claws ripping flesh from its back.

Hunter was violently shoving rounds into the rifle as Ben's fangs descended into the Scimitar's neck and it howled in rage. In a tremendous twist it struck Ben once, twice, three times to the head and neck before hurling him into the towering front doors.

With a roar the Scimitar whirled into Hunter.

As the window exploded and a prehistoric wolf equal to Ben's raging ferocity landed beside Hunter.

* * *

Blackthorn already had the rifle set in his shoulder as the black shape of the last Amphicyon crashed through the front window. For a split-second the gigantic beast filled the entire room wall to wall before it descended to hit the floor, instantly rebounding.

The detective fired two rounds point blank into the wolf as it fell from the crest of its leap but nothing could change its direction and Blackthorn whirled to push the major from its path but it was too late. With a quick twist of its head the wolf wildly blasted the detective to the side as Cathcart fired her rifle, hitting it on the flank. Then with a snarl it lashed out with a foreleg to hurl her with stunning force into the wall. As Cathcart crashed to the floor it stepped into Milton as the old man surged up, firing the rifle.

"*NEVER!*" roared Milton.

Then there was a movement too quick to follow – a fiendish savaging – and the wolf stepped back, blood falling from fangs. Without even looking at Milton as he fell, Blackthorn frantically reloaded and fired both barrels from the hip. The beast flinched.

Eyes wide, gasping for breath, Blackthorn fumbled to reload as the black, monolithic creature swung its head toward him.

* * *

"*Get Emily!*" roared Hunter as the Scimitar vaulted over his head, landing on the second floor of the staircase.

Ben whirled and charged toward the trophy room as Hunter raised his face, searching for the Scimitar. He knew that he had it on the run and couldn't let it get away. Even though it was night he would have to pursue the Scimitar into the moor and finish the fight.

Swinging around the first-floor post of the stairway, Hunter ascended the steps three at a time until he landed in a crouch on the threshold, his rifle aimed down the corridor. He saw nothing but that also meant nothing. The Scimitar could be hiding inside the first room waiting for him to run recklessly forward. Then it would tear out his throat – probably with the first blow – and descend to help the wolf finish the family. Everything within Hunter compelled him to corner Vang inside the walls. Then Emily screamed and any thoughts he had of chasing it vanished.

Vaulting over the rail, Hunter landed on the floor in time to see Ben rise on his hindlegs in the trophy room, bellowing. The Amphicyon heard the challenge, turned into it, and they collided in a thunderstorm of blows. Stretched on its hindlegs, the gigantic wolf was equally as tall as Ben. Then Ben twisted violently, all his weight and might behind it, whipping the Amphicyon to the floor. It kicked up, tearing Ben's face, and he spun away. Reaching its feet, the great wolf's eyes darted to the window.

"*NO!*" Hunter shouted.

He fired at its face and whatever he hit was vital because it screamed and twisted. Then Ben landed fully on its back, bearing it to the floor again. In a cacophony of rending blows they revolved across the stone foundation demolishing everything in their path. And not for one tenth of a second did either of them stop striking and tearing with fang and claw. All wounds received were ignored; the only thought was to kill.

Ben would not allow it to escape. He smothered it, crushed it, and his blows fell like trees pinwheeling in a whirlwind. For a breath they separated and then crashed forward again, wresting as fangs rose with torrents of blood only to instantly fall again.

In the chaotic moment Hunter finally saw Milton on the floor before his chair, his head laid back, his throat torn open. But Hunter had no time to feel anything. He dimly saw Cathcart lying unconscious and the rest of the family flattened against the walls. Bronte and Barron, as well as Flora, were standing with rifles outstretched, but none had fired a shot. Then Hunter sensed Blackthorn.

The detective was standing on the far side of the hall with the rifle set solidly in his shoulder, his eyes keyed along the sights, waiting for a clear shot at the wolf. But in the whirling, twisting maelstrom of blows exchanged between Ben and the Amphicyon there was little chance for a shot.

It was only then that Hunter realized his mistake and whirled back to see the Scimitar descending.

It crashed into the floor sending shattered stone flying.

Almost face to face, Hunter ripped out the .454 and hit the Scimitar dead in the chest. And, like before, it staggered back. Before it could recover fully, Hunter fired again and again and again until the pistol was empty. Not even thinking of reloading, Hunter raised the rifle in one hand and fired from the waist. Then the Amphicyon disengaged from Ben and leaped forward and an impact Hunter never saw coming sent him sprawling along the hall. Only with the bleakest edge of consciousness did Hunter maintain a grip on the rifle.

Dizzy, Hunter pushed up on an arm, staring as Blackthorn fired the elephant gun, hitting the Amphicyon high. Still, the wolf didn't break stride as it closed on the others and lashed out, hurling Flora across the room. But when Flora's body hit the wall, her head had already struck the floor, rolling to Blackthorn's feet. Then Barron Milton screamed and fired his rifle, striking the wall beside its face, and it swung jagged fangs in his direction.

Hunter pushed off the floor snatching up the rifle and lifting aim when Ben collided with the wolf in the center of the trophy hall. Ben's momentum carried them the full length of the gigantic room scattering furniture and trophies until they fell in a heap once again.

Of a sudden they separated and fell back, each growling and breathing in harsh, coarse blasts of vaporized blood. Hunter could see Ben was badly ravaged with wounds, but so was the Amphicyon. Then the wolf charged and smashed Ben into the wall and the bear locked his foreleg solidly around its neck, pulling its head close.

With a deafening roar Ben slammed his gigantic paw down onto the top of the wolf's head. The impact sounded like a meat cleaver striking the bones of an ox and suddenly the Amphicyon paused as Ben raised his foreleg and slammed his paw down again into its skull. And as if life had left its body with the impact, the Amphicyon fell limp.

With an enraged scream Ben hurled the body aside as the Scimitar leaped into the trophy hall, having recovered from Hunter's wound. Whirling at the sound, Hunter knew Vang was attempting to confirm that Major Milton was dead. If the old man were dead, then Vang's plan was almost finished. Hunter fired and hit Vang solidly in the head, literally cartwheeling him. But he recovered on his feet, in a crouch, and spun into Hunter as he roared. Then Blackthorn fired two shots to hit it as another impact knocked Hunter aside and Ben rushed past. The Scimitar heard the approach and turned into the Grizzly and they met in the hall beside the major's desk.

They instantly locked up, each straining with unbelievable strength to overpower the other. They rocked in place, the Grizzly struggling with a primordial might that had not been seen on the earth in eons. Then Ben put all his weight into a twist and threw the Scimitar to the floor, fangs following to tear open its shoulder.

Sending spent shells flying, Blackthorn reloaded like lightning to slam in two more. He walked toward the battle as Ben and the Scimitar rolled along the floor, each fighting demoniacally.

Hunter sensed that now, perhaps, they stood a chance. The Amphicyon was dead and the Scimitar was injured with Ben wounding him even more every moment. He joined Blackthorn and they walked forward together, Hunter shoving cartridges quickly into the Marlin. Then the Scimitar sank fangs into Ben's throat and he screamed and tore himself away, staggering across the room. For a moment the Scimitar stood alone, silhouetted against flames.

Blackthorn and Hunter raised aim and fired. With four direct hits from rounds that could drop an elephant, the Scimitar retreated and then he leaned forward with a shriek. With a quick turn, Vang launched himself through the demolished window carrying shattered shards of glass onto the cobblestone drive. As Hunter raised his rifle, it cut to the side and was gone.

Far too stunned to feel relief, Hunter could only watch as Ben reached his feet and cascaded across the shattered front doors chasing the Scimitar into the night. Ben was not giving up this fight. He would keep attacking the Scimitar until it was stone dead.

Refusing to let this battle end with anything less than death and bleeding from a dozen wounds, Hunter turned to Blackthorn, who seemed to be maintaining superhuman control. The detective looked neither enraged nor frightened as he calmly lowered his weapon. His face was covered in blood from some wound he didn't seem to notice.

With a frown Blackthorn walked forward and stood over Milton's body. He did not look at Hunter as he asked, "Now what?"

Hunter turned, dragging a key from his vest. "I have to go after him." He unlocked the gun cabinet and removed five sticks of dynamite already taped in a cylindrical mass.

"In the dark?" followed Blackthorn.

"Yeah."

"You said that was suicide."

"It is."

"He's wounded! He has no place to hide! In the morning we can take him from the air!"

Hunter began shoving cartridges in the Marlin. "He'll be gone by morning."

Finally recovering and – remarkably – still holding her rifle, Cathcart stammered, "How do you know that?" She gazed fitfully across the room as if searching for help before she added, "Hunter! Listen to me! Blackthorn's right! Wait until tomorrow and you can hunt him from the air!"

Shaking his head to scattering sweat and blood from his face, Hunter began reloading the Ruger with exacting precision as he said, "He'll be gone by then. Vang has a backup plan. Maybe even a vehicle. And I think he's got at least one change left in him. He can go back to human, and then he'll be a thousand miles from here by morning." He lifted and racked the rifle. "He's *not* getting away!"

Blackthorn gasped, "You *assume* he's running!"

"I *know* he's running!" Hunter slid the Ruger in the holster. "But there's still a chance Vang will double back to try and finish this, so be ready." He swiped blood from his brow. "I won't be far behind him, so if he doubles back, I'll know real quick and I'll be on top of him."

Raising her hands, Cathcart *insisted*, "This is *not* a good idea! Look! You said yourself you can't track him in the dark! I say we just take our chances and hunt him later! Where can he hide? The whole world knows what he looks like now! The police or the FBI or Interpol will put his picture out! They'll have to! He killed Milton! They don't have any choice!"

Glancing up, Hunter said tersely, "Vang's not stupid, Eve. He'll have a way out of here and a place to lay low. He set it up before he ever came here in case this whole thing went south. He's not insane yet."

"He's pretty damn close!"

"Not close enough!"

Holding his rifle in a hand, Hunter walked toward the door. "Blackthorn, you have the house! I doubt I'll get a mile before I catch him or he catches me, so I'll be close. Just fire a shot if you hear anything outside or inside and I'll come running. You got it?"

"Do I have a choice?"

Hunter slid past the broken door and stood on the porch staring at the moor, feeling the wind so cold on his blood-streaked face. It would have moved for the closest cover of forest, so Hunter ran around the front outcropping of the library and knelt. From his bag Hunter withdrew a palm sized maglight and read where Ben had torn through this patch of grass. Then he lifted his head as an angry roar rose in the darkness.

It was Ben, and he was close.

This was worse than Hunter's battle with Luther and it had taken him a year to heal from that fight. Hunter wasn't certain whether he could measure up to that battle again. Maybe he would hesitate or stumble when the moment came.

If the Scimitar struck him down, it'd hit like a flash of lightning from the east to the west and the contest would be decided that fast. Hunter estimated he would have one more chance to kill this thing. But if he made a mistake, he'd die. And so would the rest.

He rose and loped toward the forest and was swallowed by the wall of black. He decided to move toward Ben's last location before using the maglight. He didn't know whether the Scimitar was close but Hunter wasn't going to advertise his presence. The thought occurred to him that he could perhaps come up on the beast with no flashlight, but he knew that was unlikely. At some point Hunter would be forced to use it and that would totally change the game because Vang would see the glow for miles.

Lifting his face, Hunter paused to stare at the blood-red Hunter's Moon blazing in the night sky. It seemed to declare that death was here and would claim who it had come to claim, and no one could dispute its decision.

"*Let's do it*," Hunter whispered.

Hunter knew he should be moving but he took a moment to slow his breathing, to calm down. The night had set him on fire and that was the wrong mindset because it could make you rash, impatient, and careless. He had to slow everything down, to bring it under the coldest control because brute force would not win this. He had to outthink Vang and questions of whether the doctor had gone completely insane or not were meaningless. In this blood-hued forest, in this dead night, savagery and instinct would settle this.

Use what he does not know …

With the thought Hunter began moving swiftly through the moor, forgetting Ben's location even though the bear was hunting the Scimitar by scent and would not lose it even in this morass.

Hunter remembered where the expansive stand of cypress stood and what it held that might, in a last-chance gambit, kill the Scimitar. Hunter didn't even attempt to consider the odds. He knew, without thinking, they were astronomical. But it was the best …

No! It was the *only* move he had!

As he moved, ignoring the sound he made violently sweeping branches aside, charging through water and mud, Hunter mentally recalled all the items in his bag and knew it was enough if he was cunning. But there would be only one chance to lure the Scimitar to the place where it might be killed. And Hunter would have to use himself as bait.

Moving faster through the thinning trees Hunter fiercely fought the rage and fear. He no longer cared whether Vang was still sane. In Hunter's mind the Scimitar was a murderer, a monster, and a human tiger that needed to be put down like a rabid dog.

There would be no mercy.

Trees swept past Hunter indifferent to yet another life and death battle fought in their shadows. And by reflex Hunter remembered that the jungle was always indifferent to who lived or died and would consume them both, in the end. But it was the world Hunter knew best and he was at home with it. Then he reached lower terrain and knelt, studying the lay of the land to get his bearings.

Yeah …

Not far …

Instinct moved Hunter as a force lashed out from shadow.

CHAPTER TWENTY-SEVEN

Hurling himself forward, Hunter rolled and came up raising the rifle because, although he hadn't actually seen it, he knew what it was. Then he targeted the shape standing so close, lit by the crimson glow of Hunter's Moon, and pulled the trigger.

The rifle flare exploded inside the red sphere like lightning and all Hunter heard was primeval rage as the shadow halted in stride. And in that brief, flashing moment where some men might have turned to run, Hunter didn't even think of it. He didn't care to survive.

He wanted its blood.

The Scimitar was bent with his right arm crossed over his guts and then it slowly straightened, breathing in ghastly moans that indicated it was hurt far worse than Hunter anticipated. It was as if this endless fight were finally wearing it down. As if its all but inexhaustible strength and healing power had reached its zenith and was descending like a satellite decaying in flames as it fell to the earth. And for the first split-second Hunter dared to hope he had a chance. But that was the only thought he had as he fired four remaining rounds from the rifle dead into its chest.

The consecutive blasts struck with the thunder of an earthquake, the detonations condensed and amplified by the surrounding trees and, with each bullet, Vang twisted and screamed as if he were frustrated from destroying his most hated enemy by a single step. Then the rifle was empty but Hunter didn't attempt to reload. As he'd done before, he fast-drew the .454 and fired in an attempt to hit Vang in the head.

Vang's bestial face recoiled violently with the blast and a massive hand grabbed his face. But he made no sound as he staggered back one, two, three steps into the imprisoning muck. Then Vang lashed out so fast that Hunter barely saw the move and didn't understand what –

Something colossal smashed into Hunter with the force of a freight train blasting him thirty feet into the trees where he was only barely aware that he was crashing from one unforgiving trunk to the next until he hit the mud and continued sprawling. Only when he came to a grinding stop did Hunter realize Vang had swiped out to hit a fallen tree, hurling the trunk into him like a missile. He had no idea where Vang was as he unsteadily reached his feet.

Again, it was Hunter's instinct that saved him as he threw himself on his back but he didn't *know* he'd moved until he was staring up at the Hunter's Moon. Then the crimson circle vanished framing the fearsome, wild-haired head of the Scimitar. It reached down and grasped Hunter's leather shirt, talons curling with the most demonic delight – a glee that was all the more horrible not because it was so bestial but because it was so human.

Slowly Vang pulled Hunter close to the tusks that gleamed red in the night. But it was not from blood. It was a scarlet hue cast by the moon as if to herald Hunter's death.

Vang bent, his fist tightening as he gasped, "*I told you I would feast on your bones!*"

In a flash Hunter thrust the barrel of the big .454 directly under the Scimitar's chin and pulled the trigger. The concussion of the blast, so close to Hunter's face, annihilated every sense so that he was only dimly aware of falling back deaf and blind. Hunter was only cognizant that he had hit the ground and rolled, painfully trying to acclimate.

Something was staggering close beside him. Then a hideous shriek exploded from the fangs of the Scimitar and Hunter blinked, fiercely trying to clear his vision, and saw the beast.

The .454 had hit the mark.

Instead of firing another round that would have been deflected by its natural armor, Hunter had thrust the tip of the barrel underneath the Scimitar's chin, where there was no bone, and fired. The bullet had traveled straight up through its brain.

It screamed, both hands clutching its head.

"*Yeah,*" gasped Hunter.

Whatever part of it that survived that gunshot would be the purest testimony to its might. It would also be a testament to Vang's unquenchable rage. Then, in a slow-motion movement that seemed like some unnamable horror rising from its grave, Vang turned his ravaged face toward Hunter.

Blood seeped from his eyes and a huge gush of black froth erupted from the fangs. And even in the meager light Hunter saw a gaping hole in the top of its head surrounded by blackened hair.

Hunter leaped into the trees, running. He angled to his right, knowing Ben's last location. He set a course where Vang would be most likely to encounter Ben, who remained his last hope. If Ben didn't hit Vang from ambush and slow him down, Hunter wouldn't be the one to finish this fight. Just as he knew their next encounter would be his last.

A long ridge of piled rocks rose to Hunter's left, stretching deep into the moor like a primeval fence line. The wall was exactly what he needed – a barrier the Scimitar would have to leap or climb. And, in that split-second when the beast was silhouetted, Hunter might hit it with the rifle. Hunter only needed Ben to intervene, to delay the Scimitar long enough for him to set the final trap.

Hunter raised his face to the Hunter's Moon and noticed a faint change. The crimson glow was growing brighter even he watched. Cubed by the blackest night, the moon blazed like a red sun.

Hunter turned to step away …

A mountain of irresistible strength smashed into Hunter from the darkness – an overpowering force that had come upon him in silence – and in a mass of tangled arms and legs they rolled back the way Hunter had come until they smashed into a granite slab at the base that violently blasted them apart. Utterly breathless, stunned beyond any capacity for thought, Hunter had no idea what had happened as he struggled to gain a knee, a hand.

He couldn't breathe and all he could see was red mud beneath his face. It was pure adrenaline and fear that enabled him to raise his head inch by inch, and as his gaze rose with it, he saw the awesome shape of the Scimitar striding slowly forward. It seemed in no hurry as claws of a single hand clicked.

It was over.

Hunter couldn't even stand. He could only stare as the Scimitar closed on him and grated, *"Hunting season is over …"*

Like lightning the Scimitar suddenly whirled, both arms rising as a colossal shape descended into it with a roar. The shape – and Hunter knew it was Ben – smashed into the Scimitar carrying both of them far down the ravine where they were instantly locked in the most fiendish battle Hunter knew he would ever see. It was a battle of titans so that any one of them might finish the fight with any single blow. Each was a mirror image of the other as they evaded and rolled from blows while simultaneously returning their own with equal fury.

By instinct Hunter turned, and in the scarlet light of the moon, saw his rifle close. He crawled, picked it up, and began scrambling awkwardly up the slope. It felt like forever but Hunter made it to the crest. Only then did he turn to stare back and saw the Scimitar and the Grizzly silhouetted against the lesser darkness of the crimson night trading blows like weary boxers in the last round of a fight that had come down to this one, final exchange, and both were willing to die before surrendering.

Using the rock wall to stand, Hunter was shocked to see his pack laying close to his feet. With his mind following every howl and shriek raging so close in the ravine, he numbly snatched it up. Blinking, he removed the dynamite and laid it on the far side of the wall. Then he slung the bag and fell over the wall himself. In his mind Hunter knew he had stood, but it felt as if he were standing on dead legs that would move no more.

Then he reached the edge of the cypress stand and knelt, shoving cartridges into the Marlin. He didn't even search for a shooting rest. He simply shoved his arm through the rifle strap, tightening it behind his elbow as he set the stock in his shoulder, and raised his gaze to the wall. He would have time for one quick shot as it came over the barrier and, if he missed, the Scimitar would cover this meager ground in seconds.

There was no time to assess anything more. No time to think ahead of where he was. From here it would be instinct, reflex, and courage. Then Hunter shut down his mind and squinted, immediately sighting the dynamite. It stood black against the white granite.

Suddenly there was the wounded roar of a Grizzly – a roar that rose to a shriek and was cut short.

And nothing.

CHAPTER TWENTY-EIGHT

There was no time for emotion; Hunter knew he would be heartbroken but not now. He had to focus. He dropped to a knee and pulled the rifle tight, concentrating on the wall. It was like watching a flat lake waiting for a fish to rise. Hunter didn't know where it would break, but he would see it. He took deeper breaths to reduce the oxygen in his blood, to still his heart and steady his hands. Everything depended on a single shot. If he didn't hit the dynamite, the Scimitar would instantly cover this distance.

A long time passed and no sound emerged from the depthless black. Hunter no longer heard Ben. Even the night had fallen silent.

A shadow topped the ridge near the dynamite.

Hunter fired before he gave his mind the command and the dynamite detonated in a devastating blast that reached him a split-second later in a concussion that knocked him flat. As the superheated wave passed over him, Hunter was scrambling down the far side of the slope. He didn't make the mistake of looking back to see if the Scimitar had been killed. As he reached the cypress, he began stepping with the greatest care over sparse sandstone, knowing the bog here was death. And his only chance.

A wounded howl erupted in the night and before Hunter realized what he was doing he'd spun in place, staring back with eyes on fire, searching everything. But nothing was near. Not bothering to recognize more than that, he unslung his rope and grappling hook. He snapped the hook open and hurled it hard into a giant cypress on the edge of the pit. It caught instantly and he pulled down, anchoring the hook.

There was no time to test it as a horrifying growl emerged from the night directly behind him and, blinking blood and sweat, Hunter slowly turned his head, staring with wide eyes.

The Scimitar stood before him bent and torn with blood cloaking its entire form. Another creature would have been dead, but the Scimitar's unnatural strength kept it on its feet. Then, off balance and swaying, it began forward, fangs snapping hungrily.

Subtly Hunter wrapped the rope around his right wrist and aimed the rifle at its chest and at the movement the Scimitar stopped as if it dreaded another wound in this endless, frustrating fight. And that was *not* good because it meant caution had entered what was left of Vang's brain.

Hunter had to provoke him.

"It's over!" he gasped.

"*Nothing is over!*"

"You've lost, Vang!"

"*No stone age hunter can kill me, you fool! In my age I feasted on a thousand of your kind! You're just one more!*"

As Vang closed this final time, Hunter vividly saw gaping wounds in his chest and neck and face. He was dying. Not even that prehistoric healing power could keep up with the damage. But he wasn't going to die before he tore Hunter to pieces. Without looking, Hunter stepped back, keeping the rifle trained on Vang's chest because this would happen fast.

"*What is it to you if I live a thousand years?*" Vang managed as he staggered. "*Why are you hunting me!*"

Hunter muttered, "Because you killed my bear."

Vang threw back his head in a ghastly laugh that grew more hideous with each breath before he lowered his face again, staring with wide, blood-red eyes. *"You're going to die a fool!"*

Hunter had backed up as far as he dared. He knew by scent and sound exactly where he stood and hoped desperately Vang was wounded so grievously that his senses didn't alert him to the same. He looped the rope around his fist again, shutting off the blood.

"You were betrayed, Vang!"

Vang stopped and straightened, glaring. His fangs gleamed as he rasped, *"Do you think your pathetic lies will save you now?"*

"It's the truth!"

"NO!" he roared. *"I gave her eternal life! She would never betray me! I am a god to her!"*

Hunter spat, "A god can't be wounded!"

The incommensurate rage of the Scimitar rose like a flood as Vang growled, *"I am forever ..."*

"I took Luther's head!" gasped Hunter as his fist locked tightly on the rope. "Now I'll take yours!"

Vang roared and Hunter leaped pulling up on the rope to swing twenty feet over the quicksand. He threw the rifle as he frantically pulled higher and he heard a massive crash behind him.

As Hunter swung in a circle he twisted to gaze down and saw Vang had landed fifteen feet inside the quicksand. He was staring down as if he didn't comprehend what was happening. And then, with a shriek, he lashed out with both arms to barely miss Hunter's legs. But, in this, Vang could come no closer, and Hunter quickly hauled himself up.

As Vang realized that Hunter had ascended beyond his reach, he brought his clawed hands across the surface of the mud blasting chunks to the sides. His body, now buried to the waist, twisted violently. And Hunter knew that with each violent movement he tore mud from the river of quicksand beneath him, sinking him deeper into the morass.

Ignoring for a moment the struggle, Hunter ascended the rope to the overhanging branch of the cypress and dropped to solid ground. Then he looked back to see Vang up to his neck and sinking with visible speed. His endless rage was preventing the ragged remaining shreds of his mind from realizing the one thing that could save him.

All he had to do was stop fighting.

As Hunter watched, Vang continued to struggle, to fight, to overcome with pure brute strength. But not even such primordial might as the Scimitar possessed could defeat what could not be touched. And at last Vang seemed to accept that he could not win. Finally, all but his head was submerged. His misshaped face turned to Hunter, and if bitterness could be seen in a tiger's face, it was there. He glared, hating, to the last.

And was gone.

Bowing his head, Hunter took a deep breath and released with an exhausted moan. He turned to walk away as a tiny rise broke the smoothness of the quicksand. And then the rise began to swell, and Hunter knew that Vang, in the final seconds, had somehow reached the bottom of the pit and was struggling to climb out.

The rise mounted and mounted more until it finally began to subside because, just as Vang had destroyed his expendable Scimitars by depriving them of oxygen, the same had destroyed him.

Hunter stared a long time at what still constituted a small crest in the surface. Then a fearful doubt arose, and he knew he had to be certain. So he cautiously stepped into the quicksand and found the edge was solid to the depth of his knees. He walked out on solid footing and thrust an arm deep, searching. Then, in the unseen depths, he found Vang's bowed head. Grasping the hair, Hunter stepped back, struggling for purchase on the slippery slope, until he dragged Vang free to the neck.

Make sure …

With a frown Hunter pulled his bowie, one hand holding Vang's neck above the surface. Then he brought the blade back on a line level with the Scimitar's neck. The words that emerged from Hunter didn't come from his mind; they came from love.

"You killed my bear!" he rasped.

Vang's eyes opened.

He screamed.

Hunter struck.

* * *

Tossing the head into the quicksand, Hunter walked slowly to where Ben had battled the Scimitar and, as he crested a small knoll, saw a mountainous hulk lying unmoving in the dark. He carefully descended the hillside and fell on his knees beside the Grizzly.

In moments Hunter confirmed – with a surprise – that Ben was still breathing. But it was clear that he wouldn't be walking far. The sky was clearing and Hunter's Moon burned like a scarlet sea over the tarn. For now, there was nothing Hunter could do for Ben. His wounds were too great, and he couldn't move. Hunter affectionately laid a hand Ben's massive head. "Don't be afraid, buddy. I'll be back with help."

One more thing to do.

It took Hunter thirty minutes tracking deep into the mist using his flashlight, but he began to find traces of a well-worn trail torn by hominid scratches until he came upon what he sought.

Before him stood a small hut buried deeply within an all-but-impenetrable covering of vine that not even thermal vision would have revealed. Holding the light low, searching the ground for a deadfall, Hunter cautiously entered the structure and found the rudiments of primitive survival. And then he saw what Blackthorn told him would be there.

He took it.

CHAPTER TWENTY-NINE

After walking with increasing pain toward the house for an hour, Hunter emerged from the black forest to see the gigantic silhouette of the iron fence. He entered the gate and, finally, walked into the house to find what he expected – a heartbroken family sitting in shocked silence.

Only Bronte still held her rifle haplessly across her lap, head down, as the gothic image of Blackthorn towering over them. There was something biblical to the whole scene and then the detective turned his head to stoically address Hunter: "Did you get him?"

"Yeah," Hunter nodded wearily, "I got him."

"Was it there?"

"Here," said Hunter, and reached out.

The investigator took it.

With a deep breath Blackthorn turned to the family, and spoke in a grave tone, "There was only one means by which Vang's confederate could have told him that the old will was vacated, that a new will had been signed, and that it was time to finish this masquerade. All of you were under my observation. Not one of you left my sight except to lock the doors and windows."

Blackthorn raised his hand, and he held a cell phone stained green and discolored by muck. He hit the last number dialed.

Although neither Barron, Emily, nor Bronte moved, there was a faint vibration present beneath the soft rustling of cloth. Yet it was a glaring pronouncement of guilt just the same.

Bronte turned and resolutely pointed her rifle at Blackthorn's chest. At the stance Barron, along with Cathcart, threw themselves against the walls. Only Emily remained unmoved, head bowed, as if she had known all along. Frowning bitterly, Bronte removed a cell phone from her sweater and tossed it aside.

Without expression Blackthorn placed the second cell phone in his overcoat. "I suppose your motives are easily enough understood," he said. "Unless, of course, there are motives more powerful than immortality and an inexhaustible fortune."

Bronte grunted with contempt as she said, "I wasn't about to live at the whim of my overbearing sister, inspector. That's all you need to know."

"That rifle is unloaded," said Blackthorn evenly. "I suspected you were involved when I questioned you in the kitchen, Ms. Milton. That's why I asked to inspect your firearm. I removed the rounds."

"I know," Bronte said and fired the rifle, blasting the chest out of a Grizzly carcass standing at Blackthorn's side. "I reloaded it. Now, drop your guns."

Hunter and Blackthorn tossed aside their weapons as the investigator sternly added, "What truly transpired in the kitchen? Were you attempting to allow Vang into the house?"

"Of course not." Bronte lowered the heavy rifle as she removed a revolver from her cardigan and thumbed back the hammer. "Dr. Vang could get into the house any time he wanted. That mess in the kitchen was just an accident thanks to my idiot brother. But after he started shooting, what was I to do? I knew he could never hurt Dr. Vang. And

I knew it didn't matter if I were shooting beside him." A satisfied smile. "I had to look innocent, right?"

"So your true purpose in going to the kitchen was to call Vang and tell him it was time to finish this?'"

"No, commander, the reason I wasn't in the kitchen when my brother opened the door was because I was coming down the back stairs from my special room on the third floor."

"From your altar? Why did you go there?"

"To tie a candle to a box of dynamite."

Blackthorn nodded, "Of course. That was what told Vang it was safe to attack." He stared. "When did you take the dynamite?"

Bronte tossed back a lock of hair, "I took it from the shed today. But I wasn't sure how I was going to use it. Then my poor sister gave me a chance when she ordered me to lock the kitchen door. That's when I ran up the back stairs and lit the candle in the window and set it on top of the dynamite. It was the signal Dr. Vang was anticipating. After that, it was just a matter of time."

Blackthorn expressed distaste as he pressed, "And that demonic shrine? What is its purpose?"

Bronte's face twisted bitterly, "You call him evil. A madman. Dr. Jekyll and Mr. Hyde. But he was going to be a god." She laughed, "They've always been worshipped as gods. Yes, I know about them. I saw the major's records. My nannies told me of their power. Told me how they were worshipped. And when Dr. Vang explained the purpose of the machines that I was insuring, I understood immediately what he was doing. That's how this began."

"You would betray your family so easily?"

Bronte reacted violently, "What family! I had a father who cared only for Emily and a domineering sister who treated me like a child! Do you think the major would have left me anything when he died? No! He thought I was too young and stupid to have anything for myself! He would have left everything to my sister!" Her teeth clenched. "When I discovered what Dr. Vang was doing in his private lab I couldn't believe my luck! I asked him if I could join him and he told me what I had to do. And if you think it was a difficult decision, inspector, think again. Choosing between eternal life with unlimited wealth or living under the thumb of my sister was no choice at all."

From her position against the wall, with a hand pressed flat over her chest, Cathcart managed, "Do you really believe Vang was some kind of *god*?"

"What difference does it make!" screamed Bronte. "*To live a thousand years makes you a god*!"

Sending an electrifying thrill through Hunter, Blackthorn boldly stepped forward and contested, "He was an animal, Ms. Milton. A bloodthirsty animal that killed for the sake of killing. And he deserved to be shot down like the dog he was!"

At his impetuous stride Bronte jerked the pistol toward the inspector and, to prevent her from firing, Hunter demanded, "What was Vang doing in the attic, Bronte?"

She truculently lifted her chin as if remembering where she was. Then she answered, "He went to the attic to inspect the major's books. I kept telling him that the major had changed his will and it was done. But he wouldn't listen. He was growing impatient and … and *strange*. So he used the tunnel and went up there to make sure I was telling him the truth."

Very slowly Hunter stepped forward. "When did Vang stop hiding in the house?"

"The day you arrived."

"Why?"

"Dr. Vang hated you, Mr. Hunter. But he also feared you. He was afraid your bear would know he was hiding in here and ruin his plan, so he left the east wing to hide in the moor. That's when I gave him a spare phone in case he was unable to see the candle."

"That's a degenerate way of saying it," muttered Blackthorn.

"Of saying what!"

"Of admitting you told that madman it was time to slaughter your entire family." Blackthorn didn't blink. "You are a monster, Ms. Milton. No less than him. But now the game is up. You're finished. That is, unless you can explain five gunshot deaths to London Metropolitan Police."

Bronte cackled before she raged, "You said it yourself, inspector! This belongs to Special Branch now! Nobody is going to arrest me no matter how many of you die because they can't let their secret get out! Oh, yes, detective, they'll come and collect your bodies! And then this will be buried like all of England's secrets! I'm not a fool! And once the dynamite reduces this miserable house to ruins there won't even be any evidence that I've been here. You'll be dead. Vang will be dead. And I'll be free."

"You call this 'free?'" grunted Cathcart.

"It's a shame you're gonna miss out on immortality," commented Hunter. "That doesn't upset you?"

Steadily holding aim with a single hand, Bronte reached into her sweater to remove a syringe. It was capped and appeared to be filled with an amber liquid. "I hold immorality in my hand, Mr. Hunter. Dr. Vang thought I needed it for inspiration. I didn't. And when all of you are dead, I'll have all the money I need to enjoy it forever."

Hunter asked mildly, "Is that what the dynamite is for? To destroy us and this house? Leave nothing for the authorities?"

"Vang warned me about how smart you are, Mr. Hunter." She leveled aim at Hunter's chest. "I'm sorry I can't say the same for all of –"

Bronte screamed and fired the pistol and Blackthorn fell back with a shout. But as the detective hit the floor Hunter snatched up the Ruger and his finger tightened on the trigger before he saw the gun fall from Bronte's hand. She staggered forward half a dozen steps, eyes open in shock, gaping mutely, and fell on her face.

Emily, her white nightgown red with blood, stood behind her. Hunter saw a knife buried to the hilt in Bronte's spine. Then Hunter raised his astonished gaze to Emily, who was staring down with contemptuous, dead eyes from a porcelain face.

"*Ekibe*," she whispered.

Struggling and groaning, Blackthorn rose to a knee, a bloody hand clutching his shoulder. His teeth gleamed in anger as he saw what was before him. Then he shook his head and bowed his face.

He groaned, "Oh, my god …" Then, suddenly, Blackthorn flung out an arm. "Barron! Hurry upstairs and extinguish that candle, boy! *Hurry*!"

Barron rushed up the stairs.

Within minutes it was obvious that someone official had heard the entire thing as the roar of uncountable helicopters surrounded the estate, some circling, some landing. Walking forward, Hunter bent to pick up what was even yet held in Bronte's hand, then took a chair beside Cathcart, who was leaning forward, head down, dark hair shrouding her face.

"You all right?" he asked.

"*Nope*."

"Me, either. Here. Take this."

Cathcart dismally raised her face. Her eyes flared as she saw Bronte's syringe in Hunter's hand and she snatched it up, stuffing it in her shirt. Her eyes darted over the demolished trophy room.

"They didn't see anything," muttered Hunter.

She leaned closer. "Why are you doing this? This thing has caused you nothing but pain."

As a stampede approached the manor, Hunter sighed, "Because there's no stopping this science. Too many people have it now. But maybe you can do something good with it." He paused. "Maybe cure all those diseases you talked about."

She laughed, "I'll do my best."

"That's good enough for me."

CHAPTER THIRTY

A dozen black-clad soldiers entered the front door and swept the room. After one radioed that the house was secure, the severe shape of Commissioner Rafferty stalked around the corner. The highest-ranking officer of London Metropolitan Police took a moment to calmly assess the situation before he set an unreadable gaze on Blackthorn.

"What is the status, commander?"

Blackthorn briefly lifted an arm in Hunter's direction and Rafferty reset his focus. "Mr. Hunter?" he inquired with a shade of respect. "Have you finished the job?"

"Vang's dead," Hunter said dully. "About a mile to the north."

"We'll find him."

"He's all yours."

Rafferty snapped his fingers and a military officer stepped forward as the commissioner continued, "Take all the bodies to the base. And scour the moor for Vang."

Rafferty squared off with Blackthorn. "Your position as Deputy Assistant Commissioner in Charge of Special Operations is finalized, commander. You may assume your new detail after you recuperate from your injuries." He extended a hand. "Congratulations, Winston."

They shook hands as a team carried Bronte somewhat unceremoniously from the room. Then Rafferty turned to Hunter, "A security contract is ready for your signature, Mr.

Hunter. And a generous renumeration will be paid to your account before you depart London."

"You know," Hunter began, blinking tiredly, "you can keep your money, Rafferty. And your contract." He held his gaze. "I think someone should tell the world about this. I think Milton deserves that much."

Rafferty angrily answered, "This was *not* the work of the British Empire, Mr. Hunter! An entire country should not be tarnished because of the act of a lone madman! We've done our best to contain this carnage and save the rest of the world the horror!"

"Tell that to the world," Hunter said as he turned away. "I'm sure they'll sleep better."

Hunter had only taken three steps before Blackthorn called, "Where you off to, mate?"

He didn't look back.

"I can't leave a fallen man behind."

* * *

It was late and the night was in the last stage of what glowing red light remained of Hunter's Moon.

Hunter leaned against the window frame, staring up.

Behind him on the floor Emily was carefully cleaning Ben's massive wounds with a pyramid of rags and a bowl of hot water that Zelda and the house staff had prepared for her.

Everyone official had almost disappeared when Hunter returned with Ben limping beside him. Hunter exchanged a few words with Blackthorn. The detective's arm was braced in a sling as he reiterated his vow to help Hunter in any way, at any time. Then Hunter wished Cathcart the best, and they departed with the last of the team, lifting into the slow sunrise.

But long before the golden morning had broken, Blackthorn dispatched a platoon of constables to nearby villages to retrieve what house staff cared to return to their war-torn estate, and it turned out to be all of them, in the end. So now Emily and Barron would not be alone in this wilderness. They would be cared for as they should be. And although it was not the perfect ending, it was good enough.

Everything was as back to normal as it was likely to become without carpenters and masons finishing repairs. But "Young Milton," as Blackthorn affectionately called him, assured Hunter that the estate would be rebuilt to its former grandeur and he would watch over Emily forever.

Hunter was done here, and he was more tired than he could ever remember. Every muscle was torn, slashed, or bruised. He was cut with so many wounds, it would be a long time, if ever, before he was whole. And Ben was in far worse condition, barely hanging onto life, wounded as badly as a Grizzly could be, and live.

Hunter would be eternally grateful that iron-hearted Blackthorn, in an unexpected kindness, had also ordered his men to bring back the only veterinarian within fifty miles in the coldest, closest hours before dawn. And after meticulously sewing shut Ben's most grievous wounds and administering a host of medications, the old vet stated that Ben was "the healthiest Grizzly I've treated all week." Although, he added, Ben would need several months to fully recover from the Scimitar's slashes. Then he recommended plenty of rest, good food, and kindness, and departed.

But Hunter had no worries; Ben was in the tenderest of hands. And, gazing across the room, with Emily sitting so close and loving beside the giant Grizzly, Hunter recognized and accepted that they belonged together because they were the same in so many ways that weren't easy to explain. But they were the same, and that's all that mattered.

As Emily sang softly to Ben, he rolled his head to lay it beside her, his eyes closed in peaceful sleep as she delicately tended his wounds. After watching them a while, Hunter said, "Yeah. I think Ben loves you, kid."

"And I love Ben," Emily said without looking up. "I'll be sad when he has to go home."

Hunter smiled faintly, "You know, Emily, I think Ben is too hurt to go home."

Her eyes widened. "Really?"

Turning, Hunter put his back to what remained of the night. He didn't need time to consider what he wanted to say. He just wanted to feel it because he knew it would never come again. "Yeah, I think I'm gonna have to leave him here with you. That is, if you don't mind Ben watching over you."

She froze.

Her voice was a whisper, "He can stay with me?"

"Yeah," Hunter smiled, "it's gonna be a long time before he can travel again. And he's going to need someone who loves him to help him get better. Just promise me you'll take him for long walks in the woods, okay? He loves to do that. And you might like to get out a little bit, too."

She embraced Ben's head, and her words floated up.

"Will you miss him?"

A screech turned Hunter's head.

The silhouette of a gigantic Eagle Owl, spectral against Hunter's Moon, soared across the fading sphere and called out as storm clouds gathered to battle the light, and Hunter bowed his head.

"Yeah," he said softly, "I'll miss both of you …"

The End

ACKNOWLEDGEMENTS

I always say no book is ever the work of any one person. Rather, it's a collaboration between author, editor, and publisher. And, often enough, it's impossible to say where the achievement of one person ends and the other begins. But one thing is certain: all the efforts merge together to eventually achieve the work for which everyone has striven to achieve. And so, I wish to thank those to whom I feel a very special sense of gratitude, beginning with Michael Cordova, Steven Jackson, and Elijah Toten, who are the heart and soul of Wildblue Publishing – a publishing house to which I gladly deliver this novel because they had a hand in creating it. I also wish to thank my endlessly talented editor, Rowe Carenen, who made this book much more beautiful and powerful than I could have ever achieved alone. And then there is everyone else at Wildblue Publishing – those who labor silently in the shadows to turn what is merely good into something great. And as far as the nature and content of this novel, I freely accept any mistakes as mine alone.

*For More News About James Byron
Huggins, Signup For Our Newsletter:*

http://wbp.bz/newsletter

*Word-of-mouth is critical to an author's long-term success.
If you appreciated this book please leave a review on the
Amazon sales page:*

https://wbp.bz/huntersmoonr